ATX: Outbreak

A Novel

Michael S. Finley, DVM

Copyright © 2017 by Michael S. Finley, DVM

ISBN: 9781549986093

First Edition

All rights reserved. No part of this book may be reproduced, scanned, or distributed in any printed or electronic form without permission, except by a reviewer who may quote brief passages in a review.

This is a work of fiction. Names, characters, places, events, locales, businesses, organizations, and incidents are a product of the author's imagination or are used fictitiously. Any resemblance to actual persons, living or dead, businesses, or establishments is entirely coincidental.

Published in the United States of America

Table of Contents

Chapter 1	5
Chapter 2	9
Chapter 3	16
Chapter 4	26
Chapter 5	46
Chapter 6	50
Chapter 7	60
Chapter 8	68
Chapter 9	73
Chapter 10	89
Chapter 11	100
Chapter 12	116
Chapter 13	137
Chapter 14	143
Chapter 15	152
Chapter 16	172
Chapter 17	190
Chapter 18	201
Chapter 19	213
Chapter 20	223
Chapter 21	228
Chapter 22	232
Chapter 23	243
Chapter 24	251
Chapter 25	254
Chapter 26	270
Chapter 27	275
Chapter 28	280
Chapter 29	294
Chapter 30	309
Chapter 31	324
Chapter 32	341
Chapter 33	346
Chapter 34	354
Chapter 35	369
Chapter 36	380

Chapter 37	390
Chapter 38	398
Chapter 39	413
Chapter 40	420
Chapter 41	435
Chapter 42	438
Chapter 43	450
Chapter 44	457
Chapter 45	467
Chapter 46	470
Chapter 47	483
Chapter 48	496
Chapter 49	503
Chapter 50	510
Chapter 51	521
Chapter 52	533
Acknowledgements	540

Chapter 1

Dr. Glen Rogers was driving between Amarillo and Canyon, Texas when he received a call from a colleague, Dr. Jim Bob Marsh, ATX's feedlot veterinarian.

"Glen, we've had a rash of cattle at the Hereford feedlot begin to show signs of central nervous system disease. We've got seventeen head isolated in the treatment pens. Lethargy and facial twitching are the primary symptoms; but, there're are four head displaying more advanced symptoms."

"Jim Bob, tell me more about the four displaying more advanced symptoms", said Dr. Rogers.

"One is generally disoriented and blind. Another is pressing its head against a fence. The third is high stepping with its front legs; while the fourth has a left head tilt and is ataxic. They've all been on feed for more than three months and come from different pens. We've had no similar problems; then today the pen riders pulled out seventeen. These symptoms are different than those I would expect with other disease processes. If you have time, you might want to look at them. Maybe they should be sampled for bovine spongiform encephalopathy."

"Although it would be unusual to have more than one showing symptoms, I'd better look at them", said Dr. Rogers. "That's USDA protocol for CNS disease. I'll be there in about forty-five minutes".

"That sounds great. I called Randy; he's on his way too."

Dr. Randy Bennett, ATX's Director of Feedlot Operations, is a veterinary school classmate of Dr. Rogers and holds an advanced degree in production veterinary medicine.

Once Randy and Glen arrived, they slowly walked through the cattle observing them at rest and while moving. The four feeder cattle were displaying the most advanced CNS symptoms. They decided to euthanize the four animals, harvest the brains, and send them to Texas A&M's Vet Diagnostic Laboratory in College Station for BSE or mad cow disease testing. The remaining thirteen remained in the hospital pens for further observation.

ATX's vet hospital is well designed and contemporary. There is separate room for performing necropsies. Its equipment includes ceiling-mounted hoists, stainless steel tables, white cutting boards, and all the instruments for treating sick cattle and performing diagnostic necropsies.

Dr. Rogers and Dr. Marsh volunteered to harvest the samples. They placed the brainstem and beginning part of the spinal cord in a plastic screw cap tube of about one inch in diameter and four inches long. The ensured the obex was intact for BSE testing. Next, they sliced the cerebral cortex and cerebellum longitudinally with one half placed in a plastic container of formalin solution to fix the tissue. The other half placed in a plastic zip-lock bag, and placed in the cooler portion of the shipping container. All four samples were separately boxed.

While Glen and Jim Bob removed the brains, Randy Bennett logged into the feedlot's computer system. ATX's state-of-the-art computerized feedlot management system tracks each animal by both an ear tag and electronic identification device (EID) tag. Within minutes Randy printed each animals' health records. The animals had been at the ATX feedlot between 106 and 132 days. With the laboratory submittal forms complete and the brain stem samples packaged, the feedlot foreman drove the samples to ATX Feeders corporate office in Canyon for FedEx pick up.

The three veterinarians discussed a bigger concern. What would be best thing to do with the cattle remaining at the Hereford feedlot? Their dilemma was the Hereford feedlot had fifteen pens of cattle (over 3,800 head) scheduled for shipping to packing houses in the next week. ATX's five other feedlots in the Amarillo area provided Randy with flexibility. Randy said, "I think it's prudent to voluntarily quarantine the

Hereford feedlot. We won't ship anything to slaughter from this lot until the test results come back. Instead, I'll arrange for us to ship additional cattle from our other feedlots. This will prevent any diseased animals from entering the food chain. It will avoid the potential of a recall should one or more of the animals be positive for BSE. We should have lab results back in four to five days."

Five days later there were no results reported. However, the USDA notified ATX's Hereford feedlot it was under federal quarantine. Over two weeks passed with no official test results reported.

Glen called the lab twice with no information about the results. The lab said the results were pending. In his experience, a delay in sample results meant the animals were positive for BSE.

****

In Washington, D.C. high ranking USDA-Animal and Plant Health Inspection Service (APHIS) officials held a video conference call to determine how best to conduct efficient and comprehensive investigations of quarantined premises. Dr. Laporte, APHIS' Administrator, recognized the urgency to get a handle on whatever was affecting these cattle. He needed to detail investigative teams to the quarantined premises soon. The investigative teams would consist of specialized professionals and support staff. The specialized portion of the team would consist of an epidemiologist, an experienced veterinary generalist familiar with the local area, and a veterinary pathologist. The support team included an IT specialist and two veterinary technicians. Dr. Yu suggested the epidemiologists as team leaders. They selected additional teams to participate in the investigation if the outbreak expanded. Existing electronic epidemiological questionnaires required modification to meet the needs of this investigation. The investigative teams would utilize these questionnaires to facilitate data comparison. IT integrated an electronic version of the standard Laboratory Submission Form into the software for use by the veterinary pathologists. At this stage,

APHIS would keep the investigations low profile and confidential.

Dr. Sam Yu, Western Regional Director, was selected incident manager providing management oversight. Veterinary pathologists all came from the National Veterinary Services Laboratory (NVSL). The Center for Epidemiology and Animal Health (CEAH) would serve as the centralized location for data collection. Notification of The USDA Office of Emergency Preparedness and Response, the Office of the Inspector General, and the FBI was a requirement when the cause of the outbreak was unknown. The Office of Emergency Preparedness detailed two investigators to Fort Collins, Colorado. One representative going to CEAH and the other to the Western Region office to review and assist with the investigations from a Homeland Security/bioterrorism perspective.

Chapter 2

Dr. Rex Yoder, the Western Regional Epidemiologist, was to lead the team investigating ATX's Hereford feedlot. He met Dr. Penny Adams from the NVSL in Ames, Iowa at Dallas International Airport. They both were waiting to catch a flight to Amarillo. Prior to this outbreak, they presented papers at National Animal Health conferences and worked together on an Avian Influenza task force. In Amarillo, they would rent a Suburban and travel to the Amarillo Suites where they would meet Dr. Glen Rogers and the rest of the team.

Dr. Rogers waited for Dr. Yoder and Dr. Adams in the breakfast area of the motel near the front desk. Leaning back, he was reading the sports section of the Amarillo Globe-News when they arrived. He welcomed them to Texas and relayed the rest of the team had arrived and were in their rooms. Sammi Downey from Wichita Falls and Sonny Kelly from Plainview were the veterinary technicians. Cheri Alverez from CEAH served as the team's IT specialist. They decided Dr. Yoder and Dr. Adams would go to their rooms; then everyone would meet back in breakfast area in about an hour. Meanwhile, Dr. Rogers would contact the rest of the team to advise them of the plan.

Dr. Yoder was the last to arrive at the team meeting. The team relocated to a distant table out of earshot of the motel lobby and registration desk. He'd been on a call with Dr. Yu who provided him with current information on the outbreak and a call-in number for a daily conference call that would occur at 7:00 AM daily. After introducing himself to Sammi Downey and Sonny Kelly, Dr. Yoder sat down in the only vacant chair. There was look of intensity and concern on his brow.

Cheri Alverez started by announcing, "I have gifts from CEAH." She then handed out new iPads with wireless ear buds. After everyone received their iPad, Cheri said, "The investigative teams will be the first to use this technology. These tablets are the latest version. They're touchscreen; so,

I've loaded touch screen versions of the epidemiological questionnaires Dr. Yoder compiled. They also have voice-to-word logic software where you can dictate your comments into a microphone in the ear bud. It will show up as written dialog in the investigation reports and laboratory submission forms. I've loaded them with statistical and epidemiological software. I think you will find they greatly enhance efficiency."

"Speaking of efficiency", said Dr. Yoder, "I'm amazed Cheri has already loaded the questionnaire. I completed it right before boarding the plane in Denver. Well done, Cheri."

Dr. Yoder opened his notepad referring to the notes he'd taken when he spoke with Dr. Yu. "These are the most current details on our investigation. ATX Feeders owns the premise we're going to. It is a large progressive corporate fat cattle feedlot located about four miles north and three miles east of Hereford. ATX Feeders corporate office is in Canyon. ATX owns numerous large ranches in the north Texas as well as in northern New Mexico, Colorado, Wyoming, Kansas, and Nebraska. They operate six feedlots in the Amarillo area. The Hereford feedlot ATX feeds its own cattle, cattle ATX owned in partnership with other cattle raisers, and custom feeds cattle for other cattlemen. In total, the Hereford yard has the capacity to hold about sixty-five thousand animals and currently has a population of 62,487 head. Each of ATX's other five feedlots have the same capacity."

"While we were traveling to Amarillo, an additional 27 animals displayed central nervous system signs including ataxia, disorientation, and gait irregularities. BSE tests from Texas A&M University on an additional four head euthanized after the quarantine are "Inconclusive". Those samples sent the National Veterinary Services Laboratory for confirmatory testing. We're having daily conference calls at 7:00AM (central time) in my room. The purpose of the call is to maintain communications regarding the latest news and assessments concerning the outbreak. Tomorrow morning about 8:30AM we're scheduled to meet with ATX ownership and management at ATX Feeders corporate office before we go to the feedlot. We need to be cognizant this investigation is very high profile within APHIS. We must maintain strict confidentiality.

Dr. Rogers said, "I've been involved with the ATX outbreak since the beginning, over two weeks ago. ATX management has not received any laboratory results on the BSE samples sent to Texas A&M. Management is anxious to get some answers. I think that's one reason why our first stop tomorrow morning is at their headquarters in Canyon."

Dr. Adams spoke. "I sent a lot of supplies from the NVSL to the motel. In total, there are 82 boxes. On arrival, the motel delivered them to my room. I was part of the NVSL pathology team viewing the immunohistochemical slides. All the results were inconclusive. There is conjecture this may be a novel agent. With this in mind, we need to maintain biosecurity and be as careful as possible. If this is a novel agent, we don't know if it's infectious. It could possibly be transmissible humans. Therefore, I sent various sizes of disposable coveralls, gloves, masks, eye shields, boot covers, and head cover, instruments, several sizes of Whirl Pac bags for collecting specimens, and large shipping containers. Some of the containers hold additional equipment and supplies. Now that both Suburbans are at the motel, I'm open for volunteers to help me move some of the boxes into the two Suburbans."

Everyone volunteered to help.

After filling the Suburbans with equipment and supplies, the team drove to a quaint nearby Mexican restaurant known by locals to have the best Mexican food in Amarillo. After eating, they spent nearly an hour of visiting about a broad range of topics. But nothing regarding the investigation. Once back at the motel, everyone went to their rooms.

Dr. Yoder inquired at the front desk about renting a small conference room to store the remaining boxes of supplies and equipment. He and Dr. Rogers knocked on Dr. Adams door with clothing carts in tow to remove the excess boxes from

Dr. Adams room and transport them to the newly rented conference room. While unexpected, Dr. Adams was happy to have them removed from her room.

"My room already feels more relaxing", said Dr. Adams. "It no longer had the ambiance of the NVSL supply warehouse."

****

On a misty predawn morning, Graeme Pennington arrived at the Animal Health and Veterinary Laboratories in Worcester, England. He walked down the hallway listening to his solitary footsteps on the slate floor. It was not unusual for Graeme, as chief executive officer, to work on Saturday. Entering his office, he turned on a hotplate under an old-fashioned tea kettle in the corner of his office after filling the vessel with fresh filtered water.

After taking off his damp oil-tanned field coat he hung it on the nearby coat rack, sat down, turned on his computer, and entered security pass codes. While the computer was booting up, he poured a cup of tea and reflected on the unexpected conference call he received the prior evening.

Richard Coy, the British Minister of State for Agriculture and Food, called about 9:00 PM asking him to join a call with representatives from the United States Department of Agriculture. On the call were the U.S. Secretary of Agriculture, Clare Johansen; Animal and APHIS Administrator, Dr. Bobby Laporte; and NVSL Director, Dr. Pat Rhodes-Voss. The participants were a forum of international foreign animal disease experts with expertise at the political, governmental, and diagnostic levels.

Dr. Laporte summarized an emerging animal disease outbreak affecting five U.S. states. "During the past 18 days, cattle of both dairy and beef breeds, have developed a variety of nonspecific central nervous system signs. The cattle range from 11 to 62 months of age. Seven premises are currently involved. In total, APHIS has euthanized 122 animals. Their brain tissues tested for BSE. All test results have been inconclusive. The seven premises are currently under quarantine. Teams of investigative veterinary clinicians, pathologists, and epidemiologists are at each premise. They are onsite and will begin work tomorrow morning. Their aim is to identify common source material or an infectious agent. It's also important to note we have not briefed the press on this outbreak."

"The screening tests at our network laboratories were all reported as inconclusive. Next, we had the samples forwarded to the NVSL in Ames, Iowa for confirmatory testing. NVSL veterinary pathologists repeated the screening tests as well confirmatory ICH and Western Blot testing. Screening test results were consistent between the network laboratories and the NVSL. They were all again inconclusive. Histological abnormalities consistently noted were discrete to locally diffuse very small vacuoles. However, the presence of Bovine Spongiform Encephalopathy prion antigen has not been decisively identified. Confirmatory testing results essentially mirrored the screening test results. They were all inconclusive."

"You now have the contemporary facts concerning the U.S. outbreak. Additional animals on some of the premises are displaying clinical signs. Tissues from 36 animals are in various stages of testing. We request your assistance in determining the etiological agent. I'll be sending Graeme a series of e-mails with further detail. I'm concerned we may be dealing with a novel agent."

The English laboratory is an international reference laboratory and agreed to assist in identifying the infectious agent.

Secretary Johansen said, "This outbreak not only has U.S. domestic ramifications, but potentially significant international implications. I intend to brief the President of the United States and the U.S. Cabinet at our next cabinet meeting."

Underscoring the importance of England's help, Secretary Johansen advised, "The laboratory samples will be arriving at about 8:30 AM tomorrow morning at the Animal Health Veterinary Laboratory in Worcester. I'm sending the samples via military courier. After this call, I will authorize a U.S. Air Force pilot to depart for the Birmingham airport. A military attaché will transport the samples to Worcester. What kind of timeframe are we looking at for you to run the cadre of tests and provide us with results and interpretation?"

Graeme responded, "It will take about five days considering the depth of testing. It will be our top priority."

Secretary Johansen continued, "Given the potentially significant animal health, economical, and political ramifications, I propose we have a follow-up call once we have sample results." At 1:00 PM Washington time on day five they would talk again. Secretary Johansen thanked everyone and the call concluded.

After the call, Graeme Pennington phoned Ian McLaughlin to brief him. Ian, a friend, colleague, and Director of the Spongiform Encephalopathy section of the lab, is an international expert on spongiform encephalopathies (diseases causing sponge-like pathology in the brain). Among his previous research efforts were the development of the ICH and Western Blot testing procedures for BSE and other spongiform encephalitic diseases. Like Graeme, Ian is a veterinary surgeon with PhDs in pathology and immunology. Both are fellows in the England College of Veterinary Pathology. They have collaborated on scores of research projects during the past two decades and work well together. Briefly, they discussed the U.S. outbreak agreeing to meet at the lab the following morning to log in the samples and initiate testing. They planned to further discuss the outbreak and review the detailed information sent electronically.

Graeme poured another cup of tea and considered the magnitude of the U.S. outbreak compared to the one the British Isles endured almost two decades earlier. Opening his e-mail account, Graeme tabbed down to an e-mail having attached photomicrographs of the histology slides. As the first attachment opened; Ian knocked on Graeme's office door. Entering, the smell of fresh warm sausage rolls effused the office. They reviewed a few arbitrarily selected histology photos while they munched and commented on their observations. "Unmistakably, there are distinct non-coalescing vacuoles with no amyloidal plaque formation. These are not classic spongiform changes in the brain that would lead me to a histological diagnosis of BSE", said Ian. "However, I cannot recall viewing similar pathology." It became apparent to both men they were becoming involved in some professionally exciting and very important work. Perhaps they were dealing with a new disease entity.

Chapter 3

The smell of fresh brewed coffee permeated the motel hallway when Dr. Adams opened her room door at 6:15AM. She noticed Dr. Yoder's room door was open and the kitchenette light wandered into the dimly lit hallway. Walking toward the open door she heard Dr. Roger's voice. Penny poked her head in the door. "I'm heading down to get something to eat. Do either of you want anything?"

Glen responded; "No thanks; we just came from there. We picked up another pot of coffee and some other goodies."

"OK, I'll see you in a few", commented Penny as she headed toward the elevator.

"Good morning", said Cheri Alverez as she walked into Dr. Yoder's room with an empty coffee cup in hand.

"Good morning, help yourself to coffee. There's creamer in the bowl and we have bread for toast, butter, cream cheese, and bagels. Help yourself." Both Rex and Glen were near the window watching the orange and deep blue sunrise.

Sammi Downey, a single mother of a teenage daughter, waved as she entered Dr. Yoder's room while talking to her daughter on her cell phone. "Yes dear, you can wear my blue blouse...I've got to go now, we have a conference call in a few minutes." Following Sammi through the doorway was Sonny Kelly, who also gave a quick wave, while munching on a crisp apple and carrying a travel mug of hot black coffee.

Rex walked back to his desk to call into the conference. He then put the phone on speaker and muted the call to eliminate the background noise in the room.

Soon, Dr. Yu greeted everyone. "Good morning! Thank you all for participating in this investigation on such short notice. I cannot over-emphasize the importance of this investigation. You all are experienced experts in your fields of expertise and high performers. I want you to be thorough in your investigations and reports, it may be the commonality of little details that becomes the significant key to figuring out what is going on. With that said, I'll turn the remainder of the call to Clare Johansen, the Secretary of Agriculture. Secretary Johansen, please go ahead."

"Good morning. While you all were traveling and getting ready for today, I want to share with you the essence of a call that I made to Richard Coy, the British Minister of State for Agriculture and Food. Also on the call were APHIS Administrator Dr. Bobby Laporte, NVSL Director Dr. Pat Rhodes-Voss as well and Dr. Graeme Pennington, the CEO for Animal Health and Veterinary Laboratories in Worchester, England."

"Dr. Laporte factually explained what we've been dealing with for over two weeks. I asked Dr. Pennington for his assistance as the director of an international reference laboratory. A military courier jet delivered the tissue samples laboratory overnight. I also asked for their upmost confidentiality. I ask you for the same; do not talk with the press and do not share your professional opinions with the owners or staff of the premise you will be investigating. The Worcester lab is treating our request as top priority. We anticipate results in about five days."

"Tomorrow I will be briefing the President Smyth and my cabinet colleagues on the situation. I anticipate as you do your investigations more facts will become available which may initiate other departments or agencies to become involved. I plan to avert outside departmental involvement until we have test results from England. However, I informed the Office of the Inspector General, the FBI, and the Department of Homeland Security. That's a legal requirement when we don't know if this is an act of terrorism. USDA's Office of Emergency Preparedness and Response has detailed a person to CEAH and another to the Western Region office to assist with the investigations. OIG, FBI, and Homeland have agreed to this arrangement for now; at least until we have information or test results suggesting a possible act of terrorism."

"Earlier this morning, I called each of the owners or CEOs of the seven operations involved in the investigation. I asked for their cooperation. I spoke with each individually and did not share that there was more than one premise involved. I shared with them the results of testing remained inconclusive; and we've sent the samples to Worcester, England an international reference laboratory for review and interpretation. Once we received the test results, we will share them. Everyone said they would cooperate fully with your investigations and requests for information. We spoke of the need for their confidentiality until we had results. Everyone assured their confidentiality. I am confident this will allow you to work more efficiently."

"Lastly, I want you to know you have the full resources of the Department available to assist you. If you need *anything* request it through your chain of command. We want you to be able to conduct your investigations in the most efficient manner possible. We have five days to gather the available facts, make our assessments, and hopefully determine what's killing these cattle. Good luck and Godspeed to you all!"

Dr. Yu thanked Secretary Johansen and then said; "If there are no questions, I will let you all get to work. We'll talk again tomorrow at the same time. If, however, anyone uncovers something they think is significant, please call me immediately. Have a good day."

****

Traveling south on highway 87 from Amarillo the two Suburbans slowed as they crossed the intersection with First Avenue in Canyon. Turning right into a small parking lot mostly filled with white pickup trucks they parked in adjacent parking spaces identified as visitor. Flanking the parking lot to the south appeared to be an 1880's vintage two story brick structure. The investigative team walked to a large oak-framed beveled glass door with gold lettering identifying ATX Feeders. As the team entered the reception area, a beautiful dark haired young woman said; "Hi, Dr. Rogers. I bet y'all are here for the meeting about what's been goin' on at the Hereford lot".

"That's right Sarita", responded Dr. Rogers.

About that time Dr. Randy Bennett walked out of his office saying; "Hi Glen, it's good to see you. The others from ATX are already in the conference room. Why don't we wait until we join them and then make our introductions? Follow me."

While the outside of the building appeared to be a nineteenth century structure, the inside, although rustic in decor, was contemporary. Computer screens and keyboards garnished every desktop. The wooden flooring was well worn lumber. The walls adorned with ranch themed oil paintings and large aerial photographs of feedlots filled with cattle. The conference room housed a highly polished dark wooden table about five feet wide and at least 15 feet long. Attached along the sidewalls were blued-metal horseshoes bent at ninety-degree angles and spaced with one horseshoe hook behind each of the 12 chairs positioned along the table. On about half of the hooks hung dusty silver-gray or black western felt hats. The upholstery of the chair backs and cushions was hair-on cowhide, each with an ATX brand embellishing the chair back. Hung from the far wall of the room was a 90-inch flat screen TV scrolling through photographs of ATX properties, men working cattle, and pens and pastures filled with cattle and horses. Two hefty antique brass ceiling fans silently lumbered above. Adjacent to the door was a table holding a large coffee pot, earthenware coffee mugs and plates embellished with the ATX brand, and a large sterling silver serving tray heaped with wrapped breakfast burritos. There were six coffee mugs at the far end of the table and five men were standing behind their chairs. A ruddy faced man in his late 60's wearing lightweight plaid linen shirt and jeans stood behind his chair at the far end of the table said; "Y'all come in, grab a cup of coffee, and have a seat. We'll save the introductions until everyone has had an opportunity to get some coffee and be seated."

The investigative team each poured a mug of coffee and found chairs at the near end of the table. After everyone sat the man began; "I'm Randall Bennett, chairman of ATX Holdings. To my left is Dr. Jim Bob Marsh, ATX's feedlot veterinarian. To his left is my son, Dr. Randy Bennett. Randy is a veterinarian. He oversees our feedlot operations. Directly across the table from me is Philip Granger, our attorney. To Philip's right is John Downey the head of our IT department. To John's right is Dennis Young, the general manager of the Hereford yard."

As Mr. Bennett sat down Dr. Yoder stood introducing himself saying; "We are all with APHIS, an agency within the USDA. We all have our own areas of expertise and responsibility in this investigation. I am a veterinary epidemiologist based out of Fort Collins, Colorado. I'm the team leader. To my right is Dr. Glen Rogers, who I am sure most of you know. He serves as the team's veterinary generalist. At the end of the table is Mr. Sonny Kelly from Plainview. He is a veterinary technician. Sitting next to Mr. Young is Dr. Penny Adams, a veterinary pathologist from the National Veterinary Services Laboratory in Ames, Iowa. Seated next to Dr. Adams is Sammi Downey a veterinary technician from Wichita Falls. At the end of the table is Cheri Alverez. She is from the Center for Epidemiology and Animal Health in Fort Collins, Colorado. Cheri is our IT Specialist."

Dr. Yoder continued; "Let me provide you with an overview of our investigation and what we expect to accomplish. APHIS has been using this sort of a multidisciplinary team approach to investigate animal health concerns for over 20 years. Team expertise changes to fit each situation. Some of us have worked with each other over the years. The agency has found this approach to problem solving to be efficient and expeditious. We expect our investigation to last about five days, although it can extend depending upon what we find. During this time, we will depend on ATX management personnel to provide us with detailed specific information considering all aspects of your operation. Other subject matter experts and USDA management will review our information in real time. Our focus is on collecting factual information. Once we have gathered the information, we will begin to interpret the data collaboratively with the subject matter experts and USDA management. They may expand our investigation in an area, or send in additional expert personnel to follow up or expand in some area. We will be collecting many samples for laboratory analysis. Our samples have the highest priority for testing and analysis. When we receive results, we will share them with you. I want to thank you for your hospitable welcome."

"Dr. Yoder thanks for stopping by on your way to the yard", said Randall. "It's great to meet you and your team. As you may know, I got a call early this morning from Clare Johansen. She and I have been friends for many years. She shared USDA's most current test results for the Hereford yard. Before you arrived, I briefed the guys here and we want you to know you will have our full cooperation. Anything we can do to help, we will do. Whatever help you need, our feedlot manager or veterinarians will expedite resources; just let us know. I have asked Dr. Marsh, Randy, as well as Dennis Young to be at the Hereford yard to answer your questions or facilitate getting you answers. From the perspective of data, John Downey will be your man. I think you will find that we have innovative software concerning the feeding operations. We've invested a lot of capital and manpower into IT, just in case we found ourselves in a position we are now facing. John offices in Amarillo at the ATX bank. Our personnel know how to contact him. Give him a call anytime you need him. Providing you with data will be his top priority. Let me assure you we want to find out what's affecting our cattle; we share this common goal."

"I ask you take a few minutes so we all can get to know each other a little. For those of you that may need to use the restrooms, they're located to your left as you exit this room."

"With that said, there is a tray of breakfast burritos next to the coffee pot. Please help yourselves. They come from

Rosa's, here in Canyon. Rosa's has the reputation of making the best burritos in the panhandle. There are a couple of codes written on the foil that will take the guess work out of what's inside. "P" stands for plain-eggs and potatoes. "S" stands for sausage, egg, and potatoes. The green stripes in the foil designate mildly seasoned burritos and those in red striped foil are spicier, with jalapeños."

With the formal part of the meeting concluded, everyone congregated initially around the coffee pot, then broke off into smaller groups.

Dr. Yoder and Dr. Rogers visited with Dr. Bennett, Dr. Marsh, and Dennis Young. Dr. Bennett asked; "Dr. Yoder, how can we best split up to assist you in your investigation?"

"Glen is the one who knows the most about this operation. He will be investigating the operational aspects of your feedlot. I will focus on the more general aspects of the operation and on what's been going on from an epidemiological perspective. Penny's focus will be on postmortem examinations, collecting tissue samples, and general diagnostics. So, maybe if you want to work with me Randy. Dennis can work with Glen; and Jim Bob can work with Penny. Jim Bob, Penny is the best pathologist I have ever worked with. I think you will find it educational and impressive. She knows cattle production, disease processes, pathology, and anatomy as well as anyone I've ever met. She is also an expert in prion diseases."

"That sounds like a plan", responded Randy. "We'll do it just that way. If we need some additional help we'll get it."

Rex, contemplating the individual aspects of the operation, suggested; "It would be worthwhile to have a Bobcat with a bucket available as well as a dump truck to collect the carcasses once they have been posted by Penny. She prefers to work out of a Bobcat bucket rather than on a table or a stationary cradle on the floor. It saves her time. She's *really* fast at sample collection and doing necropsies."

Dennis Young affirmed; "I'll call the lot a on the radio and we'll have a Bobcat and dump truck at the vet clinic when everyone arrives."

"That would be great! We have the back of both of our Suburbans filled with boxes of supplies and equipment. We'll need to drop them off at the vet clinic, then we can all get to work", said Glen.

"Why so much equipment and supplies", asked Jim Bob.

"We're going to be taking lots of samples; so, there are lots of prepared sample boxes. Penny and Sammi will be wearing full biological containment apparel. Penny sent enough for several changes daily for everyone on our team as well as enough for any of your personnel who might want them", responded Glen.

"We're approaching this event as if we are dealing with a novel agent; we don't know if it could be transmissible to humans", added Rex. "Once we get conclusive lab results back; hopefully, we'll have a better idea what we're dealing with, then we'll modify the protective gear accordingly."

Sonny Kelly and Sammi Downey filled their coffee mugs and grabbed a burrito before sitting down at the table adjacent to where the APHIS vets were visiting with the ATX folks. Neither said anything, but were in earshot of the conversation and listening to the discussion.

Dr. Adams and Randall Bennett conversed near the coffee pot. "This building is quite interesting. From the outside, it appears to late 19th century construction. On the inside, it is modern with a western contemporary design. Collectively it is unique, beautiful, and functional."

Thank you, Dr. Adams. "Actually, this building was constructed about three years ago by my son Tony who operates our construction business. There's a story to its construction. The bricks on the outside are from an old downtown Amarillo hotel we purchased in the 50's; then replaced it with the ATX bank building. My eldest daughter, Mary, runs the bank and manages the building's commercial property. The bricks came from the old Therber Brick Company in Therber, TX. There's a little scavenger in the Bennett DNA. When we tore down the old Hotel, we saved the brick, all the windows that were sound, most of the solid oak and mahogany doors, wood paneling, tin ceiling tiles, the main bar, and other contents we thought we could eventually repurpose. The interior plank flooring is hand hewn mesquite from an old big barn on one of ranches we purchased about 15 years ago. The interior wainscoting is from the exterior wood of another barn up near Dumas, TX. The copper ceiling tiles came from the old hotel as did our front door. The overhead timbers and some of the framing wood are from an old bridge down by Olton, TX. Tony made the cabinets, desks, credenzas, this conference room table, picture frames, etc. in his cabinet shop from mesquite wood originally used as barn floor planking. I must say you have quite an eye for design", said Mr. Bennett.

"My mother is an architect. For a while architecture interested me. Later my interests drifted more toward my dad's. He's a pediatric cardiothoracic surgeon", responded Dr. Adams while holding her coffee cup between her hands as if to warm them. "You have the three children then; Randy, Tony, and Mary," asked Dr. Adams.

"Oh, my no," exclaimed Randall Bennett. I have eight children. There's Mike, he's a petroleum engineer and runs ATX Oil. Bobby is a mechanical engineer and runs our salvage and industrial design company. Rose is a radiologist; she's married to Larry Shelton, who oversees our farming operations and commodity trading business. Then there's Kate; she is a homemaker with five of my grandchildren. She's married to Harold Ruoff who runs our equipment (Caterpillar and John Deere dealerships) and transportation businesses (Peterbilt and GM dealerships), and ATX Trucking. And our youngest, Skip, is the MBA of the family; he oversees the ranching portion-ATX Land and Livestock. Each business group is a subsidiary of ATX Holdings. Dr. Adams, I don't mean to be rude, but I see Philip Granger has finished his conference call. He's my ride back to Amarillo. I've enjoyed visiting with you. I hope we can visit more as your investigation progresses."

Cheri Alverez and John Downey sat about mid-table chatting about computer systems. They were trying to determine compatibility of ATX's data and the software loaded into the I-pads. Cheri could not believe the sheer volume and breadth of the information ATX kept on each individual animal. She had no doubts ATX had collected all data that she would need. Astonishingly, they were using the same epidemiological and statistical software. The CEAH server is also the same model and size as the one used by ATX.

Cheri with a big smile on her face commented, "This is going to save us sooo much time. When we get on site at the feedlot, I'll send you an e-mail if we need additional reports or data."

Chapter 4

The entrance to the Hereford Feedlot was impressive. The entire front was white ten-foot-high twenty feet wide wrought iron sections set into red flagstone masonry pillars. Larger flagstone pillars and flagstone fencing bordered the wide gated entrance. Electronic monitors sat on the two main gate pillars. Each white wrought iron gate was about twenty feet wide and moved laterally in tracks to allow vehicular traffic in and out. On top of every eighth smaller pillar sat security cameras. Signage after the entrance gates directed traffic to the appropriate location. The outside of the feedlot office, maintenance shop, and vet clinic used the same bricks as those on the exterior of ATX Feeders' office building. The caravan of two Suburbans and three white ATX diesel pickup trucks pulled up to the vet clinic. A Bobcat idled at the side of the building; its driver visiting with two mounted cowboys in an adjacent alleyway. There were literally miles and miles of pipe fencing separating the pens, alleyways, and other locations within the feedlot perimeter.

Dennis Young hopped out of his pickup, opened the back of one of the Suburbans and with a box under each arm walked through the vet clinic's open overhead door onto the necropsy floor.

Dr. Penny Adams met him inside as Dennis said, "I grabbed a couple of boxes on my way in; let me show you around and you can determine where you want to store things so they'll be handy."

"Thanks Dennis. This operation and these facilities are wonderful. I'm not used to having this type of equipment and facilities to work in."

"If you're not planning on using the pipe bed to lay down the carcasses in during your postmortem exams, we can move it over next to that wall and put a couple of pallets on it to store sample boxes. Through the double swinging doors there's a bathroom with a shower. Next to the door by the double sinks, we can move those extra paper towels and replace them with the boxes of disposable protective clothing. I think it's big enough to hold several sizes along with an assortment of protective gloves and masks", said Dennis.

"Dennis, it sounds like you've been through this before", commented Penny.

"Not here, ma'am; but in another life, I was an army medic. We had routine trainings like what is going on here. We had to suit up in full protective gear. Ma'am we also have a store room behind the door on the east side of the necropsy room for overflow. There's also plenty of storage in the main office building", said Dennis.

"You're the man with the plan. Let's arrange things as you have suggested. Back at the motel we have additional supplies and boxes stored in a conference room we rented. Maybe we can bring them out tomorrow to cut down on expenses", said Penny.

"By all means", commented Dennis while directing the others where to put their boxes. Within five minutes the boxes sat in the clinic, sorted, and arranged in a manner facilitating use.

"Before we separate into our groups, I have a couple of questions", said Rex Yoder. "First, we will be taking numerous samples today. What time will we need to have them ready for FedEx pick up? Secondly, how are the carcasses disposed of?"

Randy fielded both questions responding; "If we take the samples back to the Canyon office, FedEx picks up there around 4:00 PM. However, if we request to have them picked up here at the yard, they generally arrive around 5:00 PM."

"Let's give them a call and have them pick up the samples here'" said Rex. "It will give us more time to get them collected, boxed, and ready of pick up."

"To answer your second question Rex, all ATX feedlots burn their carcasses in crematoriums. Their capacity is about 60 to 65 carcasses", said Randy.

"Wow", responded Rex. "I've never seen one that large. Maybe we could look at it on the way to the office", said Rex.

"Sure", responded Randy.

"Does anyone else have anything?" asked Rex.

Dennis commented he had the leftover burritos in his pickup if anyone wanted one before they got down to work. The two cowboys horseback and the forklift driver departed the necropsy room heading for the pickup.

Rex asked Cheri Alverez to drive the Suburban to the office stating that he would jump in with Randy and see the crematorium; then, they would join her at the office.

Arriving at the office Dennis Young ushered Cheri Alverez into a brightly colored, well-lit reception area. Stopping at a desk he said, "Cheri Alverez, this is Juana Gomez our administrative assistant. She's the gal we all go to for help and information. Juana, Cheri is with APHIS and is an IT expert. She's going be requesting specific data for their investigation. Juana will likely be able to provide you with much of the information you'll need. She inputs most of the data here and has a solid understanding of ATX's feedlot software and the management reports it generates."

"Juana, it's nice to meet you. I'm sure we'll be working closely during the next few days. I can't help but to notice your beautiful turquoise and silver necklace. Is it a Hopi design?"

"It's nice to meet you, Cheri. The necklace is Zuni. It is a gift from my great grandmother when I graduated from Texas Tech a couple of years ago. It's been in our family for six generations. Dennis asked me to be available to help you during your stay. We have a comfortable conference room located beyond the wall behind me. It should be comfortable for you and Dr. Yoder to work in. Let me show you. Our wireless modem should provide you with internet access."

Cheri and Juana followed Dennis into the spacious conference room where he dropped the box of leftover burritos on the counter exiting through the rear door of the conference room.

"This is a wonderful work area for Dr. Yoder and me. It's much more spacious and comfortable than the cubicle I normally work out of in Fort Collins. I'll get laptop, purse, and a couple of tablet computers and be right back to set things up."

From the vet clinic Randy Bennett and Rex Yoder drove north on one of two wider paved alleyways between the pens and toward five large grain silos on the horizon of a small hill. At the top of the hill Randy turned the truck to the left passing the feed mill and several five-ton feed trucks, then turned right again past the feed silos and feed mill. He turned right again about a hundred yards further north. Isolated from other equipment and buildings, was a large blackish grey cylinder that appeared to sit on its side somewhat submerged into the ground. In its top were two large horizontally hinged steel doors sitting open giving the appearance of a giant clam wedged into the cylinder. A concrete pit with about 50 feet clearance on each side and the east end surrounded the cylinder. It was open on the west side with a concrete apron extending from the concrete bottom of the pit about 200 feet from the end of the cylinder. The cylinder had a flat internal live bottom and a hinged door with a large locking device like the seal of a door on a bank vault. A ramp extended from the concrete apron up about four feet to the flat live bottom. It was large enough to drive a Bobcat with a front bucket into the cylinder. The concrete walls on the north, south, and east sides were about twenty feet high and approximately two feet thick. A single four-inch pipe extended from the east wall into the east end of the cylinder. Extending from the bottom of the cylinder were numerous lateral pipes attached to a larger pipe that ran the entire length of the cylinder. Driving around to the top mounted doors, Rex observed two large diameter hydraulic cylinders that operated the doors.

"Randy, I've never seen anything like this crematorium. It's ominous looking, but I'll bet it gets the job done", said Rex.

"My brother, Bobby, designed and built it. We have one just like it at all our feedlots. When I returned from A&M and took over the feeding operation, it was one thing I insisted we have. I wanted a method, on a commercial scale, to be able to dispose of carcasses in a manner that would ensure there was no chance of disease transmission. Incineration was the only viable option. Each of our feedlots is on land near ATX oil and gas production. Bobby has the crematoriums fueled by our own natural gas production through high pressure lines. The line also fuels our feed mill. Bobby designed the crematoriums to pull off the water and oils from the carcasses. We use oils, once treated to remove any solids and water, to fuel our diesel vehicles and equipment. We don't like to have much of a supply on hand; it means we're losing cattle. That's about all we can see for now. If you have time later, we can come back when they're loading carcasses into it and watch them fire it up."

"I will make time. I'm sure Penny would also like to see it in use", said Rex.

Returning from the crematorium, Randy stopped the pickup at the crest of the hill where there was a good overview of the feedlot pens and explained the operational aspects of the feedlot. "All traffic both entering and exiting the feedlot come through the main gate we came through. That is the only way in and out of the premises. We have video cameras at the gate as well as motion activated cameras at intervals around the perimeter fence. They record what they observe; it's monitored by an outside security service. Strategically placed cameras record the license plates of both entering and exiting vehicles. Incoming cattle turn west as they enter the main gate and unload onto the docks and alleys that supply this first section of cattle pens. That's the first two rows of back-to-back pens and there are twenty pens per row. Those pens hold our lightweight cattle. Across the wide alleyway are two back-to-back rows of pens for middleweight cattle. Across the next wide alleyway are the heavyweight pens. On the east side, there are a set of shipping pens and loading docks used for outgoing cattle. Our cowboys take finished cattle from their heavyweight pen and bring them to a shipping pen awaiting load-out and shipping to a terminal market. Also notice, the pen size and feed bunk length increases as the cattle grow. It's designed so ideally we have about 270-275 head in each pen."

"Notice the pens have a good slope to them so they drain well. There is also a grade from west to east; so, drainage caught at the south end of the pens drains to the east. That drainage goes into our waste settling pond, gets treated, and eventually reused for washing alleyways and holding pens, spraying pens to keep cattle cool in hot weather, and irrigation. To the west of the incoming docks is the horse barn and paddocks. Incoming grain trucks enter through the west wide alleyway drop their loads and then exit through the east alleyway. Incoming hay, haylage, and fresh chopped grains for silage enter through the east wide alleyway drop their loads and then exit through the west wide alleyway. We've paved the alleyways and the perimeter due to the volume of traffic; it also aids with dust control. The vet clinic is located toward the south end of the lot because the prevalent wind direction is out of the north to northwest; thus, minimizing the potential for airborne spread of pathogens. We also use the alleyways to drive sick cattle down to three separated hospital pens. Each hospital pen does not share a common fence or water source. There's one hospital pen for each weight of cattle; hopefully, further reducing cross contamination. Convalescent cattle return to the pen they came from. We steam roll our grain rations then blend them with the appropriate roughage source (ground alfalfa hay, haylage, or silage)."

"Thanks for stopping and talking me through the operation; it gives me a much clearer visual image of how your operation flows and why. There's been a lot of thought put into the design of this feedlot. It appears to be very efficient and designed with herd health and ease of handling further reducing environmental stressors. I don't think I have ever seen such a well-designed operation", commented Rex.

****

"Well you two appear to be hard at it", said Randy as he and Rex walked into the conference room. Both Juana and Cheri were busy staring at their laptop screens.

"We're transferring data from the ATX system over to Cheri's system", said Juana looking up and noticing Rex standing beside Randy.

"Hi, I'm Rex Yoder", offered Rex while extending his hand.

"Juana Gomez", said Juana reaching to shake Rex's hand.

"Doc, we're downloading data you will need to begin your epi survey. The compatibility of the two systems has made data transfer a breeze", commented Cheri. "The data is downloading both to my laptop and your tablet simultaneously through Wi-Fi connections. "Dr. Bennett, do you have an electronic copy of the feedlot's pen identification system that we can use for mapping where the animals were located when they became ill?"

"I have something that will work. I'll need to get into my PowerPoint files; then, I'll e-mail it to you and Rex. Does anyone want a bottle of water or a Coke?" Three hands synchronously waved in the air. "OK, who wants what; we have a pretty good selection. Water requested Cheri and Rex, while Juana requested a diet Dr. Pepper.

Rex sat down first checking for new e-mails on his phone. Scanning them he noticed one was from Dr. Yu requesting further information on mildly symptomatic cattle. Rex recanted Dr. Rogers's summary of when the ATX Hereford feedlot initially observed CNS signs in 17 head of their cattle affirming no cattle traveled to slaughter. Continuing through the e-mails, he read the e-mail trail documenting 'spent dairy cows' may have been harvested with their parts and pieces possibly entering both the human and pet food chains. Sam Yu notified USDA's Food Safety and Inspection Service (FSIS). They initiated their own investigation at a slaughter and processing facility in New Mexico. The FSIS investigation would soon trigger a recall of all products shipped from the slaughter plant. After reading the remainder of his e-mails, Rex turned his attention to his portion of the investigation.

About two hours later, Dr. Yu called Dr. Yoder. An issue related to his previous e-mail needed immediate clarification. Dr. Yu asked, "Rex, what happened to those cattle that were euthanized at the ATX feedlot? Were they taken to a pet food manufacturer, composted either on-site or off-site? An issue has come up at some of the other investigation sites. We must gather this information quickly.

"Sam, all ATX feedlots have on-site crematoriums. They moved the sampled cattle to the crematorium and burned them. A little while ago I went to look at it. Its capacity is about 65 head and it takes three to four hours to cremate the carcasses. They harvest and further process the oils for use as equipment fuel. The water that's separated out is essentially sterile due to the high temperatures in the crematorium; however, it's piped as influent into the feedlot's sewage treatment system, chemically treated, then used for washing alleyways, holding pens, and for irrigation of adjacent farm land."

"Thanks for the thorough description, Rex. We'll take them off the list of possible secondary introduction into pet foods. I don't think I have ever heard of a crematorium as large as you describe. If you get a chance, and if management will let you, please take some photos so we can all have an idea of what it looks like. Now, I better let you get back to work. Thanks again."

****

After introducing Cheri Alverez to Juana Gomez, Dennis exited the office through the back door returning to his pickup where Dr. Rogers and Sonny waited. "Ok Doc", Dennis said, "what's the plan?"

"We have two things we need to accomplish. First, we need to take several samples of your feed components. We also need to take water samples from several locations. Once we get these samples taken and ready for pick up by FedEx, we will start our second objective. That is to carefully look at all the cattle in the feedlot to identify any additional cattle displaying neurological signs."

"Now I see why we'll need all the sample boxes in the back of my pickup", said Dennis as they collected samples of each feed component.

Glen explained, "We're going to be taking three samples from all sources of feedstuffs and sending them to three separate laboratories. Each laboratory is part of a large university and a veterinary school. Therefore, we get a broad-spectrum analysis of the feedstuffs done on a rush basis. If they find something, we will have some of the best academic and research minds in the country involved."

Each lab will receive three boxes containing the feed components and one box of water samples. Glen powered on his new tablet computer, put the ear-bud in his ear, tapped a few icons and dictated a summary of all the samples taken and packaged. After sealing and labeling all twelve boxes, they stacked them in the shade outside the vet clinic awaiting the FedEx truck.

While at the vet clinic Glen suggested the team look at the animals in the sick pens showing signs of CNS disease. Then, they would observe each animal in the lightweight pens.

They observed each animal individually while they moved out slowly of their pen, into an adjacent alleyway, and back into the pen. They would separate those showing signs of CNS disease and move them to appropriate sick pen.

Before looking at cattle, Dennis drove to the office. Arriving Dennis said, "While I get a pen report, why don't you guys take a short break; use the bathroom, if needed, and get some water or cold coke. I'll meet you in the conference room and we can see if Cheri, Randy, or Rex have any insights that might help us."

"That is a great idea", said Sonny. "I'm a little parched and could use some water. I'll get everyone's. What do y'all want to drink?"

Dennis and Glen in unison said, "water". Dennis suggested getting several bottles to put into the ice chest behind the seat of his extended cab pickup.

Picking up the report Dennis met the others in the conference room. "We're about to start looking at cattle", said Glen. "Is there anything the data is showing that may be important for us to keep in mind?"

Rex responded, "We're just getting a start at looking at the data; however, probably the most significant thing we've come across is when we've looked at the amount of time on feed before showing clinical signs of CNS disease. The range has widened. The range is now between 68 days on feed to 239 days. As we get further into the data this may widen somewhat. Hopefully we'll be able to identify a historical event time that initiated onset of symptoms."

"That's helpful information", commented Glen. "We are going to start looking at the lightweight cattle; there were none in the sick pen. That led us to think it might not affect light weight cattle. We'll check back in later to see if y'all have more information."

Juan Garcia riding a stout red roan gelding and Philippe Ramos on a good looking gray gelding were in front of pen one. One of the cowboys previously closed the gate at the far end of the alleyway. Both cowboys sat with one knee over the saddle horn looking at the cattle in pen one. Dennis got out of the pickup reached in the front of the box grabbing a plastic gallon water jug wrapped with a wet burlap sack. He handed it over the fence to Philippe who immediately unscrewed the top and took a big guzzle, then handed it to Juan who also took a couple of big swigs before returning it to Philippe. Sonny and Dennis both put their ear buds in their ears and powered on their tablets getting them set up in the correct part of the investigation program. They positioned themselves near the gate where they would have optimum visibility of the cattle as they walked out of the pen and then returned. Dennis opened the gate allowing Juan and Philippe to ride slowly into the pen. He stood behind the open gate affording him a good view and in position to separate out anything identified as displaying CNS signs. The cowboys split up, slowly meandering through the pen as the steers walked through the open gate and down the alleyway affording everyone excellent visibility of each animal. Once all the steers were in the alleyway the cowboys pushed them slowly back into the pen.

Continuing to the next pen, everyone positioned themselves identically as the lightweight cattle moved out and then back into the pen. Methodically the men moved from pen to pen taking about four to five minutes per pen. Examining the cattle housed in the eighty lightweight pens took the men almost seven hours. They finished as the sun set. They identified 11 head showing very mild to moderate CNS signs. An abnormal movement of the eyes from side to side (lateral nystagmus) was the most prevalent sign noticed. A very slight nose or ear twitch was the second most prevalent sign. The cowboys drove the sorted-out animals to the lightweight hospital pen for further scrutiny and observation tomorrow morning.

****

As soon as the other teams departed the vet clinic, Dr. Adams asked Sammi and Jim Bob to help her arrange the examining tables and move a few mailing boxes near the smaller table, so she could work efficiently. After arranging the tables, Penny explained what each person would be doing.

"Once we all get into our personal protection equipment (PPE), Sammi I would like you to handle the samples I collect and package them. Jim Bob, I noticed all the cattle have electronic identification device (EID) tags in their ear. I would like you to euthanize the animals, read the tag with your hand-held EID tag reader, then take it over near Sammi who can wirelessly read the number on her computer and incorporate it into the Laboratory Submission Form she will be completing. Once I have collected all the samples from an animal and completed my postmortem exam, I will dictate my gross pathological findings using my ear bud. That dictation will complete the Laboratory Submission Form on both of our computers. Jim Bob, after the animal is euthanized, have the Bobcat driver pick it up in the bucket with the animal's left side laying in the bucket and its head flexed toward its chest." Penny continued to laid her equipment on the postmortem table. She attached a homemade looking contraption to the end of the hose. It had a squeeze type valve and a conical nozzle. Looking around to check that everything was in place Penny said; "If everyone's ready, I suggest we go to the bathroom. We'll then put on our PPE. It never fails that if I don't go first, it's just after I finish putting on (donning) the PPE that the urge strikes. Then I must go through the procedures for taking off (doffing) the protective equipment. Then repeat the donning procedures again."

After a few minutes Penny said; "I've laid out PPE for everyone. Jim Bob, I thought you might want the Bobcat driver to suit-up as well since he will be moving around with the carcasses and would be at higher risk for exposure."

"Good idea, I'll go get him. Jorge, please come in here, we're going to have you put on some extra gear for added protection."

With Jorge joining the group, Penny put on the white disposable coveralls while talking to the group. "You want them to fit a little large so that it is comfortable for you to move, bend, and maneuver. Once you have your legs and arms in the coveralls, do not put the hood on yet. Next, we put on the mask, being sure it covers both your chin and nostrils. Then, we put the face shield on our head. Now we're ready to zip up the coveralls and put on the hood. Once that's all done, put on the rubber boot covers followed by the inner lightweight gloves. Make sure not to tuck your pant legs in the boot tops, let them hang outside. Avoid tucking your sleeves into the gloves. Jorge, we are going to put on a rubber outer aprons, but you will not need to do this. I'll also be putting on two rubber shoulder length gloves rather than the heavy nitrile gloves; that will work better for me when I'm doing the postmortem exams and collecting samples."

Jorge walked outside to cat calls from the two mounted cowboys, one horse spooked. Seeing Jorge, the horse lowered his head, snorted, and walked backwards.

Penny explained to Sammi and Jim Bob; "I'll be doing minimally invasive postmortems and sampling. I'll be taking samples of brain, tonsils, lymph nodes, lung, heart, liver, kidney, ileum with Peyer's patches, spleen, and fat. Jim Bob, would you please take three tubes of blood? We need one red top tube and two purple top tubes. I think that's it. Do you have any questions?"

Sammi asked; "Is that why there are larger sample jars than we normally have? How am I to handle the brain?"

"Good questions! There are two sizes of sample jars; there's medium size filled with formalin and a large size also filled with formalin. I will remove the brain through the foramen magnum on the back side of the skull and cut it lengthwise. Sammi I want you to put half of the brain in the large jar and seal it. The other hemisphere goes into a medium size Whirl-Pac bag, seal it, and then put that bag into a larger size Whirl-Pac bag and seal that one too. Once double bagged, put into the cooler sample box. Make sure there's cardboard between the bagged brain and the frozen coolant. We'll keep the brain and spinal cord samples separate. All the other samples can be placed in the medium size jar of formalin."

"Let's get started", said Penny.

Jim Bob placed the captive bolt knocking gun in the appropriate position and humanely euthanized the first steer. Pushing a lever, the side of the chute opened horizontally from the top causing the steer to roll out on the alleyway floor. Jim Bob inserted a Vacutainer needle into the steer's jugular vein collecting the blood samples. Jorge picked up the steer in the Bobcat bucket elevating the bucket. Jim Bob scanned the EID tag in the animals' right ear and flexed the steer's neck where the top of the nose was resting against the inside of the bucket. Jorge turned the Bobcat and drove about ten feet into the postmortem room. Penny signaled Jorge to lower the bucket to a more comfortable working height. When the top of the steer's head was about waist high to Penny, she waved to Jorge that was the correct elevation. Without hesitation Penny pulled a sharp pointed knife out of her scabbard and made an incision through the skin from the midline down about five inches and extended the incision down the opposite side. Next, she made a deeper incision across the midline just behind the skull cutting through a large ligament and the muscles just to the side of the ligament. With a slight twist of Penny's wrist, the blade went between the skull and the first cervical vertebrae as she incised the spinal cord and loosened the connection of the top of the head to the neck cutting none of the major vessels. Reaching for the hose she placed the conical end firmly in the hole made in the forehead by the captive bolt. She slowly released the squeeze valve and water flowed out of the hose and into the steer's cranium. The brain began slowly to protrude through the foramen magnum in the back part of the skull. Remarkably the entire brain squeezed through the foramen magnum, then an outpouring of water. Penny picked up the brain, placing it on the cutting board where she sliced the brain lengthwise. One hemisphere went into the large jar of formalin Sammi was holding. Then she placed the other hemisphere into the Whirl-Pac bag.

Allowing the animal's nose to come free from the inner edge of the bucket, Penny made additional incisions behind and below the jaw to expose and sample the tonsils and lymph nodes of the head, pharynx, and tongue. Sammi held the medium sized jar of formalin near where Penny was working and she dropped in the sampled tissues after harvesting them.

Walking around to the front of the loader bucket Penny stopped at the steer's ribs. She made an incision about eighteen inches long between two ribs just behind the shoulder. This incision went through the skin, rib muscles, and entered the thoracic cavity. Next, she grasped a stainless-steel instrument, after placing it between the ribs Penny ratcheted. When the ribs spread apart about five inches, Penny reached into the chest cavity sampling lung, heart muscle, and two lymph nodes. As her left arm came out of the chest cavity, she gripped the side of the rib spreader releasing it and returning the ribs to their original position.

Next, Penny side stepped making about an eight-inch incision slightly off-midline through the abdominal wall, being careful not to nick the underlying intestines. Reaching into abdominal cavity Penny collected small tissue samples of the spleen, a portion of the distal small intestine, the liver, and kidney.

The postmortem exam and sample collection procedures from euthanasia to when Jorge was backing out of the postmortem room took less than four minutes. As Jorge took the carcass to the dump truck, Jim Bob euthanized the next animal. As Penny dictated into her ear bud, Sammi boxed the samples from that animal and put FedEx shipping labels on the box. And so, it went for almost four hours as the team worked through 16 middleweights and 12 from the heavyweight pen. When finished, Penny washed her equipment, sharpened her knives. Two other workers appeared and cleaned the necropsy room. Penny, Jim Bob, Sammi, and Jorge doffed their PPE sealing the protective clothing into red bio-hazard bags. Jorge took the bio-hazard bags to the dump truck and drove the carcasses and bio-hazard bags to the crematorium.

"I don't know about everyone else, but I am really parched", said Penny as she walked to the refrigerator pulling out three bottles of water. Everyone drank down one bottle quickly. Everyone drank another bottle.

"Let's walk over to the office to see how Rex, Randy, and Cheri are progressing", said Jim Bob.

"That would be great" said Penny. "Maybe they have come up with something."

Randy greeted the three as they walked into the conference room saying, "Did y'all decide to finally take a break?"

"Randy, we're finished!" said Jim Bob. "The carcasses are in the dump truck and heading to the crematorium. I wouldn't have believed it; if I had not been there to see it. I've never seen anyone do 28 necropsies in less than four hours! That's averaging less than eight minutes per necropsy including donning and doffing the protective clothing. Penny is remarkable. Her knife is sharper than a scalpel and she has such knowledge of anatomy and pathology. I have never seen someone work so efficiently. Watching Penny is like watching a gifted surgeon."

"I thought you would be impressed", said Rex. "Glen texted me a while ago while they were looking at lightweight cattle. He said they had found a few exhibiting lateral nystagmus and some subtle nose twitches. They've sorted them out and will be moving them to the lightweight sick pen later this afternoon. Maybe we should all make a point of looking at them tomorrow morning. Cheri and Juana are getting me lots of good data. I'm running it through the statistical and epi programs. My analysis is incomplete; so, I don't have much information yet. Perhaps in a few hours I will have something. Randy, is now a good time to go back to the crematorium and look before it becomes operational?"

"It's an ideal time to head up there and take another look. Jorge and Lupe should have the dump truck about emptied. Penny, do you have an interest in seeing the grey monster fire up? I also have some news I will share with you as we drive up there."

Penny walked toward Randy's pickup. She slid into middle of the front bench seat. Rex slipped in next to her as Randy started the noisy diesel. As the pickup headed up the middle alleyway Randy said, "Within the last 15 minutes I have gotten e-mails from two of our other feedlots. One lot is located south of here near Dimmitt and the other is east of there, near Tulia. The Dimmitt yard identified two middleweights and the Tulia yard has identified five showing possible CNS signs. I knew you would want to know. I thought perhaps you would need to go look and possibly take samples at both places."

With a thoughtful look Rex said, "That's all we need; more premises breaking with CNS disease. Before I can give you an answer, I'd better contact Dr. Yu, the incident coordinator. He's managing this outbreak. He may want to send additional teams down. When we get back to the office, I'll give him a call. What kind of distances are we talking about from here to the Dimmit feedlot and then to the Tulia feedlot? Is there a possibility that if we sample at one or both feedlots that the samples can be picked up by FedEx today?"

"It's about twenty miles from here to the Dimmitt yard", said Randy. "I can have everything ready so we can just pull in, look at the two animals, euthanize them, and take samples. It's about fifty-five miles from the Dimmitt yard to the Tulia yard and we can do the same thing there. I know we can get FedEx to come to the Tulia yard, if we contact them right away. But I don't know what time it would be. Let me call Shelly at the office and have her work on it." Randy picked up the two-way radio from its hook on his dash board. "Six to Canyon base, come in."

"Go ahead six, this is Canyon base", responded Shelly.

"Shelly, would you please contact FedEx and see if they would be able to pick-up some sample boxes at the Tulia yard this afternoon? If they can, ask them about what time they would be there. There will be as many as seven boxes. Thanks, six out."

"Will do, Randy", replied Shelly.

They were unloading the last carcass as Randy's pickup rounded the corner behind the silos. A large winch mounted on an "A" frame picked up the carcass by a hind leg lowering it into the crematorium. Once the cable was slack and free from the hind limb, the dump truck pulled forward. Jorge sprinted back to help Lupe close the hydraulically driven thick metal clam-shell doors. Randy stopped his truck near the dump truck where they all had a good view. Lupe walked over to a wheel type valve rising out of the ground adjacent to a pressurized tank about twenty feet tall and fifteen feet in diameter. Once Lupe opened the first valve, Jorge, who had walked into a small nearby cinder block building, opened a second valve causing a brief loud hissing sound almost immediately followed by gas ignition. They felt the gas ignite as they sat in the pickup. Jorge flipped a lever mounted on the wall. Randy identified it as an automatic flue control. For about two minutes the smoke rising out of a pipe chimney was blue-black in color having an odor of burning hair and hide. The thunderous sound was continual. It would not decrease until after the unit shut down. When complete, the only thing remaining from the twenty-eight carcasses would be fine gray ash and the remnants of a few teeth. Randy explained they had never cremated this number before. He estimated it would take about three hours. Then another two hours for the unit to cool down enough for people to safely work around it. As Jorge exited the control shack he turned on bright red rotating lights all around the concrete bunker. Without doubt, it is a dangerous area when the crematorium is operational.

Randy returned the way he had come. "Base to six" called the feedlot two-way. "What do you have for me Shelly", said Randy.

"FedEx can pick up at the Tulia yard this afternoon. "They said they should be there between 5:30 and 6:00 this afternoon. The truck will be coming from Plainview. It's scheduled to leave there shortly after 5:00, with one stop to make before coming to the yard. I've scheduled them to stop. If you don't want them to come, let me know and I will cancel. The driver is my cousin, Frank. So, I'll just call him on his cell."

"Thanks, Shelly. You're the best! Six out."

Returning to the conference room, Rex walked into Dennis' office to make the call to Dr. Yu. "Hi, Sam", said Rex. "We've received reports an additional two ATX feedlots, one near Dimmitt and the other near Tulia, have seven head displaying CNS signs. Two animals reported at the Dimmitt feedlot and five at the Tulia feedlot. It's about twenty miles to Dimmitt and about an hour from Dimmitt to Tulia. We can take samples today, if you wish, and have them picked up today by FedEx. Penny has finished her postmortems and sampling here for today. I anticipate more tomorrow. I thought I would give you a call to see how you wanted to handle this. I thought you might want to dispatch additional teams."

Dr. Yu hesitated before responding, "Rex, all hell has broken loose this afternoon. We've gotten reports of new CNS cases at thirty-two different premises in eleven states. Your report makes premises thirty-three and thirty-four; and we still have a few hours left in the day. If Penny can sample those two premises this afternoon it would be great. We do not have the resources to detail additional people to your area. I was about to call you to update you on the situation. Your team needs to collect data from the additional two feedlots and incorporate the additional two feedlots into your investigation. Can you get it done?"

"Sam, we can get it done. It will take longer; but we're making great headway today. Glen and Sonny Kelley are still out looking at cattle. Cheri and I are making good progress in the office. ATX uses the same hardware and software for their computer systems as we do. All the feedlots report their data in this manner, so it won't present a major problem to collect the additional data and get it ready for analysis and interpretation. If you don't have anything else, I'm going to send Penny and Sammi with Randy Bennett to the other two feedlots right away so they will have time to sample and get things ready for FedEx."

"That's all I know for now", said Sam. "Thanks for your help!"

Chapter 5

Walking back to the conference room Rex asked, "Penny could you and Sammi hitch a ride with Randy or Jim Bob to the Dimmitt and Tulia feedlots?"

"Sure", said both Penny and Sammi.

Randy responded, "Jim Bob and I were just talking about what's going on. We're both going to head that way. Penny why don't you ride with me. Sammi and Jim Bob can load up everything in Jim Bob's truck and follow us. Why don't you grab some soft drinks and water? *I hope my suggestion didn't sound too obvious. Penny is beautiful with her blue eyes and long blond hair, she is very bright, talented, and she has a great body,* Randy thought. *I must get to know her better.*

"That sounds great", said Penny grabbing a plastic sack and filling it with cold water and soda. Did I see a chest type cooler behind the seat in your pickup?" *This is going to work out great! I want to get to know Randy better. He's tall, good looking, well mannered, we have a lot in common, and he's single,* thought Penny.

"You sure did. It's a necessity during the summer. Let me open the door for you", said Randy. Penny put the water bottles and soda into the cooler as Randy fired up the diesel. About fifteen minutes later, Randy pulled into the ATX Dimmitt feedlot. Randy drove directly to the Dimmitt vet clinic where Sonny Thompson, the feedlot manager, met him. Sonny appeared to be in his early thirties with a big blond handlebar mustache. He stood six feet eight weighing around two-hundred-eighty pounds. Had it not been for his deeply tanned face, the dusty Stetson, and high-topped boots with spurs affixed, Sonny looked like he could be playing for the Dallas Cowboys.

Getting out of the pickup Randy and Penny walked toward Sonny. "Sonny, meet Dr. Penny Adams. Dr. Adams is a pathologist with APHIS and is going to look at the two middleweights you pulled out", said Randy.

Lifting the brim of his Stetson, Sonny responded, "Nice to meet you Dr. Adams. I just spoke to Jim Bob and he's about 2 minutes behind you. There's one steer and one heifer. I've have them in the alleyway behind the chute. You can get a good look at them there; if necessary, we can catch them in the chute."

"Nice to meet you Sonny", said Penny. "You lead the way and we'll be right behind you."

Sonny walked around the end of the vet clinic adjacent to the alleyway. A Santa Gertrudis steer stood there looking at them. His droopy ears were facing forward listening as the three moved down the outside of the alleyway. "I think he's blind and he 'wobbles' behind as he walks. Let me get him to move a little. He's kinda reluctant because he doesn't know where he is", Sonny described as he climbed over the fence. Sonny slowly walked toward the steer with an arm extended.

Waving his arm about six inches from the left eye and the steer did not move away from his menacing hand. Sonny spoke quietly so the steer could hear how near he was. The steer quickly backed up, pivoted, and walked into the pipe fence on the far side of the alleyway. His rear legs appeared to lack the coordination of his front legs. He almost fell when he ran into the fence. "The baldy heifer standing at the opposite end of the pen acts like she doesn't know where her front feet are. She kinda 'goose steps' and if you put a little pressure on her, she's easy to get on the fight".

"Sonny, you are exactly right in your assessment of both animals", said Penny. "I've noticed both have mild twitching of their noses. Randy, I also think I'm seeing a very mild lateral nystagmus affecting both animals. What do you think?"

"I see what you are seeing. If you had not made me look closely, I would have missed it. Sonny, what Dr. Adams is talking about is how their eyes are moving to the right and left almost like they are vibrating side to side. It's really subtle."

"I see what you're talking about", Sonny exclaimed as he carefully looked at both animals. "I hadn't noticed that before. Hey, here's Jim Bob pulling in."

"Let's sample both", said Penny. It will take us a few minutes to get ready; but with both Sammi and Jim Bob already knowing what to do, it won't take us long."

"Junior is coming with the loader", said Sonny. "I'll go open the gate for him and swing around to help unload your supplies."

Penny and Randy walked in the postmortem room door. Randy opened the overhead door and Penny noticed Sonny had set up the tables like she had arranged them at Hereford earlier this morning. The EID tag reader was already out as was the knocking gun to euthanize the animals. There was a hose already hung over the end of the table used by Penny.

A thought crossed Penny's mind-*I hope Sammi had remembered to get the pressure nozzle from Hereford*. Jim Bob and Sammi exited their pickup introducing Sammi to Sonny. Jim Bob, Sammi, and Sonny each walked into the postmortem room carrying boxes. Sammi placed a box containing Penny's knives, scissors, hemostats, and the pressure nozzle on the postmortem table. Penny thanked Sammi for remembering the device as she'd left attached it to the hose. Sammi also carried a box with PPE equipment through the postmortem room and into the wash sink area. Sonny and Jim Bob carried the sample boxes which they placed on the other table. Sammi and Jim Bob walked into the wash sink area. Everyone donned their protective equipment. Penny finished and walked out into the postmortem room suggesting to Randy he move into the wash sink area where he could watch through the window protecting himself. Sonny announced he would push the cattle into the chute. He climbed into the alleyway, opened a gate, and positioned the heifer to go into the chute first and then slowly allowed the blind steer to follow the heifer into the narrow alley behind the chute. Simultaneously Jim Bob explained to Junior how to position the loader and the animal in the bucket.

After Sonny loaded the heifer into the chute, Jim Bob euthanized the animal and Junior picked it up in the loader bucket. They harvested and handled the samples the same way as in Hereford. Fifteen minutes after making her first incision Penny was washing her equipment and putting it back into the box at the end of the table. Doffing her PPE, Penny walked into the wash sink area asking Randy, "How much time do we have to get to Tulia and collect the remaining five samples?"

"We're doing good 'Speedy'; we've got over two hours before FedEx should be there. If we are close to finishing when Frank arrives, he'll wait a few minutes. He's a good guy, and would enjoy a cold coke at his last stop. He used to work for ATX trucking. He understands. That said, we still need to hurry every chance we get."

"I'm ready when you are, slow-poke," giggled Penny as she walked out the door in a subtly flirtatious manner. *I hope that wasn't too obvious, but hopefully he got the message that I'm interested in him.*

"Sonny, thanks for all your help and having everything set up when we arrived", Penny said as she exited the postmortem room with perhaps a little more wiggle in her step than normal. It did not go unnoticed by Randy who waved to Sonny as he departed.

Sonny, grinned to himself thinking; *It looks like one of Amarillo's most eligible bachelors is off the market.*

Chapter 6

Randy pulled out of the ATX Dimmitt feedlot heading south. After traveling three miles he turned left on Highway 82 toward Dimmitt and then Tulia. Penny picked up her cell phone; apologizing for needing to make a call.

"Diane Kaminski please. Hi Diane, it's Penny Adams. I apologize for calling so late, but I need more sampling boxes. Yes, yes, the boxes sent last week arrived at the motel just fine and a few remain, but not enough. If possible, about one hundred more boxes-whatever you can get on two pallets. No, I'm not kidding. I've used 35 today of the 50 shipped and they're on their way back. You should receive them in tomorrow's early FedEx delivery. We've found two other ATX feedlots with cattle showing symptoms. Dr. Yu asked us to investigate those feedlots as well. What about the smaller sampling boxes with two medium jars of formalin? I could use those and just sample spinal cord, obex, and midbrain. Dr. Rogers will also need two additional sets of boxes for sampling feed and water at the two new premises. Well, send what you can and we'll improvise. Don't worry Diane, I understand. Also, please change the delivery destination to the ATX Feedlot in Hereford, Texas? Yes, that's it. Thanks. Bye."

"Are you going to have enough sampling supplies for tomorrow?" asked Randy.

"Probably...not really", responded Penny. "If we begin to run short, I've got some ideas that will get us through. Reaching into the cooler behind the seat Penny asked, "Do you want a pop? I'm in need of caffeine."

"A Dr. Pepper would be fine", said Randy.

Penny sorted out a Dr. Pepper, popped the top, and set it in the empty beverage holder on his side of the console. "Randy, I enjoyed talking with your Dad this morning. He's an amazing man. He's put together a diverse, yet integrated, empire using the talents of his children or their spouses. That's an extraordinary accomplishment during one lifetime. I'm sure you are proud of his accomplishments."

"I am very proud, but if you ask Dad, he'll tell you he's just been lucky. I'm here to tell you, he's been willing to take risks when he thinks it's the right thing to do. ATX Oil revenues are the foundation of our businesses. My brother Mike has made some good calls and is a good manager; but, it was Dad who took the risks. When we were all kids Dad laid down a solid production platform for Mike to expand. Dad invested the revenues from that business into the other business units; first into the bank, then into the others over time. My grandfather was a rancher and Dad was an only child. He first took over the ATX ranch when his dad died. The original ranch bordered the north and east sides of Amarillo. As Amarillo grew, the original ranch became development property. When the developers wanted a piece of the original ranch, Dad didn't sell the land. Rather, he traded the real estate value acquiring a bigger, better ranch somewhere. Later, ATX Oil explored that property. Dad didn't drill too many dry wells. Mike has carried on that development and has been more successful than Dad. That allowed further expansion. Currently all ATX business units are mature. We're expected to independently generate a profit annually. Collectively, we invest sixty-five percent of our net profits back into one or more business units for expansion and further development. It has worked out to be a good business model."

"What I'm most proud of are the things Dad has done behind the scenes. Dad and a group of primarily Texas horsemen and ranchers were instrumental in influencing the American Quarter Horse Association to locate their headquarters in Amarillo. He donated the land for the airport, the bank underwrote the bond issue, and invested in the airport bonds. The city and county officials wanted to name the airport after him; but he would have no part of it. Amarillo is rather isolated and needed a new hospital. Dad and a few of his cronies, including Philip Granger, took on that task a few years ago. My brothers Tony and Bobby collaborated on the design, materials, and built the hospital. Now Amarillo has a new state of the art hospital attracting some of most talented medical specialists in Texas. The hospital also serves as a teaching hospital affiliated with Texas Tech University's medical school. Amarillo now serves as the medical hub for the Texas panhandle, western Oklahoma, and eastern New Mexico. Dad will tell you that all of those things were just the right things to do, avoiding any credit."

"I know Dad would not say so, but we're worried this CNS disease. Whatever it is. It could be devastating not only for ATX's feeding operations, but to ATX in general. ATX owns some interest in approximately half of the cattle in our feedlots. We have over 400 million invested in cattle, feed, facilities, etc."

"Your Dad is a great man, much more so than I imagined when I met him this morning. From what I have seen today, I think you're cut from that same bolt of cloth. Hopefully we can get this malady figured out quickly."

"Penny thanks for everything you're doing and your kind words. I've told you a lot about my family. I don't know a thing about you or your family. To be as considerate and talented as you are, you must have great parents. Tell me about them."

"My folks live in Denver. Dad is a cardiothoracic surgeon specializing in pediatrics. He's on the staff at the CU Medical School as well as Denver's Children's Hospital. Mom is an architect with her own small company. Before the recession, Mom did a lot of office and large commercial buildings. Now, she delegates most of that work to the other two architects who work with her. For the last few years, she has primarily designed custom houses which my brothers build. I have two older brothers; they are identical twins and both engineers. They co-own a construction company specializing in high-end custom single-family housing. Before the economy took the dive in 2008, their construction business flourished. They also did some light commercial buildings. Their business model is Mom designs the houses; my brothers build them, and my Dad bankrolls the operation until the houses sell. I think Mom's enjoyed not working so hard. She's been able to travel with Dad to meetings and they have taken a couple of cruises."

"It sounds like you too have been blessed with a close family. I'm surprised that you didn't go into human medicine because of your Dad. I'll bet he attempted to influence you in that direction."

"Dad certainly provided the information and subtle influence. As a teenager, I watched him do surgery and rounds. But I also observed his frustration with government involvement in decision making, insurance companies, and the other not so fun aspects of medicine. I worked in his office during the summers while in college and veterinary school. It was his influence that made me direct my career toward veterinary medicine and pathology rather than human medicine. The dedication he has for his career and his patients often translates into long pressure filled hours, and not much time for family. That also influenced my brothers. They are both married with families. While they work hard, at the end of most days, they go home and spend time with their wives and children. I wanted a career like that as well, particularly if I were to get married and have a family."

Turning right at the sign identifying ATX Tulia Feedlot Randy announced, "We're here. It seemed like time flew by as we visited. I enjoyed getting to know more about you and your family." *And I want to get to know you better,* Randy thought.

"I know, it seemed like only a few minutes ago we left Dimmitt", confirmed Penny. "Well let's see what these critters look like."

"Dr. Adams, meet Bud Thomas", said Randy. "Bud is the manager here in Tulia."

Penny smiled and extended her hand to shake Bud's hand. "It's nice to meet you, Bud."

Bud's left hand held the crown of his black Stetson lifting it off his mostly bald head. "The pleasure is mine Dr. Adams." Bud was about five ten and weighted about two hundred pounds. His deeply tanned face, neck, and hands displayed the many hours he's spent in the sun. The contrast between his forehead below the hat brim and where the Stetson protected the top of his head was remarkable. Bud was about sixty years old and his exposed skin had the leathered look of a cowboy, as did his faded Wrangler jeans and pale denim shirt. Penny would learn Bud talked little. A single rein hung over the top pipe rail securing his good looking blue roan gelding to the outside the alleyway fence.

"We've got them all in the alleyway for you to look at", said Bud to Randy. About that time Jim Bob and Sammi pulled up. Jim Bob introduced Sammi to Bud. As Penny watched the introductions, Bud seemed almost shy around women, but exhibited impeccable manners. Addressing Jim Bob, Bud asked, "Is there anything I can haul into the clinic?" Jim Bob handed Bud three sample boxes while he carried two additional sample boxes and the box of PPE gear. Sammi grabbed Penny's supplies. Penny and Randy walked to the alleyway. Penny commenting that all AXT feedlots seemed to have identical layouts.

Like Sonny, Bud walked slowly through the cattle allowing them to move slowly; each carefully evaluated separately. All displayed CNS signs. Randy was first to say, "All of them are showing nystagmus and discrete nose twitches. Ataxia affected two others, one displayed an abnormal gait. Another showed a head tilt to the right. The final one, the black steer, is reluctant to rise and appears to be weak and unsteady on his feet."

As the team got ready to sample, Randy also donned the PPE protective gear; he wanted closely watch Penny's sampling and necropsy techniques. Two cowboys came to the vet clinic as they donned their protective gear. One was horseback. He reached over picking up the rein hung over the fence advising Bud he would put his horse up and feed him. The other delivered a Bobcat. Bud elected to drive the Bobcat and the cowboy ran the feeder cattle into the chute for euthanasia. The sampling team worked efficiently, with Penny describing what she was doing as she took her samples. Randy watched in amazement, offering accolades at each stage. Randy, it appeared, was exceptionally impressed when Penny removed the brains and spinal cords using water pressure. Once the sampling was complete, Penny finished dictation of her gross postmortem findings on the last animal. Then she washed and disinfected her knives and other sampling instruments. She stoned and steeled her knives until they were both sharpened to her satisfaction. Sammi finished up packaging the last samples into the sample box and affixed a FedEx label. After everyone doffed their PPE, two other workers came into the postmortem room and washed and sanitized the room. Everyone except the two workers exited the building carrying boxes of something. They set the sample boxes on the ground in the shade and the other supplies into the bed of Jim Bob's pickup.

Penny reached into Randy's pickup grabbing her phone to call Rex. "Rex", we just finished up at Tulia. I was wondering if you had left Hereford yet... I'm glad you are still there. I was thinking maybe you and Cheri could pick Sammi and me up at the ATX Feeders office in Canyon. Jim Bob mentioned he lives northwest of Tulia and Randy lives near Happy, which is about fifteen miles south of Canyon. It would save Randy extra drive time."

"I have a few more minutes to work and then I will be at a logical stopping place", said Rex. "Cheri and Juana are shutting down their computers now. Cheri and I will be glad to pick you and Sammi up in Canyon. I agree there's no point in having Randy take you back to Amarillo. We'll be going right by their headquarters. We will see you in about 45 minutes. Dennis and Sonny can drive the other Suburban back to Amarillo when they finish. They're almost finished with the lightweights."

"Thanks, Rex", said Penny.

Penny placed several bottles of water and cans of coke in a plastic sack to take to the others. "Is anyone else thirsty", asked Penny. Everyone grabbed a cold drink and quenched their thirst.

"That really hits the spot", said Bud as he drained about half the bottle of water. "Here comes Frank now", acknowledged Bud as he walked toward the samples. Frank, Jim Bob, and Bud loaded the samples.

Frank joined the group greeting Randy. "Hi Doc" said Frank. "Late afternoon samples I see from the labels. Problems? I noticed the pickup bed full of carcasses."

"We've got some sort of disease that's affected a few cattle. We're just trying to figure out what's going on", responded Randy. "How about a coke for the road?"

"Yeah, that would be great", said Frank. "It's been a hot one; a cold Coke would be great as I head back to Amarillo. Thanks, Randy. Good to see you again."

Penny stood next to Randy as everyone formed a loose circle. Bud asked when test results would be available. Penny commented, "The samples should all arrive mid-morning tomorrow. The receiving process begins immediately. First, they will be examined by Dr. Rhodes-Voss grossly. She'll dissect the brain and attached spinal cord looking for gross lesions. They will arrive fixed in formalin, which preserves the tissue. Next, they put them in a fluid to dehydrate, clear, and infiltrate the CNS tissue with paraffin wax. Subsequently they're embedded in a block of wax. That makes them easy to section as well as facilitating storage and handling. Cutting very thin sections using a microtome comes next. After mounting staining comes next. Stains include hematoxylin/eosin (H&E) stain, a silver stain, and maybe GIEMSA stain after imbedding it in plastic. Dr. Rhodes-Voss will read all the stained sections. Preparation of sections of fresh brain tissue for immunohistochemical (IHC) and Western Blot testing is next in the sequence. IHC testing takes three to five days to read depending upon results. Confirmation of a positive takes five days. A negative test is complete in three days. Western Blot testing takes about four hours from start to finish using the Snap Protein Detection System. As Dr. Rhodes-Voss reads the slides, she will take photographs of microscopic fields using a digital camera attached to the microscope. She will e-mail those images to me to for a second interpretation. Long story short, we get negative results in three days; but, if the test is positive or inconclusive, it takes five days. The test results so far have all been inconclusive. Thus, the samples were sent to the National Veterinary Services Lab (NVSL) and later sent to international reference lab in England."

"Now I understand why we were not getting results reported back on the earlier samples", said Randy. Jim Bob nodded his head in agreement. "We erroneously thought the NVSL had a problem reporting results or had lost them. I better understand why you're here investigating this issue."

Randy commented. "If you'll help Sammi get what she needs out of Jim Bob's truck, I'll wrap things up here and meet y'all at my pickup."

Sammi and Penny met Randy at the pickup. Shortly it pulled out of the Tulia feedlot headed north on I 27. Penny did not miss the opportunity to sit in the middle of the front seat next to Randy. At Happy, Randy turned on to Highway 87, a more direct route to Canyon. It took about 30 minutes to travel to Canyon.

Pulling into the AXT headquarters parking lot Randy commented, "I'll bet you are both starving; I know I am. We all missed lunch and the burrito I ate on the way to Hereford is long gone."

"I'm famished", said Penny.

Sammi said, "Me too!"

Randy said, "I know a good place near here that serves really good food. It's about a block from the campus and caters to the college crowd; the food is good and prices are in line with what college kids can afford. Do you want to ask Rex if he and Cheri would like to stop there?"

Both girls were nodding yes as Rex pulled up in one of the Suburbans and parked next to Randy's side of the pickup. "Hey, do you guys want to catch a bite to eat at a restaurant near here? The food is good and the portions are healthy."

"Sure", said Rex and Cheri simultaneously.

"Follow me", said Randy. "It's called the Lone Star; it's a block south of campus."

Walking into the Lone Star Randy was immediately greeted by the hostess/owner, Mavis. She seated everyone at a large circular table in the back of the restaurant near the kitchen. The smell of the food was appetizing. A look at the plates of those who sat at nearby tables displayed many foods. It was not long before Glen and Sonny joined them. It seemed like only a few minutes before steaming plates filled the table. They delivered everything from cheeseburgers and fries, to enchiladas, and chicken fried steaks. The social talking that had preceded delivery of their meals dissipated. As the group satisfied its initial hunger, light conversations again sprung up and everyone got to know one another better. After dinner Randy received accolades for suggesting the Lone Star. As the group left the restaurant with their hunger extinguished, getting sleep now became the next objective.

Randy walked Penny to his pickup separate from the others. Reaching in Penny got both her purse and Sammi's, while Randy lifted the boxes of supplies out of back seat putting them in the back of a Suburban. "I've really enjoyed this afternoon and getting to know a little about you", commented Randy. "I'd like to get to know you better; perhaps tomorrow I will be able to be your chauffer again."

"I'd like that too", said Penny. "I can't think when I have had such a wonderful day and met so many wonderful people. You're at the top of that list! Historically, these investigations keep us all very busy for a few days, then we all go back home. With the other two lots breaking, we'll be here a little longer; hopefully we'll get some private time together", Penny quietly commented so only Randy would hear. Feeling her face blush, Penny opened the rear door saying "good night". *Well, now he knows how I feel. We'll see if he shares those feelings.*

Before Randy closed the Suburban's rear door he leaned in and asked, "Do you know about what time you'll be at Hereford tomorrow morning?"

Rex responded, "We have a conference call at 7:00AM. As soon as it's over we'll head your way." Randy nodded and gave him a thumbs-up closing the door. The two Suburbans headed toward Amarillo driving directly to the motel. Arriving at the motel, everyone helped move the remainder of the supplies out of the conference room and into the Suburbans.

With both vehicles resupplied, everyone went to their rooms. Day one of the investigation was complete.

Chapter 7

Arriving at the west side of the White House, Secretary Johansen walked in the side entrance and up to the cabinet room in the west wing. Sitting down, Clare booted up her tablet placing it in front of her. Momentarily President John Smyth entered the room. The room quieted, a Secret Service agent closed the door. The cabinet meeting began. President Smyth's cabinet meetings were issue driven. They began with national security issues, followed by international issues, and followed up with domestic issues.

Late last night Clare e-mailed President Smyth briefly outlining the outbreak and requesting time at the cabinet meeting to brief everyone.

After discussing the nation's security and international issues, President Smyth said; "Clare, there is an issue with some sick cattle you wanted to tell us about. What's going on?"

"Thank you Mr. President", said Clare. "We have an emerging animal disease outbreak in five states: California, New Mexico, Texas, Kansas, and Colorado. In the past eighteen days cattle, of dairy and beef breeds, have developed a variety of initially vague central nervous system signs. Seven premises are currently involved. In total, the National Veterinary Services Laboratory received 122 brain samples. The results from all these samples were inconclusive for BSE. The seven premises are currently under quarantine and investigative teams are onsite beginning work this morning in hopes of identifying a common source material or infectious agent. A couple of days ago, I initiated a conference call with an international reference laboratory in England. Subsequently a military courier delivered the samples to the laboratory. The samples arrived and testing is underway.

This outbreak has potentially significant animal health, economic, and political ramifications. Therefore, we have not briefed the press on the outbreak. I plan to wait until we have the results back before we go public. The day after tomorrow at 1:00PM I have a conference call with my counterpart Minister Coy to discuss the test results and their ramifications. Because of the remote possibility of terrorism, I have notified the Agricultural Inspector General's Office, the FBI, and others. We simply do not know if a terrorist act has occurred. We should have a better idea when we speak in two days."

President Smyth listened intently and then commented, "Thank you Secretary Johansen for bringing us up to date with this emerging issue. While we do not have all the facts yet, would you share any further thoughts you may have, but cannot substantiate?"

Clare gathered her thoughts and began; "Mr. President, there are many aspects of this outbreak that are disturbing. Historically, epidemics do not begin in this manner. Rather, they begin in a focal point and spread from that foci. This outbreak started in multiple spots essentially simultaneously. Its clinical symptoms are many vague central nervous system disease signs. The brain and spinal cord pathology is puzzling. It has similarities to BSE or 'Mad Cow Disease'. However, the pathology somewhat different; BSE occurs sporadically, not with multiple cases on one farm or feedlot. The results from our laboratories are consistent. All results are inconclusive for BSE. This leaves me, and some of the best and most experienced veterinary scientists we have, to conclude we may be dealing with a novel disease. What causes this malady? How it spreads? Where it came from? How did it get here? What kind of morbidity and mortality we are to expect in the nation's cattle herd? Does it affect other species of animals? Does it affect humans? We don't know the answers to these questions. These are all questions we must answer. We are proceeding in a logical scientific manner attempting to answer these questions. After that we hope to determine if there is a cure. However, as we proceed down this path there may be other questions that arise."

"I am particularly concerned about food safety. The food safety act prohibits slaughter and consumption of animals displaying central nervous system disease. We don't know if this disease affects other animals or if their brains are infected before they become symptomatic. There may be a need to enact a temporary moratorium on cattle slaughter in interest of the public health."

"I'm concerned what effect the knowledge of this disease may have on the commodities market and on equities in general. Specifically, I'm concerned what this will do to our nation's cattle producers and dairies. We need to consider an indemnification program to prevent economic devastation to the nation's cattle producers. Recall, we indemnified producers after initially confirming BSE in the state of Washington and with subsequent positive cattle. The size of this incident is over twenty-fold the size of all previous BSE incidents combined."

"It is a given when we make a public announcement, our international trading partners will prohibit the export of beef. I recommend we be proactive announcing we are disallowing further exportation of cattle, beef, and beef by-products simultaneously with notifying the press. Disallowing export of beef and beef byproducts will have a negative effect on our GDP, and the national economy. The overall movement of livestock may need to stop temporarily until we can determine risk and a source of the agent. While I am hopeful many of my concerns will not come to fruition, I think we must be ready to implement precautionary measures. These thoughts are running around in my head as I attempt to patiently wait for the international reference lab and USDA's investigative teams to provide us with further information. It is possible this outbreak will affect areas of responsibility of others sitting around this table."

"Thank you for candidly sharing your thoughts and concerns Secretary Johansen. You have given us all a great deal to mull over. I agree that we should not inform the press until we know more. Until then folks, mum is the word. I want no leaks. Madam Secretary, I would like to listen in on the call. After this meeting, let's get you on my calendar. I want the Secretaries of Commerce, Health and Human Services, State, and Homeland Security to reflect on this issue. There may be things you must implement regarding Secretary Johansen's concerns."

"Does anyone have anything else? If not, let's adjourn. We will meet again Wednesday", said President Smyth.

The president waited for Clare in the hallway outside the cabinet room. Resting her purse strap on her shoulder, she cleared the doorway. The president said, "Clare you made an excellent presentation. We don't often hear from Agriculture, but when you bring something to us, it is clearly an issue. I want to check with Martha, my scheduling secretary, to see if perhaps we can have lunch together here prior to your call." They walked partway down the hallway leading to the oval office. The president stopped at the third desk and said, "Martha, what's the schedule look like Wednesday? I would like to have lunch with Secretary Johansen and then we have a call scheduled for 1:00PM. The call should probably take no longer than an hour. Please make any needed adjustments to my schedule. Thanks." He then turned smiling and said, "Clare I'll see you about 12:15 Wednesday for lunch." Clare turned rather suddenly, side-stepping a Secret Service agent quietly standing immediately behind her.

As Clare walked out of the west wing exit, her driver waited under the portico. He opened the rear passenger side door of the Lincoln Town Car assisting her in. Clare asked him to take her back to her office in the Agricultural Building.

While traveling back to her office she phoned Dr. Bobby Laporte, APHIS Administrator, asking him to meet her in her office in about twenty minutes. She wanted to brief him on the cabinet meeting and check on the status of the field investigations.

"Come on in Bobby", said Clare. "The cabinet meeting went well. I presented the facts that you and I had discussed yesterday afternoon. By the way, thank you for taking the time to go over them with me. It provided me a much more thorough understanding of the entire issue and some of the ramifications. The president agrees with not informing the press until we had the laboratory results from England. I laid out the possibilities of temporarily ceasing the slaughter of beef and halting transportation of cattle. I also suggested we be proactive regarding shutting down exports of beef and beef byproducts and make that announcement when we brief the press on the outbreak. Everyone listened; but, there was no further discussion from the cabinet. However, the President Smyth wants me to join him for lunch Wednesday. He wants to listen in on the conference call. I would also like for you to also be on that call from your office in case we need technical advice. Will you be able to fit that into your schedule?"

"Yes Ma'am", responded Dr. Laporte.

"Great", Clare said as she continued. "Bobby, what's been going on with the investigative teams in the field this morning?"

"Well Ma'am", Bobby started. "For the most part, everyone is off to a good start. We identified an issue in eastern New Mexico regarding the slaughter of one or more spent dairy cows although they displayed very mild CNS symptoms. I handed that issue off to Dr. Zwirn (Food Safety and Inspection Service Administrator); he has sent a team to the plant to investigate. It sounds like the slaughter plant management is confrontational when dealing with inspection personnel, and an inexperienced veterinarian may have allowed slaughter of one or more animals that were perhaps showing very mild CNS signs. As you know FSIS has effective recall protocols in place to deal with adulteration."

"We are also finding some of the carcasses that were euthanized at the feedlots were transported to pet food plants. Currently, Dr. Yu is questioning the investigative teams to ferret out the extent of that issue. We'll have to send some field personnel not involved in the investigations to further investigate those operations and divert affected product appropriately. I do not know how many producers are involved in this issue."

"Your personal phone calls to the producers have been very effective. All teams report a high degree of cooperation with the investigative teams. Thank you for your help."

"There is really not too much else to report. The investigative teams are at work and we're getting in bits and pieces of information. The computerized program is working as designed. The investigators like using the new tablets. As you know, during the first day we take a lot of samples and get them to the laboratories. We'll be getting information back from the labs starting early tomorrow afternoon. Then, we'll have significantly more information. If possible, I think we should meet at that time to review the early data and formulate some sort of an announcement for the press."

"Thanks for your brief Bobby", said Clare as she walked him to the door. "Let me know if anything significant comes up."

About three hours later Bobby called the Secretary's office. She was on a call and would return his call soon.

About a half hour later, his phone rang. "Hi Bobby, its Clare."

"Madam Secretary, it's been a busy afternoon for Dr. Yu. Starting about noon his phone has been ringing off the hook. This afternoon we've learned of thirty-nine additional premises with cattle showing CNS signs. Now, there's twelve states involved. The newly involved states are Arizona, Oklahoma, Arkansas, Missouri, Utah, Wyoming, and Tennessee. Both dairies and feedlots are involved. This outbreak has started to 'pop'. Dr. Yu detailed an additional eighteen investigative teams to the field. The newly detailed teams are traveling this afternoon and evening and will begin their investigations tomorrow morning."

"I received a call from Dr. Rhodes-Voss at the lab. She's worried about having enough sample boxes and reagents to do the testing. Because of the rapid expansion, we're considering amending the tissue sampling we are doing. I have my staff making calls to the feed testing laboratories to see if they can handle the additional volume and to forewarn them of what's coming."

"I have a conference call to discuss this in about 45 minutes. All the pathologists are participating in the investigations. There will be a cadre of scientific folks here at headquarters, and technical experts from the Centers for Epidemiology and Animal Health in the call. We must consider changes from two perspectives. One, the volume of sampling and testing we are doing; second, if we are not dealing with BSE, how do we use our resources efficiently."

The conference call began with Dr. Laporte framing the discussion saying, "We are all aware that the emerging CNS outbreak has started to pop. This afternoon we must address two issues:"

"One, our pathologists are doing limited postmortem examinations and collecting a significant number of samples. When those samples arrive at the laboratory the volume magnifies when one considers the special stains we use to evaluate existing pathology. Further complicating matters, the NVSL pathologists are working in the investigative teams. We've 'borrowed' pathologists from our headquarters' staff, FSIS's lab in Athens, our Plum Island campus, and from our National Animal Health Lab Network staffs' in California, Colorado, and Texas. Recall, when we decided on sampling these tissues we wanted to get a broad baseline of information if we were dealing with a novel agent. While we don't know if we are dealing with a novel agent, we have overwhelmed our laboratory capacity."

A lively discussion ensued regarding the amount of laboratory sampling and testing protocols required. Collectively, the group came to consensus that the initial protocol for sampling and testing should continue through tomorrow. By that time, the group thought there would be enough samples collected to establish sufficient baseline data. The risk assessment group began to work up the statistics on this size baseline sample to assure it's statistically significant. It was the group's thought it would be large enough to support the pathogenesis and maybe the identity of a future a novel agent. Once the results from today's sampling and tomorrow's testing became available, they could make better decisions about sampling and testing.

Dr. Laporte then identified the second issue. "If we eliminated BSE as a possibility, how should we proceed to identify the agent and manage this ever-expanding outbreak? We don't need to discuss this now, but I want everyone thinking about what may need to do with relation to depopulation, animal exposures, quarantines, health certifications, transportation, etc. Let's make sure we keep the regulatory requirements foremost in our minds as we make future decisions. We want to be on solid legal footing. Let's make sure we put our best collective foot forward to make sound, supportable, and fair decisions."

"Thank you for your time. Let's get together later. I'll send an e-mail to everyone, once I determine a call time. With that, let's go home folks...it's been a long day and we're going to have another one tomorrow."

Chapter 8

Graeme Pennington sat in his office reviewing photomicrographs of histological sections from the U.S. outbreak on his computer immediately after Ian McLaughlin read and photographed representative sections on the microscope in his laboratory. Just a few slides required interpretation to complete their examinations of all the samples.

Twenty minutes later, Ian walked into Graeme's office pouring himself a cup of tea as Graeme finished the last slide. Graeme got up from his desk rubbing his eyes as he sat in an adjacent wingback leather upholstered chair. He asked, "Now that we have finished looking at all of the slides and read the ELISA, IHC, and Western Blot tests what are your thoughts?"

Ian responded, "First, I don't think we are dealing with BSE. Second, I have never seen such consistent histopathology, a diffuse vacuolating encephalopathy without the presence of amyloid. Third, all the samples demonstrated non-negative or inconclusive results to the Enzyme-Linked Immunosorbent Assay (ELISA) test. Immunohistochemical testing also showed inconclusive results as did Western Blot testing. I do not think we have seen this agent before. The agent, in my interpretation of the immunology results, appears to share some, but not all, of the antigenic markers of a transmissible spongiform encephalopathy. I think we have a novel agent, due to the partial sharing of antigenic markers. It's most likely a misfolded protein-an infectious prion protein."

"I concur wholly", said Graeme. "As a next step, what do you think about looking at a few slides under the electron microscope? Increased magnification might provide more information. I would like to give the Americans more of an answer than we know what it is not."

"I agree", said Ian as he finished his tea. "I'll go back to the lab and ask Geraldine to select twelve samples from different specimens, prepare and stain the slides, and take them to the EM room. They should be ready in about an hour."

"I'll go down to the EM room to power up the microscope. Twelve slides would roughly represent a 10% sample. That is a statistically significant sample from which we can make sound interpretation. I'll meet you at the door to the parking lot. We'll get a bit of lunch. After lunch, we can look at the slides", Graeme said.

After lunch, there were twelve prepared slides sitting on the stage of the scanning electron microscope. Both men pulled up chairs and sat in front of a thirty-two-inch flat screen monitor. Ian placed a slide into the aperture and set the power on one-thousand magnification and focused to where the image was clear and crisp. Increasing magnification to six-thousand, the image in the focal spot vividly displayed more detail. Ian began, "We are seeing an abnormal increase in the number of astrocytes, due to the destruction of nearby neurons and vacuolation of selected nuclei of the brain stem; but there are no changes in the form of membrane-bound vacuoles separated by membranes curled into secondary chambers, as we would expect with spongiform pathology. As I look at these vacuoles, they appear to be very consistent in size. Let's increase magnification to twelve-thousand. Associated fibrils or 'prion rods' are not visualized, as we would expect with spongiform disease." Graeme turned the magnification to thirty-thousand. Ian continued, "We're seeing a dense astrocytic reaction accompanied by plentiful elongated microglial cells. There are numerous astrocytic processes in close conjunction with microglial cells. Neuronal degeneration is presented as autophagic vacuoles. The autophagic vacuoles appear as a part or parts of the neuronal cytoplasm."

Graeme again turned the magnification to fifty-thousand magnification commenting, "We begin to observe tubulovesicular structures; I would quantify as copious. I think we can conclude, based upon the histopathology of this first slide, that we are dealing with a novel infectious prion protein disease characterized by neuropil astrocytosis, vacuolation of nuclei, no evidence of fibrils or prion rods, and therefore no distinctive clumping, autophagic vacuoles of neuronal cytoplasm, and copious tubulovesicular structures. Ian, what are your observations?"

"I concur with your observations and synopsis", Ian said. "Let's see what the other slides show."

As the two international experts efficiently read the next eleven slides the histopathology was essentially identical. Ian said as the last slide was put back into the case; "There is no doubt in my mind that we are dealing with a novel prion agent. I'm amazed at the absolute consistency of the histopathology we observed as well as the apparent propensity the agent has for the brain stem. Because of the way this disease presented itself in multiple geographic areas, affecting numerous animals on the same premise, and essentially in a relatively short timeframe, I must conclude the agent is viciously infectious and maybe contagious as well. I am glad that we took photomicrographs of all the slides. I think we need to e-mail Dr. Rhodes-Voss the EM photomicrographs, then call her."

"Let's go up to my office", said Graeme, "and give her a call. I want Pat to know our results and have the photomicrographs to review before we get on the conference call."

In Graeme's office, they uploaded the photomicrographs into an e-mail and sent them to Dr. Rhodes-Voss. Then, they dialed her number.

A moment later Pat answered, "Hello Graeme I hope you are going to tell me that you and Ian have everything figured out."

"Pat, Ian is with me. We do have some results; sadly, it has led us to more questions than answers. I must say that your samples all arrived in superb condition. You made it easy for us to open each sequentially numbered box and set up our samples on this end. Sending the e-mailed histological samples also facilitated a quick view and comparison of what we were seeing to what you viewed. We both commented, at various points in our testing, the histopathology and immunochemistry has been unusually consistent. From your test results and our re-testing of the sampled tissues, we can conclusively say that all the samples are inconclusive for BSE. When we initially viewed the e-mailed photomicrographs, the tissues did not appear to be consistent with BSE. The agent, in our interpretation of the ELISA and IHC test results, share some, but not all, of the antigenic markers of a TSE. Early this afternoon we randomly selected twelve samples, about 10% of the whole, to view under our electron microscope. We took a few digital photomicrographs of each sample. Those photomicrographs should be in your inbox. You might want to open the e-mail and bring the first one into view. What we observed was a neuropil astrocytosis, vacuolation of nuclei, an absence of fibrils or prion rods; therefore, no distinctive clumping, autophagic vacuoles of neuronal cytoplasm, and copious tubulovesicular structures. It is not BSE or any of the associated TSEs of animals or man. Collectively, we have not observed anything like this agent. This led us to surmise we are dealing with a novel prion agent. We described the histopathology attributed to this agent as a diffuse vacuolating encephalopathy."

"Ian and I have considerable interest in this agent and are willing to help you in any way that we can. Regrettably, due to time constraints, we were unable to delve deeper into biochemistry, size, weight, or structure of this agent."

Dr. Rhodes-Voss listened to Graeme intently as he explained his test results and interpretations while taking notes of their comments. After Graeme finished Pat said, "Graeme and Ian, thank you for all of your hard work and thoughtful interpretations. I'm viewing the EM photomicrographs now. I certainly did not expect you would take time to view and interpret EM slides. This is going to assist us in making some difficult decisions later today."

"Let me give you a brief update on the status of our outbreak. Yesterday was a banner day for what you describe as diffuse vacuolating encephalopathy. The investigative teams identified 125 new cases yesterday and the outbreak now involves 12 states. It has really started to pop. We've sent all our pathologists into the field to help with the investigations, so I'm operating with a minimal staff. We're in the process of doing the histopathology on those samples today as well as setting up ELISA and IHC tests. Thanks again for the information. I better get back to work. The first set of slides are ready for me to read."

"Don't work too hard, Pat", said Graeme.

Chapter 9

It was a short night for Dr. Bobby Laporte who took an early Metro train into Washington, DC from his Virginia home. He was in his office at 6:00AM sipping on a tall cappuccino. He needed to prepare for his meeting with Secretary Johansen at 9:00AM to update her on the status of the outbreak and talk with Dr. Yu and Dr. Rhodes-Voss before the meeting. Clicking on a desktop icon on his computer he accessed the outbreak summary file. After leaving yesterday, another two premises were identified-a large dairy in southern California and a large feedlot in northeastern Colorado. Dr. Yu assigned investigative teams positioned relatively close to investigate these outbreaks. Whether the teams could collect diagnostic samples from affected animals, depended on the inventory of sample supplies the teams already had in their possession.

Opening a summary report on the outbreak Dr. Laporte looked at data similarities hoping to spot something significant. He thought. *Clinical signs of CNS disease were obviously a common thread. However, the distribution of CNS signs is relatively even. Specific clinical signs did not appear to be of any significant help. Days on feed has a wide distribution. These data suggest cattle showing signs are on a concentrated high energy high protein ration; however, both producing dairy cows and feeder cattle require concentrated diets. Feed sources varied widely as expected in a multistate outbreak. There appeared to be a trend toward cattle in more southern states vs. those in more northern states. Cattle density also trended to be a factor. Cattle in highly concentrated environments were most affected, but the data only studied cattle with CNS signs. There could be non-symptomatic cattle on highly concentrated diets in concentrated environments nearby those displaying CNS. Cattle density is not an important factor. Feed, water, histopathology data are not available yet. He was hopeful these testing results would point the team toward a cause or an infectious agent. Overall, the quantity and quality of data collected during the first day of* the investigation pleased Dr. Laporte. The standardized investigational format is working as intended. There appears to be no glitches in the software or their integration.

After reviewing the outbreak summary data, he deduced there may be a southern predilection of disease incidence. He can gain nothing else from the data. Sitting back in his high-backed chair Dr. Laporte thought. *We have not had such widespread acute devastating outbreaks since the days of Hog Cholera (1900-1960). The FDA initiated its feed ban of feeding rendered cattle by-products back to cattle in 1997 and enhanced it in 2008. Washington state initially diagnosed BSE in 2003, and the United Kingdom had a devastating outbreak from 1986-2001. In the US and Canada BSE has identified sporadic cases, never as an outbreak. We can exclude other CNS disease entities such as Listeriosis, polio, rabies, and parasitic migrations based upon presenting CNS signs and age. I trust our national laboratory system. ELISA and immunohistochemical tests suggest sharing of antigen markers with BSE, but it's not conclusive. Histopathology differs from BSE. For now, I speculate it's likely to be a novel agent. I must prepare for a press conference following the Secretary's conference call. Now, I must call Dr. Rhodes-Voss to see how things are going at the lab and what information she can share.*

"Hi Pat, its Bobby. How are things going?"

"Bobby, we're overwhelmed with the testing. After your call yesterday, I picked up some fast food and returned to the lab working until about 10:30PM. By that time my eyes were starting to cross. I headed home, got a few hours of sleep, and returned early this morning. I seem to be able to get things done more efficiently when there are no interruptions. I've viewed the histopathology slides from the non-nervous tissues. I wanted to get them finished before we started on specimens we will receive today."

"Do you have any impressions now that you have looked at the tissues", asked Bobby.

"I awakened to those thoughts this morning", said Pat. "Across the board, the slides of the hearts, livers, kidneys, lungs, abdominal fat, and spleens were essentially normal. However, I noticed many follicles with extended follicular dendritic cell networks in most ileal Peyer's patches. Previous studies suggest this involvement is due to the invasion and replication of infectious prions, specifically in the suprafollicular dome, T cell area, and germinal centers. Before I would make this comment publicly, I want the input of Penny Adams. She's on the investigative team based out of Amarillo, Texas. I did not appreciate any pathological changes in the lymph nodes and tonsil tissues submitted. However, before I make any blanket statements regarding the tonsillar tissues and lymph nodes, I want Penny to also read them. She knows more about prions and prion diseases than anyone in our lab. She did her PhD work on prions at a molecular level and she is probably the best histologist in the lab. I e-mailed her digital photomicrographs of sections asking her to look at them on her computer. Maybe she will get time to look at them today or this evening. Yesterday she performed 35 limited necropsies at three feedlots. She's been a very busy girl."

"Pat, we need to make the decisions we spoke about yesterday afternoon. I think we need to let the investigative teams know we will change sampling directions, probably tomorrow. You're overwhelmed and need relief. From what you just told me we should discontinue sampling heart, lung, abdominal fat, liver, kidney, and spleen. We will continue sampling tonsils and lymph nodes until Penny Adams weighs in. Brainstem and anterior spinal cord as well as ileal Peyer's patches may need continued sampling. Are there any additional tissues we need to instruct the investigative teams to sample?"

"The only thing I can think of is nerves, one peripheral like maybe the Maxillary nerve. It's easy to identify and excise. The other would be a section of the Vegas nerve; however, it may be difficult to identify when removing the brain and it's too much work to isolate it in the thoracic or abdominal cavities. We could make it optional-if it's there, harvest it, but if it's not easily recognizable, don't waste time hunting for it. What do you think?"

"Pat, I think that's a good suggestion. Peripheral demyelination would be important to know as would pathology resulting from migration of prions. I know it's postulated, but not described. You and your team will have enough tissues to keep you busy during the slack times studying some of these questions. I'll make sure the lab has the funds to support those efforts."

"By the way, the conference call is at 10:30AM this morning. We need to discuss exactly how much sampling we need to be doing at large dairies and feedlots. With the outbreak expanding like it is, should we be sampling hundreds of cattle to arrive at a diagnosis? Maybe we can come up with a statistically significant, but much lower number to sample. We need to use our resources prudently. Significant sampling numbers and effectively using our teams' expertise should leave us on firm ground. I'll let you mull that over. I'd better go now and let you get back to work while it's still quiet at your shop."

****

"Sam, Bobby here. I thought I'd catch you before your conference call. I wanted to share a little information with you. I think it's going to be a busy day for us. I spoke with Pat earlier this morning. She's looked at all the histological samples received yesterday. This outbreak is popping, big time. The number of samples received exceeds NVSL's capacity. You've reassigned the pathologists on her staff to the additional investigative teams. After conferring with Pat, we're going to discontinue many of the tissues we're currently sampling. I'll e-mail the tissues to discontinue sampling. We're adding sampling the Maxillary nerve and the Vegas nerve, if identified readily. Pat wants Penny Adams to look at photomicrographs of some of the other tissue samples. They may drop them from sampling as well. She's going to have

Penny look the ileal Peyer's patches samples; Pat thinks she may have identified some pathology there. Pat has e-mailed Penny the images. Apparently, Penny knows more about prions than anyone we have. Pat thinks highly of her. We won't make those changes today, probably tomorrow. I'm meeting with the biostatisticians today. We need them to quickly develop a statistically significant sampling methodology to cut down on the number of samples we're collecting from the large dairies and feedlots. We need to use our field pathologists efficiently, if this thing continues to expand. Please let the investigative teams know tissue sampling is going to change tomorrow, as well as the number of samples that need to be harvested."

"Secondly, for your information only, the Secretary has a conference call at 1:00PM Washington time with the folks in England. The Secretary briefed the president and the cabinet. President Smyth wants to listen in on today's conference call. He's taking this outbreak very seriously. I anticipate a press conference later this afternoon, after the conference call. We need to stay ahead of the press on this issue. I think we should deal with the press at the DC level. What are your thoughts regarding handling the press at the headquarters level?"

"Bobby, I think that's the best way to handle this issue. There are too many people with various levels of expertise involved in the investigation to manage press communications any other way and hope for any degree of message consistency. We need to provide the investigative team leaders a prepared statement that's shared with the affected producers, referring the press to APHIS in DC. Hopefully, this will ensure consistency and prevent all sorts of press people wandering around the premises bothering everyone."

"Good idea, Sam. I'll run that by the Secretary. As you know, she personally spoke with the initial seven producers. She'll have an opinion on how the producers will respond. I like the idea."

"In the interest of allowing you a few minutes to prepare the conference call, I'll let you go."

"Thanks Bobby, have a good day."

****

As Bobby waited in the Secretary's outer office, his phone rang; it was Dr. Rhodes-Voss. "Hi Pat. What's up?"

"Bobby, I just got off the phone with Graeme Pennington and Ian McLaughlin. I'm drafting a summary e-mail to you and Sam; but I wanted to catch you before you met with the Secretary. Graeme and Ian say the agent is a novel prion protein. They have conclusively ruled out BSE. They are calling it diffuse vacuolating encephalopathy or DVE for short. They looked at sections of brain stem using electron microscopy. I thought this information would be important to discuss with the Secretary."

"Indeed. I had a hunch they would determine it is novel. You and your lab are just too good, and the results were too consistent for it to be anything else. I'm glad you called. It will help us as we proceed with the day. I anticipate a press conference sometime this afternoon, after we decide how best to manage things."

Clare Johansen opened her office door saying, "Good morning, Bobby. Come in and sit down." After Bobby entered, she seated herself in one of the leather winged backed chairs adjacent to her desk. Bobby sat down in a similar chair at the opposite end of her desk.

"Good morning, Ma'am. I just received a call from Pat Rhodes-Voss. She spoke with Graeme Peterson and Ian McLaughlin. There's more detailed information coming, but they are calling this disease a novel prion disease. They've named it diffuse vacuolating encephalopathy or DVE for short. BSE has been conclusively ruled out."

"OK Bobby, if I understand things properly, we're dealing with a unique disease. They think it's caused by a prion that's not BSE."

"Yes ma'am, that's correct. So, we're first going to discuss prions. Scientifically, we divide prions, or more correctly, prion proteins into two groups. The first group are those naturally occurring in all mammals, including humans. Molecular biologists refer to this group as PrP^c. It is a very small protein. The second group are infective prion proteins. We refer to this group as PrP^{Sc}. This too is a very small protein; but it's abnormally folded. When an infectious prion protein enters a nerve cell, it binds with a normal prion protein causing the normal prion protein to abnormally fold. Then, the two infectious prion proteins break apart with both looking for normal prion proteins to bind to causing them fold abnormally. It's how they replicate exponentially until the cell dies. As the nerve cell dies, its cell membrane ruptures releasing all the infectious prion proteins to invade and replicate in other nerve cells. When there is sufficient cell death in an area, the area becomes a vacuole or small hole devoid of cells. In peripheral nerves, those outside the central nervous system, cell death also results causing demyelization. This results in loss of the nerve sheath conductivity causing the nerve to malfunction. The brain vacuoles or nerve demyelization, results in the array of clinical signs or symptoms we are observing. Are you with me so far?"

"Yes, Bobby. It's very technical."

"Yes, ma'am, it is technical. Now that we have spoken of normal and infectious prion proteins, and how infectious prion proteins replicate resulting in brain vacuoles and nerve sheath demyelization, let's discuss the size of infectious prion proteins. They are much smaller than the smallest known virus. In fact, they are so small we cannot visualize them using the most powerful electron microscope. Therefore, we deduce their presence by visualizing histopathology using the microscope, and the intracellular pathology using an electron microscope. Infectious prions are exclusively protein. Thus, they are not live organisms because they are of protein. They do not contain the nucleic acids necessary for genetic reproduction. If you're still with me, that's all you need to know about infectious prion proteins."

"Next, let's discuss some important questions I think you may be asked", said Bobby. "Where did DVE come from? Can humans or other animals develop DVE? How does DVE spread? What kind of morbidity and mortality are we to expect in the nation's cattle herd? The answer to all these questions is we don't know."

"Ma'am, let's talk about the name DVE or diffuse vacuolating encephalopathy. It's medically descriptive of the resulting pathology. The first spongiform disease identified was Kuru. It affected humans and resulted from cannibalism, a ritualistic method of disposing of the dead in New Guinea. Later we identified animal diseases. The first being Scrapie in sheep. Then BSE in cattle, then Chronic Wasting Disease in deer and elk, then in cats. Now, we bulk all those diseases under the heading of Transmissible Spongiform Encephalopathies or TSEs. Like the TSEs, DVE is the starting place for this novel disease entity. We need to avoid allowing the press to give it a nickname, like Mad Cow Disease. I think we can get that done by providing consistent dialog with the press and by centralizing the information regarding DVE to APHIS's spokespersons only. When Dr. Yu and I spoke this morning, he suggested we prepare a statement which the producers involved in the outbreak can use. This statement essentially refers the press to APHIS personnel for technical and general information regarding DVE. I liked his suggestion. What are your thoughts?"

"I think it's a wonderful idea. As you know our nation's farmers and ranchers are an independent lot; but, what we're dealing with is novel. They know virtually nothing about it. If it's presented in the manner we are not taking their opinions away from them, but rather acting as a technical support center for them, it's likely to work. I'm also wondering if it would be worthwhile to have a conference call with them, academia, and some of the major industry groups informing them of what we know and what we don't. Maybe you could quickly put together a webpage of information, news, and frequently asked questions about DVE. I would be glad to host the call. You'll need some subject matter experts available and our IT people will need to get the webpage up quickly."

I'll get to work on that while you're at the White House. I'll also put together some talking points for you. I'm guessing you will hold a press conference later this afternoon."

"Bobby, I like our briefing sessions. You keep me informed, I can ask questions to clarify my understanding, and I always feel like I'm smarter after of our meetings. We also accomplish a lot. Is there anything else for now?"

"We had another two premises identified late yesterday afternoon, one in southern California, the other in northeastern Colorado. That brings our total to 41 premises in 12 states. I think it's time we discuss regulatory actions. Such as putting a temporary ban on transporting cattle; a temporary moratorium on beef slaughter, until we know more; export of live cattle, beef, and beef by-products, etc. APHIS and FSIS have the regulatory authority to take those actions on your behalf. There may be other actions you may think advisable. Perhaps we can touch base after your conference call."

"On my return from the White House, I'll give you a call", said Clare. "If we're going to have a press conference, we'll have more work to do this afternoon. I would like you to be at the press conference to field the technical questions."

"Thanks for coming down this morning. I better get ready to head over to the White House. I can't be late for lunch with President Smyth."

****

Secretary Johansen arrived at the White House a few minutes ahead of her 12:15PM scheduled lunch. She walked to the area adjacent to oval office housing the gauntlet of the President's secretaries.

President Smyth walked out of the oval office. Seeing Secretary Johansen, he said, "Hello Clare, I hope I did not keep you waiting. Are you ready for lunch?"

"Mr. President, I've only been here a couple of minutes, and yes I am ready."

"Why don't we walk through the oval office to a small dining room?"

"Please lead the way, Mr. President."

"It's a small private dining room where we can have lunch and chat."

Arriving at the small dining room, Secretary Johansen observed a round table that could comfortably seat four. The table, set for two, already had ice water poured in crystal glasses. "I told the chef to surprise us with a lunch of his choice", said the President as they sat down. Soon a porter served seafood minestrone soup with shrimp and bay scallops and poured iced tea.

"This soup is absolutely delicious, Mr. President. At risk of not following protocol, perhaps I should bring you up to date on where we stand with the emerging outbreak. The director of our lab in Ames, IA received a call this morning from the lab in Worcester. They conclusively ruled out BSE. It's a novel infectious prion protein. They describe the disease as diffuse vacuolating encephalopathy or DVE. We know hardly anything about this infectious prion protein."

"In our upcoming conference call, I anticipate we will learn as much detail as is available. I expect it to be minimal. However, recall the United Kingdom dealt with an outbreak of

BSE from 1986 to 1990. During that period, over 180,000 animals became diseased. I am planning on asking them what they learned dealing with outbreak that they think is germane to our dealing with this one. Because BSE and DVE are both caused by infectious prion proteins, hopefully we can prevent making the same mistakes."

"Clare, I anticipated we may be dealing with a novel agent from your briefing. I think we must initiate all measures necessary to protect public and animal health, our economy, and the health and wellbeing of all our citizens and trading partners. We should hold a press conference as soon as possible to make the public aware of what we're dealing with."

The porter arrived to serve the main course. It was chicken breast with Tasso ham and peppers in a chipotle sauce served with cumin-scented rice, and roasted zucchini. Clare and the president ate as they continued their discussion.

"Dr. Laporte's working on proposed actions as well as a statement for the press conference. I plan to have Dr. Laporte involved in the press conference as a subject matter expert."

"Clare, I want to participate in the press conference. As this outbreak goes forward, I foresee multiple departments being involved. I want the public to understand that initially this is an agricultural issue, but as it progresses the full resources of the government may be required and are available to see it through."

"Thank you, Mr. President. Your presence is always welcome. As far as immediate actions, I think we should temporarily have a moratorium on all beef slaughter to protect public health. We will need to expedite an indemnification plan for cattle and dairy producers affected to protect their financial interests. Other actions include suspending the exportation of live cattle, beef and beef byproducts, curtailing transportation of cattle so we can capture the extent of the outbreak. The last action I recommend is to suspend the change of ownership of cattle including trading feeder and live cattle commodities as well as private and public cattle sales. I foresee this announcement will have a negative impact on the commodities and futures markets. Given a little time, the markets will find a level, almost certainly lower than present day, but it will serve to prevent reactionary trading. This will further help protect our economy. However, the Commodity Futures Trading Commission and not the Department of Agriculture holds authority to take such action."

"Clare, I agree with your recommended actions. As I said earlier, we need to protect public and animal health, our economy, and the health and wellbeing of all the public and our trading partners. Your proposal addresses each of those mandates. I'll contact Dick Kline. He's the Chairman of the Commodity Futures Trading Commission to get his help suspending commodity and futures trading of cattle for an indefinite period. There will be some squawk from the traders and investment folks, but I will handle that backlash. When do you want to hold the press conference?"

"Mr. President, I think we should see what Richard Coy has to say before we finalize a press conference time. I'm thinking later this afternoon, if there are no major changes in our plan of action. Also, I would like to conference in Dr. Laporte and Dr. Rhodes-Voss on the call if that's alright with you? I anticipate their counterparts will be participating on the call. They are our subject matter experts; so, I think they should be involved."

"That fine with me. It's your call, I just want to listen as you conduct the call", said President Smyth.

"There's one more thing we need to discuss briefly", said Secretary Johansen. "That's how we manage the press and the general message that gets relayed to the public. I want my field investigators to continue to do their jobs, and not have to take time to deal with various members of the press. That said; I want to handle all the press releases, interviews, etc. out of the APHIS headquarters, if this meets your approval. Secondly, I plan to host a large conference call tomorrow with the owners of all premises currently involved in the outbreak, as well as deans of all our land grant universities, and some of the major industry representatives. I plan to inform them of what we know and what we don't. We're quickly developing a webpage of information, news, and frequently asked questions, etc. about DVE. What are your thoughts regarding this approach?"

"Clare, it's unique. In this case it's very beneficial for everyone involved. It's an excellent way to manage the message to ensure the public is well informed, particularly since this disease agent is novel and information regarding infectious prion proteins is so limited."

"Mr. President, thank you for the delicious lunch and, of course, your time. It is time for us to initiate the call."

Secretary Johansen had given her secretary all the numbers for the participants to participate in the conference call. Once all the participants were on the call she forwarded it to President Smyth's secretary and the call rang through to the oval office. The identical participants were on this call that had participated in the call five days earlier. Much occurred in five days. Dr. Laporte provided everyone with an up to date status of the outbreak. Dr. Graeme Pennington confirmed the disease was not Bovine Spongiform Encephalopathy adding he considered the disease novel and caused by an infectious prion. He described the disease as diffuse vacuolating encephalopathy or DVE. Graeme clarified the absence of amyloid was unusual.

Secretary Johansen questioned England's lessons learned while dealing with their outbreaks of BSE. Richard Coy said the U.K. vastly underestimated the funding required for producer indemnification and general research efforts. Second, the U.K. learned carcasses testing positive required disposal to destroy the prion. That meant that all animals diagnosed with BSE required incineration or rendering with the byproducts incinerated. In the U.K., initially there were inadequate facilities to handle the volume of diseased animals. He closed by commenting that dealing with a novel agent would be much more complex and expensive.

Secretary Johansen's final question was unexpected. She asked if the cause of such a widespread outbreak could be an act of terrorism. The line was quiet for a moment; then Graeme Peterson responded, "Infectious prion proteins are very tough agents to destroy and there are no published reports of an infectious prion protein being used in such a way. While it is theoretically possible, one would need to know much more about this novel agent or discover a common source of infection. I am unaware of reports concerning propagation of prions." Dr. McLaughlin commented he was unaware of anyone attempting to propagate infectious proteins also commenting propagation would require a highly-trained scientist and a sophisticated laboratory. From that perspective, he thought such a possibility was unlikely.

The conference call ended at 1:40PM. Secretary Johansen thanked Dr. Peterson and Dr. McLaughlin for their extra hours of work to provide this information expediently. She said that the United States was indebted to United Kingdom for their expert advice and assistance in identifying DVE. She closed saying the U.S. would keep everyone updated to the progress of the outbreak.

****

President Smyth and Secretary Johansen agreed to hold the press conference at 4:00PM in the White House. The president said his staff would notify the press and setup the conference. Secretary Johansen agreed to prepare the information and to provide written text for the reporters in attendance.

On her way back to her office, she called Bobby asking him to meet her in her office in ten minutes. There was lots of work to complete in the next two hours.

As Clare walked into the atrium of her office, Bobby was waiting. In her office, they sat at a small table so they could work together compiling the information for the press conference. Bobby had his laptop containing a draft of the press release he drafted while Clare was at the White House.

"Ma'am", Bobby said, "If you want to review my draft, it's here on the computer screen for you. I've spoken to our IT people. They're working on getting the website setup. It should be up and running within the next hour or so. Of course, we'll need to load it with current scientific information. I expect it will be loaded by the time the press conference has ended."

"President Smyth and I discussed two items which need to be added to your press release", said Clare. "The first thing we spoke of was expediting an emergency supplemental budget request for an indemnification plan. We also need to include within that sufficient funds to conduct research on DVE. I did some very rough calculating on the way back from the White House. I calculated the total cost of this outbreak to be 28.9 billion to indemnify, if we added fifteen percent to that exclusively earmarked for research. Total research funds would be 3.8 billion."

"The second item that needs to be included in the press release is a temporary suspension in the change of ownership of all cattle. This statement may require wordsmithing, because its intent is to include live cattle commodity trading as well as private and public cattle sales. President Smyth is contacting Dick Kline. He's going to have him suspend commodity and futures trading of cattle for an indefinite period. Dick holds the regulatory authority for this aspect of our actions."

"Other than these two additions and including the contact web address for the new webpage, I think the press release is outstanding. You've done an excellent job of capturing the information regarding the outbreak and our actions both concisely and precisely within a tight timeframe. By the way, I want to confirm you will be present at the press conference to serve as our technical expert."

"Yes Ma'am, it is my intent to accompany you to the press conference. In fact, it will be my first time to visit the White House. I'm looking forward to it."

The press conference began promptly at 4:00PM with the introduction of President Smyth. Then he introduced Secretary Johansen and Dr. Laporte. The press response to the announcement was one of surprise-surprise there had been no leaks regarding the outbreak. Follow-up questioning became redundant regarding information about the outbreak. There were numerous questions regarding the DVE agent and infectious prion proteins. The press conference concluded at 5:00PM. Secretary Johansen met briefly in the hallway outside of the press room to set a time to meet with President Smyth to discuss an indemnification plan and research funding incorporated into an emergency funding supplemental bill. They decided to meet Thursday morning after the cabinet meeting.

Chapter 10

The morning conference call was brief. Dr. Yu identified the newly affected states in the outbreak. Many of the new investigative teams traveled into the early morning hours so he excused them from the call. Dr. Yu explained the NVSL situation. With the expected samples arriving today, a modified sampling plan was upcoming. Dr. Yu commented data transfer from the field was arriving without glitches and thanked everyone on the investigative teams for the detail in their reports. Dr. Yu said he expected that the agency would likely have a press conference this afternoon. When he found out more detail, he would notify everyone.

The team arrived at the ATX Hereford feedlot about 7:45AM to find Dennis Young horseback working with three other cowboys carefully and slowly moving cattle out and back in the last section of the heavyweight pens. Dennis waved to the investigative team while continuing to work. The Suburbans pulled up to the vet clinic unloading the supplies and sample boxes. Penny made a quick count of the sampling boxes finding 17 boxes remained from the initial shipment. She slowly walked through twenty-six lightweights observing the spectrum of CNS signs displayed when Jim Bob opened the gate to join her.

"Good morning Penny, Glen, Dennis, and Sonny identified twenty head yesterday when they went through the lightweight pens."

"Good morning, Jim Bob. I counted twenty-six head. If my number is correct, Dennis and his crew must have added six to those they had cut out yesterday. Let's look through the middleweights as Dennis finishes going through the heavyweight pens."

As they meandered through the middleweight pen they counted forty-two head. Two were down, but would rise with stimuli. By the time Penny and Jim Bob completed observing the middleweights, Dennis rode down to the vet clinic setting the gates so the cowboys could drive the heavyweights they cut out down to their hospital pen. Jim Bob and Penny moved to the end of the alleyway. From this vantage, they could see the cattle moving toward them and away from them. As the cattle moved by the two veterinarians, they vigilantly observed each animal. The cowboys walked the cattle into the clinic heavyweight pen, locking the gate without dismounting. It impressed Penny how well the horses worked the cattle.

"Dennis how many heavyweights did you bring us", asked Jim Bob.

"There's thirty-seven head", responded Dennis. "Jorge is on the way down with the Bobcat, two cowboys will stay to help Jim Bob and your team. The other cowboy will take my horse back to the horse barn and bring back a second dump truck. Sonny and I will walk up to the office to see what Glen has in store for us today. I calculate there is a total of 105 head to work. That will be two loads for the crematorium. Penny, can you do that many in a day?"

"I've never had to do that many in a day. We'll see; I think so, but it's going to be a busy day and we can't waste any time." Walking into the postmortem room she noticed that Sammi and Sonny had everything set up and Sammi had donned her PPE.

"We're ready to go ma'am", said Sammi.

"Stop it with that ma'am stuff! It's Penny or Doc, but not ma'am. That makes me feel old!" said Penny. As she donned her PPE, she remembered her advice from yesterday and stepped out of her coveralls walking toward the restroom.

Jim Bob was walking out when he heard Penny. "Forget something, ma'am?" he teased with a big grin on his face. Sammi giggled.

Jim Bob, Penny, and Jorge finished donning. As Penny strapped on her scabbard, Jorge fired up the Bobcat and Jim

Bob was ready to knock the first lightweight animal. From the start the team fell into an efficient groove at perhaps a pace slightly faster than the previous day. In about two hours they had completed the lightweight pen and started on the middleweights. Penny already switched to an alternative method of handling the samples, as they knew they would likely run out of sample supplies if the FedEx truck didn't arrive soon with more boxes. They were about a quarter of the way into the middleweights when the FedEx truck arrived. Penny suggested this would be an ideal time to take a break, rehydrate, and put the new sampling boxes and supplies away. Jorge asked if he just drank a bottle of water if he would have to doff his PPE and then don new PPE. Concluding that he had not been real close to the potentially contaminated carcasses, Penny advised that he could raise his face shield and carefully drink the bottled water. Jorge's smile told he was happy with the answer.

Two kinds of sample boxes arrived in the shipment. One contained the same supplies as sent and the second were smaller boxes containing two medium size bottles of formalin and medium sized Whirl Pac bags for shipment of one hemisphere of the brain. There were 100 sample boxes...just what Penny had ordered. She calculated she should have enough boxes for today's sampling and a few extra for Dimmitt or Tulia. Additional PPE gear in all sizes also arrived. It would keep everyone supplied for at least another ten days.

After everyone drank two bottles of water and used the restroom, Sammi, Penny, and Jim Bob donned new PPE and got back to work. Everyone needed the short break and water to refresh. Getting back to the task at hand, they fell into the same efficient groove working about another four hours. After finishing the middleweight cattle, they started on the heavyweights. About half way through the heavyweights, everyone was slowing down. It was time for a break and lunch. Earlier, Sonny came down saying Juana Gomez had gotten cheeseburgers and fries from Mom's Cafe in Hereford. Mom's was famous for their cheeseburgers.

They went to the office after everyone doffed their gear. Penny downed a bottle of water between leaving the vet clinic and arriving at the office. Jorge was taking the first dump truck up to the crematorium and then he would have his lunch. Jim Bob asked Jorge and the two cowboys to be ready to finish the heavyweight sick pen when they returned from lunch in about 45 minutes.

Penny walked into the office conference room greeting everyone and looking around for Randy. He was in Dennis' office on the telephone. The cheeseburgers and fries kept warm in the oven. Sammi took three cheeseburgers and three orders of fries out of the oven placing them on the conference table with three paper towels to use as napkins. Jim Bob was the last to enter the conference room after stopping to check his e-mails. He walked directly to the refrigerator and picked up a bottle of water asking what everyone wanted to drink? Jim Bob took the drink orders and delivered to everyone. Penny sat at the conference table next to Sammi and ate her lunch.

Randy walked out of the office and sat next to Penny asking, "Have you finished sampling?"

Before Penny could empty her mouth of the bite of cheeseburger, Jim Bob responded, "We have 17 head left in the heavyweight pen. Are there any at Dimmitt or Tulia?"

"Yep, there are three at Dimmitt and eight at Tulia", Randy said. "I'd also like Penny to look at my roping steers at Happy, if she has time today. I cut five out this morning. Bud hauled them to a hospital pen at Tulia."

Penny responded, "We should be done here in less than two hours; then we can head Dimmitt and Tulia. We have about an hour and a half of sampling work at the two places exclusive of travel time. Do you think you have the same issue in your roping steers at Happy?"

"I'm not sure… maybe so", said Randy. "I thought we could first look at the five head I cut off at Tulia where there's better facilities. Each year I buy 25 head of Mexican Corriente roping steers to rope." With a big grin Randy continued, "If I could talk you into looking at them, I'll cook you some dinner at my place. What do you think?"

Penny got a big smile on her face and somewhat flirtatiously said, "Well I suppose I could do that; if you're a good cook!"

"That's too much pressure to put on a poor bachelor, but we'll try to round up something that's edible", Randy joked. "Do you like Mexican food and maybe a Corona?"

"I love Mexican food; that sounds wonderful", said Penny. Finishing the last of her fries she said, "Well gang, we'd better head back and finish up the sampling, so we can head to Dimmitt and Tulia." With that comment Penny got up from the conference room table and started walk to the door. Jim Bob and Sammi followed.

"Wait a minute you guys", said Rex. "There something I need to tell. Secretary Johansen having a press conference at 4:00 PM Washington time this afternoon. The outbreak is the main topic. Dr. Laporte's also be involved. I'm told that it will preempt programming. I don't have any other information now. It's at 3:00PM Texas time. If you think you can fit it into your schedule, Dennis will have a TV set up in the conference room."

"Thanks Rex", said Penny. "We'll have to see if we get done with the heavyweights in time. Once we start, I don't want to stop and then don and doff again. If we are unable to make it, I'm sure you and Cheri will take good notes and can fill us in later."

Penny walked from the office back to the vet clinic lost in her thoughts. *Dinner at Randy's, I wish I had time to clean up and take a shower. I'll smell like a dead horse by the time we sit down to dinner. This came a lot sooner than I expected. He must be interested; I know I want to spend more time with him.*

The cowboys rode up with Jorge riding double behind one cowboy. Simultaneously Penny, Jim Bob, and Sammi were donning their PPE gear. They fell back into their efficient groove. When the press conference started they had not finished with the heavyweights. It took an hour and forty-five minutes to finish the 17 heavyweights. Sammi and Jim Bob finished putting the boxes out for FedEx, loaded sample boxes, supplies, and equipment needed at Dimmitt and Tulia, and met Penny at the office.

Penny walked to the office getting drinks for everyone and listened to the press conference in progress. Glancing at the TV Penny first noticed President Smyth standing next to the podium on one side and Dr. Laporte stood on the other as Secretary Johansen responded to questions from the press. She answered some, while Dr. Laporte responded to the technical questions. Randy's full attention was on the press conference and he in deep concentration. He turned in his chair and briefly smiled as Penny sat in the chair next to him. Randy watched a few more minutes, then asked Penny if she ready to go to Dimmitt. Penny suggested they watch for a few more minutes as the press conference was not over. The questions became redundant. Dr. Laporte was repetitively responding, "Unfortunately that is currently unknown" to most questions being asked.

"This is getting stupid", said Randy. "Why don't we get on the road and I'll fill you in on what was said."

"Sounds good to me", said Penny. "I need to check my phone and order some more sample supplies." Checking her phone there were several e-mails regarding the press conference. There was an e-mail from Dr. Rhodes-Voss with the subject of Diffuse Vacuolating Encephalopathy. Penny opened the e-mail finding it was essentially a summary of the verbal report from Graeme Pennington and Ian McLaughlin. Attached were photomicrographs of the EM images from the twelve slides they had reviewed. Penny called Diane Kaminski to order another a hundred more small sampling boxes. Diane shared with Penny that the lab was running out of sampling supplies and reagents for the ELISA and IHC test kits. They requested the labs in the network to send half of their supplies to the NVSL. Penny thanked Diane and hung up her phone.

"OK Randy, I've gotten my things taken care of", said Penny. "Please fill me in on the press conference."

Randy began, "Well the first thing that struck me was it started out with President Smyth speaking about an emerging animal disease outbreak. I had no idea other premises were involved. It's spread to fourteen states and more than fifty premises. I thought we were the only ones having problems. In a perverse way, it made me feel good that we were not the only ones with this problem. President Smyth said he and Secretary Johansen were going to work on an indemnification program for those producers with infected herds. He further said he would expedite emergency supplemental funding bill to congress. After the president gave the overview, he turned it over to Secretary Johansen. This morning the reference lab reported we are not dealing with BSE or any other TSE. They are saying this is a novel prion disease as evidenced by histopathology and electron microscopy. They are calling this disease Diffuse Vacuolating Encephalopathy or DVE. Secretary Johansen also said she is putting a temporary, but indefinite, moratorium on the slaughter of all cattle. The Secretary emphasized no animals displaying CNS signs of disease ever reached the food or animal food chain. She stated the existing meat supply is safe to consume; telling the public any animal presented for slaughter having CNS signs is immediately condemned, euthanized, and brain samples tested. Also, she said she's temporarily prohibiting the transfer of ownership and the transport of cattle, both intrastate and interstate. The USDA is disallowing export of cattle, beef, and beef byproducts. This all goes into effect tomorrow morning at 12:01AM. Dr. Laporte spoke about spongiform diseases caused by prions, and the similarities and differences of them to DVE. He said this is the first known vacuolating encephalopathy. He explained there are many unanswered questions that will take diligent work on behalf of the USDA, academia, and industry to answer. Dr.

Laporte said they don't know how it spreads, where it came from, how it got here, what kind of morbidity and mortality to expect, if it affects other species of animals, or if it affects humans. Then they opened it up for the press to ask questions. Then the really dumb questions began. It's also when you sat down at the table."

"Well that's the most significant press conference during the three years I have been with the agency...and I missed it", Penny said. "This is probably the most significant disease process to be identified since Kuru or Scrapie, which started identification of all spongiform diseases. It's really frightening when you think about it."

Everything was ready when they arrived at Dimmitt. Jim Bob and Sammi were talking with Sonny and everything ready for Penny. "We're ready for you ma'a...I mean Penny" said Sammi with a smile.

Penny said, "Thanks everyone. I suppose you all heard about the news conference?"

"Yes, we did, in fact we listened to it on our way down on public radio", Jim Bob commented. "It sounds like we're dealing with something novel. We were just visiting with Sonny about it. Can prions mutate?"

As everyone walked toward the alleyway near the vet clinic, Penny finally responded to Jim Bob's question. "To my knowledge, there's never been anything reported suggesting a mutation. All the TSE diseases are quite similar in pathology. The TSE diseases are known not to be contagious, but they are infectious and transmission may occur through oral transfer of infectious particles. Because prions lack nucleic acid, they're not considered alive; therefore, they cannot mutate."

Sample collection went remarkably well. Within twenty minutes Penny and Randy were pulling out of the Dimmitt feedlot with Jim Bob and Sammi following close behind.

Both Penny and Randy quietly traveled down the highway on the way to Tulia. Penny broke the silence; "A penny for your thoughts handsome."

Randy smiled and responded, "My thoughts are kind of selfish. I was thinking about the indemnification program. If the program is fair and large enough to cover the losses of large producers, like us, it could save our operation. Without it, I don't know what we'll do. What were your thoughts?"

"I was thinking about this new disease, that led me to think it would be interesting to research it in more detail. Then, I began to think about what would be the first thing I'd do. We need further information on its epidemiology to determine the source of the outbreak. We need a lot of specific research done to better understand prion proteins."

"Would you really consider redirecting your career toward research? I'm a little surprised. You're a great pathologist; I thought you would continue in that direction."

"No", Penny replied, "if I was able to get a tenure track position doing worthwhile research at a well-respected university, I think it would be ultimately more fulfilling than sampling and reading histopathology slides. In a way, I'm getting a little stale. Working with this investigative team has made me reevaluate my life's compass."

Randy smiled, not saying anything. He thought privately. *Wow, Penny just clarified she's open to a major shift in her life. That pearl of knowledge that requires more thought.*

"Want to know what I'm thinking about now?" Penny playfully inquired. "I'm thinking what kind of a Mexican dinner is this guy going to cook me tonight? TV dinners don't count."

Randy laughed, then developed a very serious expression. "I have a confession to make. When you said you liked Mexican food, I asked Sarita if she would make enchiladas for us tonight."

Quickly Penny inquired, "Who is Sarita?"

Randy picked up more than a little concern in Penny's voice and the quickness of her response. Trying to defuse the situation Randy responded, "Oh she's a girl that lives at my place." Immediately recognizing his response was anything but clarifying he continued, "I have a little guest house at my place. Sarita lives in the guest house; sometimes she picks up around my house while doing her laundry. She's just finished her junior year in accounting at North Texas A&M in Canyon. During the summers, she works at the Canyon office. During the school term, she works part time. You'll like her; she's a really nice girl. In fact, you saw her when y'all came to the office. She was sitting in for our receptionist."

Penny didn't immediately respond. Rather, she thought. *That girl was gorgeous. She could be a big-time model...and she lives at Randy's house...cleans his house sometimes. I wonder what's going on there. No, I'm not so sure I will like her. I don't even know if I like Randy right now!*

The two pickups pulled into the Tulia feedlot driving directly to the vet clinic. Bud had the cattle in the alleyway by the chute. The tables were ready for everyone. They observed the cattle from the fence. All were showing signs, but the roping steers' signs were very mild. They displayed mild nystagmus and nose twitching. The other three were showing more advanced signs. All three were ataxic appearing more excitable. They collected the samples and packaged efficiently. Soon they were ready to observe the roping steers at Randy's house.

Jim Bob said, "I'm going to take these samples as well as those from Dimmitt back to Canyon. It's too late for FedEx to pick them up here. Sammi has made arrangements to meet Sonny, Cheri, Glen, and Rex at the office."

Chapter 11

Randy with an easy-going smile looked toward Penny and said, "Well, Miss Penny, they've gotten everything worked out. We need to head toward Happy so can get a look at the steers before the sun goes down."

She jumped into the pickup and sang, "On the road again". As they pulled out of Tulia and headed north she said, "I need to check my phone again. I'm hoping that Dr. Rhodes-Voss has reported on the samples we submitted yesterday. Now that we know kind of what we are dealing with, the histopathology on the supplemental samples might be useful in determining a method of transmission. But, we may not know anything using a light microscope. No, there are no reports from Pat." Penny placed her phone back into her purse.

Randy looked over at her saying, "I hope you're not angry that I am not cooking your dinner. Actuality, I can't cook a lick. I wanted to spend some time with you and that was the best excuse I could come up with at the time."

Penny laughed nervously and said, "Randy, I'm not angry; the Sarita thing just caught me off guard. I wanted to spend time with you and... Oh God, I just got a whiff of myself. I smell like a goat that's been dead for a week. Maybe we should have dinner another time or we could have dinner outside and you could put me down wind."

"Penny", Randy explained, "let me briefly tell you about Sarita. About six years ago Sarita's mother died of breast cancer. She is the oldest of three children. Her father, Manuel Torres, worked for us at the feed mill at Hereford. About four years ago, on the night of her senior prom, Sarita went to prom with her date. Her younger sister, Juanita, wanted to go to prom and see her sister, as did her father. It's a common thing for parents to visit the prom and see their children in this part of the country. Well, Manuel and Sarita's two siblings came to the prom watching Sarita dance with her date. Manuel was so proud of his eldest daughter. She had taken over the household responsibilities after her mother died, along with keeping her straight A average in school. On the way home from visiting Sarita at the prom, a semi hit Manuel's car head on. The truck's driver had fallen asleep at the wheel. Everyone in the car died on impact. Sarita has no relatives living in the U.S. She had scholarships and planned to attend college in Canyon. Mom and Dad moved her into their house in Amarillo for the summer. She became close to my parents, but Sarita was frightened about driving back and forth to Canyon to attend college."

"Mom gave Sarita her car as a graduation gift from high school; then Dad bought Mom a new one. Anyway, I had a guest house at my place and did not use it. I have a five-bedroom house, so if someone comes, they just stay in my house. Sarita moved into my guest house before starting her first year of college and has been there ever since. When I'm gone, she watches the place, picks up the mail, and feeds the steers and horses. She also uses my washer and dryer; so, while she's doing her laundry, she sometimes cleans my house. I really don't want her to think she needs to clean and pick up the house, but I think she feels compelled. A couple times a week she cooks something at her house and we have dinner together at mine. Sarita is really a nice girl and a good cook. She's going to have dinner with us tonight. You'll get a chance to know her a little better. Does that help set your mind at ease?"

"Oh Randy", Penny said apologetically, "Sarita has been through so much; you and your family have been so kind to her. I feel embarrassed."

"Not to worry. Sarita is like my little sister. She has a boyfriend and I've been keeping a close watch on him. He works for an oil company as a petroleum engineer. I think they may be getting a little serious, but Sarita says not. If they do get serious and get married, I plan to introduce him to my brother Mike and see if Mike can hire him away from Rim Rock Oil. Sarita, nor anyone else, knows this; but I've spoken to my sister Mary, she runs the bank. When Sarita graduates and gets her CPA licensure, she's going to transfer from the feeding operation to the bank's trust department. The VP in charge of the trust department is about three years from retiring. So, when he retires, and Sarita has gotten some trust experience, she can slide into that position. If Sarita continues to work hard, that position will provide her a nice living."

"We're here", exclaimed Randy. An understated automatic gate opened and they drove in on a paved lane. Off to the right was a large stone and log ranch style home. Randy drove past the home to the left and up to an old looking stone barn. "Behind the barn is the arena. At the end of the arena are the cattle pens." They walked down the aisle way extending the length of the barn separating one row of eight stalls from another row of the same number. Penny noted the stalls were spacious, probably 16 feet by 16 feet. The aisle way being about that same width. White painted pipe fencing extended from both sides of the barn providing a paddock for each horse. Randy turned on the barn and arena lights to provide better illumination as they walked to the cattle pens. Penny's eyes were actively trying to take in each detail while they walked. The arena ground was soft and a tractor with a harrow sat outside the arena. As they walked the length of the arena Randy said, "We can turn on the lights to the pens if it gets too dark to see. There's a light switch on one of the poles."

Penny commented, "I don't think I have ever seen such a nice facility. You must be quite a horseman."

"No, not really. I'm just a cowboy at heart, who likes to rope in my spare time. I travel to a few rodeos each year to compete in the steer roping. It's one of my many bad habits."

"When I was young, I was in 4H and had a horse. I rode him at the county fair; one year I did well enough to go to the Colorado State Fair. We did not win anything there, but it is a fond memory", commented Penny.

Penny and Randy slowly walked through the roping steers carefully looking at them from behind, both sides, and the front. They observed them as they walked and trotted away from a hayrack a filled with a big bale of fresh green alfalfa hay.

"I don't see anything worrisome", Penny said.

"I don't either", said Randy. "I'm going to have Bud send a couple of his guys over to take them to Tulia this evening. We'll be able to look at them there daily. If they start showing CNS signs, we'll have them in a better place to collect samples and dispose of the carcasses."

Penny responded, "This may be bad advice, but I don't see APHIS continuing to do as much sampling in the coming days. Nationally, the demand is just too great and it's overwhelming the lab's capacity. Secondly, the steers you cut out today were showing very minimal signs-a slight nose twitch and mild nystagmus. Maybe you should wait and see if any others start to display signs. It may be that none of the others break with signs. That way you could rope them when you have time."

"That's a good thought", Randy said. "At least that way I could get a little practice in. I have a rodeo coming up in late July; I'm going to Cheyenne."

Closing the gate to the cattle pen and walking back across the arena, Penny asked; "Do you feed them any grain?"

"No, I don't want them to get too heavy too quickly. I just give them alfalfa hay free choice. That's what's puzzling me. The only thing I've fed them since they arrived here about three months ago is alfalfa hay. I started them on some third cutting hay I had left over from last year. When the first cutting came off our irrigated fields, about two months ago; I switched them over to this year's alfalfa. That's all they've had."

"So, there's nothing different in their ration, except that a couple of months ago you switched to this year's alfalfa? And the alfalfa came essentially from the same source as last year's crop?"

"Yeah, actually I think from the same field. We have a farm about halfway between Tulia and here. We raise alfalfa and corn on it. Larry round-baled part of the alfalfa for my steers, the other he chopped for haylage. We have about ten farms in this general area that supply crops to our 'southern' feedlots. We have other farms north and east of Amarillo where our other three feedlots are located."

"It would be interesting to know if anything was done differently between the southern and northern farms", said Penny.

Randy replied, "Indeed it would. Partly in response to Secretary Johansen's announcement, we're having a holding company board meeting tomorrow morning. I'll ask Larry Shelton, he's my sister Rose's husband. He oversees the farm operations. It may be meaningful that all of the CNS problems have been localized to our southern feedlots as well."

By this time, Penny was walking through the barn carefully looking at the old barn. In the middle on one side was a tack room. On the other side was an area used to store small bales of grass hay. In the spacious tack room were two fifty-five-gallon metal barrels with heavy metal lids hinged top with a handle to lift the lid. One barrel held rolled oats, the other was empty. While Penny looked around, Randy fed the two horses in the barn. The barn was setup so Randy could grab about a foot of flaked hay and throw it into a feeder attached to the outside barn wall next to the stall door leading from the stall into the outdoor paddock. A well-used three-pound coffee can portioned the oats into the rounded bottom of the hayrack. Each horse received the same amount of hay and oats. "That's it, we're done feeding", said Randy.

Penny walked out of the barn getting into the pickup. Randy turned off the barn and arena lights then followed. They drove to his house where Randy pulled the pickup into the garage. He opened the door leading from his garage into a short hallway. On the left was a half bathroom, while on the right the laundry room contained a washer and dryer and a set of cabinets with a counter top along the opposite wall. The hall exited into a large country kitchen. There stood Sarita, a dark haired stunningly beautiful, slender girl with a hot pad over her right hand standing in front an oven.

She looked up with a warm smile and said, "I've just put the enchiladas into the oven."

Randy introduced Penny to Sarita. Shaking Sarita's hand Penny said, "Sarita it is so nice to meet you. Please excuse my appearance I have been working all day. I feel dirty and must smell horrible. It's embarrassing for me to meet you looking and smelling this way."

Sarita smiled saying, "Penny it is a pleasure to meet you as well. You look like you're about the same size as I am. I wear a size six. How about you?"

"Generally, a size six fits me well", responded Penny.

"Randy", said Sarita, "a lady does not feel comfortable when she feels unclean; regardless of how beautiful she is. We'll be back in a few minutes. There's beer in the refrigerator and iced tea on the counter."

Sarita placed Penny's hand in hers and led her out of the kitchen and through a double patio door to a pathway leading from Randy's house to her bungalow. Sarita's actions happened so quickly it startled Penny. "I'm sure I have something that will fit you. It'll make you feel more comfortable and we have about 30 minutes or so before dinner."

Startled, Penny, didn't know how to respond as Sarita quickly led her out of the house. Walking into the bungalow she noticed that while small, it was spotlessly clean. There was a small kitchenette area with a counter separating it from a small living room. Immediately to the right as she walked through the entry door was a bathroom and adjacent to it and the living room was a small bedroom with a closet and two chests of drawers.

"I have slacks and jeans, but you might be more comfortable in shorts", said Sarita as they walked into the bedroom.

"Shorts would be fine. Actually, anything is fine. Sarita thank you for sharing one of your clean outfits with me".

"I have a pair of yellow linen shorts that are lined. I think they would look cute on you Penny. Here they are. What do you think?"

"Oh, they are cute and not too short. I've always liked yellow", Penny said holding them up next to her while looking in a full-length mirror attached to the door.

"I don't think I have a bra that will fit you; you're a little larger than I am. So, let's find a top that won't be too revealing", Sarita said opening the bottom drawer of the dresser. I'm thinking maybe a sweatshirt. The air conditioning in the dining room can make the room a little cool. What do you think about this ivory one? It should fit loosely, and yet not be revealing."

Penny held up the sweatshirt and viewed herself in the mirror. On the front of the sweatshirt it said Red Raiders in worn red lettering. "It looks great. Who are the Red Raiders?"

"That's Texas Tech University in Lubbock. I have small feet, but I have a pair of thongs that are a little too big for me, said Sarita while reaching into the closet and pulling out the thongs with light leather straps."

After loosening the laces on her running shoe and removing her sock, Penny tried on one of the thongs saying, "It's perfect! Sarita, you are like the sister I never had. How can I thank you for letting me borrow an outfit? You're so sweet."

Sarita smiled and said, "I'm going to tell you something that Randy would kill me for, if he knew. I have lived here in this guest house for almost four years. In all that time, Randy has never asked me to cook a meal for him or any of his guests. You are very special to Randy; he wants everything to be perfect for you."

Penny softly blushed and said, "We've only known each other for a little while, but Randy is becoming very special to me as well". She followed Sarita into her bathroom for a much-needed shower.

"Well, I feel like I washed off about a pound of dirt and five pounds of stink", Penny said as she walked into the kitchenette area. Sarita laughed.

Walking into the dining room at Randy's house a few minutes later, the two women found Randy sipping iced tea while standing in front of a flat screen TV in the living room watching CNN.

Sarita set the table as Penny placed a bowl of homemade tortilla chips, a bowl of freshly prepared guacamole and a smaller container of Pico de Gallo on the table. A pitcher of iced tea sat on the table with large glasses half filled with ice.

Randy watched CNN's report of the emerging disease outbreak. Penny walked up to his side and put her arm around his waist saying, "Hi there, cowboy."

Randy looked to his side, and then turned his body. Penny had washed her hair and had pulled the still damp long blonde hair back into a loose pony tail. "Wow", exclaimed Randy. "You sure do clean up well! You really do look much more relaxed and comfortable."

"It's all thanks to Sarita", responded Penny. "She truly saved the evening."

Sarita looked up when she heard her name mentioned saying, "Penny you do look beautiful. If you can pull Randy away from the TV, dinner is ready."

Sarita seated Randy at the head of the oak dining table with his back toward the TV. Penny sat to Randy's right and Sarita to his left. The enchiladas were on a hot plate between Penny and Sarita. The aroma infiltrating the dining room was appetizing. Sarita suggested, "The enchiladas are very hot and messy to plate. If you will hand me your plate Randy I will put them on your plate, then I will plate some for Penny and me. Oh, I forgot the frijoles; they're still on the stove. I'll serve everyone their enchiladas, then get the frijoles."

While Sarita put the beans into a large bowl, Randy poured everyone a tall glass of iced tea. Sarita returned to the table with the frijoles moving a small bowl containing sliced lemon and fresh mint toward Randy so he could add a slice of lemon to his tea. Penny did the same. She slightly crushed a mint leaf between her fingers and placed it into the tea glass. Randy served himself beans asking Penny if she would like him to spoon some onto her plate. After serving Penny, Randy also served frijoles to Sarita.

After eating the first bite Penny commented, "Sarita, these enchiladas are so good; they are the best I have ever eaten. Wherever did you learn to cook so well?"

"When my mother got sick and was taking chemo, she lost her appetite. Her sense of taste diminished. She started showing me how to cook for our family. She had a three-ring binder of recipes, mostly hand written, which were her mother's and grandmother's. It was there for me to use as a guide. She supervised me making many different meals. When she got sicker, I did all the cooking. After Mom passed away, I inherited the cookbook. It also became one of my responsibilities to cook for our family and I began to enjoy cooking. It gave me time each day to think of my mother and helped me mourn her death. I cooked almost every day from the time I was twelve until the accident that took my Dad, brother, and sister from me when I was eighteen. I still like to cook, but it's less satisfying to cook only for myself. Sometimes I'll cook something at my house and bring it over after Randy gets home and we eat it together. That's about the only time I cook anymore. It was fun for me to cook this meal; it brought back many pleasant memories. I am happy you are enjoying it. If you would like, I will share the recipe with you. It's one of Randy's favorites."

"I would really love to have your enchilada recipe, and the one for the frijoles and guacamole as well. I hope I'm not being too bold."

"If you will leave me one of your business cards before you leave tonight, I will e-mail all of them to you", said Sarita.

Randy and Penny were hungry when they sat down at the table. Everyone found the meal to be delicious. There was little conversation while everyone enjoyed the meal. After dinner, everyone's plate was clean. Randy had a second helping of enchiladas and frijoles. Penny displayed more restraint. Sarita cleaned the dishes from the table putting the leftovers in containers and filling the dishwasher with cooking utensils, silverware, and flatware. Both Penny and Randy were sipping their tea after giving high praise to Sarita for the dinner.

Randy commented, "I need to know more about prions and the diseases they cause. I'm sure I will have to describe what's been happening to our cattle at the board meeting tomorrow morning. Can you help me out?"

"There's more we don't know about prion proteins than what we do know, said Penny. Prion proteins occur naturally in nerve cells. They are exclusively protein molecules. While their physiological function remains controversial, recent research suggests prion proteins in peripheral nerves causes activation of myelin repair in Schwann cells that insulate individual nerve fibers. The lack of prion proteins results in demyelination. There are studies demonstrating prion proteins may have a normal function in maintaining long-term memory. Mice without normal prion protein show altered long-term potentiation in the hippocampal portion of the brain. Other studies have shown prion protein expression on stem cells is necessary for the self-renewal of bone marrow. This study showed all long-term hematopoietic stem cells expressed prion proteins on their cell membrane and that hematopoietic stem cells without prion proteins demonstrate an increased sensitivity to cell depletion."

"When a prion protein folds abnormally it becomes an infectious prion protein. These infectious prions cause diseases like Scrapie, BSE, Chronic Wasting Disease, and other transmissible spongiform encephalopathies. And now Diffuse Vacuolating Encephalopathy. Most contemporary investigators accept prion replication defies the rules of nature because they do not possess nucleic acids, which are necessary for all other living organisms to replicate. Therefore, we do not consider prions to be alive like viruses, bacteria, fungi, etc. We know the enzyme proteinase digests normal prion protein. However, infectious prion proteins are proteinase-resistant. In fact, exposure to concentrated formalin, high temperature and pressure autoclaving, exposure to intense radiation, and ultra-violet light all destroy nucleic acids—and inactivate known viruses and bacteria. Yet these treatments have no effect on infectious prions. They can and have caused disease in a new host. Propagation of infectious prions depends on the presence of normally folded protein in which the prion can induce misfolding. Once induced to misfold, it becomes an infectious prion and growth occurs exponentially. The incubation period of prion diseases is determined by the exponential growth rate of prion replication, which is a balance between the linear growth and the misfolding of aggregates."

"The exact structure of prion protein is unknown. Infectious prions are 17 to 27 nanometers in size and weigh between 300-600 kilodaltons. They are really tiny, but nasty agents."

"My God, Penny the board will never understand that, even if I could spit it out verbatim", responded Randy. "I was able to keep up with your description; and I will be able to dumb it down so the others will have a general understanding. I learned none of this in vet school or anywhere else. Thank you."

"Penny you're so smart", said Sarita. "While I didn't understand much of what you said, I can appreciate why Randy and you are working so hard to try to figure out what's happening."

Penny, mildly embarrassed by the praise, responded; "When I did my masters work, it was in molecular biology. Then when I was doing my pathology residency my major professor was studying chronic wasting disease in elk. So, I ended up getting kind of a double dose. I really enjoy working in the lab with complex problems like this."

Randy started a round of uncontrollable yawning affecting Sarita, then Penny. Penny stood and said, "Randy, you better get me back to the motel; we're both tired and need to rest. Sarita, thank you for a delicious meal and the clean clothes. I'll get them back to you as soon as I get them cleaned. I have never had a sister, but I could only wish if I did that she would be just like you. I had a very wonderful and relaxing evening. Thank you both!"

Sarita walked them out to Randy's pickup and when they left she walked back to her cabin. She reflected, *it was a wonderful night and Penny is so charming. She's just the kind of girl that Randy needs. I could tell she adores him and he's smitten with her. I could not have picked someone that could complement Randy as well as Penny does...time will tell.*

As Randy pulled onto the highway Penny pushed up the console between them and moved over toward Randy resting her head on his shoulder. "I had a wonderful evening. Sarita is so sweet and considerate. She is a marvelous cook; I have never had a better meal", Penny said as she lightly wrapped her arms around Randy's upper arm.

Randy responded, "I could tell Sarita really likes you; and I have found her to be an excellent judge of people. For that matter, as I get to know you I am beginning to think you are very special as well. I worry your investigation will soon end and you will go back to Ames. I've never been involved in a long-distance relationship, but I'm not very fond of the idea."

"I, too, know the day is coming. I am already dreading leaving more than you may know. But I don't think there's anything around here for me", said Penny disappointingly.

"We're you serious when you said you would consider moving into a research position", asked Randy.

"Yes, I was serious, but I'm unaware of any such positions. What are you thinking", Penny asked.

"Well, someone is going to need to study the prion protein that is responsible for DVE. Maybe that person should be you. You certainly have the education and experience to do the work."

"Randy, there is no funding for DVE, nor a position. If there were, and if it's in this general area, I would be all over it."

"I understand what you are saying. I agree there's nothing right now. However, that could change in a few months. With such a devastating agent, I think industry and government will fast track funding. As far as a position goes, let me begin to lay a foundation for that as well", commented Randy.

"You're way ahead of me Randy. I don't understand what you're thinking. In the bureaucratic world that I live in, funding takes time, approvals, and congressional action to acquire the funds. Please enlighten me", said Penny.

"Secretary Johansen and President Smyth are currently working on an indemnification plan. I'm thinking they will include funds for research, since we are dealing with a novel disease. I anticipate their plan will pass through congress with broad based support because so many states are involved and there is significant risk to this nation's cattle herd."

"Secondly, industry groups view this outbreak as potentially catastrophic. They too will make research funds available. The large packers and other various large agribusiness corporations will also contribute."

"Most large universities have researchers who will compete for research funding. Some of the proposals will be germane, others will likely lack relevance. There is a large well-respected university about ninety miles south of Happy that may be interested in hiring someone like you for prion research. That university is Texas Tech-in fact you're wearing one of their sweatshirts."

Penny was now sitting up next to Randy listening with interest. "How long have you been thinking about this? I'm amazed at the scope of your answer and how well thought out it is. However, I do not know anyone at Texas Tech to even make an informal inquiry."

I've been mulling it over since earlier today when you mentioned if the right job at a university were available, you would find the research rewarding and would be interested. You need not know someone at Texas Tech. My family has developed influential relationships at Tech over the years. I will see what we can get done."

"Sure. I'm kind of dumbstruck. I don't know what to say. Randy, you have a way of blowing my mind", Penny said leaning over and kissing him on the cheek.

"Where is your meeting tomorrow", Penny asked as they pulled into the motel.

"It's at the bank here in Amarillo. I'm delegated to stop at Rosa's on my way in to pick up the breakfast burritos", said Randy.

"Will I see you tomorrow", Penny asked.

"I hope so, the meeting starts at 7:30 and it should be over by noon. I'll check in at the office, then head to Hereford to meet up with you."

Penny reached for her purse pulling it open; she got out two business cards giving them to Randy. "One is for Sarita; she's going to e-mail me the recipes. The other, she said reaching into Randy's shirt pocket for his pen, is for you. I'm writing my personal cell phone and home phone numbers, address in Ames as well as my home e-mail address. That way, you'll have all my contact information." Penny replaced his pen and put the cards in his pocket.

Randy reached in his back pocket for his wallet writing down his home telephone number and address. "This address works for both Sarita and me." Looking in Penny's eyes Randy said, "This has been an extraordinary night. I've really enjoyed being with you."

Penny leaned forward kissing him, this time tenderly on the lips. Randy placed his hand on the back of Penny's neck extending the kiss. "Sweet dreams", said Randy.

Penny slid over to the passenger side of the seat and climbed out of the pickup. She waved as she entered the lobby. Randy waved and drove back toward Happy.

Penny thought, *this is crazy; but I think I have found the man of my dreams.*

Chapter 12

The investigative team gathered in Rex's room for the daily conference call. The smell of fresh brewed coffee permeated the living room/kitchen area. The Texas investigative team was eager to hear what Dr. Yu would have to say after President Smyth's and Secretary Johansen's press conference.

"Good morning everyone", Dr. Yu began the call. "I am sure all of you either heard or read about the press conference yesterday. We at least know what we're dealing with now. Regrettably, we don't know much else about the agent. Our charge is to drill down gathering as much germane information as possible."

"With that in mind, I need to inform you all that you are not to speak with the press as an agency or government representative regarding DVE. Dr. Laporte wants all communications with the press to go through headquarters. This is for two reasons. First, so you all do not have to spend valuable time speaking with the press. Secondly, because we are dealing with a novel agent, headquarters wants the message to be consistent. As you might imagine, having a discussion with a reporter regarding an infectious prion protein would soon become a highly technical conversation and easily misunderstood by someone lacking scientific background. To assist in providing accurate detailed information, the agency has developed a website for additional information. Each of you will receive this information soon by e-mail. The website is up and running this morning and I have been able to access it. On the website, there are telephone numbers for headquarters staff who are available to converse with the press. The website also has a link providing basic information concerning prions, specific up to date information regarding this outbreak, and frequently asked questions. I encourage all of you to spend a few minutes accessing the site and perusing around the web pages."

"The next item of business is we are changing the tissues we need to harvest for sampling. I received an e-mail concerning this change just prior to joining the call, so it's hot off the press. We are to discontinue taking heart, lung, liver, kidney, abdominal fat, and spleen samples. Additionally, we need to collect samples of the maxillary nerve and a section of the Vegas nerve, if it is readily identifiable when excising the atlanto-axial joint. If you cannot readily identify the vegas nerve, do not waste time hunting for it."

"The amount of sampling to be done at each premise has also changed, effective today. The population of cattle on the premise will determine the number of samples to collect. Rather than sampling all symptomatic cattle like we initially instructed, we now want to sample only a statistically significant number for that premise. I'll e-mail everyone the specific number of samples to take from symptomatic cattle on a given premise after this call. I'll not bore you with the details."

"This morning at 11:00AM eastern there is going to be a large conference call hosted by Secretary Johansen. Invited participants include the owners of the premises currently involved in the outbreak, the deans of agriculture at all our land grant universities, and some of the major industry groups. The purpose of the call is to inform them of what we know and what we don't. Additionally, the Secretary will offer to address press inquiries. Secretary Johansen feels the premises owners are currently dealing with enough. She is making this offer of APHIS' expertise and man hours to lessen their collective loads during this hectic time. We're offering our assistance in appreciation for the extraordinary cooperation and help the owners/managers have provided everyone. Please contact premise management this morning and advise them of this call. Provide them with the call-in number. Also, look for an e-mail with the details of the call soon after this call ends. Agency representatives on the call will be Dr. Laporte, Dr. Rhodes-Voss, and me.

"Dr. Adams are you listening in this morning," asked Dr. Yu.

Rex hurriedly un-muted the call as Penny walked toward the speaker phone. "Yes sir", said Penny.

"Dr. Adams, would you please give Dr. Rhodes-Voss a call when this call ends? She asked if she could borrow your expertise this morning. I told her I would have you give her a call. Thanks, Penny."

"That's all the news I have this morning. Thank you all for working so hard. Your efforts are providing the additional information we'll need to figure this out and get things under control. Those of you working with cattle, please continue to work safely and don't take any chances."

"Are there any questions or comments? If not, I hope you all have a good day."

****

Penny stepped out in the hallway next to Rex's room to call Dr. Rhodes-Voss. "Hi Pat", said Penny. "Dr. Yu asked me to give you a call."

"Penny, I spoke with Dr. Yu instead of directly talking with you because I need your help, and officially you are now assigned to an investigation team. There are decisions we're going to need to make based upon our histopathological interpretations. You know more about prion disease than anyone I know. Thus, I would like your input. I have sent you several photomicrographs. Some are EM slides from Worcester. Next, I have sent you photomicrographs of all ileal Peyer's patch sections from symptomatic cattle. I have looked at all of them. I think I'm seeing numerous follicles with extended follicular dendritic cell networks. I'm wondering if this could be due to the invasion and replication of the infectious prions, specifically in the suprafollicular dome, T cell area, and germinal centers. Your experience with prions will hopefully help set my mind at ease regarding quantification of what I'm seeing. I have also included about

50 sections each of tonsillar tissues and lymph nodes. Please provide your interpretation."

"I also e-mailed you an attachment containing another piece of software that integrates into the outbreak investigation software. It provides you the opportunity to dictate your observations into your ear-bud. It integrates those comments, using the voice to text technology, into the histopathology report for that animal. I think you will love using this program; it makes reporting much more efficient. Do you think Rex will mind if I 'steal' you from the investigation team for today?"

"Pat, I don't think Rex will mind. After listening to what Dr. Yu said about just collecting statistically representative sample numbers, I am ahead of the game at the Hereford feedlot and I can catch up on the sampling at Dimmitt and Tulia either this afternoon or tomorrow. I have not yet read the e-mail regarding the numbers to sample based upon herd size."

"Good, I'm glad that Rex will not mind. You might have your IT person install the software package into the investigation software; it will probably save time."

"I'll do that Pat; however, the team is about to leave, I need to catch them. I'd better let you go for now. I'll call you after I'm finished looking at the photomicrographs."

"Rex, Pat asked if she could use me today to look at a whole bunch of histopathology photomicrographs today. I think it would be less distractive and efficient if I stayed here. When I get through, if it's early enough, I'll meet you at Hereford. Also, she's sent me a software program that integrates into the investigational software program. I'm wondering if Cheri could take time to install it before she leaves?"

Rex responded, "Sure it's OK. I looked at the new sampling e-mail after the morning conference call. You've taken more than enough samples at Hereford. Both Dimmitt and Tulia will need more samples collected, but that can wait. I'm wondering how we can get Cheri and potentially you to Hereford. I don't want her to have to wait for you and I don't want you to be without transportation."

"I've thought about that", said Penny. "Cheri can take the other Suburban. Randy has a meeting in Amarillo this morning. I'll give him a call and he can pick me up on his way to Hereford, or maybe we can meet Jim Bob and Sammi at Tulia or Dimmitt."

"That should work. Why don't you give Randy a call now and see if it's OK with him? Maybe you could also tell him about the mega conference call Secretary Johansen is hosting".

"I'd better do that right away. His meeting starts at 7:30." She walked back to her room and dialed Randy's cell phone.

"Good morning pretty lady", Randy answered.

"Well good morning to you, handsome", Penny responded. "Randy I've got some work to do this morning at my motel room. I was wondering if I might catch a ride with you to Hereford, if I get finished early enough."

"So, you're inviting me to your motel room, huh? How could I say no to that request?"

"Well maybe", she teasingly responded. "But only if I finish my work in time." Penny's mind raced, *that sounds pretty good too...I'll make sure I get my work done.*

"Seriously Penny, I would be glad to give you a ride. Do you want me to call you when we're finished?"

"That would be great. Also, Secretary Johansen is hosting a conference call with all the producers who are involved in this outbreak as well as the deans of agriculture at all land grant colleges, and some industry groups. The call is at 10:00AM Texas time. If you like, I'll text you the call-in number. You will probably be getting an e-mail from the Secretary's office also."

"Please text me the number, that way I'm sure I'll have it. I'm certain the board wants to listen in", said Randy. "I need to let you go, the meeting is ready to start."

Cheri walked into Penny's room as she was talking to Randy. She listened. When Penny hung up her phone Cheri said, "Sounds like he's captured your interest?"

"Yes, he has. Randy is so nice, considerate, and has such a big heart; his eyes are such a deep blue."

"Yeah, and as they say here in Texas, he fills out a pair of Wranglers nicely", Cheri said teasingly.

Penny blushed, slightly rolled her eyes, and with a devilish smile said, "That he does."

It took only a few minutes to load the program and verify it was working as intended. Cheri soon left in the Suburban heading toward Hereford. Penny viewed the digital EM photomicrographs first. She appreciated the intracellular pathology described by Graeme and Ian. She found the lack of amyloid deposits to be puzzling. When she had time, she promised herself she would study that further.

Next, she read the ileal Peyer's patch photomicrographs finding the dictation to text saved significant time. After viewing all the Peyer's patch photos, she randomly went back through about 40 of the slides to better quantify the number of follicles with extended follicular dendritic networks. As she viewed the photos, Pat's observation of seeing a 'large' number was correct; in fact, Penny thought she might consider there to be a 'preponderance' of follicles with extended follicular dendritic cell networks. While Penny felt Pat's reasoning for this could be due to the invasion and replication of the infectious prions, she would not make a written comment without looking closer at the tissues through an electron microscope. Penny reasoned under higher magnification, while she could not visualize the actual prions, there would likely be subcellular pathology to help support the comment.

As Penny viewed the e-mailed digital photomicrographs of the tonsillar and lymph node tissue, she thought about what was going on at Randy's board meeting. She felt sympathetic towards Randy. Thinking he may have to respond to numerous questions to which there are no answers. She thought it would be hard when your family depended upon you and your education to provide answers to those questions.

Penny thought, *I must focus and stay on task.* She poured another cup of coffee and continued interpreting the tonsillar and lymph node slides. Penny considered, *the infective titers of prions in tonsils are much lower than in brain. They used H/E stain to stain these tissues. They all appear to be within normal limits. However, using different stains, there may be a possibility of identifying prion disease.* Penny supposed the group discussing sampling tonsils and lymph nodes did not consider the need for special testing techniques. While NVSL could perform these special techniques, they would be time consuming. When dealing with a novel outbreak, they're just not practical. Conversely, in a research study, their inclusion would be good science.

Penny finished her cup of now lukewarm coffee and called Pat Rhodes-Voss.

****

ATX's holding company board of directors' meetings were casual. Randall Bennett, its chairman, often described the meetings as a cross between a family brunch and a full-blown bull session. The demeanor at today's meeting was somewhat staid, with a breeze of concern drifting through the boardroom. Philip Granger, ATX's attorney, was the only one in attendance not on the board of directors. At these meetings, he served as sergeant-at-arms moving the agenda along in a relaxed and thoughtful manner. Without his direction, the meeting could run off the tracks. All the Bennett men wore jeans, boots, and Stetson hats to the meeting. Mary wore a navy blue tailored pantsuit appropriate for the bank president she is. Rose dressed in an attractive ivory pantsuit with contrasting turquoise jewelry. Her husband, Larry, accompanied her. Larry's responsibilities included overseeing ATX's farming operations and commodities businesses. Kate Bennett-Nafzger did not attend the meeting; rather, her husband Harold who runs the equipment and transportation businesses was in attendance.

"Everyone please get something to drink and a burrito and have a seat", said Philip Granger. Once everyone sat around the conference table, the conversation died down. "We have a lot to talk about today so let's get started. As you all know ATX has had an outbreak of a nervous system disease affecting cattle in three of our feedlots. Yesterday, President Smyth and Secretary of Agriculture Clare Johansen held a press conference regarding this disease, now called DVE. One of the things that we learned from the press conference was ATX was not the only one affected. Over 50 producers in 14 states have confirmed DVE. With that introduction, maybe Randy can provide us with more information."

Randy began, "DVE is a disease of the brain and maybe peripheral nerves thought to be caused by a very small misfolded protein called a prion. This prion's existence was not known until this disease outbreak. The Hereford lot was one of the first places identified. A prion is so small one cannot visualize it even using a powerful electron microscope. Because it is so small, it's identified by the pathology it causes primarily within nerve cells in the brain. One of our primary concerns was that we were dealing with BSE; or what some describe as Mad Cow Disease. When our feeders first started showing signs of central nervous system disease, we called the USDA and they came out, removed the brains from the feeders, and sent it to A&M for testing. Those tests were "inconclusive" and the lab forwarded the tissues to the USDA's national vet lab in Ames, IA. They repeated the tests and inconclusive results again obtained. In turn, USDA's Iowa lab forwarded tissue samples to an international reference lab in Worcester, England. Testing at this lab yielded essentially the same results-inconclusive. The Worcester lab also looked at specially stained brain tissue samples under an electron microscope. They determined conclusively it was not BSE. Rather, it is a novel prion causing similar, but uniquely different pathology in brain cells. Is everyone with me so far?"

No one responded and Rose, the radiologist, nodded her head. Randy continued. "That information was reported to the USDA yesterday morning. Of course, we all heard or read about the press conference yesterday afternoon. President Smyth and Secretary Johansen are developing an indemnification plan to submit to congress as part of an emergency supplemental funding bill to cover the outbreak's expense. There has been a temporary suspension of beef slaughter; a temporary prohibition on transporting cattle both intrastate and interstate; a temporary ban on the exportation of beef and beef byproducts. There is also a temporary ban on the transfer of ownership of cattle. This is pretty much what we know for fact."

There is a lot about DVE and infectious prions we don't know. The exact structure of prion protein is unknown. We don't know how it spreads. We don't its mortality and morbidity. We don't know if it affects other animals or humans. We don't know how it got here. And if you delve deeply into prions, there is more we don't know than we know.

Next, let's discuss where ATX fits into this. Before we get into this discussion, we received an invitation to participate in a large conference call Secretary Johansen is hosting. It's specifically for all producers affected by DVE, the deans of agriculture at all land grant universities, and some industry representatives. The call starts in about 30 minutes, so this may be a good time for a restroom break and to get refreshments. If it's OK we'll break now."

The ATX board room evacuated in a relatively orderly fashion as would a school with the fire alarm ringing. After a few minutes, the Bennett family drifted back into the boardroom. Mary asked Randy for the conference call number, saying her secretary would place the call and ring it into the board room when it began. Randy noticed Larry Shelton and Harold Nafzger were both standing outside in the hall making calls on their cell phones. The rest of the board had returned to their seats quietly visiting while waiting.

Soon the boardroom phone rang. Mary placed it on speaker. Secretary Johansen began by introducing the others from USDA on the call; saying they were technical experts she would defer to, if their questions were technical. Next, she briefly covered the points that were the basis of the press briefing the previous day. She then spoke about how the field investigative teams, laboratory personnel, and APHIS veterinarians were all focused on obtaining information about the DVE outbreak. Secretary Johansen offered the producers to direct their press calls to APHIS, if they wanted to, saying the USDA would respond to affected producers press inquiries. She concluded saying she felt it important that the press have accurate and timely information regarding DVE, which became a very technical topic to discuss and communicate to the public. Secretary Johansen then opened the call up to questions from producers, deans, and industry representatives.

There were several questions asking for specific information regarding the indemnification plan. The response was that the indemnification plan was in essentially the pre-draft stage. Secretary Johansen and President Smyth were to have meet about indemnification tomorrow. However, the Secretary did not think it would take too long to put the plan together as USDA had experience drafting emergency supplemental requests. Previously the USDA had done them for extensive forest fire fighting efforts. She relayed there was already strong bipartisan support in both the house and senate.

One dean of agriculture asked if the bill would include monies for research. The Secretary responded that because so little was known about infectious prions, and that essentially nothing was known about the DVE agent, a portion of the bill would specifically be earmarked toward prion research. She added the details of how to attain research grants will be forthcoming after the bill passed and indemnification of producer losses would take top priority.

A representative of the National Cattlemen's Beef Association thanked the Secretary for including industry representatives; saying he thought he could speak for all industry representatives in saying if they could help by communicating information to their memberships, they would be happy to do so.

On that note, the Secretary thanked all those who took time out of their day to participate in the call and reminded them that USDA/APHIS was available to respond to their press inquiries.

Philip Granger called the meeting back to order in a casual manner by saying, "Before we listened in on the conference call, Randy was going to discuss where ATX fits into all of this. Randy do you want to proceed?

Randy began, "We know infectious prion spongiform diseases infect animals and humans through oral transmission. If this novel disease uses the same route of transmission, and it's a reasonable assumption, then I think we need to be zeroing in on what our feedlot cattle have been consuming. We also know that cattle in three of our six feedlots are confirmed to have DVE. Interestingly, it's the three southern feedlots. There's also a fourth premise you don't know about. That is the roping steers at my house. Yesterday, I cut off five steers that were displaying very subtle signs. Bud took them to the Tulia lot for examination and sampling by the USDA. Those results will be available tomorrow."

"Importantly, since the roping steers arrived at my house, they have been fed only alfalfa hay. When they arrived about three months ago, I started feeding them alfalfa bales left over from last year. About two months ago, one of Harold's trucks delivered a load of fresh first cutting alfalfa from a farm located east of Dimmitt. The Tulia, Dimmitt, and Hereford lots received first cutting alfalfa large round bales and chopped alfalfa for haylage. Hereford received its alfalfa about a week before the other two lots. Weather delayed baling and chopping for about a week."

"I spoke with Larry to inquire if there was anything done differently at this farm or the other southern farms, that was not done at the northern feedlots. Larry reminded me this is the initial year of new crop rotation plan using alfalfa and corn. This year Larry planted alfalfa in ground used in corn production last year and vice versa for corn planting. Part of the strategy is to utilize a new alfalfa plant variety developed by USDA to increase biomass yield, disease resistance, and it's significantly more drought resistant; thus, requiring less irrigation. Larry also implemented a new fertilization strategy on the southern farms. Supposedly, the new fertilizer is more environmentally friendly. The new fertilizer uses surfactant which allows for better absorption and the fertilizer contains nanoparticles of titanium dioxide. Titanium dioxide nanoparticle (NPs) biosynthesis is a low cost; ecofriendly approach. A study using titanium dioxide nanoparticles on young alfalfa plants showed significant improvement on shoot length, root length, root area, root nodule, and chlorophyll content. Total soluble leaf protein almost doubled after application. I reviewed this new plan last fall, as well as the research that supported its use. I thought it seemed to be a sound plan with solid research behind it. I recommended Larry implement it this spring. Perhaps Larry can provide further information regarding the new crop rotation plan, the new variety of alfalfa plants, and the new titanium dioxide nanoparticle fertilizer."

Larry began, "After I sent the information to Randy and received his OK, I sent the plan to my brother Ray, who heads the crop science department at the University of

Wyoming. I asked him to look it over. Ray was familiar with the variety of alfalfa we chose. He said it was a very hearty variety and he thought we would see good results with it. He was not familiar with the surfactant and titanium dioxide fertilizer; so, he did a library search for information, but found no information. I sent him copies of the scientific articles I had received and provided to Randy. Based on those copies, Ray concluded the fertilizer was efficacious and ecologically friendlier than continued applications of nitrogen based fertilizers. Additionally, the North Texas Farm Coop was handling the new fertilizer. Its price about 35% less per acre than liquid nitrogen based fertilizers. Considering this information, I decided to use the new alfalfa plant variety and the titanium dioxide nanoparticle fertilizer. However, as with most things that are new, I was unwilling to go all-in with this new program. I tried it on the southern farms, while continuing the old, established rotation and fertilization program with the northern farms. If things worked out as well as projected, I was going to compare northern farm production with that of the southern farms. First cutting alfalfa yields on the southern farms out produced the northern farms by almost 20%. I thought we had a good thing going until Randy called."

"Earlier this morning I collected four boxes of first cutting alfalfa produced from the same farm where Tulia, Dimmitt, Hereford, and Randy's steer hay was produced. I'm shipping it and five gallons of unopened surfactant/titanium dioxide nanoparticle fertilizer to Ray by FedEx. I'm leaving on an afternoon flight to Denver and then on to Laramie. I plan to spend a few days with Ray and his colleagues to see if we can resolve our concerns. The University of Wyoming has a Neuroscience Center Core Grant from the National Institutes of Health. Ray has interested his colleagues there in what we're dealing with. Hopefully, it will be time well spent. Does anyone have questions for me?

Skip Bennett asked, "Does anyone know if plants become infected with infectious prions or do such prion diseases happen in plants?

Larry responded, "Skip that's a great question, but I don't have an answer for you. How about you Randy?"

The board sat looking at Randy for a few seconds; then Randy spoke, "I seem to remember some papers written a few years ago regarding this issue. As I recall someone tried to infect several species of plants with chronic wasting disease prions tagged with a fluorescing chemical. If memory serves, plants took up the infectious prions. Their basic premise was to investigate if infected deer or elk were to urinate on or near the plants would the plants have uptake of the infectious prions. However, the investigators used macerated brain tissue infected with CWD in water; flawing the study. It was to applied on and around the plants. They found uptake, fed the plants to mice and none became symptomatic. It's been a few years ago, and my specific memory of the articles is obscure."

Philip Granger said, "We all know more about DVE and infectious prions than when we walked in this morning. Secretary Johansen has offered the USDA's assistance in handling the press and updated us regarding the indemnification plan. Randy and Larry have identified the southern production of alfalfa may be the cause or secondary to a new fertilizer. Larry's investigating this issue. It looks like ATX for now is in somewhat of a holding pattern. Randy what are your plans?

"Well", Randy said, "I'm going to take the Secretary of Agriculture up on her offer and let USDA handle the press. This issue is way too technical for me to attempt to handle. The best information will come from DC. I plan to continue to cooperate with the USDA investigative team as they study this issue. With all the slaughter houses shut down and transportation of cattle temporarily prohibited, we're not going to be too busy, except for incinerating diseased cattle. I do have a related question for Larry before he leaves. Do we have commodity hedges in place on the feeder cattle owned by ATX?"

"I'm glad you brought that up Randy. We hedge all ATX owned cattle, so we have an identified floor to minimize losses. I do that as soon as new cattle enter your feedlots. When I was on the phone at break, I found out the Chicago Board of Trade is not trading in cattle futures. That is part of what Secretary Johansen meant when she said there was a temporary prohibition on change of ownership of cattle. She's indefinitely suspended trading in cattle futures and options. I'm guessing this action is to help the market stabilize, and prevent speculators from artificially influencing the market. She's one smart lady; I didn't pick up on that when I listened to the press conference."

Philip Granger asked, "Any other questions from anyone?"

Randall Bennett then spoke. "Thanks everyone for coming this morning, I feel better knowing we have all put our heads together on this issue and know we are now in a holding pattern until we have further information. Randy, I think that it's a smart move to let the USDA handle the press. Keep up your hard work, Son. Things will get better for the feeding operation."

After Randall's comments, the meeting adjourned. The Bennett family members cleaned up the table and room filing out visiting with one another.

As everyone stood to leave, Randy asked his father, "Dad can I speak with you before you leave, after everyone else has gone?" Philip Granger began to walk away and Randy commented, "Philip, you can stay too."

As everyone vacated the boardroom, Randy walked to where Randall and Philip were sitting and slid up a chair. "I want to ask you both for some help. It's personal, not business. A few days ago, I met someone. She is a veterinary pathologist on the USDA team. I have never had such strong feelings toward anyone. Her name is Penny Adams and she's special. Anyway, we both know this investigation is going to end sooner than later. Neither of us want to have a long-distance relationship. She's willing to move closer so we can continue get to know one another. However, she wants to continue her career. Her education and experience would allow her to be a professor at a university and teach while continuing her research. She is a well-respected pathologist with expertise in prion diseases. It's my thought there's going to be lots of long term research money that will be coming available soon to fund a major research project. I thought maybe Texas Tech would have an interest in pursuing prion diseases as a field of study. I was wondering if you two could feel Tech out and see if they might have an interest. We would both appreciate it."

"Randy, the short answer is yes. The longer answer is let's discuss this more over lunch."

****

Randy called Penny after checking in at the office and speaking with Dennis Young at the Hereford feedlot. Attempting to disguise his voice Randy said, "Dr. Adams, please."

Penny responded quickly, "Randy, it's not going to work; caller ID gives you away every time. I just finished my work a little while ago and just finished reading the paper. How was your meeting?"

"The meeting went well. We listened to Secretary Johansen's conference call. For the most part, she said about the same thing that she said during the press conference; but there were no dumbass follow-up questions. There was a new item that got my interest."

"Oh, yeah; what?"

"Why don't I tell you in a couple of minutes? I just parked my pickup in front of your motel. Are you decent?

"Always decent, most of the time much better than that", Penny teased.

"Well, I guess I will have to make that decision for myself".

Penny soon heard a knock on the door and walked from her couch to open the door. "Hi there, handsome", she said with a big smile while batting her eyes. Come on in and have a seat on the couch. Do you want anything to drink? She was wearing a pair of pale green shorts and an oversize sweatshirt.

"Howdy, good looking", Randy said as he leaned down and gave her a quick kiss, reaching back to close the entry door. "You're in a playful mood I see."

Penny sat down on the opposite end of the couch crossing her legs under her. "Yeah, I finished my work and just finished getting cleaned up. Your timing is perfect. Glen texted a couple of hours ago to say he, Jim Bob, and Sammi were on the way to Dimmitt and then Tulia to collect some samples. I think he said there were six at Dimmitt and Tulia had four. They said they could get them without my help. Now tell me more about the meeting, and what got your interest."

"The first thing was Secretary Johansen offered to handle all press inquiries for the producers who have DVE cattle. Secondly, one of the deans of agriculture asked about research funding and the Secretary said the DVE indemnification bill would include funding for research."

"Both of those things are good. Tell me about the board meeting."

"The meeting went well. Basically, I gave them a history of the outbreak in our feedlots and explained how they diagnose DVE. I told them a little about infectious prions, after the conference call I told them about how the southern feedlots seemed to be the ones affected. Then I told them about some of my roping steers showing CNS signs and we sampled them as well. This led the discussion to the hay as a potential causative source. My brother-in-law, Larry Shelton, spoke specifically about the southern farming operations. I forgot last fall Larry presented me with a new alfalfa/corn plant rotation plan. He implemented the plan this year on the southern feedlots. Irrigated land that was in corn last year is in a new variety of alfalfa this year. The Agricultural Research Service developed and researched the new variety. Another part of the plan was using a more environmentally friendly method of fertilization using a new fertilizer containing surfactant and titanium dioxide nanoparticles. I looked this plan over last fall and reviewed the research for both the new alfalfa variety and the new fertilizer. Anyway, all three feedlots, as well as my steers, received this new variety of alfalfa fertilized with the new fertilizer. I called Larry last night on my way home after dropping you off. We had a good discussion. Early this morning Larry took several samples of the alfalfa...everything from pulling up healthy plants to samples of baled hay and samples of haylage. He also picked up an unopened five-gallon bucket of the new fertilizer and is sending them FedEx to his brother Ray at the University of Wyoming. Larry is also heading up to Laramie to spend a few days."

"Why is Larry involving the University of Wyoming in a Texas problem and what does Larry's brother Ray have to do with the University of Wyoming?"

"I'm sorry. Ray is a professor of crop science at the University of Wyoming and department head. Ray also reviewed the new alfalfa/corn plant rotation plan Larry gave him as well as the new fertilization method. Ray also gave the plan his blessings, so he was familiar with what was happening. Apparently, the University of Wyoming has a Neuroscience Center Core Grant from NIH. Ray has interested some colleagues at the center in what we're dealing with. They have a new microscopy center that supports the neuroscience center with two electron microscopes."

"Actually, I am familiar with the neuroscience center. The group studies the structural bases that occur in neurons and their synapses in response to numerous physiological events, development, and several neurodegenerative diseases. I can see why they showed interest. They are a solid group, who historically have done good work. ATX's problem would be right up their alley."

"After the meeting, I had lunch with Dad and Philip Granger. Your ears should have been burning as we talked a lot about you. I asked them to quietly feel Texas Tech out about getting you a job there."

"Oh my God. Randy-Tell me you didn't! When you get an idea, you just don't let it go. I should have never told you a tenured research job interested me."

"Yeah, I did. Maybe not quite that directly, but yeah, I did. Before you go off any more, let me explain. Dad and Philip Granger are both on the Board of Regents for Texas Tech. I told them that although we didn't know each other well, we were both interested in pursuing a serious relationship. With you in Ames and me in Amarillo, it would be a long-distance relationship that neither of us wanted. From what I interpreted from Secretary Johansen's response regarding research funding, it looked like it may be something that Texas Tech would have an interest in pursuing. Your education, experience, and reputation would certainly qualify you teach and do some serious research on infectious prion proteins. We discussed prion diseases had cross-over interest between veterinary medicine, production agriculture and human medicine. Dad and Philip discussed maybe a joint type of appointment with the College of Agriculture and the College of Medicine. You really impressed Dad when you visited with him about the headquarters building in Canyon and our family and your family. He found you delightful. His words, not mine. Philip just noticed that you are absolutely beautiful, and much too good for me. Philip's words, not mine."

"Quit Randy! You're embarrassing me."

"Dad already knew about you and me. Apparently, he called Mom after the meeting to let her know that he was going to have lunch with Philip and me. She told him Sarita had called her this morning to tell her about last night. Sarita really liked you, and wanted Mom to know about the girl who had stolen her son's heart. Sarita reportedly told Mom how smart and beautiful you are. You should know, Mom thinks of Sarita as a daughter since she lived with them for a while after the accident. Mom values Sarita's opinion, and shared it with Dad. Dad usually uses the speaker phone in his car when he makes calls, so I'm sure Philip overheard the conversation."

"I'm learning just how close your family really is. How does Philip Granger fit in? Is he just ATX's attorney?

"Philip and Dad were childhood friends. They were roommates at college until my grandfather became ill and dad returned to the ranch to help. My grandfather soon had a fatal heart attack. This left Dad running the ranch and unable to finish college at Texas Tech. Dad met Mom at Tech and they married after Mom graduated. Mom is a twin. Her twin sister Kay, also went to Tech, and dated Philip Granger. Kay married Philip after he got his BS, and before he went to law school. After law school Philip returned to Amarillo and started what became an extraordinarily successful law practice. He advised Dad about trading land rather than selling it to developers, and at every step along ATX's development. Early on Dad asked Philip to become partners in ATX, but Philip wanted to continue his law practice and declined the offer. Rather, Dad had Philip on a retainer. I'm told during the lean years for ATX that retainer was a dollar a year. Over the years, Philip's law practice flourished and he added several partners and specialties. His son, Philip Jr., is also an attorney and is now managing partner of the firm. Philip has essentially retired from the firm; but he continues to be on retainer to ATX and will be until he decides he doesn't want to be any longer. His retainer is now a lot more than one dollar a year. He and Dad remain best friends. Actually, Philip is our uncle."

"Now I understand how Philip fits in and why he joined you and your father for lunch. You're all one big family, and Sarita is a part of that family as well."

Randy looked at his watch and said, "Are you hungry, we could have an early dinner."

Penny got up from the couch walked to the opposite end grasping Randy's hand and pulling him to his feet. "You have not seen the rest of my suite...this is the bedroom. Actually, I have something else in mind for now", Penny cooed as she kissed him passionately. "Maybe we can have a late dinner."

Chapter 13

Larry's brother Ray met him at the Laramie airport about 10:00PM. After enjoying the cool high plains evening air while visiting on their patio, Larry retired for the evening. The next morning the two brothers caught up with each other's lives as they waited for the alfalfa samples and five-gallon bucket of fertilizer to arrive around 10:30AM. They headed to Ray's office in the College of Agriculture building on campus to await the samples. FedEx delivered the samples soon after they arrived. With samples in hand, they walked to the nearby Biology building. In a lab on the main floor Ray introduced Larry to Dr. Eugene Thorpe. Dr. Thorpe was a small, slightly built, gregarious man with a warm smile and pale blue eyes hiding behind wire framed trifocals. It was easy to perceive Dr. Thorpe was enthusiastic about being involved in this project. The boxes and fertilizer sat on a lab bench as Larry and Ray followed Dr. Thorpe to his office adjacent to the lab.

His office appeared as if two ferrets organized it during a hurricane. Neither Larry nor Ray could sit in the two chairs in front of his desk. Both chairs contained what appeared to be a random assortment of papers, file folders, and reference books. Dr. Thorpe did not recognize this until after he had sat down at his desk and peered over large stacks of paper and a large flat computer screen. He was the epitome of a brilliant, but absentminded professor.

After a few minutes of visiting, Ray and Larry followed Dr. Thorpe down a stairway to the basement level of the building and into a small room with large whiteboards on three walls. It was only minutes before two others walked into the conference room. Marty Schwartz, a rotund man in his mid-sixties, and a petite Chinese woman, Lin Fong, who appeared to be in her early to mid-twenties. They were both professors associated with the neuroscience center; Schwartz being the director. The last to arrive was Dr. Brenda Edwards, the director of the microscopy core.

After introductions, each took a chair around the table. Ray gave a brief introduction of the DVE outbreak caused by a novel infectious prion protein. All had listened to the press conference held by President Smyth and Secretary Johansen. Ray asked Larry to provide details to the group on the outbreak at the ATX feedlots.

Larry thanked everyone for taking the time to listen to ATX's problem and their willingness to help try to solve this crisis. He gave a brief history of implementing a new crop rotation program using a new very hearty variety of alfalfa. He also told of his decision to use a new titanium dioxide nanoparticle fertilizer billed as being ecologically friendlier than continued applications of nitrogen based fertilizers.

The group started a technical discussion regarding which equipment would be best suited for studying this problem. The was consensus to start with the scanning electron microscope (SEM). Perhaps later they might use the transmission electron microscope (TEM) for additional detail. The group felt studying the leaves, stems, and roots would be important to see if they could identify uptake. After considering several methods of sample preparation to maximize the chances of nanoparticle identification and hopefully identifying the titanium dioxide. The group held no hope of identifying a prion.

After arriving at a consensus on slide preparation the biologists garnered samples and headed back toward their labs where they would guide graduate students as they prepared the slides for EM examination. The group estimated the slide preparations would be ready for viewing tomorrow midmorning. They would meet in the microscopy lab the following morning at 10:00AM.

Ray and Larry, agreeing that they were hungry, walked to the faculty dining room in the Student Union building. It was quiet with a relaxed atmosphere. Both men ordered corned beef Ruben sandwiches with potato salad at Ray's suggestion.

They discussed the project. Larry asked, "Can you explain, in not too technical terms, what you anticipate we'll see if prions are so small that we can't visualize them using one of the electron microscopes?"

"Good question. To be honest, we don't know what we will see. The first thing we want to determine is whether the nanoparticle capsule is protein or carbohydrate. To do this one of the slide preparations techniques will use protease K, an enzyme that digests protein. If the nanoparticle capsule is protein, the enzyme will digest the capsule and we will see un-encapsulated titanium dioxide. If the nanoparticle capsule is carbohydrate the protease will not digest it so we'll see intact nanocapsules. The second technique will use detergent rather than protease K. Detergent will digest carbohydrate encapsulated nanoparticles. In this scenario, we should see free titanium dioxide. Should there be an infectious prion hidden in the nanoparticle, there may be protein debris. The other thing we hope to determine is the size of the nanoparticle."

"They will also use cryofixation methodology to stabilize and fix the different plant specimens. This technique takes only milliseconds to fix the specimen and immobilize the cellular components. A variation of this technique, called high pressure freezing, is the most powerful cryofixation method. Part of this method includes freeze substitution and embedding a resin to enhance ultrastructure observation."

"So why are they only using the SEM", Larry inquired.

"SEM allows for a larger sample size to be analyzed, than with TEM. SEM provides three-dimensional images whereas TEM provides a two-dimensional image; but at increased magnifications of up to 500,000 magnification. SEM is for surfaces showing only morphology using magnifications of about 100,000 magnification. On the other hand, TEM has much higher resolution; and can image tiny precipitates, magnetic domains, but the sample size is much smaller. You can liken the difference as SEM is looking at blood through a light microscope under low power, while TEM is looking at the same blood using the high-power lens."

"Do you think we will be able to decisively get some answers? I've been pulling my hair out trying to figure out what's going on. We have around 195,000 head of cattle at risk in the three feedlots."

"I could see the worry written all over your face when you stepped from the airplane last night. I can't imagine the pressure you must be under to find an answer. Thank God there is going to be an indemnification program. Hopefully that will help keep ATX solvent. I am optimistic that we will find out some things, but whether it's going to be conclusive proof, I'm not so sure. I don't think it's the alfalfa seed. It's been around too long and it's been so well researched. I can't think of a scenario of how seed could become contaminated with infectious prion protein. The fertilizer almost has to be the culprit."

"The pressure I'm under is self-inflicted. The Bennett family is, and has always been, more interested in finding the answers, and then dealing with the facts; it's not like anyone has placed blame on me. I am not only worried that somehow the alfalfa has gotten contaminated, but more importantly what about the ground. It's my understanding infectious prions are very hard to kill in the best of circumstances. Rose has told me of a patient who was known to have Creutzfeldt–Jakob disease required brain surgery. After surgery, because they could never ensure they would be free of the prions, the hospital discarded all the surgical instruments. She said there have been cases where patients developed the disease from prion contamination after sterilization using conventional methods. With that in mind, how in the hell do you sterilize farm ground; once it's been contaminated?"

"I don't have a good answer to your question. That is indeed worrisome. How much ground are you farming?"

"We have about 12,000 acres under irrigation in the southern farms and about 16,000 acres under irrigation on the northern farms. The southern farms have richer soil and produce about the same volume of crops as the northern farms. Some of the ground we lease. Think of the potential law suits resulting from ground contamination. This has the potential to be catastrophic."

As Ray looked at Larry's eyes, he could only feel empathy for his brother's predicament. Without good facts and solid scientific research to support them, Larry could not make necessary farming decisions. "Larry, let's wait until we see what the folks come up with tomorrow. They'll provide us with some answers, then we can develop a plan to study the degree of ground contamination that may be present. I read the instructions for application of the fertilizer and it appeared you needed only a fraction as much fertilizer and subsequent water as with nitrogen based fertilizer. Did you apply it as the directions suggested? To me when I read the instructions, you would be applying a mist. Most of the application was applied directly on the foliage; so maybe the degree of potential ground contamination is minimal."

"The fertilizer was applied exactly as the instructions called for. Because the volumes were so small, we put it through our center pivot irrigation systems. The same man fertilized all the fields. When I bought the fertilizer, I calculated about how much we would need and bought a little more than that amount. We have some five-gallon containers left over, maybe twenty. Whether we find out anything significant from the electron microscope testing, I would like you to put together a proposal to study ground contamination on the farms. I think that information will be important from many different perspectives. Besides, it will give you an excuse to come down and visit."

"That sounds like a plan, younger brother. We enjoy coming down to visit with you and Rose. The kids are about the same age and enjoy each other. I'll work on a proposal in collaboration with our soil scientists. We'll have results before the fall term starts."

"What do you say we get out of here and check in at the house? Maybe we can get nine holes in before Kate has dinner ready. We don't have much else to do until tomorrow at 10:00AM."

Chapter 14

After the press conference, there were several follow-up priorities USDA personnel needed to focus on. First, preparation for the meeting Secretary Johansen would be having with President Smyth in two days to discuss the DVE indemnification plan, including funding for DVE and prion research. Second, research on pricing of feeder and dairy cattle research was necessary. Third was drafting the supplementary funding bill and later its presentation to congress. Fourth was developing a method of destroying DVE infected cattle. Within a relatively short period each priority required completion.

At Thursday's cabinet meeting Secretary Johansen updated the cabinet on the status of the DVE outbreak. Clare informed the president and cabinet; "the outbreak continues to grow in terms of affected states, number of premises, and number of animals. There are now seventeen states affected with the addition of Oregon, Washington, and Idaho. The number of samples submitted to NVSL has overwhelmed their capacity. APHIS has revised the guidance to the investigative teams limiting the number of samples taken at each premise based on herd size. Sampling from a herd perspective as well as a national level, will remain robust and meet statistical significance."

"We are discontinuing the in-depth investigations and returning the specialized teams to their regular duties. The in-depth investigations have completed their purpose; which was to collect a great deal of data, analyze it in a timely manner, and provide justification for upcoming actions. The specific cause for the outbreak has yet to be determined."

"APHIS field personnel, primarily veterinarians with a tech to assist, will replace the investigative teams performing the scaled back sampling. It's a concern that APHIS may not have enough field personnel to handle the projected volume of sampling. Therefore, I plan to assign FSIS public health veterinarians and meat inspectors to supplement sampling needs, given the current ban on slaughtering beef animals."

Clare continued, "The sheer number of infected premises and animals is anticipated to grow based on epidemiological projections. This presents a huge challenge. Carcass disposal due public health concerns necessitates the total carcass destruction. Normal rendering processes of the affected animals or herds is insufficient. Infectious prions survive other chemical, pressure and heat methods for destroying fallen stock. This was also a huge challenge for the UK when they had their BSE outbreak. For most animal diseases requiring depopulation, burning carcasses using accelerant, wood, and coal is sufficient. These fires are not hot enough to result in prion destruction. The only methods to accomplish this are either through tissue digestion or incineration."

"Our primary focus is getting the indemnification plan finalized and the supplemental presented to congress. It appears outbreak indemnification and prion research funding will cost about thirty billion dollars."

"Thank you Secretary Johansen", said President Smyth. "Are there any questions?"

"I have one", said Secretary of Homeland Security, "You said the specific cause of this outbreak has not been determined. Has terrorism been considered?"

"Yes, Mr. Secretary we gave terrorism consideration. Early in the outbreak I contacted the Office of the Inspector General for Agriculture and the FBI. USDA's Office of Emergency Preparedness and Response has detailed a person to CEAH and another to the Western Region to assist with the investigations. In part, the in-depth investigative teams collect data which would help ferret out a terrorist action. In addition, when President Smyth and I spoke with representatives from the UK, I specifically asked the experts. There have been no reports of infectious prion protein used as terrorism agents according to Dr. Peterson. He said it could be theoretically possible; however, one would need to know much more about this novel agent or discover more evidence than was currently available. Dr. Peterson also commented that he was unaware of any reports of propagation of infectious prion protein in the literature. Dr. McLaughlin, his colleague, commented he was unaware of anyone trying to propagate infectious proteins saying an attempt to propagate prions would require a highly-trained scientist with a very sophisticated laboratory. Dr. McLaughlin said he thought such a possibility would be extremely unlikely. These two men are international experts on infectious prion diseases. However, should new information develop suggesting possible terrorism, I will immediately contact everyone."

"Thank you Secretary Johansen", said the Secretary of Homeland Security.

"Are there any other questions", asked President Smyth. "OK then, if there no further questions or comments, meeting adjourned."

President Smyth waited in the hall for Secretary Johansen saying, "Clare, let's go to my office and discuss the indemnification plan."

Clare, with her tablet in her purse, walked beside the president into the oval office. The president motioned for her to have a seat on one couch as he sat in a wing-backed chair.

"Clare, your brief was excellent this morning. You provide a transparent, factual, and through brief. I like your style; when you have finished, there is little room for questions. If I remember correctly, you did brief DHS at the same time as OIG-Ag and the FBI. Yet your response saved the Secretary embarrassment. I had one question, which I didn't want to ask at the meeting. Are there currently funds for carcass disposal in the DVE indemnification plan and supplemental request? If not, let's work numbers up and include this in the request.

"Honestly, Mr. President, we have not gotten that far in the supplemental. I can tell you that we had brief discussions; but, we needed more data to arrive at a good number."

"There is a policy issue that remains before we can put hard numbers to the indemnification plan. The issue, which we've just started to discuss, is whether it's best to totally depopulate DVE infected herds or to only destroy those animals showing nervous system signs. We need to do that research before we can thoughtfully make this decision."

"Once the investigative teams have returned to their regular assigned duties, I am planning to keep two pathologists in the field to conduct this research and hotshot problems. One name that keeps coming up in discussions regarding infectious prions is Dr. Penny Adams. Reportedly she knows more about infectious prions than anyone in the USDA. She's currently in north Texas at three large ATX feedlots. The person who owns ATX is a friend of mine. His wife and I are sorority sisters. She was my big sister when we both attended Texas Tech. Her name is Beth Bennett. You may know her husband, Randall. Over the years he has put together a family empire based in Amarillo. I think we'll be able to use his cattle to do the beef portion of the experimental trial."

"There's a large dairy in California that is open to allowing us to do this work there. It's called the Pinos Dairy. It's located at the very southern tip of the San Joaquin valley. Mt. Pinos sits directly south of the dairy. I'm planning on Dr. Ben Johnson sampling the cattle at Pinos Dairy. He's already in California and would perform the dairy portion of the trial."

"These two veterinarians, with two veterinary technicians each, would adequately staff the sampling portion of this trial. We plan to run these trials concurrently. Of course, we would have to indemnify the animals we used in the trial; but, we'll have results in about a week."

"You have been busy since the press conference", said President Smyth. "I agree you need to go forward with these trials. It will provide scientific justification, whichever way they turn out. Although there is broad support from both sides of the isle for DVE emergency supplemental, you should expect to spend a day or so testifying in front of the joint appropriations committee."

"You gave a rough estimate of about thirty billion. You also said you were working toward a harder number. How are you going about this process?"

"Mr. President, we are researching pricing of feeder and dairy cattle. Beef cattle pricing is dependent on various factors such as breed, sex, and weight of the individual. For dairy cattle, considerations include breed, age of cow, milk production of the individual, condition, and weight of the cow. We are working on an automated program using an electronic check off that will individually calculate the price for each animal. The aim is to use the same pricing mechanisms currently used by industry to determine the value of cattle. We should have the algorithms completed in a couple of days, add another two to three days to develop software. We want the software downloaded to field personnel's' computers who are involved in executing indemnification program."

"Dr. Laporte has people researching the availability of tissue digesters and incinerators. The problem is, although the technology exists, it's difficult to identify anything having the capacity to handle the volumes we anticipate. There is a report from the investigative team in north Texas regarding commercial scale incinerators. Dr. Laporte is following up. I should have an answer on this process later today."

"Mr. President, I anticipate that we should have the pricing of beef and dairy cattle completed in five days. The trial is necessary to determine whether complete herd depopulation is necessary. We will have answers in a week, once it begins.

We should have data on carcass disposal systems in about a week. The emergency supplemental request will include cattle indemnification, prion research, and the expense of cattle disposal. The actual numbers in the request are largely dependent upon completion of the trial on beef and dairy cattle. Therefore, I think it's reasonable to expect we should have the emergency supplemental request drafted and ready for you to submit to congress in ten days. Does that meet your approval?"

"Given what needs to be completed so solid numbers can be derived, I do not see how it can be accomplished in less time. Clare, if you see it's going to take another few days, please let me know; and we'll extend the deadline to two weeks from today. I want the bill to contain realistic solid numbers. While you are working on the emergency supplemental request, I will start greasing the political wheels in hopes of a quick approval on a clean bill, with no riders. Government and congress needs to do this for American agriculture at some of their darkest times in history."

"Thank you, Mr. President for your time and particularly your full support."

"You're welcome; but it is I who should be thanking you for all your hard work and particularly the hard work of the Department of Agriculture employees who have displayed their dedication and professionalism during this entire crisis."

****

Bobby Laporte was waiting when Secretary Johansen walked into the atrium of her office. "Come on in Bobby" she said opening the door to her office.

"How did the meeting go, ma'am?"

"It went well Bobby. At the cabinet meeting, I briefed everyone and set the foundation for a more detailed discussion with the president, just as we discussed. He is up to speed on where we are. He's agreed with the initiation of the beef and dairy research project. Please pull the trigger on getting that implemented. Let's staff the project with the two veterinarians you mentioned. Let them select the two techs they would like to have working with them. Are you planning on it starting next Monday as we discussed?"

"Yes ma'am. Dr. Yu advised the investigative teams they will be returning to their normal assignments on Monday. We're going to have them travel back home tomorrow. That will give them the full weekend once they get home. I'll talk with both Dr. Adams and Dr. Johnson regarding their new assignments. I also need to talk with Dr. Rhodes-Voss to let her know Dr. Adams and Dr. Johnson will not be returning to the NVSL quite yet. They will be directly reporting to me. Once the extra sampling completed, I'll use them as special hot-shots when problems arise. I'll have the lab send out extra sampling supplies to the ATX feedlot in Hereford and the Pinos Dairy."

"Were you able the get any further information on the carcass disposal system?"

"All the ATX feedlots have carcass incinerators. They each have a capacity of about 65 head. It takes about four hours per load of carcasses. The incinerators are natural gas powered. During processing, it separates the oils and water from the solids. Dr. Yoder said he had watched the process and it was efficient and did a good job of incineration. ATX in their Salvage and Industrial Design division made the incinerators. Bobby Bennett operates that division. I asked Dr. Yoder how much gas they used per load, but he couldn't give me an answer. Natural gas from ATX own gas wells power their incinerators. Rex said when they started they roared loudly and continued roaring throughout the entire process. I thought I would have Dr. Adams look closely at the process and draft a report to include photographs. As she won't be traveling home tomorrow, I thought she could get that accomplished tomorrow."

"That's a great idea. Please forward a copy of the report to me as well."

"That ATX operation must be very progressive to have incinerators. I have not been able to find anyone that knows of others in the US. The chemical digesters we've identified have only a two-thousand-pound capacity-that's the largest size. Digesters are not practical alternative. We did come across some data on high pressure/high temperature rendering that reportedly kills prions. We need to check that option out further. Maybe we could interest some existing rendering operations, if this turns out to be a viable alternative."

"ATX is somewhat of an empire in Texas. Randall Bennett and his wife Beth, whom I know from college, own ATX. They have a large family and each of their children or their spouses run a division. Randall is a self-made man who would be in the top 25% of the Forbes 400 if his companies were public corporations. If you didn't know it, you would never guess Randall is wealthy. He's soft spoken, always thinking, unassuming, humble, and dresses like a Texas rancher in jeans, boots, and a Stetson hat. He actively avoids recognition and publicity."

"Ma'am that information is good to know. Is there anything else I need to know or work on", asked Bobby.

"There is one thing. President Smyth commented to me as we were concluding our meeting said he particularly wanted to thank the employees of the Department for their hard work, dedication, and professionalism throughout this DVE crisis. I too want to thank you and everyone you have involved in this emerging outbreak. We still have a lot of work to do and information to find out, but you've made good progress. There's another thing. You and your staff have been working long hours; you all need to have a weekend at home with your families. Please make sure that happens for everyone, including you."

Smiling to himself, Dr. Bobby Laporte exited to his office to make calls. He thought to himself, *it will be nice to have a weekend off...maybe...I hope. Maybe I can take the kids swimming...maybe...I hope.*

Chapter 15

During the morning's conference call Dr. Yu announced the investigative teams had accomplished their missions and would returning to their regular assignments on Monday. Friday would be their travel day back home.

The north Texas investigative team was finishing up the final details of their report at Hereford. Penny and Sammi were loading enough sampling boxes to collect samples at Dimmitt and Tulia. Glen and Sonny completed their portion of the report and would soon drive home; they checked out of the motel this morning. Penny, Sammi, and Jim Bob would finish the required sampling for Tulia and Dimmitt early this afternoon.

About 11:00AM Thursday Penny received a call from Bobby. "Good morning Dr. Adams, I'm sure by now you know we are sending the investigative teams back to their duty stations. I'm calling to discuss a special assignment I would like you to do for the agency. It will necessitate you continue to stay in north Texas."

After listening Penny thought; *this means Randy and I can spend more time together. Hell yes, I will stay in north Texas longer. How could things work out this well for us?*

"What does the new assignment entail", asked Penny.

"Dr. Adams, we need to gather additional information necessary for us to make some important decisions. I have heard nothing but praise regarding your work; and that you're probably the most knowledgeable veterinary pathologist in the agency when it comes to prion diseases."

"What I need for you to do is collect brainstem samples from three hundred head of clinically normal appearing beef cattle. We'll be having one of your colleagues, Dr. Ben Johnson, collect a like number of samples from dairy cattle in California. We're planning on collecting the beef samples at

ATX, although we have not asked them yet. We'll use these data to determine whether to depopulate entire premises, or to indemnify only symptomatic cattle. Do you have an interest in collecting the samples from the beef cattle at AXT?"

"Certainly, this is important work. The agency needs this information to appropriately determine how compensate producers for their losses. I would like to be part of it. Have you spoken with Dr. Rhodes-Voss about me staying in Texas longer," asked Penny.

"Yes, I have spoken with Pat. While she certainly misses you at the lab, she has offered to take photomicrographs of your sample slides and e-mail them for you a second interpretation. She says you have done that during the investigation and she wants your interpretations included in the analysis. We plan on you keeping a couple of the techs on your team to help you with the collection process to facilitate sample collection. If you will ask two techs, of your choosing, to stay for a few days. Let me know who you select, I'll clear it with their supervisors."

"Dr. Laporte, if it's OK, I will only need one tech, Sammi Downey. Our team included Sammi and Dr. Rogers, ATX's feedlot veterinarian. I'm sure he will want to continue to be involved, so we might as well put him to work and save on the expenses of an extra person, if that's OK with you?"

"That's OK with me. I want to keep you and Dr. Johnson on special assignment for an indefinite period after you have concluded the additional sampling. I want you two to serve as experts to hotshot issues that may come up during indemnification. During the time, you're serving as an agency expert, you will report directly to me, although you'll need to copy Pat on our e-mail correspondence. I specifically selected you for your expertise and ability to work independently. Do you have questions?"

"If it's OK with you", Penny said. "I would like to give Sammi the opportunity to take tomorrow off as a travel day.

She lives in Wichita Falls, and has a teenage daughter there. This will allow Sammi to see her daughter and have the weekend off. When she returns on Monday, she could bring her GSA issued vehicle and save on rental vehicle expense."

"I think it's a great idea. You all have worked hard during the investigation. Both of you must take the weekend off. However, I want you to keep one of the rented Suburbans. Tomorrow, while everyone else is traveling, I want you to gather additional information on the carcass disposal incinerators used at the ATX feedlots. Write up a brief report and include photos. You can use your phone or tablet to take them. Carcass disposal will present a significant problem with this outbreak. The agency is exploring practical methods for carcass disposal. Your evaluation of the cremation process is a key component to determining the practicality of using incineration for carcass disposal. If you have any experience with high pressure/high temperature rendering, I would appreciate your assessment of that process. I'm wondering if using this process is a viable alternative to cremation."

"Sadly, Dr. Laporte, I don't have much experience with high pressure/high temperature rendering. I know carcass disposal of scrapie infected sheep used this method, but the volume of infected product is not comparable. I don't know which rendering companies use this process, but I'll research it."

"That's great, Dr. Adams. I am looking forward to working with you on this project. If you have any questions or need any help, equipment, or anything else, please contact me day or night. I will send you an e-mail containing my contact information. I look for you to be a primary source of information; so, we'll need to keep in close communication."

"Thank you Dr. Laporte. I also look forward to working with you. I will also send you my contact information. I think this project is going to be a significant learning opportunity, both for me and for the agency. It's going to be fun!"

"Dr. Adams, I'll look forward to your e-mail confirming Sammi Downey will be working with you during the upcoming sampling of normal cattle. Enjoy your weekend off."

Thank you Dr. Laporte. Please call me Penny."

"Likewise, please call me Bobby. That's what everyone calls me. Everyone from my secretary to the Secretary of Agriculture."

"OK, Bobby it is! Look for my e-mail soon. Thanks again."

****

"Hi there; what are you doing", Penny asked Randy as she walked into Dennis' office. "It looks like you were deeply concentrating about something. Do you want me to come back later?"

"Oh no, I was just checking to make sure I made motel reservations for the rodeo I'm going to in Cheyenne. It's coming up next week. Sonny and I always go up together; with everything that has been going on here, I couldn't remember if I made reservations. I've found the confirmation; so, we're good. What's up with you?"

Penny could hardly contain her excitement. "How would you like it if I were able to stick around a while longer?"

Randy looked over the top of his laptop. "That would be great! I thought you said your team completed its work and everyone is heading home tomorrow. What's up?"

"I just got off the phone with APHIS's Administrator. He wants me to do some additional sampling here, then I'll be one of two veterinarians on an indefinite special assignment as an agency expert to hotshot DVE issues. The agency wants to sample exposed, but clinically normal cattle, to see if there is preexisting pathology before cattle become symptomatic. Dr. Laporte said Secretary Johansen is going to call your Dad to see if APHIS can collect the samples at ATX. They want additional data to determine if total herd depopulation is going to be necessary. Sammi's going to be staying to help me. If we could use Jim Bob for a couple of days, we would have our team together."

"I see no problem with using Jim Bob to collect the samples. He really enjoys working with you and Sammi. How many cattle are they planning on sampling?"

"Dr. Laporte said six hundred; split between here and a dairy in California. Dr. Johnson will be doing the sampling at a dairy. We're just going to sample the brainstem. That will take a lot less time. When are you leaving for Cheyenne?"

"I've got to leave Tuesday evening. I rope Wednesday morning in the slack. They run the whole first go-around Wednesday morning. The slack starts at 7:00AM. You want to go?"

"I would love to go, but I don't know if we will be finished sampling by then. It is possible, but things would have to go just right. Are you and Sonny going to drive up there? That seems like a long way if you're not leaving until Tuesday evening. I suppose after I finish the sampling I could request a few days off, maybe by then I can think of a way to justify going to Fort Collins to the Regional Office to see Dr. Yu. If not, I want to visit my parents in Denver."

"Sonny and I are flying out of Amarillo that evening. We'll rent a car in Denver, and then drive to Cheyenne. Bud Thomas' son, Junior, is hauling our horses to Cheyenne. He's going to leave Monday morning and will arrive in Cheyenne that evening. Junior has driven the horses up for the last few years. He likes making the trip. It allows us to jump on a plane. If something goes haywire down here, we can just hop a plane and be back. Junior also ropes pretty well. This year he's taking his horse. It will be his first time competing at Cheyenne."

"I'll make a plane reservation for you. Do you like western art? Next Wednesday evening there's a Western Art Exhibit and Sale that kind of kicks off the rodeo. If you're coming, I'll get us tickets. Over the years, I have bought some art at the sale; so, I always get an invitation. It's a fun time; an open bar and steak dinner goes along with the show and sale."

"You smooth talker you, get me a plane reservation. If I've not finished the sampling, I'll cancel and stay here until we've finished. Then, I'll meet you in Cheyenne for the art show. I do want to see my parents, maybe over the weekend. Do you want to meet them?"

"Yes, I would like to meet your folks. Who was it that said; 'I love it when a plan comes together'?"

"That was Hannibal on the A-Team. Bet you didn't think I would know that", said Penny. "My brothers were big A-Team fans when we were kids. I watched it with them."

"I need to go out and confirm Sammi will come back for a couple of days next week; then we need to get to Dimmitt and Tulia to finish up sampling at both places. Are you going to be my chauffer, or do I need to take one of the Suburbans?"

"I'd love to be your chauffer, but there are conditions. Sonny and Junior are coming to my place to rope this evening. If I am your chauffer, you and Sammi are going to have to stop at Happy while we rope. Then we'll have a supper, and I'll take you both back to Amarillo."

"I can agree with that. But I too have conditions."

"And what are your conditions, Dr. Adams," Randy asked teasingly.

"First, and most important; you will not call Sarita and make her cook for us", Penny said with a smile. "We'll pick up something for dinner. The second condition is you will not tell Sonny that Sammi has a crush on him."

"I can agree to both of your conditions; but, you should know that Sonny is kinda sweet on Sammi as well. I won't tell, if you won't tell."

Penny motioned for Sammi to meet her outside. Out of earshot of the others, Penny asked Sammi if she would return to Amarillo to help her and Jim Bob do the additional sampling. Penny explained the additional sampling and that she had chosen Sammi to help her. And Sammy could travel home on Friday, spend most of the weekend with her daughter. However, she would have to return to Hereford early Monday morning. Penny told Sammi she would push to get all the sampling completed on Monday and Tuesday. Sammi was agreeable to helping with the sampling. Penny also asked Sammi if she would mind stopping at Randy's place in Happy on their way back to the motel while Randy and Sonny roped steers. Sammi was agreeable, particularly when she found out that Sonny would be there. Sammi told Penny Sonny had called her a few times at the motel in the evening. Seeing Sonny outside of work excited Sammi.

The two walked back into the office to see Randy, laptop in hand, talking with Jim Bob. They were both laughing and walking toward the doorway. Penny wondered what they had been saying, but guessed she would probably find out on the way to Dimmitt. Maybe it was Randy asking Jim Bob to help with the additional sampling.

Penny spoke with Rex Yoder before she leaving for Dimmitt. She sat down next to him saying, "Rex, please don't turn in both Suburbans. I just found out Sammi and I will be staying to do some additional sampling. Sammi is going to go home and return Sunday evening. Tomorrow I'll need one of the Suburbans, but I will gladly drop anyone off at the airport who needs a ride."

"If you're not going home, that only leaves Cheri and me to travel to the airport. We both have the same flight, so we can use the same vehicle. Do you have a preference which Suburban we leave for you?"

"It really doesn't matter to me", responded Penny. "It's been really great to work with you again...Cheri, thank you for all you have done to help us work efficiently. If I need to contact you about an IT problem, may I do so? I don't know of anyone who knows more about this software than you."

"You've been so sweet and considerate", commented Cheri. "Of course, you can call. I'll leave a business card under your door, if I don't see you tomorrow morning. My home and cell numbers will be on the back. You can call me anytime. If you're ever in Fort Collins, please call or stop by CEAH and see me. I have really enjoyed working with you. Although we've put in some long hours, it's been fun; but now, I'm ready to get home to my husband and get out of this scorching heat." Penny and Cheri stood up walking to the end of the table they gave each other a hug.

****

Penny, Jim Bob, and Sammi sampled seven head of symptomatic cattle at Dimmitt. While they were sampling Sonny and Randy were discussing the upcoming trip to Cheyenne and roping practice tonight. Randy suggested Sonny bring the four-horse trailer over and leave it and his horse at Randy's until they left for Cheyenne. Randy said he would offer the same to Junior. They planned to rope Friday, Saturday, and Sunday evening. With Sonny's trailer and the horses already at Randy's, he thought that Junior could head to Cheyenne from Happy on Monday morning. Randy also mentioned Penny would be flying with them on Tuesday evening, if she completed her additional sampling. Sonny raised his eyebrows slightly and grinned, widening his handlebar mustache. Randy then mentioned that Sammi would be at Happy this evening while they practiced. "That will be nice", said Sonny grinning. The width of his mustache extended further.

After leaving Dimmitt, Penny to made a few calls. Penny called the lab to assure delivery of lab sample boxes Saturday. Diane Kaminski confirmed three hundred sample boxes would arrive tomorrow. Penny asked to talk with Dr. Rhodes-Voss. Penny told Pat she intended to take a few days off after sending the samples to the lab; but she would make time to read the slides on Wednesday and Thursday. Next, she called the Amarillo Suites asking if she could extend her stay. The motel responded they were full Tuesday through Sunday nights next week, but could extend her stay through Monday night. Penny said, "That will work, if I can get back in the following Monday night for another week or more." The motel made future reservations for her.

Penny looked at Randy saying, "OK I'm done with all my calls. I have one more item of business, then I'm 100% yours."

"Really", asked Randy teasingly. "This may be a short roping practice session for me; I've never had opportunity like this."

"Seriously Randy, temporarily you need to take your mind off my body. After we discuss this one business item, you can put it back on my body. Dr. Laporte asked me to write a report about the ATX crematoriums and to include photos with the report. Apparently, the agency is struggling with carcass disposal methods for DVE nationally. Do you mind if I take some photos to include in my report? I don't want to do anything that you would consider releasing proprietary information."

"I don't mind. You should know that my brother Bobby did get the design patented. It was his hope major feeders and large dairies would have an interest in purchasing them."

"Thanks", cooed Penny. "Now you can put your mind back on my body...my mind is already on yours...and I like what I see."

****

After pulling through his gate, Randy parked in the driveway near the garage. "I'm going to put on some old boots and a T-shirt".

"If you have a large water container, I'll make some iced tea to take down to the arena", said Penny. Should I also take beer down?"

"Nah, there's a refrigerator in the tack room that's full of beer. If anyone wants some, they can get it from there. I appreciate you asking, but we don't want to spoil them", Randy replied laughingly.

Before Penny had the iced tea made, a gooseneck trailer pulled through the gate and drove down near the barn. Sonny and Junior had arrived and unloaded their saddled horses. Both men took the halters off their horses replacing them with bridles. They hopped aboard riding through the barn and into the arena. After warming up their horses, Junior rode into the steer pen at the end of the arena and brought the steers up into a small holding pen adjacent the roping chute. By this time, Randy saddled his big heavy muscled blue roan gelding and started to warm him up. Penny was loading the container of iced tea onto the back of an ATV that Randy backed into the garage. Jim Bob and Sammi pulled up with his two boys riding in the back seat. Sammi jumped out of the truck and walked into the garage. "Is there anything I can do to help?"

"There is a tray sitting on the kitchen counter with some plastic iced tea glasses, a covered plastic container of sliced lemons, another with sugar, and a bunch of plastic spoons. If you want to get them, that would be great", responded Penny. A few minutes later, Sammi returned with the tray and placed it adjacent to tea on the rack on the back of the ATV.

"Wow, what a house. I was not expecting a bachelor to have such a big house with a gourmet kitchen. I need to make a potty stop, but I didn't want to go wandering through the house. Can you show me?"

"Sure", answered Penny. "Follow me."

Penny walked Sammi through the kitchen, dining room and into the living room. She pointed down the hallway saying, "There are two bedrooms on each side of the hallway. Each bedroom has an attached bathroom. You can use anyone of them. The door at the end of the hall leads into the master bedroom." Penny waited in the living room for Sammi and looked at the western art hanging on the walls. She noted all the art appeared to be originals in different mediums. Penny looked at the artist's names, but did not recognize any. She was not familiar with western artists. However, she found the art tastefully displayed and adding a warm ambiance to the living room.

Sammi walked into the living room also beginning to looking around. Most of the furniture was leather covered and appeared to be very expensive. "We waited until FedEx arrived then Jim Bob drove home to pick up the boys. Jim Bob's wife is doing some volunteer work. He's taking care of the boys until she returns home. Jim Bob's house is only about five miles from here. The older boy's name is Jim Bob, Jr. He goes by JR. The younger one's name is Paul. They both like to watch the men rope. Randy is their role model. Jim Bob told me Junior is Bud Thomas' son and is Sonny's foreman at the Dimmitt lot. He also told me Sonny is actually kinda shy, but he's smitten with me".

"Penny, are you in here?" It was Sarita who entered the kitchen with an armload of Styrofoam boxes from the Lone Star.

"We're in the living room, Sarita." Entering the kitchen, she observed Sarita placing the boxes on the marble counter next to the oven. "Do you have any others in your car", asked Penny.

"Yeah, this was about half of them. I thought there was too many for one trip." Turning she noticed Sammi and extended her hand saying, "Hi, I'm Sarita.

Penny said, "Sarita this is Sammi; she has been working with me helping with sample collection."

"Nice to meet you Sammi, you're the one that Sonny thinks is so wonderful. I can see why, you are so pretty and petite."

Sammi found herself a little bit embarrassed and blushed. Quickly she said, "Thank you; I'll go out and get the rest of the food" and promptly walked to the garage. Walking toward the car Sammi thought, *everyone knows about Sonny and me. Well, Sonny for sure. I'm glad that Sonny likes me, but I don't know how to show my feelings without making Sonny feel uncomfortable. If I come on too strong, I risk the chance of scaring him off...and I don't want that to happen. I guess I'll just play it by ear.*

With Sammi getting the additional food, Sarita and Penny hugged each other. "I'm so glad you're here tonight; you will get to meet my Thomas. He's coming over tonight. I am dreading you going back to Iowa tomorrow. I will miss you; and I know you will be leaving a big hole in Randy's heart."

"You haven't heard. I got a call this morning. I will be staying here for a while. I have more sampling to do. Then I will remain in Amarillo doing some additional work. I am also planning on traveling up to Cheyenne with Randy; then we're going to Denver to see my parents."

Sarita hugged Penny again and said, "I am so happy you will have more time here. Does Randy know you love him?

"I haven't told him in so many words yet." Sarita's matter-of-fact question startled Penny. She thought; *I didn't realize my feelings were that apparent.*

Penny and Sammi both jumped on the ATV slowly driving to the barn. Sarita drove to her bungalow to change clothes before Thomas arrived. Penny noticed metal fencing panels extending down the arena resulting in the arena being about two-thirds its normal width. Junior roped the first steer tying one front foot and the back two together. Junior then walked to his horse, turned him around and rode forward about two steps, where there was slack in the rope. Sonny rode up, dismounted, took the rope off the steer's horns, and untied the steer's three legs.

"Junior", Sonny said, "that was a nice run; but Thumper drug the steer about five feet too far. You had to run back up to the steer when ole Thumper decided to stop. It cost you about three seconds. You might try dragging a jerk line on your next steer, and giving it a little tug just as you get to the steer."

"OK Sonny, he's been doing that lately and I didn't know how to stop it. Do you have a jerk line I can borrow?"

"Yeah, there's one in the tack box of the trailer. If you have never used one before, I'll help you set it up."

"That would be great. I've used one roping calves, but not steers. I would appreciate the help. I don't want to get tangled up or cause Thumper to stop too soon."

Randy rode up to the fence just outside the left box saying to Penny and Sammi, "Well, that's going to spoil us. Cold iced tea with all the trimmings served up right behind the arena." Teasingly Randy asked Sammi, "Didn't you bring the linen tablecloth I laid out?"

Sammi nervously said, "I'll run back up to the house and bring it. I didn't see a tablecloth. Where did you put it?"

Penny and Randy laughed. Sonny rode up and asked, "What's so funny?" Randy told him and Sonny too laughed. "Sammi, don't let Randy get to you, he'll take every opportunity he gets to tease someone."

Penny asked, "So why did you guys narrow the arena?

Sonny responded, "At Cheyenne the arena is narrow down by the roping chute, about half the ropers ride out of the left box which is unusual. We put the panels up to simulate the narrower arena; because once you have the steer roped, you must ride toward the fence and jump from your horse. This way, our horses are familiar with seeing a fence coming up soon and will angle left after you've stepped from your horse. If you're lucky, after you rope the horns, the steer will veer to the right. If the steer does that, you won't have to worry about the fence and you can be really fast." Then Sonny uncoiled his rope forming a loop with his right hand. He backed his horse, Gus, into the left-hand box and nodded his head. Jim Bob's older son, JR, opened the chute gate and out ran the steer. Sonny let the steer run out some distance before he spurred Gus who quickly ran up behind the steer. Sonny roped both horns, threw his slack over the steer's right hip, riding to the left. When the rope came tight, the steer switched directions in the air landing flatly on the ground. Sonny stepped off his horse, stepped over the steer and tied one front leg and the two back legs. Sonny had roped, tripped, and tied the steer very smoothly; but it did not appear he was moving fast. However, the time was faster than it appeared, because there was no wasted motion.

Randy, rode out to where the steer was laying on the ground, removed the rope from his horns, and untied his feet. Handing the piggin' string back to Sonny, Randy said; "really nice run. Gus worked perfectly."

It was now Randy's turn to rope. He also rode into the left-hand box. He nodded his head and JR released the head gate and the steer slowly loped out quite a way before Randy's horse, Blue, ran out of the box. Randy caught up with the steer much sooner, roped both horns, set his trip jerking the steer off his feet. He stepped off his horse and yelled "whoa" as he put his piggin' string over the steer's front foot. Blue stopped dead in his tracks, but leaned forward keeping the rope taunt between the saddle horn and the steer's horns. Randy lifted the hind legs slightly and slipped the piggin' string under both rear feet, made two wraps around the three legs securing the steer's legs with a half-hitch. Randy moved smoothly and his time was faster than Sonny's. Junior rode up to untie the steer's legs saying, "Wow, I wish I could rope like that." Sonny whistled loudly.

Randy rode back up to the right side of the fence adjacent to the right-hand box, dismounted, loosened his saddle's cinches, loosely placing the rein over the top rail of the fence. "I'm done", announced Randy. "Blue worked great, so did I. I'm not going to give him or me a chance to mess up."

Randy walked through a gate, poured himself a glass of tea adding lemon. Penny walked to him putting her hand around his waist and said, "My, my, you are a man of many talents, Randy Bennett. I had no idea you were such a good roper. I'm impressed!"

"I just got lucky", Randy commented. "Did Sarita get home yet?"

"Yes, she got home while I was making the iced tea. We put the fajita meat, rice, beans, and tortillas in the oven in dishes on low heat. Dinner will be ready whenever you and the guys finish roping. Sarita told me Thomas is coming to see her tonight. I'm guessing she's cleaning up and getting ready. I can go check, if you want?"

"No, that's fine. I just wanted to make sure she got home OK. Usually she'll come down to the arena after she changes clothes."

"My guess is she's avoiding the dust and standing in the hot sun. I doubt she wants Thomas seeing her dusty and sweaty. It's what we gals do to be beautiful for our men!"

Randy grinned, "As I recall you went as far as taking a shower and borrowing clothes."

"Randy, I smelled like a goat! I couldn't even stand myself. Thank God Sarita understood and we're about the same size! Have you met Thomas before?"

"Yes, but only to be introduced and visit a few minutes while he was waiting for Sarita. He's a good kid. I look forward to getting to know him better. He's probably gone home to change clothes before coming out. He works and lives in Amarillo, so there's a little travel time."

Sonny roped and tied two more steers, then said, "I'm finished for today." Junior roped and tied four steers prior to finishing. Sonny and Junior checked the hay feeders and ensured the water tank was full. They road back to the barn stopping to get a glass of tea. The guys were unsaddling their horses and visiting. Penny and Sammi, each carrying one handle of the iced tea container, walked through the barn until Sonny observed what they were doing. He stopped immediately; grasping the container he finished carrying the tea to the ATV. Penny returned for the tray with the other items on it. As she walked back through the barn, Penny asked if anyone wanted more tea before she took it to the house. Sonny was filling his glass when Sammi took it, filling it again, and then returning it to him. Jim Bob and his boys listened to the conversation. As the ropers unsaddled their horses and took the saddles to the tack room, JR told his brother to follow him. They walked to the middle of the barn and got a bale of hay and fed the horses. With Sonny's and Junior's horses there were four horses in the barn. The boys fed hay to them all. Jim Bob was proud his boys had thought to help without his urging. Each man fed his own mount grain and checked to make sure the automatic water basin was working. Jim Bob and his boys walked with Randy to the house. Sonny and Junior unhooked the trailer from the pickup, then drove the truck to the house.

Penny set the food out on a counter top with plates, silverware, etc. The vessel of iced tea sat on the opposite side of the kitchen counter near the sink. Clean glassware sat next to the iced tea. As Randy entered Penny said, "I thought we would have dinner buffet style."

"That's great", and gave Penny hug. "I've got to wash my hands, but a shower will have to wait until later." Randy led the way to a small bathroom off the kitchen as Jim Bob's kids followed. By the time the boys had washed up, Sonny and Junior fell in line to wash their hands before dinner. Sarita and Thomas walked in through the patio door introducing Thomas to everyone beginning with Randy and Penny. Penny noticed the dining room table appeared lengthened. Penny guessed Sarita had come back over to put an extra leaf in the table. There were also extra chairs set around the table, plus three folding chairs leaning against a wall. Penny looked at Sarita who just winked at her as if to say *this is our little secret*.

Dinner was laid back and pleasant. The food, especially the fajitas cooked over a mesquite wood fire, was excellent. It was obvious everyone enjoyed each other's company. Outbursts of laughter mixed with snippets of serious discussion filled the dining room. Penny asked Sarita where she could find a pitcher to serve more tea. Penny poured iced tea refills. Randy had a good visit with Thomas, getting to know more about him. He learned Thomas graduated a year ago from Texas Tech in petroleum engineering. Thomas said he enjoyed his work, but hoped that he would have more responsibility after completing college and working for Rim Rock for over a year.

Sonny and Junior discussed the finer points of steer roping; however, it was clear Sonny wanted to get to know Sammi better, often answering Junior's questions as briefly as was polite. Then he would ask Sammi an open-ended question to learn more about her. He discovered Sammi grew up on a cattle ranch near Shamrock, TX. She learned Sonny came from Childress, TX. While Sonny attended Texas Tech in Lubbock on a football scholarship, Sammi went to Visalia College, also in Lubbock.

Penny sat next to Jim Bob for a few minutes asking if he was OK with helping them collect the additional brain samples. Jim Bob said he was looking forward to it; saying he enjoyed participating in research projects. He asked how many samples they would be collecting and where. Penny said that she had thought about it and thought they would take one hundred samples each at Hereford, Dimmitt, and Tulia. Further, to make it random she suggested splitting the hundred samples evenly between normal appearing lightweight, middleweight, and heavyweight cattle, with an even number of steers and heifers. Penny said she thought if each feedlot lot would choose fifty head (twenty-five steers and twenty-five heifers) for each weight group, they could then just run in the first thirty-three or thirty-four head from each weight-group pen near the vet clinic. Jim Bob liked that idea. It was practical while still achieving the randomness they were looking for. Penny's thought was to collect as many samples as they could on Monday, then finish up on Tuesday. He said that maybe they should try to have two Bobcats; so, while one was taking a sampled carcass to a dump truck, the other could be picking up the next carcass to sample. Further, he thought they would need two dump trucks initially; after the first one was full, they would load into the second.

Jim Bob said he'd deliver the sample boxes to each feedlot with PPE gear, etc. That way all Penny and Sammi would have to do would be to drive to the vet clinic and everything would be ready to go. Cattle would be in the alleyway ready for euthanasia and sampling. Penny asked what time Jim Bob thought they should start. He said, the earlier the better, noting the cattle work better earlier in the morning when it would be cooler. Penny liked that idea and they decided to start at 5:30AM both mornings. That allowed more time if something went wrong. It also increased the odds of Penny making her evening flight. After finalizing the arrangements, Jim Bob said he would take care of communicating the details to Dennis, Sonny, and Bud when he delivered the sample boxes.

Dinner lasted almost two hours. Saying he needed to get the boys home to bed, Jim Bob and the boys took their leave. Sonny followed commenting he and Junior needed to get back to Dimmitt. Thomas thanked Randy and Penny for inviting him, the meal was wonderful, and he needed to get back to Amarillo before too long. Randy, the ever-gracious host, thanked everyone for coming saying he was glad Thomas came to dinner. He enjoyed visiting with him. Then Randy looked at Penny and Sammi saying, "I better take you and Sammi back to the motel before you're late for curfew."

Junior asked if federal employees really had curfews.

Randy replied before anyone else could answer; "they sure do, they have to be in their motel rooms by 10:00PM and lights out by 11:00PM on weeknights and midnight on weekends."

Junior looked at Sonny and Sammi and said, "Really?"

Penny, hardly kept from laughing saying, "Really! It's kind of a pain, but the government wants its employees fresh and ready to work the next day." Then everyone laughed.

After seeing everyone to the door except for Sarita, Sammi, and Penny, they cleaned off the table, loaded the dishwasher, putting the leftovers in proper containers before putting them in the refrigerator. Sarita walked to Thomas putting her hand in his; they exited through the patio door back to Sarita's bungalow. Penny and Sammi walked into the garage as Randy held the door open.

Penny sat next to Randy while Sammi rode "shotgun". "Thank you for dinner, Randy. It was really a fun time. Sonny is a funny guy; I like him. I'm glad I'm coming back Sunday afternoon. He's going to come into Amarillo. We're going to a movie."

Randy's pickup hardly stopped before Sammi jumped out heading for the door. It was obvious she did not want to encroach on Penny and Randy's time together.

Randy asked, "Do I really smell that badly?"

Penny laughingly commented, "Well you're a little gamey, cowboy." Then she reached over to put her hand around his neck and kissed him passionately on the lips. Then she said, "Until tomorrow."

"What, you're not going to invite me up," Randy asked in a dejected voice.

Penny replied, "Only if you promise not to say no, and we take a shower first."

"OK, then", Randy said. "Until tomorrow, but tomorrow I'm going to take you up on it."

"Well then", Penny said smiling, "Until tomorrow and there's no backing out."

Chapter 16

Penny put her overnight bag in the back of the Suburban with her laptop. Going back inside she poured a cup of coffee and toasted a bagel which she topped with cream cheese before driving to the Hereford feedlot. Arriving a few minutes before 7:00AM, she set up her laptop in the conference room and booted it up. Soon, Dennis walked in saying, "My, you're up and at 'em early this morning."

"Good morning, Dennis. I woke up early. With there being no conference call to delay me, I got an early start. Today I need to learn as much as I can about the crematorium and take some photos with my phone. Then, I need to draft a report about carcass destruction using the crematorium."

"Randy called me this morning saying you were coming. He stopped by the office to get you additional information for your report. He was going to have Shelly fax it, but I needed to stop by the office this morning, so I picked it up. He told me to tell you that you could use, photocopy, or scan any or all of it. He said he was going to the northern feedlots this morning, but he would be back in Canyon about 2:00PM. He asked that I tell you to meet him there, whenever you completed your work."

"Randy thinks a lot of you, Penny", said Dennis. "Sonny called me the first day after you went to the Dimmit lot with Randy. He said Amarillo's most eligible bachelor was officially off the market. The next day I watched Randy when you were here. I called Sonny back saying, damned if he wasn't right. Randy's happier than I have ever seen him, even with all the cattle dying. In the time I have been around you, I'm impressed with your intellect, work ethic, communications with everyone, and you've become an ex officio member of ATX Feeders. I think Randy has chosen well. During my career with ATX, I have gotten to know Randy very well. I have found him to be an even tempered, thoughtful, caring, hard-working. He deserves someone like you. In all seriousness, I thought you should know what we think; 'we' being Jim Bob, Sonny, Bud and I." Smiling Dennis said, "And if you tell Randy I said any of this, I will deny it."

"Thank you for your kind words. They mean a great deal coming from you guys. I think you know I think he's a special guy. I feel it was divine intervention that I get to stay around here longer. We both need to get to know each other better. Next week, I'm going to go to Cheyenne with him. While we're there Randy will meet my folks. We're both old enough to know what we want. So far, I don't think either of us has found any deal-breakers."

Dennis handed a thick file folder to Penny saying, "This's all the information we have on the crematoriums. If you have any questions, let me know. Maybe I can provide some clarity. When you're ready to take your photos, let me know and I will drive you up there. If you want to catch them loading it, it should be about another two hours before the process is complete and cooled down enough that it's safe to get close. I'm guessing around 9:30 to 10:00AM."

Penny reviewed the file folder. *My God,* she thought, *everything is in here. There is a copy of the patent, rough sketches, blueprints, calculations for temperatures and pressures, the oil scrubbing operation that results in diesel fuel, drawings of the doors, hydraulics, cement work, elevation drawings...everything. I have everything I need to write a detailed report.*

Penny thought a moment and began drafting the report. She referred to the patent, blueprints, and elevation drawings in her draft because she intended to scan them and include them as supporting data. She covered processing the fatty rich oils, a rendering by-product, for fuel. Conversely, the protein fraction of DVE infected cattle is prion rich potentially contaminating soil or plant life, if not destroyed. Therefore, Penny recommended destruction of the protein fraction by incineration.

She addressed high temperature/high pressure rendering operations and the advantages and disadvantages of such systems. She included a link to specific British research data and historical data explaining the size of the rendering industry. Which, over the last twenty years had declined in independent ownership and increased in facilities owned and integrated into large slaughter plants.

After seeking input from Dennis, Penny included cost estimates for using a cremation system. She recommended additional modifications to the cremation system that would decrease unit cost and increase efficiency. Her specific recommendations were carcasses should have the hide removed, be eviscerated, and then run through a pre-breaker and hasher prior to placement in the incinerating cylinder. Penny's final recommendation was to make some of the incinerators mobile by modularizing them on flatbed trailers.

Penny completed her draft in about two hours. She asked Dennis if he thought the crew might be about to load the crematorium. Dennis agreed it was about time. Dennis and Penny drove to the crematorium where she took photos. Dennis asked one guy to open the large end door on the crematorium; so, Penny could get photos of the inside of the machine. She photographed from a distance to capture the placement of the tube in relation to the surrounding terrain and concrete safety walls. They moved to the top level where she captured the natural gas piping from a pressurized storage tank into the device. She photographed how carcasses were top loaded into the vessel. Feeling it was important to photograph the supporting equipment, she captured images of the 'A' frame and hoist as well as safety equipment. Penny included closeup photos of the hydraulically operated top clamshell doors and vessel safety features. Additional photographs visually described the two-valve system gas system, the small cinder block control building, and the automatic flue control system. Penny also incorporated images of the tallow collection system including the vertical centrifuge, the tallow filtration system, and the biodiesel storage tank.

Arriving back at the office, Penny planned to scan in the materials she wanted to include from the ATX's file. Penny had just started when Juana Gomez asked if she could help her scan the materials to save Penny time. Juana said when she finished her daily work and she would e-mail the scanned documents to Penny. With Juana doing the scanning, Penny edited her draft and put it in final form. Within another hour, Penny had the report finalized with the supporting documents attached in a zip file including the photographs she had taken with her phone's camera. At 12:45PM Penny sent her e-mail to Dr. Laporte and Dr. Rhodes-Voss.

Before heading to Canyon, Penny entered Dennis' office. "Dennis, I'll take the folder back to Canyon. I want to know if you would like me to print out a copy of my report for the file; or I can forward you a copy of my e-mail to Dr. Laporte."

"An e-mail would be fine. I'll forward it to a girl in the office who does the filing after reading it."

As Penny drove toward Canyon she thought, *it will be at least an hour after I arrive before Randy returns to his office. I might stop at the office and ask if Sarita wants to join us for dinner tonight. I'm in the mood for marinated steak cooked on the grill.*

Soon Penny arrived in Canyon and walked into the office. Sarita was sitting at the receptionist's desk. She had a welcoming smile and said, "Hi Penny you're here early. I just spoke with Randy and he's running about thirty minutes late."

"Sarita, I stopped by early to return this file. Randy sent it out to Hereford for me." Penny handed the file back to Sarita. "I also wanted to ask if you would like to join Randy and me for dinner tonight. I am going to stop by the grocery store to pick up some steaks and vegetables to make a salad."

"I'm so excited. Last night Thomas asked me to go to Lubbock with him this weekend. He wants to introduce me to his parents. We're supposed to leave soon after we both leave work. While I won't be able to join you for dinner, I'm sure that you will think of something to keep Randy entertained", Sarita said teasingly as she winked. "Don't buy any steaks; there is a freezer full of beef at the house. When you pull them out, put them on the patio table; they will thaw out while the guys are roping. If you're going to make a tossed salad, Randy likes blue cheese dressing. I don't think there is any in the refrigerator. And he doesn't like peas."

"Things must be getting serious between you and Thomas if he's taking you down to meet his parents. I am so happy for you. Thomas is a first-rate gentleman. His dark wavy hair and puppy dog brown eyes are so cute. Thank you for your advice on the steaks. I'm going to look on my phone to see how difficult it is to make homemade blue cheese dressing. Maybe I'll also get a cheesecake as well. I hope you and Thomas have a wonderful time in Lubbock. I'll see you in a little while."

As Penny walked to the Suburban she thought she would call Dr. Laporte to see if he had questions regarding the report and ask him for a few days off. She dialed while pulling out of the ATX parking lot.

"Dr. Laporte, here", he answered the phone.

"Hi, this is Penny. How are you this afternoon?"

"Penny, I'm doing great. I finished reading your report a few minutes ago. It's a great report! I'm surprised it included blueprints, drawings, the patent, as well supporting documentation. Your photos were excellent; after reading the report and reviewing the drawings and blueprints, the photos just put the whole thing together. How does the designer, Bobby Bennett, fit into the ATX organization?"

"Bobby runs ATX Salvage and Industrial Design. He is a mechanical engineer and designed the crematoriums. ATX has one at each of their feedlots. They use them for carcass disposal. He's Randy Bennett's older brother. Randy oversees ATX's feedlot operations. He's a veterinarian."

"You made three recommendations. Please tell me more about them", said Dr. Laporte.

"The first two recommendations are related. The removal of the hides, evisceration, incorporating a pre-breaker and hasher at the front end of the system are to decrease particle size. I think reducing particle size will allow the crematorium to function more efficiently. It should increase capacity and reduce cycle time. Skinning will eliminate the noxious odor of burning hair and hide. It may increase the need for cleaning up around the new equipment. An outside contractor might buy the green hides for further processing. I don't know if my third recommendation, modularizing one or more mobile units, is possible. My thought is that while the DVE outbreak is wide spread, smaller operators may not justify a large-scale crematorium. Thus, mobile units could arrive at a temporarily location and serve multiple smaller operations. When incineration of all the carcasses in an area is complete, the modular unit would disassemble, move locations to serve other smaller producers. All three of my recommendations will become more practical, if the upcoming research data suggests total herd depopulation is necessary."

"Thanks for clarifying the rationale behind your recommendations. That helped me understand your perspective."

"I have a request for you. After I complete the sampling of non-symptomatic beef cattle, I would like to take a few days off. Specifically, I was thinking of taking off next Wednesday through Friday. I've spoken to Pat and she wants me to interpret the results of my sampling. That will provide two histopathological interpretations per sample. She's going to e-mail photomicrographs of each slide. I can provide my interpretations using the outbreak software. We have done this before, it works well, and it's really efficient. Anyway, I'll take my laptop with me and read those slides on Wednesday and Thursday, if that's OK?"

"You know you will be collecting 300 brainstem samples?

"Yes, sir", responded Penny.

"And you plan to accomplish that in two days?"

"Yes, sir. ATX has great facilities, plenty of equipment, and good help. We're only sampling brainstem. My sampling team works very efficiently. ATX will provide additional experienced personnel to assist with sampling. A hundred and fifty samples per day is certainly doable."

"Penny, provided your sampling is complete, I think you should enjoy a few days off. Where are you planning to go?"

"My parents live in Denver; and I thought I would go see them; and I also plan to spend a couple of days in Cheyenne at the rodeo."

"That sounds like fun. I'm thinking, I need to go see Dr. Yu; if you were to hang around Colorado another day or two, I could meet you in Fort Collins at the Regional office. I want to meet you in person. This would be a great opportunity. We'll talk about DVE and you will have read all the slides by then. We need to do a postmortem on how effective we were responding to the outbreak. Your input would be invaluable. Would meeting with Sam and I on Monday afternoon and Tuesday work for you?"

"That sounds exciting! I will plan on meeting you at the Western Regional Office at 1:00PM Monday after next and all-day Tuesday."

"Penny, thank you for calling. I am looking forward to meeting you. I hope your sampling goes well next week. Safe travels."

"I'm looking forward to meeting you as well, Bobby. Thanks for approving my leave."

Penny walked into the Canyon Super Savers grocery starting in the produce department. She chose fresh corn on the cob and a head of lettuce, tomatoes, carrots, fresh spinach, a cucumber, and two lemons. Then she pulled out her phone and looked up what she would need for homemade blue cheese dressing. The recipe looked simple enough, so she selected fresh blue cheese, a small jar of mayonnaise, a quart of milk, and a container of sour cream and a bottle of Worcestershire sauce. At the bakery, she planned on getting a cheesecake, but instead chose a German Chocolate cake.

After loading the groceries in the Suburban, she noticed the gas gauge was nearly on empty. She filled the tank at a nearby service station, then returned to the ATX office. Randy pulled into the parking lot just in front of her. He walked over giving Penny a light kiss on the lips and said, "You're timing is perfect. I need to stop at the office for a few minutes, then we can head to Happy."

"Sounds good to me."

Randy walked into his office putting papers on his desk. He looked through notes of phone calls that had come in, sorted them, and put three of the small orange sheets in his left shirt pocket. Randy put the Wall Street Journal and Amarillo Globe-News under his arm as he walked to Shelly's desk to update her on what she needed to accomplish next week. He told her he would be in town on Monday and Tuesday, but would be in Cheyenne, for at least the remainder of the week. As Randy spoke with Shelly, Penny spoke with Sarita telling her about the German Chocolate cake, and that it appeared blue cheese dressing was easy to make. Sarita informed Penny German Chocolate was Randy's favorite. Randy came to Sarita's desk and put his arm around Penny's waist. Sarita told Randy about going to Lubbock with Thomas to meet his parents.

Randy in his pickup and Penny in her rented Suburban headed south toward Happy. About 15 minutes later Penny pulled into the garage. She unloaded her computer and the groceries. She left her overnight bag for later, when Randy was at the arena roping. After unloading the groceries, Penny went to the freezer and selected two tenderloin steaks and placed them on the patio table as Sarita suggested. The patio was on the west side of the house and it was hot in the afternoon sun. Penny thought it wouldn't take long for the two steaks to thaw. Randy changed into a faded pair of Wranglers, a tee-shirt, replacing his straw hat with a cap, wearing his old boots, with spurs attached. He sat at the table reading the Wall Street Journal while sipping a tall glass of ice water relaxing while he waited for Sonny and Junior to arrive. Penny peeled a carrot, the sat at the table reaching for the Amarillo paper. She took a sip out of Randy's ice water after removing her work shoes and socks. Her bare feet resting across Randy's knee.

In a little while Sonny's pickup drove through the gate and down to the barn. Randy said to Penny, "The guys are here. I better head toward the barn and get Blue saddled. Are you going to come down and watch us while we practice?"

"I thought I would make some iced tea and bring it down later. Then, I think I'll take a nice warm shower and wash my hair."

"Why don't you skip the iced tea tonight. We'll grab a beer. It's Friday, and a beer would taste good as hot as it is."

"Sounds good to me. I've got a couple of tenderloins thawing, I thought we could grill them. Does that sound good to you?"

"Steak always sounds good. Steak at home with you, sounds like it couldn't get any better."

After Randy left for the arena, Penny continued reading the paper until she finished the article. She walked out to the Suburban taking her overnight bag to the master bedroom. She had not been in this room before. Penny took a little time to look around. As she walked into the bedroom there was a large king size bed adorned with a tasteful satin comforter and matching bed skirt.

To the right of the entryway, a door opened into a large walk-in closet largely unused, except six or seven new trophy saddles stacked on the floor in the back.

Another door on the right wall led to an adjacent room Randy used as his home office. It contained a large cherry wood desk with a marble top and matching credenza. On the desk sat a large flat screen monitor with a docking station for his laptop, a telephone, computer mouse, and three stacks of paper. On the credenza sat an all-in-one printer, fax, and scanner. Between the desk and credenza was a high-backed leather executive chair. Cherry wood book shelves adorned the perimeter walls holding both reference books, stacks of journals, and Randy's personal library. It appeared he enjoyed reading military history of World War II and Viet Nam.

Walking back to the bedroom entryway door there were other two doors. One lead to Randy's walk-in clothes closet. The second door led into the master bathroom. On the left side wall of the bedroom was an adjacent room. This room had a large opening rather than a doorway. The three sidewalls each held large windows and furnished with a small couch, two comfortable matching chairs, and a large flat screen plasma TV. It was a sunroom or reading room.

Penny walked into the master bath to see a large walk-in shower enclosed floor to ceiling with glass walls and rain forest type shower heads. The toilet was separate from the room by two walls and French doors. Against the far wall sat an oversized jetted whirlpool type tub. Opposite the shower was a marble topped vanity with two sinks also of matching marble. Along the vanity was a mirrored wall running the entire length of the vanity. Penny turned on the shower and walked back out into the bedroom where she placed her overnight bag on Randy's bed, selecting matching underwear she went back into the bathroom. Penny took off her clothes, adjusted the water temperature, turning on the rainforest nozzles as she stepped into the shower. The water felt like warm raindrops running down her body. *This is so relaxing; I could stay in here the entire night. This shower is large enough Randy and I could shower simultaneously. We'll have to try it some time.*

Penny put on a pair of shorts selecting a tee-shirt from Randy's closet, which fit her loosely. She picked up her dirty clothes putting them in a plastic sack she had brought from the motel placing them back in her overnight bag and the overnight bag then in the non-used walk-in closet. Back in the dining room, she took a hair brush from her purse and walked out onto the patio to brush her hair dry and check on the steaks. The steaks were thawing nicely, but not yet ready for the dry marinade. She sat down and brushed her hair. The sunlight and heat felt good on her freshly clean body. In the low humidity and sunlight, it took hardly any time for her hair to dry. She loosely braided it so it would fall down the middle of her back. *I'd better start getting things ready for dinner,* Penny thought as she walked into the kitchen.

She first made the blue cheese dressing, then the salad. After putting the salad ingredients together, she topped it with lemon zest and placed a plastic film wrap over the bowl to prevent wilting. After removing the husks from the corn, she placed them on a plate in the refrigerator. *I'll roast them on the grill while the steaks are cooking.* Penny placed the cake on a large plate and hid it in a cabinet so Randy would not see it until she was ready to serve it. She set two place settings on the table. *Now, I'm ready until Randy comes back. I need only to grill the steaks...Oh, I must check on the steaks and rub them.* With the now thawed steaks sprinkled with rub, Penny placed them in the refrigerator on a plate. *Now I'm finished.*

Later Randy walked into the house, found Penny giving her a kiss. "My you smell good".

Penny, grinning, said, "You, not so much. How did roping go?"

"I roped two steers", explained Randy. "Blue worked great, I messed up the tie on the first one, so I roped one more. The old adage of slow down and be quick is really true. On the first steer, I hurried the tie and caught the piggin' string between the toes of one leg. I was planning on taking a shower; but you've shamed me into doing it before dinner", Randy said with a grin.

"How did Sonny and Junior rope?"

"Sonny roped well. I thought Gus worked well, but Sonny said he felt a little 'chargie', so he roped another one. According to Sonny it was smoother when Gus ran up to the second steer. Sonny is roping well and so smooth. It wouldn't surprise me if he won some money at Cheyenne, if he draws good steers. Junior's horse is still running off a little, but better than last night."

As Randy walked down the hallway Penny said, "Are you ready to eat when you get out of the shower?"

"Well maybe after I get some clothes on. I don't plan on eating in my birthday suit with you fully clothed", Randy said laughingly. "Yeah, I could eat after I shower."

"I'll listen for the shower water to stop; then I'll start the steaks. They'll be about ready by the time you're dressed; although I find the picture in my mind of you eating in your birthday suit quite appealing. How do you like your steak cooked?"

"Rare to medium rare", responded Randy as he was walking down the hallway.

Penny listened, but did not hear the shower. Before she knew it, Randy was walking into the dining room. "I didn't hear the shower water at all." I'll put the steaks on as soon as the grill heats up. Do me a favor, please turn on the grill. I should have asked you how to do it before you took your shower." Penny then walked to where Randy was standing, reaching around she put her hands in his back pockets, pulling him to her. "Now you smell pretty good too-for an old cowboy," Penny said with a big grin on her face.

"Let me show you how the grill works; when we built the house, we plumbed a gas line into the patio. First, you need to turn this valve on, then turn on only one burner and hit the spark igniter. Once you have one row of burners lit, you can turn on the other burners. While it's heating up, I usually turn all the burners to heat it up quicker. Then, when I'm ready to cook, I turn some of the burners off depending on how much is on the grill. I also turn the burners all the way up while it's heating, then turn them to low so the meat cooks slowly."

After a few minutes, Penny put the marinated steaks on the grill with the two ears of corn on the top rack reasoning the radiant heat from the burners would cook the corn in about the same time as the meat.

While the steaks and corn were cooking, Penny took the salad out of the refrigerator and placed it on the table. She then placed the blue cheese dressing in a small bowl next to the salad. "Do you want another beer with dinner", Penny asked.

"No, I don't think so, but thanks", answered Randy.

"I'm having ice water", said Penny. "There's also some iced tea left from last night, and milk."

"I think I'll have ice water as well...Hey, I have some red wine; that sounds good with steak. Why don't I get a bottle and we'll have it with dinner?"

Randy walked to a cupboard near the end of the kitchen and pulled out a bottle of wine. He found a corkscrew while Penny went to the patio to turn the steaks and corn. "Dinner should be ready in about four minutes", Penny said going into the kitchen to bring a clean plate out for the steaks and corn.

Randy placed two long stemmed crystal wine glasses on the table. He then poured wine into both glasses saying, "I'm told that you should allow wine to breath before drinking it.

Truthfully, I don't understand the respiratory system of a glass of wine."

"Neither do I", Penny said laughingly. The wine I'm most used to is drunk immediately after the cap is unscrewed." Penny then looked at the bottle and saw it was a Merlot from a vineyard in Brian, TX.

"The last time I was at a meeting in College Station there was a tour of a nearby vineyard. I took a sip of this on the tour. It tasted good to me; so, I bought a case to bring back. I have not had any since I brought it home. It could be terrible; I do not have a sophisticated palate."

Penny laughed as she went to the patio setting a plate down on the side of the barbeque. After turning off the burners, she turned off the gas valve. With tongs, she placed both steaks and the ears of corn on the plate. Walking back into the dining room she said, "Mom says steaks should rest for about five minutes. I don't understand why a cooked piece of cow needs to rest!"

They both laughed and simultaneously picked up a glass of wine. "A toast, Randy said, "to resting wine and breathing steaks...or is it the other way around?" Clicking their glasses together they laughed and had a sip.

"Randy, this is really good wine! Much better than I'm used to," said Penny as she plated the steak and roasted ears of corn. Randy tossed the salad using tongs Penny had found in the silverware drawer. Reaching for her wine glass, Penny said, "Another toast-to us!"

The steaks were perfect. With a little butter, salt, and pepper the corn tasted excellent. Randy placed salad in his bowl and poured a healthy serving of blue cheese dressing over the salad. Penny did the same.

Taking a bite of salad, Randy said, "This is great blue cheese dressing! I think it's the best I have ever tasted. What brand is it?"

"It's Penny's brand. I made it while you were out roping. I've never made blue cheese dressing before, but it was easy. I like it too!" Penny found the meal turned out great. She was anxious; this being the first meal she cooked for Randy. By no means was it a flop; as evidenced by the way Randy was savoring each bite.

As Penny was finishing up and Randy had completed his meal, Penny asked, "What is the dress for the art show we're going to in Cheyenne?"

"The museum calls the dress 'western formal'; but that's wide open to interpretation. I generally wear a sports coat with a starched dress shirt and a pair of starched newer Wranglers. Generally, I'm overdressed. I've seen women in everything from a tank top and mini skirt with boots, to classy western dresses."

"I did not bring anything close to what you described. Of course, I had no idea I would be going to an art show in Cheyenne when I packed. I've got to go shopping for something to wear tomorrow. Do you know where I should go? What shops have western chic clothing?"

"I don't have a clue where to go or specific stores; but, I do know someone that can tell you and will probably go with you. My sister Rose is a classy dresser and she loves to shop. She's married to Larry Shelton who is up in Laramie. I'll give her a call and ask her to help."

"Thanks, but don't ask her to take me. If she offers, that's fine, but I don't want impose on her Saturday."

"OK, I won't ask Rose to go; but I'll bet she will want to. With Larry gone, that's about as much of an excuse as she needs. Rose likes to shop for clothes and has a lot of them. She has good taste, I think you will like her."

"Oh, I forgot to tell you earlier, I spoke with my new boss, Dr. Laporte, and he wants me to meet him and Dr. Yu in Fort

Collins at the Regional Office next Monday afternoon and Tuesday. We're going to discuss the DVE outbreak and other stuff. So, I won't have to travel home from Cheyenne on Sunday night as I planned. When were you planning on returning?"

"My return depends on how well I rope the first two head, and what's going on at the feedlots. If I do well enough to be in the top fifteen steer ropers based on two head, then I will qualify for the finals. They are two weeks from Sunday. I know I rope my first head Wednesday morning in the slack. They run the entire first go-round on Wednesday morning in the slack. I most likely will rope my second steer on Thursday morning in the slack, as that's when most of the second go-round goes. But, unlike most rodeos the Cheyenne committee selects ten ropers per day for the afternoon rodeo performances. There is an outside chance I could rope my second steer in one of the afternoon performances."

"I went to the northern lots today to make sure there were no signs of DVE breaking. They are looking closely, but no signs of DVE, at least not yet. Dennis and Bud have things under control at the southern lots. With Jim Bob looking after things, I'm not concerned about needing to return."

"While I'm in Cheyenne, I want to go to Laramie and visit with Larry's brother and the team that's working on the alfalfa/fertilizer scenario. Maybe we can both go to see what's going on?"

Penny walked toward one cupboard where she got two small plates setting them on the table with two forks. With a big grin on her face she said, "It sounds like we're going to be busy in Cheyenne; I think we're both going to need extra energy for such a busy schedule." Penny reached into the cupboard again pulling out the German Chocolate cake and placing it on the table. Penny smiled then laughing as she watched Randy's expression change from query to surprise to joyous.

Penny handed the cake knife and server, which she had skillfully hidden behind her back, to Randy. "Would you do the honors?"

While Randy cut and served a slice of cake to each of them, Penny remarked; "I spoke with Pat Rhodes-Voss today. She asked if I would read photomicrographs of the samples we'll be collecting on the normal cattle. I told her I would. It's my plan to read them on my laptop Wednesday and Thursday after you rope. It won't take long. The software is neat; it includes a voice to text application; so, while I look at the slide I dictate my observations. When I finish my dictation, the histopathology interpretation report is complete. It's efficient. So, reading the slides shouldn't take long."

Randy listened to what Penny said, but his focus was on the cake. "It's my favorite cake. How did you know?"

Smiling, Penny said, "I didn't really. I like German Chocolate. I initially thought I would get a cheese cake and some fresh fruit to top; but when I saw the cake and it looked good, so I bought it."

After finishing their cake, Penny poured the remaining wine into their glasses and began clearing off the table. Randy helped. With the table cleared and the remaining food put away, Randy reached for his glass with a wide grin saying, "If I didn't know better, I'd think you're trying to get me drunk; then take advantage of me."

Also grinning, and in a sultry voice, Penny responded, "With or without getting you drunk, I'm planning on taking advantage of you." Penny reached for Randy's hand and led him down the hallway and into the master bedroom.

Chapter 17

Larry Shelton liked to get up early in the morning to see the sun rise and drink coffee. Since his arrival and waiting for slide preparations, Larry was becoming progressively more anxious. He had too much time to think about things out of his control. Things just weren't happening fast enough. As he reflected on yesterday's meeting, he had no high comfort level with the team his brother contacted to help him find out the answers important to ATX. The technology used was far too technical for him. He'd have to depend upon his brother to interpret the science. He had faith Ray would voice his unabridged opinion.

After a delicious breakfast, Ray and Larry drove to the biology department parking lot. The microscopy lab was a short distance from where they parked. Once in the basement, they walked directly to the lab. Drs. Schwartz, Fong, and Edwards were already there. They were waiting on Dr. Thorpe. Larry thought *why am I not surprised? The absent-minded professor can't tell time any better than he can keep his office organized.*

"Good morning brothers Shelton", said Dr. Schwartz. "Dr. Thorpe called to say he would be about twenty minutes late. He's performed some additional tests and is waiting to remove the slides from the incubator. If you like, we can start. Before you arrived, we were discussing looking at the fertilizer as a starting point."

"We're going to look at a 1:1, 1:10, and 1:100 dilutions of the fertilizer using a slide preparation technique called freeze drying. What Dr. Edwards has done with the first three slides is quickly freeze the fertilizer diluents using liquid nitrogen gas. Placing the frozen samples in a high-vacuum chamber overnight allowed the sample water to evaporate. Under vacuum, the water in the fertilizer evaporates at a temperature far below zero degrees centigrade. After putting the dried samples on normal SEM stubs, they are sputter coated. We expect to observe the titanium dioxide nanoparticles. The purpose of using three different dilutions is to adequately observe the nanoparticles individually so that we can observe their structure and approximate their size", said Dr. Schwartz.

The 1:1 aliquot was in the SEM. Dr. Edwards turned on the monitor. *At low magnification, the sample looks like a pile of black sand* thought Larry. Dr. Edwards first moved the microscope stage to an area that appeared less dense; and then turned the magnification up to 15,000. This was three times the initial magnification. To Larry *the image was now larger black spheres, but the spheres piled upon one another.* They could not observe individual spheres.

Dr. Edwards took the one to one diluent off the SEM stage replacing it with the 1:100 aliquot saying, "they appear to be very small NPs, I don't think the 1:10 aliquot will show much difference, so I'm going to go directly to the 1:100 dilution." Dr. Edwards repeated the process as she had on the one to one dilution. Larry thought, *the grains of sand look less dense, but I still cannot see any individual spheres.* As Dr. Edwards slowly scanned the slide for the least dense area she saw nothing promising. "Well we're out of luck. The NPs are very small and when we evaporated the aliquot condensing the particles. We will need to make further dilutions to isolate a single particle. I'm going to start with a 1:1000 dilution and go up five dilutions to where the final dilution will be 1:32,000. Regrettably, those slides won't be available until tomorrow morning.

Dr. Thorpe entered the room as Dr. Edwards looked at the 1:100 aliquot. Everyone, including Larry, had a good view of the SEM screen. "What's next", said Ray Shelton.

Dr. Fong in a meek sounding voice said, "I have taken alfalfa leaves, stems, and roots. Hopefully I sliced them where we can observe the exterior and internal structures of each part of the plant. There is a total of twelve slides as I ran duplicates of each slide using two different plants. I prepared the slides using the CP-drying method. The samples were fixated in two percent formaldehyde, 70 percent ethanol, five percent acetic acid, dehydrated with 99 percent ethanol and CP-dried with CO2." Dr. Fong then placed a plastic SEM holder containing twelve SEM stubs in front of Dr. Edwards. "I'm hoping, if there was uptake of the titanium dioxide NPs into the plant, we will see where they're located. Because the NPs are in surfactant, I think we have a good chance to visualize uptake."

Dr. Edwards placed the first SEM stub onto the stage and focused on the alfalfa leaf. She turned the magnification to fifteen thousand and refocused the microscope's objective. Dr. Fong explained, "This sample is of the exterior of the leaf's surface. Low power scanning demonstrates the leaf surface is healthy, the epidermal cells are intact, while preserving the papillae. But the alcohol dehydration destroys the epicuticular wax microstructure. There are two areas on the leaf's surface requiring closer review. Turning up the magnification, one area demonstrated organic residue contamination. The second area viewed was a spherical shaped particle that could possibly be a NP in the process of translocation. If this image was not artifactual, it would be the first image captured of a NP translocating from the leaf surface into the leaf's stoma. Dr. Edwards increased magnification again and the image of the tissue was much larger, but did not have the clarity of detail. The magnification decreased slightly. Seventy-five thousand magnification, restored clarity allowing for clear digital photomicrographs. The image displayed what the team thought. A NP, seen as a black sphere, appeared surrounded by the epidural stoma. Dr. Fong was excited, becoming antsy, like a child waiting for desert.

Next, Dr. Edwards placed a section of stem on the SEM stage. She focused the objective under low magnification. The stem had a vertical placement so the image appeared as cross-section of the stem. Dr. Schwartz described the low image anatomy of the stem. There were several small black spherical particles below the epidermis in the palisade and spongy parenchyma. The quantity of NPs astonished the team. They viewed a NP appearing to have translocated into the stem. Increasing the magnification confirmed the exact locations of the NPs. Small spheres were located among the palisade and spongy parenchyma cells and one sphere in a stem vein in the Xylem. As magnification increased to seventy-five thousand the black sphere became more pronounced and its location verified as between the cells, not intracellular. Dr. Edwards took more digital photomicrographs.

Dr. Fong announced the next sample was from a root of the alfalfa plant. Dr. Edwards focused on cross section of the root sample. Anatomically, Dr. Fong identified the epidermis, root hairs, the cortex, and stele of the root under low magnification. Seeing no tiny black spheres, Dr. Edwards increased magnification. She scanned the root cross-section right to left, down, then left to right, and so on. The viewed entire cross section at 15,000 magnification. There was no evidence of NPs present. Dr. Edwards reached for the duplicate slide. Replacing the initial root sample with the duplicate. Turning down the magnification and focusing the SEM on the duplicate section of the root, Dr. Fong spoke. "It is known that the interaction of some metal oxide nanoparticles is relatively poor. It may be due to particle size. Maybe the nanoparticles we observed in the stem are physically too large to be absorbed into the plant root or maybe there were no nanoparticles in the soil." Dr. Edwards continued scanning the duplicate root sample observing no evidence of NPs.

"Dr. Thorpe, are your samples ready?" asked Dr. Schwartz.

"Yes", responded Dr. Thorpe. "This part of the investigation is to first determine whether the nanocapsules consist of protein or carbohydrates, which are by far the two most common substances used to form nanocapsules. To determine whether the nanocapsules are protein or carbohydrate, I prepared two slides with a composite of alfalfa plant leaves, stem, and root breaking down the plant components by ultrasonification. I also prepared duplicates of the two slides using a 1:10,000 dilution of fertilizer containing titanium dioxide nanoparticles. I treated two of the slides containing plant parts and two of the slides containing the dilute fertilizer with Protease K, an enzyme known to digest protein nanocapsules. I treated another two slides containing plant parts and two slides containing dilute fertilizer with detergent which breaks down carbohydrate nanocapsules. Very early this morning, about 2:30AM, I looked at four slides on the SEM. I found the nanocapsules used in the fertilizer are protein. Next, I wanted to ascertain whether the protein coated nanoparticles contained titanium dioxide. Next, I exposed two slides to Protease K, thus removing the protein capsule. Subsequently, I bathed the slides in fluorescein tagged chlorine. The chemical reaction resulted in the formation of titanium tetrachloride which fluoresces in the SEM. I was late because these slides had not adequately dried."

"Dr. Edwards, I have arranged the SEM stubs in the order they should be viewed." As Dr. Edwards adjusted the SEM to focus on the first slide, Dr. Thorpe explained what he saw. "This slide is of the alfalfa plant components treated with a detergent to break down carbohydrate nanocapsules. We see several individual dark spheres intermixed with plant parts. The detergent did not affect the nanocapsules. Higher magnification confirms the integrity of the sphere is intact."

"Second slide please. This slide demonstrates what happens when we expose the fertilizer with titanium dioxide nanoparticles to detergent. Again, we see individual dark spheres that enlarge in size as we increase magnification. Higher magnification confirms the integrity of the sphere. Detergent had no effect on the nanocapsules."

"Next slide please. This slide is of the alfalfa plant components exposed to protease K. We observe small vacuoles on lower magnifications. On higher magnification, we observe there are no black spheres; rather there are vacuoles some containing rock-like structures assumed to be titanium dioxide. Protease K has digested the nanocapsules. I am troubled by the vacuoles that are devoid of titanium dioxide. Let's go to as high of magnification as we can. The only thing I observe is perhaps some pinkish proteinaceous residue. Dr. Edwards, what magnification are you at?"

"The magnification currently is 100,000, Dr. Thorpe."

"Thank you, Dr. Edwards. Next slide please. Under lower scanning magnification we are now viewing the diluted fertilizer sample treated with protease K. The field of vision is devoid of what we now know to be proteinaceous nanocapsules. We again view vacuoles. In some of these vacuoles are irregular appearing structures assumed to be titanium dioxide. As magnification increases, the titanium dioxide particles become larger and the remaining vacuole is clear of any other structures or debris. Now at this magnification let's look around and find an empty vacuole. While this vacuole does not contain any particles, there is an apparent nondescript proteinaceous residue. Let's look around to see if we can find more of these empty vacuoles and see whether they contain a proteinaceous residue. As we scan around it appears those vacuoles that do not contain titanium dioxide particles do contain a proteinaceous residue. I wonder why there would be incomplete digestion of the nanocapsules only in those vacuoles that do not contain titanium dioxide. Please increase the magnification to maximum power. The residue or debris is very small, but consistently present. Higher magnifications provide us no further clarity. Could those residues contain something very small that is unaffected by protease K?"

"Next slide please. This slice contains plant parts treated with protease K and subsequently bathed in fluorescein tagged chlorine. As Dr. Edwards scans the slide at low power, we observe numerous vacuoles are fluorescing and more numerous vacuoles that are not fluorescing. Let's look at both under higher magnifications. The vacuoles with the titanium particles are now fluorescing. The empty vacuoles contain very small areas of proteinaceous debris, but they appear to be unaffected by the florescence."

"Next slide please, Dr. Edwards. This slide contains diluted fertilizer exposed to protease K and subsequently bathed in fluorescein tagged chlorine. Under low scanning magnification we observe numerous vacuoles fluorescing and numerous vacuoles that are not. Those vacuoles that contain titanium are fluorescing. Those devoid of titanium do not fluoresce. Under higher magnification we continue to visualize what I will call trace amounts of proteinaceous debris."

"That completes my portion of the investigation. Are there any questions?"

Ray commented, "Dr. Thorpe, your investigation was designed to cut to the chase with its simplistic design. You have demonstrated the nanocapsules are proteinaceous both within a plant composite and in the diluted fertilizer. You have also shown less than half of the nanoparticles contain titanium dioxide. You have also consistently demonstrated the 'vacuoles', as you refer to them, contain what appears to be a proteinaceous residue. Considering infectious prion protein is resistant to protease K, would you care to speculate on what the 'protein debris' may be inside the empty vacuoles?"

"Ray, you are a scientist as am I. We both know it is dangerous to speculate without proof. Considering we are involved in a purely academic discussion, I would have to think the protein debris could be infectious prion protein. We don't have any evidence to prove they are infectious prion protein. Conclusive evidence is problematic due to the small size of prion protein. However, candidly that is my first consideration."

"Dr. Thorpe, are you planning or would you consider quantifying the number of vacuoles that contain titanium dioxide versus those that may be described as empty vacuoles? Also, would you consider running those numbers out to where they demonstrate statistical significance? This information is important going forward, said Ray."

"Ray, I had not planned on quantification, but it is good science. I will work on providing this information. Honestly, now, my first act is to go home and go to bed. As a graduate student pulling an all-nighter was not out of the norm. Now, I can still get it done; but I am exhausted afterward."

Larry commented, "I would really like to thank all of you for the information you provided on such short notice. I think you have planned on performing some further studies that would provide further information. Do you think those studies are still germane?"

"Mr. Shelton", said Dr. Schwartz, "considering the information Drs. Thorpe and Fong provided today, I think we all need to go back to the drawing board and reevaluate what we might propose. Perhaps if we can meet with you in two or three days, we will be able to have a thoughtful answer to your question. Would that be acceptable to you and Ray? I want to make sure Dr. Thorpe gets adequate time for his battery to recharge."

"If we can make it four days, say Thursday afternoon, I would be most happy to listen to everything you present. Please consider we may use your results as evidence in litigation. We would need to present sound supportable scientifically based evidence. Does Thursday afternoon work for everyone? I may want to bring along some folks, if that is OK with you?"

Everyone around the table was nodding Thursday afternoon would be fine. Dr. Schwartz finished by saying we'll see you all on Thursday, say about 1:30PM? Larry, bring whomever you wish. We will be happy to have them."

As everyone was leaving, Ray caught Dr. Edwards in the hallway. "Would you mind making me a disk of the digital photomicrographs you took throughout the slides? Are you planning to continue the dilution trial to characterize the size of the nanoparticles? I think it's still important information."

"Yes, I think it important as well. I will get the slides set up this afternoon. They will be ready to view about 10:00AM tomorrow, if you wish. I will also try to catch Dr. Thorpe before he leaves and see if he would like me and Dr. Fong to quantify the number of nanoparticles and vacuoles that contain titanium dioxide. If he agrees, we'll have that information available tomorrow morning as well."

"Thank you", Ray said as Dr. Edwards hurried toward Dr. Thorpe's lab and office.

"Little brother, you're buying lunch", said Ray as they walked toward the parking lot.

"Do you still belong to the country club out west of town?"

"Yeah, is that where you want to eat?"

"I remember the last time Rose and I were here to visit, you and Kate took us there. I had one of the best prime rib sandwiches I have ever eaten. That sounds good to me. Do you want to call Kate and see if she wants to join us?"

"Kate's not home. She took the kids out where they keep their horses. They were going horseback riding."

Ray drove to the Trails End Country Club where they sat in the bar. Everyone was out playing golf. The bar was empty, so they chose a table adjacent to a south facing window and sat down. Larry ordered the prime rib sandwich, while Ray had a patty melt. Both were sipping iced tea when their lunches arrived.

"Ray", Larry said, "as I listened to Dr. Thorpe, his presentation was very logical and I was able to follow it very clearly. However, I also thought he was leading us very subtly to his conclusion. Could you come to an alternate conclusion given the data he presented?"

"Given the tests he ran and the results of those tests, I can think of no persuasive alternate conclusion. Particularly considering this is a novel agent. You must consider Gene has been a college professor for a long time; he laid out his investigation in a logical and orderly manner that was easy to follow, then he talked us through the results, which were straight forward. This is same methodology he uses to explain an investigation to graduate students. That format comes naturally to him. He's a great teacher and has received several teaching awards. He also has a knack for taking very complex problems and simplistically investigating them."

"Actually, I agreed with his conclusion; I wanted to give you the opportunity to play devil's advocate. Based on the evidence we have, I'm going to call Randy and tell him the source of DVE was the alfalfa produced on the southern farms. Both the fertilizer and the alfalfa contained prions", said Larry.

"Larry, remember how carefully Gene chose his words. He identified the remaining pink smudges in the vacuoles as proteinaceous residue. Then, he explained this residue was resistant to protease K treatment. Gene led us to the edge of what he concluded, but he did not make the leap to call them prions. You would be safe telling Randy there was consistently proteinaceous residue in the empty vacuoles which was not present in the vacuoles that contained titanium dioxide. When you call Randy, I would be glad to speak to the specific details, if he has questions."

"That sounds great. I'll give Randy a call after we get home. For now, I am going to continue to enjoy this sandwich. It's as good as I remembered. With my big brother across the table from me, and the cooler weather, I'm just going to concentrate on enjoying myself. Ray, thank you for your help in getting this thing figured out."

"No thanks are necessary. That's what we Shelton's do; we help each other. With enjoying the weather in mind, what do you want to do over the weekend?"

"Fishing and golf sounds good, but I don't want to capitalize your time. Kate and the kids need some too. You know this area much better than I do, is there any where you would recommend that we could also take Kate and your kids along?"

"Have you ever been to the Saratoga area? It's on the west side of the Snowy Range Mountains. There are several places over there to stay. The one I'm thinking of is the Ole Stag Inn. It's a private club, but they allow visitors as well as members to enjoy their facilities, which are first class. There is fishing all around, both public and private, and the Old Stag has an excellent golf course, so I'm told. I've haven't played golf there; however, a couple of years ago the Ag College held a retreat there. Kate and I had a fantastic time. Generally, they're full, but we can give them a call and see. They also have activities for kids. Do you want to see if we can get reservations?"

"Yeah, give them a call. But the stay will be at ATX's, expense. There's no negotiation on that caveat. With all you have done for me and ATX these last few days; whatever the cost, it's worth it."

"OK, I'll give them a call when we get home and after you call Randy. That way if something comes up we don't have to cancel."

"What's the name of the place again? I'm going to call Rose first and see if I can talk her into flying up to join us. I want to make sure I get the name right. I don't think she is on call for several days."

"The Ole Stag Inn", said Ray.

Chapter 18

"Hi Randy, it's Larry. How are things down there?"

"Larry, things are going well down here. I'm getting ready to leave for Cheyenne in a couple of days. The horses leave tomorrow with Junior. Sonny and I are flying up Tuesday evening. I'm also bringing Penny with me. What's going on up there? Are you finding out anything?"

"I spoke with Rose just before I called you. So, I know about Penny. You've been keeping her a secret; but Rose said she and Penny went shopping. Rose really likes her. She told me she hoped you don't let her get away."

"Rose is going to fly up tomorrow with the kids, if she can get plane tickets. Then my brother, his wife Kate, and both families' kids are going to go to a place where we can fish, play golf, and relax. It's west of Laramie, over the Snowy Mountain Range, in a little town called Saratoga. We're going to spend three days over there, if we can get reservations. It's called the Ole Stag Inn; Ray has been there and says it's a nice place."

"Anyway, I have some significant news regarding the fertilizer and southern alfalfa."

"Wait, let me interrupt you", said Randy. "If it's significant news, I want to get Dad on the line and we will conference you in. I want him hear what you say firsthand. I'll call you back as soon as I get Dad on the line. If he's not around, I'll call you right back."

Randy hung up his cell phone, coming in from the garage to find Penny. She was in the living room visiting with Sarita. Randy relayed that Larry had significant news asking if Penny wanted to join him on the call. He planned calling from his office in the bedroom. Penny said she would listen in. Sarita was telling Penny about her weekend with Thomas in Lubbock. Sarita said she would wait.

"Hi Mom, is Dad at home? Good, could you put him on the line? I want to conference him in with Larry. Larry is up in Laramie with his brother Ray. He says he has some significant news. I want Dad to hear it firsthand."

"Hi Randy, Mom told me what's going on, thank you for including me. Do you want me to hang on while you reach Larry?"

Randy called Larry back on the land line in his office as it had a good speakerphone. "Larry, it's Randy again. Now let me click-in Dad. Dad are you there? Larry are you there? I can hear both of you well; does anyone have a poor connection?" A unison denial was his answer.

"OK Larry, you told me that you had significant news. Please go on with the details."

"Good afternoon Randall. My brother Ray spoke with some faculty in the Neurosciences Department at the University of Wyoming. We met with them yesterday morning to explain our situation and thoughts about the fertilizer being the possible source of the DVE at the southern feedlots. After conferring about the problem, they set up a series of experiments yesterday."

"This morning we stopped in to see their results. They performed three experiments using their Scanning Electron Microscope. In one experiment, diluted fertilizer they attempted to determine the nanoparticle size. They're repeating this test using more dilute samples. The second experiment demonstrated uptake of nanoparticles into the leaf and stem, but there was no uptake by root. The third experiment was the most conclusive. Dr. Thorpe finely ground composite samples of leaf, stem, and root. Another set of samples were of very dilute fertilizer, like a 1: 10,000 dilution. He exposed one slide of each set (plant or fertilizer) to detergent. Detergent would dissolve the nanocapsules if they are carbohydrate. The detergent did not affect the nanocapsules. He exposed the second slides to protease K.

The protease K would dissolve nanocapsules made of protein. The enzyme digested the protein leaving tiny vacuoles. Some of the vacuoles contained titanium dioxide nanoparticles. However, over half of the vacuoles were empty, except for a small pink residue smudge in all the empty vacuoles. The vacuoles containing the titanium dioxide did not display these smudges. He exposed a third set of slides (one plant and one dilute fertilizer) to protease K and then bathed in fluorescein tagged chlorine. In both the fertilizer and the plant parts, there were vacuoles and a chemical reaction had taken place causing the titanium to fluoresce. There were also more empty vacuoles than those fluorescing. The empty vacuoles had the pink smudges in them, but those containing titanium did not. From this experiment, Dr. Thorpe concluded the nanocapsules are proteinaceous. He demonstrated that less than half of the nanoparticles contained titanium dioxide. He consistently demonstrated the 'empty vacuoles', as he had referred to them, contained a proteinaceous residue. Learning infectious prion protein is resistant to protease K, the protein debris could be infectious prion protein. But there is no conclusive evidence to prove that. We think the smudges or proteinaceous reside in the empty vacuoles is infectious prion protein causing DVE."

"I asked the group to consider the information the group had provided today and propose further experiments germane to providing evidence that could potentially provide overwhelming evidence to support possible litigation. Ray and I are supposed to meet with them Thursday afternoon to see what they might come up with."

"I chose Thursday afternoon because I knew Randy would be in Cheyenne roping on Wednesday morning and possibly Thursday morning. I also told the group that I may have some folks with me when we came back. I thought that would allow time for anyone who wanted to attend to get here."

"So that's what I discovered today. Tomorrow will be a follow-up day where we should find out about the size of the nanoparticles and the quantification of nanoparticles with titanium dioxide in them versus those containing protease K resistant proteinaceous residues."

"Wow, Larry you've found all that in the last two days", said Randy. "That's extraordinary; I hope Dad doesn't hold us to that standard. I think we need to let the USDA know what we found. It will save lots of time, expense, and duplicated effort."

"Why don't you boys let me notify the USDA? I've been looking for an excuse to call Clare. This will be a good note for my call. I'll call her first thing tomorrow morning."

"Larry plan on Penny and I joining you on Thursday afternoon. What is the time and location?

"The meeting is in the basement of the Biology building on the Laramie campus at 1:30PM. If you want to come earlier, maybe we can catch lunch somewhere. Let me know."

"Dad, do you want to go too?"

"Let me think about it and see what Clare has to say. What Larry, Ray, and that group of scientists pulled off, needs recognition. That's part of what I'm going to tell Clare when I speak with her tomorrow. Randy, is Penny on the line with you", inquired Randall.

"Yeah, she's been listening in. Do you want to talk with her?"

"Please. Penny, do you mind if I mention your name tomorrow when I speak with Clare Johansen?"

"No sir, I don't mind. However, I was not involved in what Larry and Ray have done."

"Thank you, dear."

"Rose and the kids are flying up tomorrow, if she can get tickets", said Larry. Both Shelton families are going to a club over by Saratoga called the Ole Stag Inn. Ray's been there before, he says the fishing is great and they have a good golf course."

"Larry, you've done a good job. Enjoy the fishing. Y'all will enjoy the Ole Stag Inn. Randy, thanks for including me on the call. Do you want to set up a conference call tomorrow to let the other board members know what Larry has found out? I'll tell Phillip tomorrow morning; we may need his services. If there isn't anything else, I will sign off."

"Larry do you have anything else? Thank you for doing such a good job in getting this train wreck placed back on the tracks. Also, you left the board meeting before I could catch you the other day. I also wanted to thank you for hedging all those cattle. That may help save my bacon."

"Randy, you don't need to thank me. That's what we do. You know that. I can tell you, I've been sweating this one out. It was me that did this new rotation plan and chose the fertilizer that contaminated our alfalfa. Although we're not out of the woods, at least we know what we're likely dealing with. I'll let you go; if Penny is listening, I look forward to meeting you soon. Rose enjoyed the shopping trip."

****

"Well what do you think about Larry's news", asked Randy.

"It's the most logical explanation I have heard", responded Penny. "While the experiments performed at the University of Wyoming were rather simple to perform, the design of their experiments collectively was brilliant. Their work provides conclusive evidence the fertilizer was adulterated."

From the perspective of an outside investigator, the U.S. was lucky Larry implemented the new corn/alfalfa rotation and specifically used the contaminated fertilizer." Randy looked puzzled at Penny's comment. Penny went on, "I cannot think of another integrated agricultural operation in the U.S. whose management, from top to bottom, is so knowledgeable in a vast spectrum of specialties, has the resources, and is well enough connected politically and otherwise, to decipher the cause of such a complexly designed act. It's likely it would have taken government and academia, acting cooperatively, truly years to get to this point. It took you and your family, acting independently, literally weeks. That's something you all should be most proud of."

"Thanks, but maybe we just got lucky", said Randy.

"Randy when we first came to Canyon we were one of seven teams tasked with carrying out investigations. Four of the other six premises were large, like ATX. All cooperated with the USDA. We all took samples of the feed and water; performed limited necropsies and sent in numerous samples. To me, when you cut out the five head of roping steers we sampled down at Tulia, that was the difference. Knowing the roping steers ration consisted exclusively of alfalfa hay, you determined the feed difference needed further investigation. You capitalized on that fact by calling Larry and eliciting his help. Together you and Larry, with the help of others, identified the source of this novel protein."

"That's a major breakthrough and will lead us to learn how we can deal with, and prevent such a malady from recurring. All the other premises, I'll bet, used the same contaminated titanium dioxide fertilizer, yet it was ATX who determined there were contaminated nanoparticles in the fertilizer. The alfalfa plants subsequently absorbed the nanoparticles. No Randy, that's not being lucky; that's being smart, having the resources to be thorough, building lasting relationships, and dealing with the facts."

"Randy, that's why I love you; I want ours to be one of those lasting relationships."

"Penny, I love you too. More than you know, I want our relationship to be loving and lasting", Randy said as he held her closely and kissed her tenderly.

"I better get back to the living room; we ran off to the conference call and left Sarita sitting there alone. She said she would wait." Penny then walked down the hallway toward the living room, stopped, walked back to Randy, and kissed him again. Then, Randy and Penny walked down the hallway and into the living room hand in hand.

"Sorry I was gone so long Sarita, the conference call was longer than I expected; Larry and his brother Ray were able to identify the source of what caused DVE to affect all the cattle. The adulterated fertilizer got into the alfalfa. When the cattle ate the alfalfa, they became sick about two months later," said Penny.

"Randy, I'm so glad you all found out the cause. Is there anything you can treat the cattle with that will make them get better", asked Sarita.

"No, unfortunately there is no treatment; but we will know not to feed any more of the adulterated alfalfa to our cattle. That's about as good as we can do for now. I'm going to go back out to the garage and finish up. I'll let you two girls visit."

"OK Sarita, start over tell me about meeting Thomas' parents."

"Thomas' Dad is a high school teacher. His name is Carlos and he teaches history and social studies. He is a laid-back kind man with thinning hair who enjoys working on old cars. He has a fifty-seven Chevy that he is in the process of restoring. It looks brand new to me, but he says he still has a lot of work to do on it. Thomas' mother, Esmeralda, is a nurse. She works for a doctor at the medical school. She assists him in surgery and works in his office. She is very nice and is a good cook. They are a very traditional Mexican couple and very religious. We went to mass together, it was very nice. That's one thing I miss; not having a family to go to mass with. I went to mass with Randall and Beth when I was living with them that summer, and I go with Randy sometimes, but it's just not the same. I liked his parents and I think they liked me too."

"Did you and Thomas do anything while you were in Lubbock", asked Penny.

"We went to the mall for a while and walked around. I bought a small bottle of perfume. We also went to a winery with Thomas' parents. That was fun. We took a short tour and then sampled some different Texas wines. I'm not much of a wine drinker, but I did buy a bottle Thomas and I liked. I'll open it some night when we have a special dinner."

"Penny, I heard you went shopping with Rose."

"I needed to get a fashionable western style dress for Cheyenne. Randy is taking me to an art show and sale. Of course, when I packed for coming on this trip, putting in clothes for an event like that was the furthest thing from my mind. I didn't know where to go that would have clothes like that. Randy said he would call his sister. He said she liked to shop and would know where I should go. Rose insisted on taking me. It was fun! She is a hoot; she's funny and knew the right stores for what I was looking for. I ended up buying a unique dress; it's made of off-white buckskin and will be perfect. I got some contrasting turquoise boots. After we finished shopping, we went to Rose and Larry's house where she loaned me some beautiful turquoise jewelry. We also went to a resale boutique that had some nice casual clothes at unbelievable prices. I bought some designer made outfits there that I can wear at work or for casual occasions. We ate lunch at a quaint restaurant. I really had a fun day with her, and I think she had fun too."

Sarita responded, "I know Rose likes you. While you were trying on clothes she called me to tell me you are nice, beautiful, smart, and had excellent taste in clothes. She thinks you are the perfect match for Randy."

"I should have known, you would have the inside scoop on what Rose thought. I keep forgetting that your part of the Bennett family. And I think you are everyone's confidant", said Penny laughingly.

****

"Good morning Clare", said Randall Bennett. "Beth says to tell you hello from her. When are you going to stop in and see us?"

"Randall, you sound bright and chipper this morning. Tell Beth I miss our long lunches. I wish I could get out of the Beltway to come see you soon. The DVE outbreak is keeping me pretty close to Washington right now."

"Clare, that's why I am calling. My son Randy, his girlfriend Dr. Penny Adams, who works for you, and my son-in-law Larry Shelton, with the help of a few other folks determined how DVE came to be. It seems a relatively new fertilizer containing nanoparticles of titanium dioxide is adulterated with prions that were encapsulated in some of the nanoparticles."

"Oh my God; that's a deliberate and purposeful...an act of bioterrorism! Randall, does anyone else know about this, other than those you named?"

"Not to my knowledge. I asked Dr. Adams to hold off telling her supervisor until after I spoke with you. I thought you should be the first to know; I didn't want you hearing about it second hand. We've been friends too long to withhold this type of information and simply allow it flow up the bureaucratic chain of command."

"Let me tell you what specific information I know. Last fall Larry Shelton, Rose's husband, who runs our farming operation considered implementing a different crop rotation program. Along with the rotation program he planted a new variety of alfalfa that some of your research folks developed several years ago. It is safe and proven to increase tonnage of forage. He also decided to try a new, more environmentally friendly type of fertilization using nanoparticles of titanium dioxide. Before Larry did this, he had my son Randy look over the program. Randy runs our feeding operation. Randy looked over the plan giving it his blessing. Larry has a brother, Ray, who is a professor of crop science at the University of Wyoming in Laramie. Larry had Ray also look over his plan. Ray too gave it his blessing."

"This spring Larry implemented the program on our southern farms which supply our southern feedlots with feed. Since we initiated the farming changes there have been two cuttings of alfalfa harvested. Part of the first cutting round baled and the other part went to producing haylage. About two months after Larry harvested the first cutting of hay cattle started showing symptoms. That spurred the USDA to investigate, as you know; the incriminating agent was identified as a novel infectious prion protein which caused DVE."

"The northern farms continued producing alfalfa as we had done in the past. The DVE outbreak has only affected our southern feedlots. In addition to the three southern feedlots, Randy had five roping steers with DVE. Randy buys 25 roping steers every spring. These steers had just crossed the border when they arrived at Randy's place. Initially, they ate some leftover alfalfa hay from last year's production. However, once the first cutting was available, Larry delivered some bales to Randy for the steers. Alfalfa hay is the only thing they've been fed. That got Randy, Dr. Adams, and Larry to think they needed to look further at the alfalfa hay. Larry collected several alfalfa samples, boxed them up and sent them to Ray in Laramie. He also sent an unopened five-gallon container of fertilizer. Then Larry jumped on a plane and headed to Laramie."

"Larry and Ray met with some of Ray's colleagues involved with electron microscopy and neuroscience. They designed some quick experiments to look at the alfalfa and fertilizer. Long story short, the UW researchers found nanoparticles of fertilizer and others with a residual protein substance inside them. I am told these tests were rather simple to perform, provided one had access to an electron microscope, but the design of the experiments was 'brilliant', according to Dr. Adams."

"At any rate, Clare, I think the team of researchers at Laramie should be recognized by the USDA. I think this type of recognition will help the USDA get broad support for the emergency supplemental funding request you and President Smyth are working on; particularly, adequate funding for research into prions."

"I am getting an appreciation for just how much we don't know about prions. The sophistication of this attack worries me. It was designed not only to eliminate a large portion of the nation's cattle herd, cause widespread national economic chaos, and lack of trust among our international trading partners."

"Lastly, I want to commend you on the initial actions you and the president implemented. In my view, they were spot on to negate as much as possible the intentions of those behind this act. You and President Smyth did indeed have the best interests of the country in mind."

"Randall, thank you very much for making this call to assure I was the first to know. I agree we need to recognize those scientists at the University of Wyoming; and I intend to do it sooner rather than later. My next call will be to President Smyth, then we will get Homeland and all the investigative agencies involved. I'm thinking maybe a national press conference in Laramie to announce this information would be in order. However, I have one caveat. Randall, you and Beth need to attend."

"While I am quite sure the Laramie folks would drop everything to accommodate your schedule, I know there is going to be a meeting Thursday afternoon between the scientists at the university and Larry, Ray, Randy, and Dr. Adams, provided you allow her to attend. They plan to discuss additional research proposals. That may be an excellent meeting to crash. I'll let you think about that for a while. If you're going to Laramie, Beth and I will be there. It will be great to see you again."

"Randall, you haven't changed a bit; you are still as crafty as you always were. You would have made an excellent politician! I will give you a call once I speak with President Smyth and get the details worked out. Randall, thank you again for calling with this information. Do you have anything else?"

"Isn't this enough for one day, Clare", teased Randall. "Actually, I do have one question, call it a curiosity. How much, in rough numbers, are you thinking about directing toward prion research?"

"Randall, don't hold me to this number, but I think it's between three and four billion dollars. We're still fine tuning the numbers for the emergency funding request."

"Thanks Clare. Three or four billion should buy a good deal of quality research. I won't take any more of your time. Good bye, Clare."

"Good bye, Randall."

Chapter 19

"Good morning, Bobby. I wanted to call to tell you Dr. Penny Adams will be giving you a call soon."

"Ma'am, I've got her on the other line. She called just before you did. What can I do for you?"

"I'll let Dr. Adams tell you what's going on. When you're done, call my office. If I'm not here, I will call you when I get back from the White House."

"Good morning, Alice. This is Secretary Johansen. Is President Smyth available? It's important."

"Hold on Madam Secretary...I'm transferring you now."

"Good morning, Clare", said President Smyth. "What's up? Alice said it was important."

"Mr. President, Randall Bennett from Amarillo called me this morning. They have determined the source product that caused the DVE outbreak. It's a new fertilizer containing nanoparticles of titanium dioxide with nanoparticles of what appears to be infectious prion protein. The alfalfa plants absorbed the fertilizer. In turn, cattle ate the alfalfa. I wanted to give you a call first; before I notify Secretary Robinson and the FBI."

"Thank you for calling me first. Why don't you come on over and we can discuss what to do next?"

Clare sat back in her chair looking at the ceiling for a moment, then called to notify Secretary Fred Robinson. He said he would notify FBI Director. Clare called for her driver to pick her up. She gathered her tablet computer and purse and walked toward the side exit. As she rode to the White House, Clare sent a text message telling Bobby Laporte to clear his schedule for Thursday.

Both Secretary Robinson and Secretary Johansen arrived at the White House simultaneously. Together they walked to President Smyth's office. As Clare walked into the secretarial office area, Alice commented, "Madam Secretary, whatever you spoke to President Smyth about has certainly put him in a good mood. You both can go on in, he's waiting for you."

"Come on in. Have a seat on the couches. Do you want a cup of fresh coffee?"

"Coffee sounds good; I'll take one please", said Clare.

"Me too", responded Secretary Robinson.

President Smyth carried a silver tray containing three cups and saucers and a coffee carafe. He poured the coffee setting the pot back on the tray. "Cream or sugar?" Both shook their heads no.

"Clare, I was most pleasantly surprised when you called this morning to advise the causative source for DVE had been found", said President Smyth. "Adulterating a new type of fertilizer containing nanoparticles is certainly a creative method. How do you think we should proceed from here?"

"Mr. President, I consider this to be an act of bioterrorism. Without doubt it was a purposeful act to place the adulterated nanocapsules in the fertilizer. In my view, we need to initiate a criminal investigation under the purview of Homeland and FBI, with the cooperation of EPA and FDA. It's interesting there is not a specific federal entity that regulates agricultural fertilizers. Their regulation falls to state regulations. Of the fifty states, two states have no fertilizer regulations; they're Hawaii and Alaska. The EPA's concern primarily deals with overuse causing high levels of residual nitrates and phosphates that may contaminate the environment. FDA's concern is primarily the contamination or adulteration of edible foodstuffs consumed by the public, not animals. There are other issues that remain for USDA to deal with concerning this outbreak. First on this list is getting the emergency supplemental funding plan approved. We also need to figure out carcass disposal methods and get them up and running. We'll need to track down all the contaminated hay and prevent further consumption. The second track of the investigation is the one Fred will oversee; that being the criminal investigation and prosecution of those responsible."

"I can assure you this act was initiated by someone, or a group, highly trained in molecular biology with expert knowledge of infective prion proteins. This factor, at some point during the investigation, will become important. This act required very sophisticated minds and expert knowledge coupled with access to a sizeable and comprehensive laboratory facility. This facility would likely include equipment, such as electron microscopes, in addition to other very technical and expensive biochemical and assay equipment."

"As a related matter, the public needs to know of our progress, without comprising an ongoing investigation. I have an idea about how to do this. Perhaps later in this meeting it will be more appropriate to proffer this thought."

"Fred, I realize you became aware of this information about an hour ago. From your perspective, how do you think we should proceed?"

"As you said Mr. President, I have not had much time to think about this information or prepare a course of action. At this point, I do not even have the names of the people identified who were responsible for this breakthrough. Initially, I plan to discuss this issue with my deputies and the Director of the FBI. Together, we will put our heads together and develop a course of action. We will begin developing an approach to how we investigate this act of terrorism. I concur with Secretary Johansen there is a need to keep the public informed; however, we have to be careful not to compromise the investigation."

"Mr. Secretary, as I said when I called you, I will provide you with the names of USDA contact personnel and others directly involved in determining this was a terrorist act. I will do that now, if you wish."

"No, Madam Secretary, it can wait; but we need to interview them."

"Not a problem. Please call me Clare."

"Clare, do you have further thoughts regarding the investigatory part of this issue", asked President Smyth. "While I recognize the criminal investigation is under homeland's purview going forward, you have been directly involved since the DVE outbreak started. I have found your thoughts and suggestions specifically helpful."

"Mr. President and Secretary Robinson, I think we made good decisions in the initial actions we took. The decision to stop the change of ownership of cattle was particularly important from a national economic perspective. It may also be an important aspect of the initial investigatory efforts. I think we need to identify those individuals who stand to profit the most, if the cattle futures and options markets were to nose dive. A close look by a group of experienced forensic accounts may prove worthwhile. It may be Dick Kline, the Chairman of the Commodity Futures Trading Commission, has already initiated a probe."

"As a suggestion, I recommend Secretary Robinson find someone, maybe from the CDC, the military, or NIH, who has expert knowledge regarding infective prion proteins and get them temporarily assigned to your staff to serve as an expert that can educate your investigators on the science of infective prion proteins; and serve as a go to reference when they have questions. I have found this subject to be very complex. Your investigators will need to know what questions to ask as well as understand the responses provided. I would look for a physician or a veterinarian with a PhD in molecular biology. I was lucky enough to have one, but I currently have her covered up in work."

"As you reach milestones, I recommend you keep the public informed. I know you would not compromise your investigation, but I would certainly be sensitive to opportunities to update the public when I could. I've always had the opinion if you don't stay ahead of the press, they will get ahead of you and provide information that may not be factual or true. I've also found misinformation breeds contempt, not against the press; but toward me or the USDA."

"Gentlemen, that's all I can think of for now", said Clare.

"That's some savvy advice", said President Smyth. "Fred, do you have any thoughts or questions before we move on?"

"No sir."

"Clare, earlier you said you had an idea regarding letting the public know our progress. Let's discuss that now."

"Ok Mr. President. As I told you earlier, Randall Bennett called to tell me further testing confirmed adulterated fertilizer is the source. He also told me the team of scientists at the University of Wyoming were the ones who conducted the experiments leading to breakthrough. Randall suggested the Department recognize them and their contribution."

"After mulling it over, I think this might be the perfect opportunity to recognize the scientists and keep the public informed on DVE developments. Randall suggested, if I could find the time, I should be the one to recognize the scientists. In his opinion and mine, it would be a good political move to make the announcement before we submit the emergency funding bill to Congress. It is likely this will assist in getting support for the supplemental bill as well as demonstrate DVE is a top priority."

"Thursday afternoon some management folks from ATX will be meeting with the Wyoming scientists to discuss further research to be conducted by this group of scientists. I'm thinking a recognition ceremony followed by a low-key press conference. I'm planning on Dr. Laporte going with me to respond to the more technical questions, like what he did at our first press conference. Leading questions, that we don't want to discuss, we will respond to as not wanting to interfere with an on-going investigation."

"I know the president of the University of Wyoming and plan to call her to get it set up. I'm thinking of having just the president of the university, the deans of the colleges the multidisciplinary team represent, and the multidisciplinary team. After a private recognition ceremony where I will present the team, including Dr. Ray Shelton, with the USDA Secretary's Honor Award and a USDA research grant for $250,000. We'll hold a small press conference. Major news channels and agencies may not choose to send a representative. They would most likely have to travel from Denver. What are your thoughts?"

"Clare, it's brilliant. It accomplishes everything you intend to do. It recognizes the important contributions of the scientists and informs the public of our progress without compromising the on-going investigation. I would like to come with you; however, whenever I go anywhere, a low-key intimate event is impossible. However, from a political perspective, I think you need to consider adding three others to the invitation list. That's Wyoming's delegation to congress. Both the house and senate will be in session being it's on a Thursday. So, the delegation might not choose to attend, but I think they would feel shunned if they weren't invited."

"That's an excellent suggestion Mr. President. I will personally call each of them as soon as we get things put together so they will know what we are trying to accomplish and will hopefully stay on message."

"Secretary Robinson, do you have any suggestions or comments", asked President Smyth.

"Not really Mr. President, I just hope the investigation does not become compromised. I worry about what the scientists might say as well as the congressional delegation."

"Mr. Secretary, Clare will minimize the comments made by each of those groups. Remember, it's her press conference, not the university's or the Wyoming delegation's. DVE is a very technical issue; the reporters who attend will not be knowledgeable enough to ask intelligent technical questions. Dr. Laporte generally responds to those questions with either very broad-based answers or will remind the press they will not compromise an on-going investigation", countered President Smyth.

****

Clare e-mailed Fred Robinson the contact information while riding between the White House and the Department of Agriculture building. She also called Bobby Laporte asking him to meet her in her office.

Both Clare and Bobby arrived at Clare's office at about the same time. Sitting down in a wingback chair Bobby said, "We certainly had a positive breakthrough on DVE delivery. I'm amazed at the sophistication of the delivery system. We're damned lucky they detected it so soon. It's amazing how quickly ATX focused on the information. Penny Adams said Randy Bennett purchased some roping steers which he only fed alfalfa hay. The source of that hay was from a field where ATX grows alfalfa as well as corn. This hay had also been fed to cattle at the Hereford, Dimmitt, and Tulia feedlots."

"There is no doubt whoever is responsible for adulterating the fertilizer meant to cause as much damage as possible. We were lucky to have ATX independently investigating their problem, and then sharing the results of their research with us. When Randall Bennett called me this morning, telling me what they found, his only request was recognition of the scientists at the University of Wyoming. That's what you and I will be doing on Thursday. Did Penny Adams tell you about the meeting that AXT and the Wyoming scientists are having on Thursday afternoon?"

"Yes, she said Larry Shelton and his brother Ray, who is a plant science professor at the university, as well as Randy Bennett will be attending the meeting to listen to further related proposals. Penny asked permission to attend. I told her it would be OK. Do you have anything specific in mind as an award or recognition?"

"Actually, I do. Determining the delivery method for DVE is a major accomplishment. I was thinking I would present the entire University of Wyoming team, including Ray Shelton, with a USDA Secretary's Honor Award and a $250,000 USDA grant to for ongoing DVE research. As I recall, private citizens who have made outstanding contributions supporting USDA's mission are eligible. I've already cleared the grant with President Smyth. In my mind, this is a significant event and we need to treat it as such."

"Oh, by the way, did you know Penny Adams is Randy Bennett's girlfriend", asked Clare.

"No, that's news to me, but it explains why she was listening to the conference call yesterday between Larry Shelton, Randy and Randall Bennett. How did you find out this information?"

"Randall Bennett told me this morning when he called. He said it in a very casual way. However, if you know Randall there's something behind everything he says; not in a devious or malicious way, he's just a man who normally doesn't say much. When he says something, you need to listen closely. You will get to meet him Thursday. Matter of fact, I need to give him a call to let him know we'll be there Thursday. Forgive me a moment, I need to give him a call now. You don't need to leave. It will be a quick call."

Dialing his number from her cell phone, "Hello again, Randall", said Clare. "I'm calling to let you know I'm planning on being in Laramie on Thursday. I'm going to present the University of Wyoming professors, including Larry's brother Ray, with the USDA Secretary's Honor Award and a research grant. It's the highest award I present. In the academic world, the Honor Award is very prestigious; we'll stipulate the grant is for ongoing DVE research. I'm also inviting the Wyoming congressional delegation. We will hold a brief press conference after a private awards ceremony. So, Randall, I'll see you and Beth on Thursday?"

"Beth and I will be there. Let's see if we can get together before hand to visit. Maybe a bunch somewhere. I know you and Beth will want to visit for a while. You make the arrangements; then let Beth know when you want us to arrive." With that, they ended the call.

"I'm sorry Bobby, but I needed to give Randall enough time to make travel arrangements. Bobby, would you please arrange the details for the award and the grant? I need to call my friend Dr. Lucy Ingram, the president of the University of Wyoming, then see if we can arrange for travel. Let's touch base tomorrow morning to make sure we have the T's crossed and I's dotted. It shouldn't take very long."

"Sounds great ma'am. I'll see you tomorrow morning."

Later that afternoon Bobby Laporte got a call from Clare. She asked how the award and grant were coming along, "Just fine, ma'am", said Bobby. "I'm glad you called there's one thing that I'm doing that we have not discussed. I need to bring you up to date. As we now know the nano-fertilizer contaminated the alfalfa, I have our Plant Protection and Quarantine (PPQ) Division investigating all the premises that have cattle positive for DVE. They're tracing back their sources of alfalfa hay or fertilizer using the data derived from the in-depth investigations. From there, we're in the process of going back to the individual alfalfa growers and quarantining their alfalfa fields. We're also in the process of getting the records of nano-fertilizer sales from individual coops and we will cross check those records of receipt against those of the national co-op distributor and the individual farming operations that bought and used the nano-fertilizer. I have also got our Investigative and Enforcement Services (IES), a staff of roughly 140 employees, providing investigative, enforcement and regulatory support. If we need more we can borrow some investigative and enforcement folks from FSIS."

"Good to hear, Bobby. You're already working on the next phase. Keep me appraised and let me know if you need any help. Now, the real reason for my call, I have spoken with Lucy Ingram. It's all arranged with the University of Wyoming. I have also gotten our air transportation finalized to Wyoming. We're going to be flying out of Andrews in an Air Force Jet with 'wheels up' at 7:45AM. We will arrive in Laramie at about 8:30AM mountain time.

Chapter 20

Randall Bennett called the four airlines servicing Amarillo attempting to make flight reservations to Denver and then on to Laramie. There was only one non-stop to Denver in the morning, and it was full. Hearing a car honking in the driveway he kissed Beth and walked out the door with a sport coat over his left shoulder and his well-worn leather briefcase in hand. "Good morning, Philip. I was trying to find us airline reservations to Laramie, but I'm having no luck. As you drive to Lubbock I'm going to call Mike. He has good connections at the airport. It looks like I'm going to have to charter a flight for Thursday."

"Hi Mike, how are you this morning? Hey, I need your help on something that just came up. Do you have a little time?"

"Good morning, Dad. What's up?"

"I need to charter an airplane, probably a business jet, to take your Mom and I and Philip and Aunt Kay to Laramie, Wyoming on Thursday. Can you arrange for the jet? We'll want to leave about 7:45AM so we can arrive in Laramie about 8:45AM. It's important we be there, so I was hoping you could use your connections to find us a charter. We'll be returning to Amarillo that evening."

"Dad, I don't know if I will be able to find anything out of Amarillo; if not, I'm sure I can find something. So, the four of you are going?"

"Yes, just the four of us, said Randall.

"Ok Dad, let me get busy finding you an airplane. Are you going to be around where I can reach you?"

"Mike, Philip and I are driving to Lubbock for a regents meeting starting in a couple of hours. After that we'll be out of touch. If I don't respond, call your mother with the information. I'll call her and let her know what's going on so she can call Aunt Kay. I appreciate your help."

Mike sat at his desk a few minutes thinking. *Who has a plane that we can use for a day? Bernie Covington has one; but, he keeps it busy running back and forth to Dallas and Oklahoma City; it may be worth a try, but I doubt it is available, particularly on short notice. Who else? I know; I'll call Rick Phillips, he's not been traveling very much since he lost his VP of operations at the refinery.*

"Hello, Rick its Mike Bennett over at ATX. How are you doing?"

"Mike it's good to talk with you. I've been busy since Sam Richards left the refinery for the CFO job with Penrod refining. It's a wonderful opportunity for Sam; I certainly don't blame him for taking it. I think it will lead to him becoming CEO in a few years when Tom Vanoy retires. We've got a search out and we're down to three good candidates. Anyway, it's been keeping me close to the refinery. What can I do for you?"

Rick, I'm looking for a jet to charter for Dad and Mom and Philip and Kay Granger. They need to go to Laramie, Wyoming early Thursday morning and will return that evening. I thought yours might be available?"

Mike, the jet's been sitting in the hanger. Both pilots are in town just twiddling their thumbs and I'm paying them like they're doing something besides playing golf. Your Dad, Philip Granger and their wives are welcome to it. Just tell me when they want to take off."

"Dad said they would want to take off around 7:45AM, so they could arrive in Laramie around 8:45AM. The return trip sounds a little more open, but he did say that they wanted to be back in Amarillo that night. If you need anything more specific, I can get in touch with Dad and get back to you. I want you to send the bill to ATX Oil and Gas."

"That's as much information as I need to file the flight plan. Let's get together with our wives and fly maybe to Fort Worth for dinner some Friday night after I get someone hired to run the refinery?"

"I would like that a lot. We've always enjoyed you and Ann. When you've got someone that can take the reins, give us a call."

"That's a deal, Mike. It's been good talking with you. We'll take good care of everyone on Thursday."

"Thanks, Rick. You saved the day. Don't work too hard."

Mike called Randall saying, "We lucked out. I found a plane. When you turn into the airport go to the private aviation building. The jet will be waiting for y'all."

"Thanks Mike. How much is it going to cost?"

"I didn't ask, I just told him to send the bill to ATX Oil and Gas. The price will be fair. I expect it to be the going rate for charter aircraft."

"Thanks again, son. I need to let your mother know before we get to our meeting."

"Bye Dad."

****

Four years ago, Randall and Philip conceived dual degree programs at Texas Tech. These programs have proven to hugely succeed. Initially, one was a dual bachelor degree program in Agriculture and Applied Economics. The other, a graduate dual degree program, led to a Master of Science in Agricultural and Applied Economics and a Doctor of Jurisprudence. Then the concept expanded to other colleges on the campus at both the undergraduate and graduate levels. The programs continue to be successful and popular; saving students' money and time obtaining their educations. Employers continue to recognize the added value of hiring dual degree graduates.

Last week, Randall and Philip sent a detailed letter to each regent and the chancellor of Texas Tech sharing their vision for a National Prion Center to be at Texas Tech University. Randall and Philip felt their proposal had a good chance at attaining board approval. While the National Prion Center would require significant capital investment, some of the technical expertise is on staff. The concept would maximize known synergies between the College of Agriculture, the School of Medicine, and the Graduate School of Biomedical Sciences. Their letter presented the proposal as a joint venture between the College of Agriculture and the Health Sciences Center.

On the drive from Amarillo to Lubbock, Randall called several of the Regents further discussing their proposal. Randall particularly wanted to respond to questions the regents may have. He also wanted to determine the support he and Philip would have for their proposal. There was considerable support for constructing the Center and developing it into one of national prominence. Of the nine regents seven were strong supporters. One regent, Ruth Murdock of San Angelo, wanted to think more about the proposal, but would likely support the initiative. The other regent, Tom Brown, an oil and gas attorney from Fort Worth, had been in Canada on business and had not yet read the letter. He said he would be at the meeting and would read the letter prior to the meeting. Philip planned to discuss the proposal with him prior to the meeting.

If the regents approved the concept, Randall and Philip recognized considerable work lie ahead. Experience from the Amarillo hospital project proved it necessary to select the right director and reach consensus on the building's design early. In both men's mind, the right director should be someone from the agricultural side with a broad education and research experience studying prions. They felt this was necessary to attract large amounts of research funding which would soon become available. By the end of the day, they sought approval a National Prion Center. They foresaw Dr. Penny Adams as the Director of Texas Tech's National Prion Center.

Chapter 21

While driving home Randy called the airline upgrading all their tickets to first class. Penny was exhausted as she boarded the plane in Amarillo. Soon after the jet was airborne she was asleep. Once in Denver, Randy took a bus to the car rental agency, while Penny and Sonny collected their luggage. Randy picked up a pearl white Cadillac Escalade ESV. He had requested a full-size SUV, anticipating a Tahoe, Explorer, or maybe Suburban. Apparently after ski season, little demand for large SUVs allowed the rental company to upgrade Randy at no additional cost.

As Randy returned to the airport, he spotted Sonny standing above the rest of the crowd with his black Stetson sitting slightly cocked over his right ear. Soon Sonny had the luggage loaded in the rear compartment. Penny climbed in the rear seat to allow Sonny maximum legroom for his 6'8" frame. As Randy headed toward Cheyenne, Penny placed Randy's sports coat, over her as if it were a blanket. Quickly she once again fell into deep sleep.

"Penny must be really tired, I have never seen anyone fall to sleep as fast as she did on the airplane; we're not yet to the E-470 turnoff, and she's fast asleep again", commented Randy.

"Think about it Randy; she removed the brains from 300 head of cattle in the last two days. She wore protective clothing all the time, and at least at Dimmitt she never took a break."

"If someone had told me Penny would be able to work all three hundred feeders in two days, I wouldn't have believed it. I actually expected you and I would be flying to Cheyenne tonight, with Penny arriving in a day or two."

"When Penny arrived at Dimmit yesterday, we had the cattle up and were ready. She got out of that Suburban, casually walking up to us saying her goal was to try to do twenty-five head per hour. That's only one head every two plus minutes", she clarified. That's a doable pace isn't it, she asked. She looked at everyone to see what the crew thought; everyone, including me, nodded their head yes. She had us bought into the pace, and then relentlessly kept us going for four hours. No one dared to say anything about being hot or tired, because Penny in that damned space suit moved at that slow appearing pace while working us into the ground. After Penny left, I got a case of beer for the crew. It was gone in a heartbeat."

Randy and Sonny continued to visit back and forth as they traveled north on I-25 toward Cheyenne. It seemed like only a few minutes had passed when the two men turned into the motel, The Cheyenne Club Inn. Randy parked under the portico to check in.

Penny walked into the registration area a few minutes later.

"Hi, sleepy head", said Randy,

"When I crawled into the back seat, I turned on the seat warmer. Within minutes the seat warmed up and I wrapped your jacket over me. I just died. I must have needed the sleep. Now, I'm badly in need of a restroom."

The receptionist overhearing Penny directed her toward the bar saying, "The restroom is just outside the bar on the right."

Randy and Sonny completed checking in when Penny returned. "Now I suppose you're all rested up and ready to party", asked Randy.

"Not really, I feel like I could go back to sleep again with no problem."

Sonny said, "What do you say, we get the luggage in the rooms and come back to the coffee shop for something to eat? Those airplane peanuts were all I've had since breakfast."

"I could eat too", said Randy as he looked toward Penny.

"Let's get unloaded; it will allow me a few more minutes to wake up. I'm a little hungry; but, I may just go back to sleep. If I do, you guys go eat. I'll be the one snoring when you get back to the room."

Penny entered the oversize room with a king bed unpacking her hanging clothes to avoid further wrinkling. She put her overnight bag under the vanity. "Randy", I think I will have something to eat; then I'm coming back here and going back to sleep. If you, Sonny, and Junior want to visit, that's OK; I just want to go to sleep. What time do we have to get up tomorrow morning?"

"We need to leave here about 5:30AM. Sonny and I must check in at the contestants' office, get our numbers, passes, saddle, and warm up our horses before the slack starts at 7:00AM. I've seen ropers be late after their steer was in the chute. They turned out their steer and the next roper was already roping. Cheyenne is known for starting on time, whether it's the slack or the afternoon performance."

"I'm going to set the alarm next to the bed for 5:00AM; that should give us enough time to get ready, don't you think?"

"Sounds good to me", said Randy. "Let's go get something to eat."

Sonny leaned up against the hood of their rental patiently waiting. They walked to a large restaurant and sat in a booth near the cash register. Everyone asked for water to drink and ordered. Sonny was the last to order and said to the waitress, "Ma'am, we've been traveling all day and will be staying here for several nights. Tonight, we're tired and we must get up early tomorrow morning. So, not to be impolite or anything, tonight we're more interested in eating, than the complete dining experience."

"You must be cowboys here for the rodeo. I completely understand what you're saying. I'll tell the chef to prepare the meals right away. Thank you for telling me."

"Thank you, ma'am", said Sonny with a pleasant smile.

"Have you spoken with Junior", asked Randy.

"Yeah, he's in the bar having a beer. He ate a hamburger in town before coming back to the motel. He said the horses settled in fine and he exercised all of them this morning. He told me he had ridden Thumper in the box and down the arena to ensure he's familiar with everything."

"You must have told him to do that", commented Randy.

"I was going to, but Bud called me this morning telling me Junior had forgotten his rope bag and spurs. Bud said he was in such a hurry to hit the road with the horses, that he walked right by them on his way out the door. I think Bud mentioned it would be good to get his horse used to the arena before he roped."

After finishing their late dinner, Randy and Penny walked back to their room while Sonny went to the bar to see Junior. The cool night air made Penny shiver. "Randy, when we get back to the room and climb in bed, I want you to hold me. I can think of nothing better than you spooning me as I fall to sleep in your arms. No hanky-panky tonight...you have to rope early tomorrow morning."

Chapter 22

Penny woke up to the alarm ringing as Randy continued sleeping; he rustled a bit. Penny got out of bed, started the coffee maker before brushing her teeth. When the coffee finished brewing, she poured two cups leaving one on the vanity counter and taking one into the bedroom. She softly sat on the bed and said; "Time to get up cowboy. Ole Blue is waiting to be saddled."

Randy rolled over and lifted his head. "Good morning, the coffee smells good." Looking when he said, "It's time, I'd better be getting up and ready. Thanks for the coffee."

Randy got out of bed putting on the same clothes he'd worn on the plane. "I'm going to clean up after I rope. No sense putting on clean clothes to go out and rope, then come back and clean up again." He pulled on his wranglers and the socks he had draped over his old boots. After pulling on his boots, he stood up walking to the bathroom. Penny finished putting on her makeup and was lightly brushing her hair before loose braiding it over her left shoulder.

Penny wore a pair of designer jeans from the resale boutique and a cute light blue linen blouse with matching blue sandals. "Will this do", asked Penny.

"You look great", responded Randy. "However, I would recommend you wear a jacket. You'll find it cool in the stands. They are in the shade until at least mid-morning. Also, be careful around the horses in the sandals. They could do some damage to your essentially bare feet. It's mostly cowboys and their families that attend the slack."

Randy and Sonny first stopped at the contestants' office got their contestant numbers, car passes, etc. Next, they went to find a parking spot close to where Junior parked the trailer. By the time, they got to the trailer Junior had all three horses tied to the trailer and was finishing saddling

Thumper. He was attaching the jerk line as Sonny had shown him.

Two hundred eighty-eight ropers entered the steer roping at Cheyenne. Each one would rope the first of their two head this morning. Junior was 16th in the order to rope. Randy and Sonny were in the second half of the order. As soon as Randy and Sonny walked up to the horse trailer, Sonny told Junior to be ready to rope right at 7:00AM; he was the 16th roper. It was evident to Randy and Sonny that Junior was tense. Randy worked steadily at brushing the hair on Blue's rump, finishing with a large toothed comb for his mane and tail. Junior was horseback and ready to warm up Thumper. Sonny said, "Junior, you're going to need a rope and your spurs", clearly, Junior was nervous roping at Cheyenne for the first time.

Sonny hurried getting Gus saddled and cinched loosely. He jumped on Gus telling Randy, "I'm going to catch up with Junior; and try to get him a little more relaxed before he ropes. I think he's letting the big arena and all the ropers intimidate him. Hopefully, I can get him focused on what he needs to do, rather than where he is."

At a more leisurely pace Randy saddled Blue, put on his spurs, and hung his rope bag over the saddle horn. He also put on a light jacket saying to Penny, "I'll lead Blue and walk over with you. There's no sense in me getting in a hurry. We'll have time to walk over, tie Blue to the fence, and get up in the stands before Junior ropes. I remember the first year I roped here, I was as nervous as Junior. Cheyenne is by far the largest steer roping of the season and everyone who can rope a set of horns enters the steer roping. After coming a few times, you look forward to coming so you can see and visit old friends you never see, except at Cheyenne. Whether at Cheyenne or at Happy, the key to doing well is maintaining focus on what you need to do, and not worrying about anyone else. They will take care of themselves, or not. Junior listens to Sonny; Sonny can help him relax and get focused."

"Now that you mention it, I can see that you're more relaxed than I would have expected. Actually, I think you were more nervous at our first meeting in Canyon than you are today."

"Well yeah, with all the cattle dying, not knowing the cause, thinking we were the only ones with this problem, and then this gorgeous blond sat across the table from me. I tried my best not to just stare with my tongue hanging out the side of my mouth. You don't know the effect you have on a guy", Randy kidded. "If Dad hadn't introduced me, I don't know if I would have remembered my name."

As Penny and Randy walked over to the roping pen area, a lot of cowboys rode by speaking to Randy. All seemed friendly to Penny, with some tipping their hats. Penny was getting excited to see Randy rope. Randy tied Blue to a fence by hanging the bridle rein over the fence. They found a place to sit in the covered bleachers closest to the roping chute. The announcer said good morning to the crowd telling everyone this was first call. He named the roper who was 'up', 'on deck', 'in the hole", and 'get ready' positions. In three minutes, exactly at 7:00AM, the first steer was in the chute and with a nod of the cowboy's head the chute gate slowly opened. The steer slowly walked out of the chute, looked around a second, and then began to trot toward the opposite end of the arena. Penny had never seen steers react so slowly. There was a length of white belting affixed to the ground in front of the roping boxes. That is the barrier or head start line given to the steers before the ropers could ride out of the box. It looked like a long head start to Penny. In the first fifteen ropers, there were only two qualifying times. One was 24.3 seconds, the other 21.9 seconds. The other ropers either did not rope the steers, or the steers got to their feet before the roper could tie their feet together.

The announcer said, "The next roper up is Junior Thompson from Tulia, Texas. It's Junior's first time roping at Cheyenne. Some of you may remember Junior's dad, Bud. Bud won the Steer Roping, Calf Roping, and All-Around titles here in 1968."

Penny's head turned toward Randy's saying, "I didn't know that. Bud certainly looks like an old cowboy; I had no idea he was a champion. Why did Bud quit roping?"

Randy responded, "Yeah, Bud was a really good roper. He traveled the circuit for several years. A few months after Cheyenne in 1968, Bud tore up his left knee badly. He had surgery to repair it; but, Bud's knee was always weak after the surgery. That's when he came to work for Dad."

Junior nodded his head, the chute gate opened slowly. A red and white steer walked out toward the line, stopped, turned his head around looked back at Junior, then slowly walked toward the white line. The steer stopped again to smell the belting, before jumping over it. Thumper, came blasting up to the steer, leveling off just as Junior roped his horns, pitched the slack over his right hip. Thumper ducked to the left tightening the rope. The trip sent the steer into the air landing flat on his right side. Once the steer was straight behind Thumper, Junior stepped off, turned, pulling the piggin string out of his belt. When Junior yelled whoa Thumper stopped immediately. Junior strung the lower front leg, pulled the rope behind the two back legs, and tied the steer using two full wraps and a half hitch. Junior threw his hands in the air and walked directly back to Thumper. He patted Thumper on the butt as he stepped into the stirrup, turning him around to slacken the rope. After six seconds, the field judge rode off. Arena hands removed the rope from the steer's horns and untied his legs. Junior coiled his rope and put his pigging string over his right shoulder as he rode out of the arena.

"Ladies and gentlemen", said the announcer, "we have a new leader. Junior Thompson of Tulia, Texas roped and tied his steer in 15.8 seconds. It appears Bud has shown Junior a thing or two about roping steers! Junior, welcome to Cheyenne, it's the daddy of 'em all."

Immediately Randy and Penny stood cheering. From behind the roping box, Sonny's huge frame was jumping up and down while hollering and waving his hands.

Randy with a deadpan look turned to Penny and said, "It looks like Sonny got Junior focused."

"Ya' think", Penny exclaimed while laughing.

"I'm going to go congratulate Junior. We'll all be up here in a few minutes, said Randy."

"I'm going to walk out of the bleachers with you to find the ladies room. Do you want some coffee; I'm going to get a cup."

By the time they were walking down the ramp to ground level. Randy commented, "See that port-a-potty over there?"

"Yeah", responded Penny.

"Avoid it at all costs. It's nasty. A couple of years ago, I had to really go and walked over there to use it. It was so bad I climbed into a pen holding some bucking bulls, and went over there by the hay rack", Randy said with a grin.

Penny, smiling, responded, "You did not. I know you better than that."

"Ever since that time if I feel the need to go, I just wet my pants and save myself the grief!"

Penny laughed slapping Randy on the shoulder.

"Seriously, if you walk up that ramp to the second level of the grandstands there are restrooms up there. I think you will find them more comfortable. When you've finished, we will meet you at the bottom of the ramp by the picnic tables. It's a food vendor; they'll have coffee as well as something to eat, if you're hungry."

"OK, I'll meet you and the guys there", said Penny walking toward the ramp.

After a cup of coffee, Sonny looked at his watch saying, "Randy it's about time for us to warm up our horses and get ready to rope."

Penny said as they were leaving, "Good luck, you guys."

Randy smiled saying, "Thanks." Sonny waved his big meaty hand.

Junior turned toward Penny and quietly said, "I was really lucky. I was getting nervous when Sonny rode up to me on the way to the arena. He just visited with me for a few minutes describing how he prepares to rope by just focusing on what he needs to do. He went through his preparation step by step. Then, he told me that there's always a lot of contestants at Cheyenne; but that didn't mean all of them really know how to rope steers. Sonny said, there's lots of variables that I couldn't control; however, if I just focus on roping as good as I can, like when we're practicing at Randy's, I'd do fine. When I backed in the box, that was all I was thinking about. Penny, I did as good as I could; and I feel good about that. So far, I'm still in the money. I know there are probably going to be some runs that will be faster; but, like Sonny says, I don't have any control over that."

"Junior", responded Penny, "Sonny is right. Doing as well as you can is all you can expect of yourself. You impressed Randy with how well you roped. He said if you have another run like that one, you will be roping a third steer in the finals."

In a little while Penny heard the announcer telling Randy he was in the 'get ready' position. Randy was standing on the ground next to Blue, checking all his equipment and pulling the saddle's chinches tight. He stepped into the saddle; made sure his rope was firmly attached to the saddle horn, cleaned the lenses of his aviator sunglasses, replaced them, and pushed down his hat. Randy was ready.

Randy rode into the box as the announcer called his name. Blue backed into the corner of the box standing still. You could see his muscles tense and ready to leap when Randy gave him the signal. Randy nodded; the chute gate opened ever so slowly, out walked a mostly white steer with red and black spots. The steer stopped to look at the line, and then jumped into the air over the line like he was jumping a small stream. Blue made a mighty leap as the barrier string sprang by his chest. Randy swung his rope twice, then threw it at the steer's horns. In the same smooth motion, pulled the slack partway out of the rope setting the trip. Without apparent cueing, Blue dropped his left shoulder. Soon the steer was airborne, landing flatly on his right side. Randy strung his top front leg with the piggin' string, brought up both hind legs, making two wraps around all three legs finishing with a half hitch to secure them. Randy pulled the piggin' string tight and threw his hands in the air. He walked somewhat quickly back to Blue, patting him on the rump he stepped into the left stirrup turning Blue around to slacken the rope. While waiting for the six seconds to expire, he loosened the rope from the saddle horn. After the rope was removed from the steer's horns, he coiled his rope. One of the untie men handed Randy his piggin' string saying, "Really nice run."

Randy rode toward the arena exit gate when the announcer said, "Ladies and gentlemen, we have a new leader. Randy Bennett from Happy, Texas tied his steer in 13.3 seconds. We're checking our historical records; Randy Bennett just set a new Cheyenne arena record with that run. The old record was 14.2 seconds set in 1974. Congratulations Randy."

Penny jumped up; her hands waving over her head she cheered loudly. A lady sitting in front of Penny turned around smiling and asked, "Your husband?"

"He's my boyfriend", said Penny.

"Even better", said the lady. "The cowboy who held the arena record Randy just broke, is now my husband. At the time we were engaged, but it sure served as good luck for us. I hope it works out that way for you."

Her sentiment touched Penny. Sitting down she touched her shoulder lightly saying, "Thank you. Between us, that means so much."

Sonny was just backing Gus into the box. Once Gus was standing squarely, Sonny nodded his head. Out trotted a rough coated black steer. He trotted past the line taking no time to examine it. Sonny quickly gathered the steer throwing his rope. With both horns roped, Sonny pulled his slack and threw his trip all in one motion. Sonny rode with both feet in his stirrups until the steer landed flat. As Sonny stepped off Gus, the steer had rolled from his right side to his left and was attempting to get back to his feet. Running down the rope, Sonny grabbed the top horn in his left hand while grasping the steer's flank with his right. Sonny literally rolled the steer back down flat, reached for the top leg, he threw the piggin' string on the top leg with it tightening above the fetlock. Pitching the piggin' string out of the way, Sonny reached back with his long right arm grabbing both hind legs and tied the steer like a calf. With his hands still in the air, Sonny walked back to Gus. Patting him on the rump, Sonny stepped on Gus turning him around and slackening the rope. Sonny coiled up his rope after taking his left foot out of the stirrup to allow the rope to come free from under his legs. Handing the piggin string back to Sonny the untie man said, "Wow, I've never seen anyone do that."

"Folks", said the announcer, "you don't see that every day, but then again you don't see a cowboy as big and agile as Sonny Thompson from Dimmitt, Texas every day. Sonny tied his steer in 15.3 seconds. That places him in second. You know the cowboys that are currently in first, second, and third place in this go round all live within about thirty miles of each other. I'll bet they practice and travel together as well. They sure can rope down south of Amarillo."

Penny and Junior got up to leave. The lady in front of Penny turned back around and said, "Have a good day dear; be careful not to get your foot stepped on by one of the horses. It really hurts when it happens...I know from experience. Y'all have fun today."

Penny joined Randy, Sonny, and Junior behind the stands. They all were standing with their horse's reins in their hands. "You waiting on me", asked Penny.

Randy smiling said, "Penny, we would wait until sundown if we had to."

"Not me", joked Junior.

"Me neither", said Sonny laughingly. "Junior and I have got horses to feed, people to see, beer to drink, and after the horses get fed, I'm going to find me one of those dining experiences and have breakfast", said Sonny.

"I'd spring for those fine dining experiences back at the motel for everyone, if you're interested", said Randy.

"You're on boss", said Sonny.

"Me too", said Junior.

"Does anyone know when we will rope next", asked Junior.

"They should have it figured out sometime this afternoon; after the first go is complete. They'll run most of the second go tomorrow morning in the slack, holding back ten ropers per day to rope in the performance. That means they hold back about eighty steer ropers, a little more than a third of the entries", said Sonny.

Since we all roped well, we might all get to rope in the performances", said Junior.

"One can hope", said Sonny. "Randy told me as soon as you and I are out of the roping, we're headed back to Dimmitt."

"I did not give any such instruction", quipped Randy.

As the men unsaddled their horses returning them to their stalls with fresh hay and grain, Penny sat in the Escalade checking her phone. She had recently received the set of histopathology slides from Pat in a large zip file. She noticed she had also received e-mails from Dr. Laporte, Pat, and both of her parents. Penny thought, *I'll call Mom after we have breakfast.* She then read her work e-mails. A few minutes later Randy climbed in the driver's side of the Escalade. "You up for breakfast after we get back to the motel", asked Randy.

"Sure", responded Penny. "After breakfast, I have some calls to make and Pat has e-mailed the histopathology slides on the non-symptomatic cattle I sampled Monday. I want to get them finished before I start getting ready to go to the art show this evening. Also, Mom sent me an e-mail that they were planning on attending the art show tonight. Apparently, Dad helped a colleague from Cheyenne with a case; she invited Mom and Dad to attend the art show with her and her husband. Mom didn't want to surprise us saying they would stay home, if I didn't want them there. Do you have a problem with it? I don't; it'll be fun and a relaxed way for you to meet them."

"Of course, I don't have a problem with your parents attending the art show. It's a fun event; I usually don't know anyone who attends. The art, however, is generally very good. You should give her a call while we drive to the motel; we don't want to let them know at the last minute. Maybe we can sit at the same table and have dinner with them. I look forward to meeting them."

"Hi Mom, I just read your e-mail. We think it's great you and Dad are coming to the art show. No, it will not be an imposition on us. Randy is looking forward to meeting you and Dad. He said maybe we can eat together. We understand you are the guests of the pediatrician. We won't impose on your time or be rude. Rest assured, we're looking forward to seeing you there. We'll see you and Dad this evening. I love you."

"Mom's excited to meet you at the art show. Her only concern was the pediatrician who gave Dad the tickets may have other colleagues who were planning on eating at the table. I told her we wouldn't impose or be rude. I really don't know what she was thinking."

"We're here. I'm going to park near the room, go wash my hands before I eat breakfast", said Randy.

"While you do that, I think I'll put on some shorts-it's getting warmer now. I was sure glad I wore the jeans and a jacket this morning. It was cool in the stands, until about the time you roped."

"This afternoon I think I'll go back out to the rodeo grounds. I want to see when we all rope again and I'll pick up our tickets to the art show. That way, I'll be out of your hair while you're reading the slides and making calls. I have some calls to make as well."

Chapter 23

Breakfast was more of a brunch. The formal dining room at Cheyenne Club Inn had set up a buffet. Randy decided it was better than ordering off the menu. Sonny, and particularly Junior, took full advantage of the all-you-can-eat buffet. Both filled their plates more than once, sampling several entrees and desserts. After Penny had eaten, she excused herself going back to the room.

Penny first called her Dad; but, he was in surgery. She asked the nurse to tell him she would see him this evening.

Next, Penny called Dr. Laporte as she got her computer set up. "Good morning, Bobby this is Penny. I read your e-mail. I'm calling as you asked."

"Penny, it's afternoon here in DC, but I know it's still morning in Wyoming. Are you having fun in Wyoming?"

"So far it's been pretty busy. We got in yesterday evening and were up early this morning to go to the slack. However, it's been fun."

"What is the slack?"

"I'm sorry, it's a rodeo term. When there are too many contestants for them all to compete during a rodeo performance; they have some of them compete before or after the scheduled rodeo performance. That's called the slack. The Cheyenne rodeo has way too many contestants; so, they run the entire first go-round in the slack as well as about two-thirds of the second go-round. The first go-round was this morning."

"I didn't realize you're such a big rodeo fan", said Dr. Laporte.

"When I was young, I had my own horse competing in 4-H horse shows. My boyfriend is a steer roper. He competed this morning."

"Did he do well?"

"When we left, he was winning the first go-round and broke an arena record for the fastest steer ever tied. So yes, he did very well. This evening, we are going to a western art show. I'm looking forward to that. Apparently, my Mom and Dad are planning on attending the art show as well; so, we will meet them there. I look for things to be a little more relaxed this evening."

"You're still planning on going to Laramie tomorrow?"

"Absolutely, we'll be there. I think it's going to be interesting to hear what they propose. I'll let you know what they're planning."

"Actually, I'll be there too. That's why I asked you to call. I wanted you to know before you arrived. Secretary Johansen is going to honor the UW scientists involved; and there will be a press conference following the recognition ceremony. I wanted to give you a heads up. The Secretary wants me there to field technical questions; however, if I don't know, I plan to defer to you, if you don't mind. Do you know what time you will be there?"

"I know the meeting starts at 1:30PM. Certainly, we will be there by that time. Randy said he had some calls to make, so it may change when we arrive. What time are you and the Secretary going to be there?"

"I think we will arrive in Laramie around 8:30AM. It's my understanding that Mr. Bennett and his wife will also be attending; however, I don't know when they'll arrive."

"If you want, I can call Randy and ask, then give you a call back?"

"No, that's not necessary. Let's try to meet up when you arrive?

"OK Bobby, that sounds good."

"Thanks for calling. I look forward to seeing you tomorrow. I feel like I already know you. Have fun at the art show this evening."

Penny unzipped the histopathology folder and read the slides while dictating her interpretations. Penny was progressively getting more proficient in reading and dictating her observations. As she reviewed each of the first two hundred slides, it was becoming obvious there was prevalent pathology, a milder form of diffuse vacuolating encephalopathy. There was no doubt in Penny's mind, based upon her histopathological observations, the non-symptomatic cattle were demonstrating mild DVE pathology in their brain stems. The vacuoles were consistently smaller; but they were present. Therefore, she would recommend complete depopulation of affected premises. Penny drafted an e-mail to Pat, copying Bobby Laporte, summarizing the prevalent pathology and her recommendations. She noted she would read the final 100 slides tomorrow; however, based on today's observations, she doubted it would influence her recommendations. Carcass disposal needed immediate consideration.

As a follow-up to her e-mail, Penny called Pat Rhodes-Voss. "Hi, Pat its Penny. How are things going?"

"Things have slowed down somewhat, except for one veterinarian who sampled two hundred fat animals on Monday and another hundred on Tuesday. That gal has got me working my tail off. The lab techs are about to revolt", Dr. Rhodes-Voss commented laughingly. "I got a call late last week from Dr. Laporte who told me what you were planning. He asked if you could really pull that off. I told him I would not bet against you. I just saw that you have sent me an e-mail."

"Pat, I looked at the first two hundred slides. There's no doubt they are developing DVE. I'm recommending complete depopulation. I was just wondering what your interpretations were?"

"Penny you and I are identical in our interpretations and recommendations. I've just read your e-mail. Carcass disposal is going to present a major problem."

"Pat, I'm going to see Bobby Laporte tomorrow. I think we need to do another experiment...call it a terminal study. As I'm going to be in Amarillo, and by the way that's working out quite well, I think it would be interesting to let these cattle live until they die, rather than euthanizing them as soon as they develop CNS signs. Of course, we won't allow anything to suffer. I'm thinking if the cattle develop signs, their progression may plateau at some point for a while, it could buy us time to gear up and develop a solid plan for carcass disposal. I know the agency is considering various methods, but I don't think there's much out there that is practical for the numbers of cattle we're talking about, except incineration. Anyway, I am going to discuss this with Bobby tomorrow; and wanted to keep you in the loop. More importantly, I wondered what your thoughts might be on such a study?"

"I think the terminal study is certainly worthwhile to perform. It would provide important information on how the pathology progresses. I mean, you never know if amyloid deposits may develop with more time. By the way, when you get back to Texas if you can make some time, I'll send you some data. We should start writing some papers regarding this outbreak."

"Pat, go ahead and send the data when you have time. I know I'm going to be busy for about another week or so, and then I don't know what I will be doing for sure. I hope to stay in Texas as long as possible."

"I heard you found a boyfriend down there. Is that why you want to stay?"

"Yeah, he's kind of the man of my dreams. He's bright, good looking, and has a great sense of humor. He's also a veterinarian."

"My sources also say he's laid back and his family owns most of the Texas panhandle. Am I going to lose you?"

"Pat, I honestly don't know. I do know long distance relationships are difficult and we really don't want that. We need to get to know each other better, and with Randy in Texas and me in Ames, that would be difficult. On the other hand, I am not independently wealthy; nor do I want to be a kept woman. I need to have a job and want to have a career. Unfortunately, there is not much demand for someone like me in the Texas panhandle. We'll just have to see how it works out. Tonight, we're going to a western art show; my parents will be there, so they'll get to meet each other. On that note, I suppose I better start to get ready, I look like a hag."

"Penny I love working with you; but I also understand. I know, however if works out, you will have given it much thought. When you have time, keep me in the loop. Have fun at the art show tonight."

Penny put down her cell phone with plans of taking a nice relaxing leisurely shower. No sooner had Penny stepped into the shower, then Randy walked in to the motel room. Hearing the water running in the shower, he shed his clothes, quietly walking into the bathroom. He stepped into the shower. Initially startling Penny, but she recovered quickly. "Hi there, handsome", she said placing a bar of soap on his upper chest.

"I thought if we showered together, we would be conserving water", Randy said as he pulled Penny toward him.

"Is water conservation the only thing on your mind", Penny cooed as her arms reached around him to pull him closer.

Without waiting for an answer from Randy, Penny said, "Apparently not. Oh, I like where this is heading."

It was a leisurely shower and no doubt relaxing as they toweled each other dry moving to lay on the king size bed. "That's without a doubt the best shower I have ever taken", remarked Randy.

"Me too, Penny said as she nestled against Randy. They continued to embrace until they both fell lightly asleep in each other's arms. Earlier, Penny set the thermostat for the air conditioning to the lowest setting and turned the fan on high before she started working. Soon the cool room temperature awakened Penny. As she moved to separate herself from Randy, he awakened. Their skin was cool to the other's touch. Penny giggled as she gently ran her hand over Randy's buttocks feeling the goose bumps that had arisen. "Up and at 'em cowboy, we have an art show to get to", Penny said as she pushed herself away from Randy. "I still need to fix my hair and put on make-up."

"I have to shave too", said Randy as he first sprawled out on the bed, then did a sit-up while rotating his legs over the side of the bed. "It's no worry to be a little late, in the past people tended to drift in over the course of a couple of hours. However, we do want to be there for the appetizers. They are usually excellent and there's a wide variety. I find I need a little something in my stomach to soak up the booze, before the art show and sale starts."

"We've got two sinks on the vanity, which one do you want?"

"It makes no difference to me; but you probably want the one closest to the outlets so that you can plug in your curling iron", said Randy.

"Well Randy Bennett, you don't think I need something like that to make my hair look good do you", Penny teased.

Randy responded, "Probably not, but you gave yourself away by placing the curling iron on the vanity."

Soon Randy wore a pair of newer starched Wranglers and a starched white western shirt. He had pulled on a pair of brown alligator boots with a matching belt and a shiny championship belt buckle. Draped over his arm was a lightweight navy blue blazer with brass buttons. "Do I look OK", asked Randy.

Penny finished combing her hair as she turned looking him up and down, as if she was highly scrutinizing his appearance. "You cleanup pretty good, cowboy", she exclaimed with a smile. "I'll be ready in a minute." Penny went to get her jewelry case containing the turquoise Rose loaned her. "Randy", she asked, "Where did you get that fancy buckle?"

"I won it at Prescott, Arizona over the fourth of July. I was lucky and drew good steers."

"There you go giving credit to luck again. Randy you're a good steer roper, and everyone knows it. And you attribute it all to luck."

"Well, if everyone knows it, and I take credit for it - that's like bragging. If you brag, your luck will change until you become humble again."

She put on the off-white buckskin dress, which Randy had not seen yet, then Rose's squash blossom necklace with matching earrings, and bracelet. As she slid her feet into the turquoise colored boots before turning toward the mirror for one final look. She adjusted her dress before stepping into the bedroom. "Do I look OK", she asked.

"My God Penny, you look absolutely stunning. I don't think I have ever seen you look as beautiful." Randy stood up and walked over to embrace her giving her a loving kiss.

"Well then, cowboy, let's go to the art show", Penny said with a smile. As they walked out the door, Penny thought *Yes, that's exactly the response I was hoping for.*

Chapter 24

After meeting with management officials at the Department of Homeland Security, the directors of the FBI, DEA, and other key investigative personnel, Secretary Fred Robinson developed a comprehensive investigative plan. Implementation of the plan was immediate. Conducting interviews with premise owners and developing a list of fertilizer suppliers fell to the FBI. The Treasury Department's Commodity Futures Trading Commission and Financial Intelligence Unit, also known as the Financial Crimes Enforcement Network (FinCEN), continued investigate possible financial links to the tainted fertilizer.

Secretary Fred Robinson called Director Dick Kline to inquire if Kline investigated potential financial improprieties. "Yes, Mr. Secretary", said Kline, "I initiated an investigation as soon as President Smyth contacted me regarding temporarily suspending trade in feeder and live cattle commodity contracts and futures trade. I also called FinCEN Director Bill Franklin. Together we began an investigation. At that time, there was nothing detected by our routine monitoring protocols. Therefore, I assigned a team of forensic accountants to look deeper into current contract holders and their trading practices. Bill Franklin assigned senior financial intelligence officers to query these investors hoping to identify additional investments made by them. FinCEN identified additional investments in Exchange Traded Funds on the London Securities Exchange. In every case the investments were in leveraged inverse ETFs purchased on live U.S. cattle. We found there were twenty investment entities globally that made identical investments, all through different foreign exchanges. As we investigated further, we discovered each entity was a new client of the exchange, and in every case the exchanges allowed on-line purchases. Additionally, we ascertained these 20 investments represented about 88 percent of the short live cattle contracts written and about the same percentage for put options purchased. This was accomplished without being detected by our established routine monitoring protocols."

"Do we know who the individual or individuals are who have made these investments", asked Secretary Robinson.

"The short answer Mr. Secretary is no, we don't have a clue. In more detail, we found the investor to be at three 'entities' such as a trust, a holding company, and an investment fund. Each of these entities is foreign, not only to the U.S., but also to where the exchange is located. For example, there was an investment that originated from the Hong Kong Exchange by an entity from Johannesburg, South Africa. Such is the case for all twenty investments. We are drilling down on what we consider to be 'true ownership'." As you can imagine it is slow going and progressively more complex the further the investigation progresses."

"In my thirty-eight years of experience, I have never encountered such complexity in determining ownership of commodity contracts and options. There is no doubt this complex investment strategy is intentionally designed to deceive and protect the principals involved."

"Mr. Franklin, I appreciate you taking the initiative to begin the investigation and getting FinCEN involved. Thank you for your patience in explaining the investment strategy you are investigating. While I understand why your investigation is progressing slowly I must remind you we are dealing with an act of terrorism. Therefore, all of us are on a short timeline to develop information that will move the investigation forward. Would more manpower help you get information more quickly? The DEA and FBI both have forensic accountants and senior financial intelligence officers. If you need additional personnel let me know. Also, know all overtime or compensatory time needed for you to proceed is approved on my authority."

"Mr. Secretary, thank you very much. Let me talk with Bill Franklin and see what he thinks about additional staff. For now, I want to give your offer additional consideration. I certainly would not want to request additional personnel; and have the learning curve of the additional personnel slow the progress of the investigation. That specifically is what I want to ponder."

"That sounds prudent. Again, you have the resources of the government at your request. We need to complete these investigations as soon as possible so we can get the cattle commodity market and related financial markets reopened to trade."

"Yes sir, thank you for your call."

Chapter 25

"I forgot to ask when you startled me in the shower. How did you and the guys end up in the 1st go-round", Penny asked.

"I ended up winning the round, Sonny was fourth, and Junior was moved to seventh. They bumped Sonny down a couple of places and Junior down four places from when we left. Overall, we turned out OK."

"When do you all rope again?"

"Junior goes Saturday afternoon in the performance. Sonny goes Wednesday afternoon in the performance. I end up going the following Saturday in the performance. It looks like since we all placed in the first go-round, the committee selected all of us to rope during performances in the rodeo."

"If you don't rope your second steer until a week from Saturday, when are the finals? I thought they were on Saturday."

"The finals are on Sunday, the final day of the rodeo. I don't particularly like waiting around here so long to rope my second steer but there is an advantage to roping right before the finals. It will tell me about how fast I have to be on two steers to qualify for the finals."

"I thought you just went out there and roped as fast as you could? Why is it important to know how fast you must be on two steers?

"We always want to rope as fast as we can; but if you know how much time you have to rope your steer second steer then it tells you whether you need to take chances. If I had to rope one in 14 seconds, then I would have to take the first throw I had and throw my trip the same time I pulled my slack, a time saving move. Where if I knew I had a little more time, I could hold Blue in a little longer to make sure I had a good trip. Does that explanation make sense to you?"

"Yes", said Penny. "In knowing how fast you need to be, you can adjust the risk level in your roping to give you the highest percentage opportunity to qualify for the finals."

You've got it", said Randy. "By the way, have I told you how beautiful you are?" They were just pulling up in front of the art museum.

Dr. Lucy Cook and her husband Howard invited Dr. Ken Adams and his wife Pam to attend the art show with them. About six months ago Dr. Cook had referred a three-year-old girl, Amy Hamilton, to Dr. Adams for evaluation and possible heart surgery. Amy was in heart failure due to a large hole between the two ventricles of her heart. It was Dr. Cook's first examination of the toddler. Dr. Cook found Amy a sweet child with a grade IV holosystolic murmur with a palpable thrill. Children's Hospital referred Dr. Cook to Dr. Adams who listened as Dr. Cook described her patient's history, physical exam, laboratory tests, and echocardiogram. Both physicians concurred the child's heart required surgical repair. Dr. Adams scheduled little Amy for surgery the following morning.

Amy and her mother, Joyce, were to travel to Denver that afternoon. On arrival Amy required hospitalization forthcoming surgery. Joyce was a single parent, Amy her only child. Joyce had no family or support network; having moved to Cheyenne only two weeks previous. Joyce's car was old and unreliable, concerning Joyce about getting Amy to Denver safely. Joyce shared her concerns with Dr. Cook. Dr. Cook's schedule showed she only worked until noon this day and little Amy was her last patient of the morning.

Dr. Cook, knowing she had nothing of importance to do that afternoon, told Joyce she would take them to Denver and pick them up when Amy was ready to come home. After completing her dictation, she took the file up to the front office and asked one of the transcriptionists to transcribe her dictation STAT as she needed it to take with the patient to Denver.

In less than five minutes Dr. Cook put the transcription into the file with copies of several pages from her computer-generated file and a copy of both the chest X-Rays and echocardiogram. While Dr. Cook gathered the medical records and other information, Joyce went out to her dilapidated old Chevy Caprice and removed the child seat from the car's back seat. Dr. Cook and Amy met Joyce at her old car, transferring the car seat into Dr. Cook's Audi A6 sedan. Once they installed Amy's car seat and fastened Amy securely in the seat, they headed toward Denver.

As Dr. Cook left Cheyenne, she stopped at a drive thru to buy lunch for herself, Joyce, and Amy. In less than two hours Dr. Cook dropped off Joyce and Amy in front of Children's Hospital saying she would go park her car and stay until they got Amy settled in her room. Amy's admission went smoothly, assigning her to a private room in the cardiac section of the hospital. As Dr. Cook was about to walk out of the room, Dr. Adams walked in wearing his surgical greens. They met briefly and Dr. Cook left the room, waiting in the hall to talk more with Dr. Adams. They quickly struck up a collegial friendship.

The following day Dr. Adams called Dr. Cook to tell her how "their" patient was doing post surgically. Dr. Adams said anticipated he would release little Amy about seven days post op. At three days' post op, Amy was recovering well; he gave Lucy Cook (they were now on a first name basis) an update. Dr. Cook cleared her day in the clinic and went to pick up Joyce and Amy. As they drove back to Cheyenne, Amy fell asleep in her car seat remaining asleep all the way back. Dr. Cook learned a great deal about Joyce. She was twenty-four years old and from Kaycee, Wyoming. Joyce had come to Cheyenne to find a job, not yet finding one. She was staying in a cheap motel with a kitchenette. Joyce talked the owner into cleaning rooms in lieu of paying rent. It was the motel owner who told Joyce to take Amy to the doctor noticing the little girl was short of breath, fatigued, and had a dry cough.

Howard Cook was Cheyenne's version of a real estate mogul who owned several apartment houses, a small construction company, and was also in the house flipping business. He learned about Joyce and Amy when Lucy called as she was driving them to Children's in Denver. On the return trip, he received another call from Lucy asking if he was still looking for a resident manager at his new twelve-unit apartment building. In less than five minutes, Howard had a new resident apartment manager and Joyce and Amy had a permanent place to call home. For extra money Joyce cleaned Howard and Lucy's house twice a week. Over the next few months Amy thrived, gaining muscle weight and endurance. She was now a normal three-and-a-half-year-old little girl.

The two physicians and their spouses were standing in the Governor's backyard sipping their drinks. Lucy and Pam were becoming fast friends. There were about 400 people in the back yard and the great room of the Governor's mansion. Traditionally, the governor invited the art show guests to his mansion for drinks and appetizers prior to the opening. The rodeo committee provided the volunteers who served the guests. Pam told Lucy and Howard they may run into their daughter, Penny, and her new boyfriend during the evening. Howard had taken Ken to introduce him to some of his friends. Pam and Lucy were standing in line to get a refill on the chardonnay they were drinking. Lucy looked at the entryway to the governor's great room from the patio; something caught her eye. "Oh my God", said Lucy, "Look at that absolutely striking dress."

Pam quickly looked at the dress and said, "That dress is gorgeous; oh my God, that's my daughter Penny!"

"I want to meet Penny, go bring her over, I'll hold our place in line. She is so beautiful."

Pam walked over to the patio area where Penny and Randy were scoping out the crowd, not recognizing anyone. Pam walked to Penny's side and said, "Penny dear, how are you?" They embraced, then Penny introduced Randy to her mother.

"Nice to meet you Mrs. Adams", said Randy lifting the brim of his black Stetson slightly.

Pam gave Randy a welcoming smile, then took Penny's hand saying, "Come with me you two, there's someone I want you to meet." They walked near a bar set up in the back yard where Pam said, "Penny and Randy, I want you to meet Dr. Lucy Cook. She is a colleague of your Dad's and we're their guests tonight."

"Nice to meet you both", said Lucy. "What do you want to drink? It's about my turn to order."

Penny said, "I think wine, like you and Mom are drinking."

"A beer sounds good", said Randy.

After everyone had a drink in their hand, Lucy led them away from the crowd by the bar and near an open-sided tent with tables displaying multiple platters of hors d'oeuvres.

"Penny", Lucy said, "I think that is the most stunning dress I have ever seen. It is so unique and yet so classy. The squash blossom and matching earrings and bracelet accent it so nicely. Of course, it doesn't hurt that you are a drop-dead gorgeous girl. Randy, you a lucky guy; you have the belle of the ball."

"Thank you, ma'am, I think so too. No offence to either of you two ladies."

Penny saw two men walking toward them. She pulled away from Randy running a couple of steps. "Dad, how are you", Penny said giving him a big hug. "I want you to meet someone. Turning around she reached for Randy's hand slightly pulling him toward her. Dad, this is Randy Bennett; Randy this is my Dad, Ken Adams."

"Hello, Randy. It's nice to meet you. Penny has spoken of you when we've visited on the phone. Your name sounds familiar for another reason, you're here competing in the rodeo; isn't that right?"

"You must be a roper", said Howard Cook, introducing himself. "They're the only ones in town this early", Howard clarified his guess.

"Yes sir", said Randy. "I also like western art. In the past, I've attended the art show several times."

"Have you competed yet", asked Lucy.

"Yes, ma'am, this morning", said Randy.

"How did you do", asked Howard.

"Well sir, I drew a really good steer and was able to put together a decent run. I was kinda lucky."

"Randy, if you're not going to tell them, I am", interrupted Penny. "Randy set a new arena record this morning besting one that had been in existence since 1974. He also won the first go-round. Randy is superstitious, he thinks if he tells people he has done well, they may think he's bragging. And if one is a braggart, his luck will leave him until he becomes humble again."

"Randy", said Ken Adams, "I've never heard it put quite that way, but I think much the same way. As a surgeon, it's easy to let people put you on a pedestal and not remain true to your craft. If you get to believing what people say, something will not go as expected and put you in your rightful place."

"Yes sir, Dr. Adams that's been my experience."

"Randy, can I get you another beer", said Howard Cook. "Does anyone else need anything?"

"Another beer would be fine; but I want Penny to try some of those hors d'oeuvres. The last time I was here, they were a highlight of my trip", said Randy.

"We will be back in a minute", said Penny as she walked with Randy to the tent.

Arriving at the appetizer tent and out of earshot, Penny commented, "Mom really likes you, I can tell. When everyone was asking you about roping, she grabbed my hand and gave me the look of approval. Dad's much like you and most of the time doesn't say much. If he didn't like you, he would not have agreed with you about humility and luck. He might have thought it, but he would not have verbalized his opinion."

Randy filled up two paper plates with various kinds of hors d'oeuvres and cheeses. Penny watched and when Randy got to the end he handed her a plate saying, "After this little ice breaker we go back to the museum to look at the new art. It's a silent auction with open bars all over the place. They aim to take away some of your inhibitions about parting with your cash. When the silent auction is well underway, they open a large tent set up in the parking lot for a delicious buffet style steak supper. I want to make sure you have the opportunity to get something on your stomach, because it's still a few hours until supper."

"I was not going to ruin my appetite with these hors d'oeuvres; but with that information, I'm going to have some. I certainly don't want to get tipsy. I'll share that information with Mom. They don't know the schedule either."

Penny and Randy joined the group as Howard and Ken returned with the drinks. "I see you kids found the appetizers", said Howard handing Randy his beer and Penny a glass of wine.

"Yes, we did", said Penny. "Mom, these are really good, you and Dad need to give them a try. I think you'll find they complement the wine very well."

"They really do look delicious", said Pam. Looking over at Lucy she said, "What do you say we go get some for us and the boys since they made the run for refills?"

"They do look good. Howard, Pam and I are going to get some appetizers for you and Ken. We'll be back in a few minutes."

Randy looked around to see a lady he recognized walking toward him. "Hi, Randy. I don't know if you remember me; three years ago, you bought an oil painting I consigned to the show. It was of some longhorn cattle grazing in a mountain meadow, there was a chuck wagon parked below a big cottonwood tree, and..."

"Certainly, I remember you. You are Lynn Ascot. I have your painting in my living room opposite the fireplace. I didn't want to get it too close to the fireplace, because of the heat and wood resins. I was afraid they might damage it. By the way, congratulations on your selection to last year's class of cowboy artists. I want you to meet my girlfriend, Penny Adams. Penny, this is Lynn Ascot. You know the painting we're talking about."

"It is nice to meet you Lynn. I do know the painting; it is my favorite in the living room. Your use of color in that painting, particularly greens and tans, brings the entire painting together for me."

"Penny it is great to meet you. I am so happy you appreciated the subtle color differences. I meant it to do just that, but I thought it may be too subtle. That is such a beautiful dress and the turquoise accents it so well. You're just gorgeous."

"Thank you. Do you have anything in the show this year", asked Penny.

"Yes, I have a couple of oils, three watercolors, and a small bronze sculpture of an Indian brave. Please come take a look."

"We sure will", said Randy. "Did Frank come up with you?"

"Sadly, no. We lost Frank in December. A bull ran him over while we were working cattle. The kids are just now getting where they can talk about it."

"I'm so sorry to hear that. I'm sure it was hard on all of you. We'll be sure to stop by tonight."

After Lynn walked away, Penny looked at Randy and said, "I expected you to be more empathetic when Lynn said Frank was run over by a bull and killed."

"Frank had the temperament of a pit viper. He was a gluttonous, ill tempered, vile bastard. The year I bought her painting, he knocked over one of the serving tables, ate four or five tenderloin steaks, and I bet two or three pounds of potatoes au gratin, then he ran off. Knowing I was a veterinarian, she asked me if I would give Frank something to make him vomit. I gave him about two ounces of hydrogen peroxide and the food show began."

"Lynn had you treat her husband?"

"Oh God no", laughed Randy. "Her husband's name is Earnest. Frank was an Australian cattle dog. He was the meanest son of a bitch I have ever been around. He bit me four times while I squirted the peroxide into his mouth; then puked on my pant leg and boots. I hated Frank. If he was here, I wasn't going to go by her exhibit. She used to let him lay underneath the display table. He would reach out and bite the ankles of people walking by who weren't paying attention."

Penny laughed so hard that she was holding her stomach. The more Penny thought about Randy's story, the funnier it became. Soon she was laughing so hard she was crying.

Randy laughed, but then again said, "I did, I hated Frank-he was pure evil!" Penny broke out laughing again.

A short time later Penny and Randy climbed aboard a school bus transporting them back to the art museum. The show was open so they walked through the museum. In the atrium sat several vintage wagons on display. Following the crowd, they entered a hallway where western relics and clothing were on display. They passed one of the many bars. Randy asked if she wanted anything to drink. Penny declined. They then walked into the art exhibition area. It was basically as an oval with a wide double sided central isle. Artists displayed their work on both sides of the isle.

Penny found the art to be of high quality, with mostly original art displayed. There were a few limited editions. The bronzes were from small castings and all numbered. Randy and Penny perused each piece, discussing what they liked. Penny thought, *Randy has a much better and more critical eye than I do.*

As they walked past the far end of the oval, a bronze of a young Indian girl caught Penny's eye. She went to examine it more closely. "Randy, this girl reminds me of Sarita. Look, see what you think."

"You're right." It captured Penny and Randy's attention. The more they looked at the detail, the more they liked the piece. Randy examined the base and noticing it was numbered four of five. The artist was well known, a charter member of the Cowboy Artists of America. The piece was relatively small; about eight inches tall with a wider base. Once Penny noticed its price of 17,500 dollars, she was no longer interested. They both visited with the artist a few minutes, then continued onward.

As they walked away, Randy said, "I'm going to the restroom since we're close. I'm also ready for something to drink. Do you want me to get you something as well?"

"Going to the restroom seems like a great idea. I think another glass of wine sounds good. What if I meet you at that bar over there when I'm through", asked Penny.

"That's fine. I'll see you in a few minutes", Randy said walking to the Men's restroom. Coming out of the restroom, Randy returned to the bronze placing a bid for the piece in a small box sitting next to the bronze.

Randy was at the bar sipping his beer and holding a glass of wine for Penny when she returned from the restroom. They continued their leisurely walk looking at each piece of art. They ran into Ken and Pam Adams as they neared the far end of the exhibition. "Are you two enjoying the art", asked Ken.

"Dad, there's some good contemporary western art here. I've discovered that Randy has a good eye for western art. I guess I should have known, since his house if full of it."

Randy responded, "I must confess my sister, Mary, has a much better eye than me. She and her husband attend a western art show and sale in Scottsdale every spring. She's the one who selected much of the art in my house. I add a little to it, when I find something I like."

"Have you found anything you like Mom", asked Penny.

"Oh yes, dear. There are several pieces that I like, particularly some of the landscapes; but they wouldn't go well with our decor."

"How about you Lynn", asked Penny.

"I found a watercolor of horses around a windmill. Howard and I both liked it. It's not real big; but I have just the spot for it in our family room.

"I'm getting hungry", said Pam, "Let's go eat."

As the three couples walked into the large walled tent they found an empty table opposite from the band. Randy placed his Stetson in the middle of the table. They joined the buffet lines, which were moving steadily. Most of the crowd remained in the museum drinking and visiting. The main course was marinated rib eye steaks served with scalloped potatoes, fresh vegetables, and numerous salad choices with warm dinner rolls. They barbequed the steaks just outside the tent. Near the dessert area sat another open bar. Water troughs containing ice cold bottles of water, beer, and pop sat next to the bar. At the end of the bar was a large copper urn filled with iced tea. While Penny picked up a bottle of water, Randy chose iced tea. Returning to the table everyone sat down to eat. Ken and Howard were in a deep discussion regarding owning and managing rental units.

Penny sat on Randy's right, next to her mother. She turned around and asked, "I forgot to ask before, what time do we have to be in Laramie tomorrow?"

"A little before 8:30AM", said Randy. "Things have changed some. Mom and Dad and Philip and Kay Granger are flying in. Dad said he has something he wants to talk with us about. I asked; however, he said it would wait until tomorrow. The meeting with the EM group is still at 1:30PM. Clare Johansen is also coming."

"I knew the Secretary would be there, as well as my new boss Bobby Laporte. I spoke with him early this afternoon. There's going to be a press conference. Dr. Laporte also wanted to see if we could meet again on Friday. I told him I would have to wait and see when you roped again. I'm not going to miss seeing you rope; when I took vacation time to come to Cheyenne."

"I don't know of much going on Friday", said Randy. "You're still planning on going to Denver to see your parents over the weekend, aren't you?"

"I think we should plan to leave after Junior ropes Saturday afternoon. Maybe we can stay down there on

Monday, if Dr. Laporte doesn't have a meeting scheduled with me. Remember, initially I was supposed to meet him Monday afternoon and Tuesday."

Randy laughed and said, "All the changes that keep happening, it's hard to keep things straight. Maybe we need a social secretary?"

Penny laughed and then turned back to join the conversation that Pam and Lynn were having. Randy listened to Ken and Howard for a couple of minutes. Ken, sensing Randy was left out of the conversation, asked Randy, "Penny said you two met when she went to Texas to investigate the CNS disease that has broken out across the country. Have you lost many cattle due to DVE?"

"We continue to lose cattle, but only in the southern feedlots. The three northern feedlots are unaffected. We're very lucky in that regard. My brother-in-law, Larry Shelton, looks over the farming operation. Last fall we decided to implement a different plant rotation and used a new fertilizer designed to increase efficiency of crop production by increasing yields while reducing environmental impact. As you know, the hay became contaminated by fertilizer adulterated with infectious prions. Luckily, Larry only implemented the program on the southern farms. Therefore, only the cattle in the southern feedlots are affected."

"You own six feedlots around Amarillo", asked Howard.

"Oh no sir, they are owned by the ATX Holdings. I'm just the Director of Feedlot Operations", said Randy.

Ken commented, "I was unaware that they had determined the source of the infectious prions. I've been trying to keep up on what's going on since Penny is working on the outbreak."

"Well sir, that information will become public tomorrow. It's not common knowledge yet. Dr. Adams, I understand you are a pediatric heart surgeon. You may not know it, but

Penny it truly a remarkable veterinary pathologist. When she performs necropsies and sampling, she is methodically quick, efficient, and decisive. She has all traits of a good surgeon. I have to think you must have shared some of your training."

"When Penny was a teenager in high school, I did my best to interest her in medicine, particularly surgery. She accompanied me in surgery, where she could get a firsthand look at what surgeons do. She had interest in the technique; but not in the commitment and dedication it takes. She wanted to be a veterinarian. I shared some broad and well-intended advice with her. I told her to be a good scientist, whether a veterinarian or physician, she had to attain an in-depth understanding of how cells work and what happens to them when they become damaged. I also told her regardless of what field in veterinary medicine she would pursue, she would need to be well grounded in anatomy. From what you have told me, she listened beyond my furthest imagination. I can only now understand what she was telling me. She wanted to also be a wife and have a family; the surgeon's life I so proudly exposed her to would simply not allow her to be a wife and mother. Randy, she as that teenager, understood what she wanted and how to get there. Penny has never brought a serious boyfriend home to meet her parents. I have never seen her act the way she has tonight. You are special to Penny, and by extension to Pam and me. Thank you for sharing Penny with us tonight. It's been truly a privilege and a pleasure meeting you tonight. I hope we will be able to spend some time together this weekend. Unfortunately, I do have a case Saturday morning and it will last into the afternoon. As soon as I can, I will be home, so we can get to know each other better."

"Several things have changed since we initially planned our itinerary", said Randy. "Our plan now is to leave Cheyenne Saturday mid-afternoon to travel to Denver. I'm hoping Mrs. Adams did not make plans for Saturday morning. If she has, I'll cancel my commitment, and we'll be there Saturday morning."

"Pam has not made any plans. We wanted to spend some relaxing time with you and Penny. Our hopes were to get to know you better and to spend time with Penny. We don't get to see her very often. Saturday late afternoon will be fine for you and Penny, as well as me. I do think that Sunday late morning Pam has arranged for us all to go to a brunch somewhere with Penny's brothers and their families so they can meet you."

"I would like that very much", said Randy. "It has been a great evening and I have enjoyed meeting you and your friends. I need to sneak back into the museum without Penny's knowledge and take care of a little business. When I return, we're going to have to excuse ourselves. We both have a very busy day tomorrow. My parents and their best friends are flying into Laramie on business. We'll spend the day with them, my sister Rose, her husband, as well as some USDA folks including Penny's boss. We both need to get a good night's sleep."

"I understand Randy. I'll cover for you if Penny asks where you are. Thank you for taking the time to let us get to know you. If we don't speak after you return, I look forward to spending more time with you over the weekend."

Randy casually got up from the table walking outside as if he were going to the restroom. He then walked into the museum to booth where the bronze sat. Briefly Randy visited with the artist and arranged to ship the bronze home. He then wrote a check for the asking price and another for a twenty-five-hundred-dollar donation to the museum. After completing his "business" he returned to join Penny.

A few minutes after returning, Randy put his hand gently on Penny's shoulder to get her attention. She turned giving Randy a loving smile. He said, "We've got an early and full day tomorrow. Perhaps we should head back to the motel?"

Penny and Randy said their good byes leaving for the motel. Randy thought; *this was a good night. Penny and I had fun. I've got a surprise for her. Penny's parents are nice folks; I look forward to spending more time with them this weekend.*

Chapter 26

Secretary of Agriculture Clare Johansen and APHIS Administrator Dr. Bobby Laporte arrived at Joint Base Andrews in the Secretary's chauffer driven Lincoln Town Car. Once inside the large reception area, Air Force personnel shuffled them to a smaller, more private area. Their luggage and briefcases made their way to an Air Force Gulfstream parked on the tarmac and they met the two Air Force pilots who would fly them to Wyoming.

"Madam Secretary, I am Lieutenant Colonel Charles Hardy. It is a pleasure to have you aboard this morning."

Shaking the Lieutenant Colonel's extended hand Clare said, "Lieutenant Colonel Hardy, it's an honor to fly with you this morning.

"Dr. Laporte, I am Major Justin Thompson. I'll be your co-pilot this morning. The weather will be unremarkable during the entire trip.

"Major Thompson, I have no doubt I'll enjoy the trip. Thank you for having me. We appreciate you taking us to Laramie."

"Well folks, it's time we get aboard and head west. Do either of you have any questions? One more thing, Madam Secretary, please call me Charlie."

"Then Charlie, it's Clare for me."

Major Thompson looked at Bobby Laporte and said, Doctor, you can call me Justin, or just swear at me; I've been in the Air Force long enough that I'll respond to either."

"Please call me Bobby", said Dr. Laporte laughingly. *He was glad to see the pilot had a good sense of humor.*

Clare heard all the tower communications when Charlie spoke to the tower. It was fascinating. Soon the aircraft taxied toward the main runway. As Clare and Bobby looked to their left; Air Force One sat on the tarmac, ever ready if an emergency occurs.

Clare felt the engines built power then they rolled down the runway accelerating. Before they were halfway Charlie pulled back and the aircraft was airborne. The rate of assent shocked Clare. She heard the landing gear retract and the aircraft turned left; however, the rate of assent did not change. Clare thought; *if he keeps this up much longer we'll be circling the moon.* Clare heard Charlie speak to the tower, "Four Charlie Eagle to Andrews tower, heading two-seven-three requesting clearance to four-zero-zero. The tower replied; " Four Charlie Eagle, copy, cleared to four-zero-zero at two-seven-three. You guys have a good day." As Clare looked out toward the ground, she could see the freeways around Washington, but could no longer discern individual vehicles. It was more like a strand of traffic.

Within minutes they were at 40,000 feet. "I wonder how fast are we going", Clare asked.

"We're now traveling about Mach 0.8 or roughly 600 miles per hour. Our flight is approximately 1650 miles. So, we'll be in Laramie roughly two hours and forty-five minutes", said Justin.

"This makes flying commercial seem like riding in a cattle car."

In about two and a half hours the Gulfstream G280 taxied up to the terminal parking on the tarmac at an angle to the small terminal building.

As Justin pushed out the stairway, a Gulfstream G550 touched down on the runway. At the far end of the runway they turned on a short ramp to the taxiway that brought the larger business jet back toward the terminal. The Gulfstream G550 parked further down the tarmac at a forty-five-degree angle to the terminal. Within a minute, the stairway near the nose of the aircraft released unfolding down to the concrete tarmac. Beth Bennett and Kay Granger walked carefully down the stairway using the handrail to stabilize them. Momentarily, Philip Granger walked down the stairway. Randall Bennett stood at the top of the stairs talking briefly with the co-pilot before he walked down the stairs while putting on his Stetson. The two couples walked toward the terminal while eyeing the sleek looking smaller jet.

Standing near the front, but off to the side of the jet's nose, Beth loudly said, "Clare?"

Turning around Clare looked down, immediately smiling and said, "Beth and Kay!"

Clare finished coming down the stairway and ran to the two women. All three hugged. The three walked toward the terminal door where Clare noticed Philip and Randall standing. She walked up to Philip give him a hug and a kiss on the cheek saying, "Philip, it has been a long time, too long, it's so nice to see you again." Turning to Randall, she hugged him and gave him a peck on the cheek. "Randall, thank you for coming, although I bribed you. It's so nice to see everyone again."

Soon Bobby and the two Air Force pilots joined Clare. She made the introductions and everyone walked into the terminal. Larry, Rose, Randy, and Penny were in the terminal. Both pilots carried the luggage they had retrieved from the storage compartment. Randall, please introduce Justin and Charlie to your family."

Randall made the introductions.

Randall smiled asking, "What brings the Air Force out this way? I can't think it is a routine thing to deliver government officials to meetings."

"We were in DC yesterday for some meetings at the Pentagon; we were traveling to Warren Air Force Base in

Cheyenne so Secretary Johansen and Dr. Laporte hitched a ride with us. The two pilots walked around their aircraft in preflight inspection and climbed the foldable stairway soon the powerful engines started to whine and they taxied on the tarmac to the south end of the runway. The jet engines roared and the jet was airborne by the time it reached the terminal. As the aircraft gently gained altitude while it turned left toward Snowy Range, and made a half circle placing them traveling east above the terminal. They rocked their wings as they approached the terminal as a way of waving goodbye to everyone.

Chapter 27

Ryan Anderson, Drug Enforcement Administration Administrator, was rereading an intelligence report from Hugo Mendez the District Manager of the Laredo, Texas District Office. He recalled a Laredo field agent reported hearing of fertilizer smuggled into the US through Mexico. Both the agent and Hugo found this unusual as importation of fertilizer from Mexico into the US was routine, requiring minimal documentation due to the North American Free Trade Agreement. He also wondered why this information would originate from a Mexican drug informant. At the time of the report, everyone thought the information to be benign and extraneous, having little intelligence value. Unfortunately, the report was eight months old and did not contain further detail.

Mendez answered his ringing phone; "Laredo DEA, Mendez can I help you?"

"Hugo, its Ryan Anderson. How are you this morning?"

"Fine Boss, what's new?"

"Hugo, I was reviewing an intelligence report you wrote about eight months ago. The report referenced an informant reporting the smuggling of fertilizer into the US through Nuevo Laredo. At the time, none of us thought much about the information. I'm wondering if you have any additional detail? Apparently, it involved several truckloads."

"Boss, let me see what I can dig up in my files and notes. Sadly, I don't think there's going to be much. Is it OK if I get back with you this afternoon, last night we made a bust; I was just leaving to attend the after-action briefing?"

"That's fine, Hugo. Thanks."

Anderson sat in his chair thinking. *Nuevo Laredo is a lucrative drug corridor because of the large volume of trucks* passing through. Over forty percent of all cargo crossings from Mexico to the United States cross through border checkpoints in Nuevo Laredo, then to I-35. But why smuggle fertilizer? What information were the smugglers trying to hide? Perhaps they did not want to divulge the originating location of the fertilizer or where it was going. Without this information, it became much more difficult track either back to the Consignor or forward to the Consignee. If the trailer making the delivery had a false bottom, it could also contain illicit drugs. I must see if there was any intelligence regarding large drug shipments around that timeframe. Nuevo Laredo is Los Zetas territory, the most vicious of the Mexican drug cartels. There must be more to this than fertilizer.

Anderson turned to his computer and searched electronically filed reports for Laredo and San Antonio for the past year. He read all the intelligence reports for the two districts to see if there were any other references to smuggled fertilizer. He could find none. However, about the same time as the smuggled fertilizer reference, a preponderance of intelligence concerned a large shipment of heroin destined for the US. Supposedly it was to go through Nuevo Laredo up I-35 to San Antonio for distribution. The DEA failed to identify the shipment or shipments; however, there were a string of deaths due to overdoses in Chicago, New Orleans, Houston, Dallas/Fort Worth, San Antonio, Phoenix, Las Vegas, San Diego, Los Angles, San Francisco, Denver, and Kansas City. Laboratory analysis showed the heroin to be pure, from a single source, and originating in Afghanistan.

"Good afternoon Boss Man", said Hugo Mendez. I checked through my notes. I had no more on the fertilizer; then it clicked in my memory. We had also gotten word of a big shipment of heroin to be coming through Nuevo Laredo. I spoke with my informant after lunch; he remembered more information. According to him, the fertilizer and the heroin were from the same source, a southwestern Asian businessman. It was a shit-load of fertilizer, like twelve to fifteen container loads. He thought the heroin came in on the same containers. The shipment arrived at the Port of Tampico. From there up to Monterrey, eventually crossing the border at Nuevo Laredo. Apparently, it was high grade pure heroin when it arrived and the Zetas cut it in Monterrey. My informant says the cartel paid a hundred million dollars for the heroin; getting the price of the fertilizer upon delivery to somewhere in the US. He said the fertilizer arrived in five-gallon plastic containers with the labels showing manufacture in the U.S. As they processed the heroin, they send it with a truckload of fertilizer.

"Did your informant know where it traveled to in the US?"

"He didn't know where it went once it got on our side of the border. He did say it was a huge deal for the Zetas. They watched things carefully on both sides of the border. I wish we could have gotten the drugs; I don't know how we could have missed that much. I'm going to do some further checking to see if I can determine why we missed that much."

"Hugo that's a good exercise, but we'll probably never find out. I'm sure all the cartel's resources went into getting that much heroin across the border and distributed. I'm betting they cleared at least three hundred million dollars. That much money will pay off lots of people."

"That's all I got for you today, Boss."

"Thank you for checking out this issue and getting additional information. I'll call you, if I need anything else. Good job, Hugo."

"Thanks Boss."

Anderson called the Monterrey, Mexico DEA office to speak with agent Felix De la Garza. He asked him to investigate a large quantity of heroin supposedly arriving in Port of Tampico and transported to Monterrey for processing about eight months ago. There may be a link between the heroin and fertilizer. The fertilizer arrived in five-gallon plastic buckets with labels stating it USA origin. Both the heroin and fertilizer may have originated in Afghanistan or Pakistan. Reportedly, the supplier was a southwestern Asian businessman.

Felix said he'd look in the matter; he'd travel to the Port of Tampico in a few days. However, Felix commented if this was a deal with the Los Zeta cartel, no one who would provide any information fearing death. He said the Zetas are ruthless with many connections in every location where they did business.

Anderson said he would not get his hopes up. De la Garza said he would contact him within a week.

"Boss, its Hugo Mendez. I was visiting with Dan Cook; he's a Texas Ranger working in their Special Operations Group. Remember when you asked me to go to Costa Rica undercover some months ago? Earlier this afternoon I was talking with Dan; he mentioned something that happened while I was gone. Their intelligence identified drug runners were crossing over the border, then trans-loading semitrailers with smuggled contraband. They were using the shipping docks at an old slaughter house and meat warehouse. The Rangers, local police, and the ATF set up a sting operation. That sting went down around the time of the fertilizer and heroin smuggling. Anyway, when they raided the dock area of the warehouse they found a five-gallon bucket of fertilizer. They still have it locked in Border Security's Operation Center as evidence in the other case. Apparently, they were smuggling weapons into Mexico. I'm going to a look at the fertilizer bucket tomorrow morning. Because it may be important to what you're working on, I thought I would give you a call. It's my intent to take some digital photographs. I'll e-mail them to you tomorrow."

"I also found out a little more about how this operation was working. Texas did a lot of surveillance before making their sting. They may have even observed the fertilizer and heroin coming in without knowledge of what was going on. At any rate, an old semi-truck with a beat-up trailer would pull into one dock. Then a couple of vans would park along the dark side of the building with several men in each van. They entered through a side door to stage whatever was in the old trailer next to an empty dock door. Later, a new truck and trailer backed into an adjacent dock door. The crew from the vans emptied the new trailer into the old one, subsequently filling the new trailer with whatever had just crossed the border. They'd change the identity of the new truck using different license plates and put magnetic signage on the truck's doors with false Department of Transportation registration numbers. Dan said the whole operation took about twenty minutes. The docks had two forklifts used for trans-loading. He said the vans pulled up accompanied by three or four dark nondescript vehicles each with two armed men. The vehicles parked around the building establishing a perimeter. When the raid took place, they took down all four perimeter vehicles, the two vans, and both truck/trailer rigs. He also said no one who was arrested has said anything; personal documents and Mexican criminal records tie them to the Los Zetas."

"I'll see if I can find out more while I'm at the Border Security Operation Center tomorrow. Hopefully this will help with what you are working on."

"Hugo, that helps a lot. I have a meeting at Homeland tomorrow. I'll share this information. To my knowledge, this is all new information. Let me know if you find out anything else. Thanks, and say hello to Maria for me when you get home."

"I will Boss, have a good night."

Chapter 28

"Where are we headed," asked Randall Bennett.

"To the Trails End Country Club for breakfast and an overdue opportunity to visit", said Clare. "I'm told it's near here; they are opening the restaurant early for us. It will be private and relaxing."

"Before we go, I need to make a quick phone call. It will only take a minute." Shortly, Randall walked back toward the group gathered around Randy's rented Escalade and Ray's Tahoe. "I called the pilots; they are going to come with us. Here they come now. Clare, why don't you and Beth and Kay jump in the backseat while Philip and I ride up front with Larry? Rose, if you would please, travel with Randy, Penny, Dr. Laporte, and the two pilots in the Escalade."

"I know where the Country Club is", said Larry. "Randy, follow me".

In ten minutes both vehicles parked in front of the Trails End Country Club. As everyone exited the vehicles Randy looked at one pilot saying, "I know you. Aren't you Rick Phillips?"

"Yes, Randy I am."

"What are you doing flying the charter? I would think you're busy enough running an oil company and refinery. What gives?

"Randy, Mike called me a few days ago asking if he could charter my jet for your Mom and Dad as well as Philip and his wife to fly up here. I've been busy at the refinery and haven't done any traveling, so I said yes. I would not have done it for anyone other than Mike and Randall."

"Last night my co-pilot was playing baseball with his 13-year-old son, his son hit him in the mouth with a line drive.

The ball broke off three upper teeth and one lower tooth. A dental emergency, he called it."

"Anyway, he's having dental surgery this morning; so, I decided to play hooky and go flying. I was about twenty-one the last time I saw your Dad; he has not recognized me. I want to surprise him when we land at Amarillo."

"While your group is off doing your thing, Buzz and I are going to rent some clubs and play golf. Let me give you my card. My cell number is on it; just give us a call when you're close to returning. We will get a ride back to the airport and be ready to take off when y'all arrive. This has been more fun than I have had in months."

Rick and Randy walked to the front door of the Country Club. Randy opened the door to walk in. Rick said, "I'm going to the pro shop to get some golfing duds. We'll see you back at the airport. Y'all have fun."

Randy walked to the club's dining room looking around. Secretary Johansen sat with his mother and Aunt Kay near a window. They were reminiscing about their college days at Texas Tech and laughing. Randall and Philip sat at another table with Larry. It appeared they were talking business, but not a serious conversation based upon their relaxed faces and body language. Penny sat with Rose and Bobby Laporte. Everyone seemed relaxed, smiling, and visiting. Randy chose an empty chair between Penny and Rose. Penny introduced Randy to Bobby as he sat down. They shook hands. Coffee carafes sat on each table and everyone sipped coffee while visiting. The kitchen staff set up a breakfast buffet line; the aroma of which slowly drifted toward the tables, whetting everyone's appetite.

Rose said to Randy, "I understand you approved of the dress Penny and I picked out for the art show."

"The dress was absolutely stunning. Penny looked gorgeous. She was much too beautiful to be accompanying me."

"You didn't look half bad either, cowboy", said Penny with a loving smile. "Rose the jewelry was the perfect accent. Thank you again."

"Bobby", Randy said, "we attended an art show and sale event in Cheyenne at the art museum last night. It's a nice, laid-back event that kicks off the rodeo which follows for the next ten days. It's always a fun time; they draw well known western artists. We had a great time, actually running into Penny's parents."

"You roped yesterday morning didn't you", asked Rose. "Did you do well?"

"Yeah, I roped yesterday morning, drew a really good steer. I did OK, but I'll need to put two good runs together to make the finals."

"When do you rope again?"

"Next Saturday."

The club manager came to the middle of the room and announced the breakfast buffet was ready, and everyone should help themselves. Randall and Philip arose, moving to the table where their wives were sitting and accompanied them and Clare to the buffet line. Larry escorted Rose. Rose introduced Larry to Bobby. After breakfast, Randall said, "Clare, when you have time this morning Philip and I would like a few minutes of your time to tell you about something we've been working on."

"Now is as good of time as any", said Clare.

Philip, who was sitting next to Clare, stood assisting her with her chair. Randall led them toward the opposite side of the dining room near a window overlooking the golf course.

With a welcoming smile Clare sat at the table saying, "OK, what have you boys got up your sleeves now?"

"Clare", Philip began, "as you may know Randall and I are on the Board of Regents at Texas Tech. With this DVE outbreak we've both come to realize there's not very much known about infectious prion proteins. The similarity between DVE and some of the human diseases is astounding; diseases such as multiple sclerosis and Alzheimer's disease. As Randall and I discussed this issue, it became clear to us there is not a centralized location devoted to research and the study infectious prion proteins. We think there should be a National Prion Center, and we think it should be located at Texas Tech. It is our vision, the center would be a joint venture between the College of Agriculture, the School of Medicine, and the Graduate School of Biomedical Sciences."

Randall continued, "We presented this concept to the board at a recent meeting. There was unanimous approval by the board and the Chancellor to proceed. We wanted you to be aware of what we are planning and hope you will support this endeavor. We think within a year we can have the program up and running, and within two years we will have a research and teaching facility up and running."

"From what you have told me, it sounds like there are many synergies within the existing university structure you intend to capitalize on", said Clare. "Bringing in the College of Agriculture is smart. That will certainly allow Tech to compete for upcoming funding that's part of emergency supplemental funding bill. I like the concept and its location. As you go forward, let me know where I can help."

"Clare, you may recall the other day when we spoke, I asked how much money would be included in the supplemental funding bill for research. I understood you to say somewhere between three and four billion. As I reflected on that number, I think it may be too much money to throw at this problem all at once. If you spread it over several years, I think you would get more bang for your buck. I would also hope there would be additional funding to follow for those researchers who significantly contributed to the main mission. One of my concerns is you can't fund a national research center with a one-time outlay of funds, or even if it's spread over three years. It may be worthy of consideration to create endowed research positions, specifically targeted toward institutions who are making long term investments into programs that specifically address the nation's research needs. Endowed positions will allow gifted researchers to focus on continuing research, rather than worrying about where funding for the next grant will originate. Philip also had a good idea; he wonders if productive Agricultural Research Service scientists could serve one to five-year postdoctoral sabbaticals at established research centers. It would serve to recharge their batteries, as well as bring new blood and ideas to academic research centers. We proffer these ideas your consideration."

"Frankly", said Clare, "we have not given the research funding details much thought at all. Our primary focus has been on getting the emergency supplemental funding bill written and to President Smyth for him to submit to congress. We need to get the bill passed as soon as possible; so, we can begin the indemnification process. Your thoughts demonstrate much more forethought than the department has given to research funding. Your thoughts are important to me. I promise you I will give them very serious consideration. Before submitting the bill to congress, I will critically read the bill ensuring the language provides me the discretion to outlay funding grants over several years, endow research positions, and create ARS postdoctoral sabbaticals. Should you fellas come up with other thoughts, please give me a call. I value your input. I need to get you two together with President Smyth. He needs advisors like you two; intelligent, straight talking, and sincerely trying to do the right thing for the right reasons.

"Clare thanks for your time", said Philip. "We appreciate you listening and your support; but, we do not want to monopolize any more of your time."

"Gentlemen, any time I have the opportunity to visit with you, I learn something. Your approach to problem solving takes a wide view of the issues and your solutions are long term and comprehensive. Thank you for sharing your ideas and plans with me. Hopefully together we can maximize the benefits from the research funds."

During Randall and Philip's private discussion with Clare, Larry and Rose joined Beth and Kay. Bobby, Penny, and Randy started a serious discussion about DVE.

Bobby asked, "Penny have you had the opportunity to look at the histopathology from the non-symptomatic cattle yet?"

"I have about thirty slides to go and it will be complete. I doubt that the last 30 slides will show anything much different than the 270 that I have already read. In general, what Pat and I have both seen is an earlier stage of DVE. The vacuoles are smaller, there's more inflammation. Based upon the consistent histopathology, I think we have no choice other than depopulation of entire premises where we have confirmed DVE or cattle have consumed tainted foodstuffs. I know this recommendation is aggressive and the most expensive regarding indemnification; but, it is the only alternative that protects public health."

"Penny, I think this is the only alternative we can scientifically justify. Doing anything less would be capricious. I'd much rather testify in front of congress supporting the decision to depopulate, than to try to justify why we did not."

"Me too", said Penny.

"That brings me to the issue of carcass disposal", said Bobby. I read Penny's report on the incinerators. It was more comprehensive than expected. By the way Randy, thank you and ATX for being so open regarding the design, specifications, etc. To my knowledge, ATX has the only carcass incinerators of any size in the U.S. I commend you on your foresight to have them installed at all your feedlots. Do either of you have any good ideas how we can properly dispose of all the carcasses from everywhere in the US other than ATX?"

"Before we get really into that discussion", commented Penny, "I think we should address an additional piece of information. We just discussed the need for premise depopulation; but, we don't know how long symptomatic and non-symptomatic cattle will remain alive. This information is important in determining approximately how much time we have to get them or something else constructed to fill the need."

"Penny, you're right", said Bobby. "I suppose you have given this some thought?"

"Actually, Randy and I discussed it a little. Randy's agreed to let us use ATX cattle at the three DVE positive lots for this trial. Other trials could go on at other locations, if there was a need. Obviously, this trial would run in unison with construction of carcass disposal units or sites."

"I agree this information is important. Hopefully, it will be a thoughtful method to buy us some time. Randy, you, and your family have put this investigation where it is today. Are you sure you want the 'terminal studies' to be done at ATX facilities?"

"I don't see a down side. On issues of animal health and feedlot operations the AXT board will defer to my judgment. We already have carcass disposal units in place and operable.

It makes common sense not to create a nuisance or public health problem. When something dies or euthanized, we can dispose of it immediately. That can't be said for the other infected premises."

"That sounds good to me. I'll let Secretary Johansen know."

Hearing her name Clare walked to the table and said, "Did I overhear my name being mentioned?"

"Yes, ma'am you did", said Bobby. He then recanted the discussion regarding the terminal studies. "Randy is agreeable to having this study done at ATX's three DVE infected feedlots. Penny will oversee the studies as part of her special assignment."

"I agree this is important information you'll need. It sounds like you have a plan in place."

Clare sat down at the table, looked at Penny and Randy and said, "While we have not been introduced, I'm Clare Johansen. Penny, I have heard so many good things about you, I want to thank you personally for all the work you have done and continue to perform regarding DVE. Your knowledge and expertise is an invaluable asset. If there is anything I can ever do for you dear, please let me know."

"Thank you, ma'am", said Penny humbly.

"Randy, I've known your Mom and Dad since our college days at Tech. I cannot tell you how much you and your family have contributed to us getting a handle on DVE; what causes it and how it came to affect this nation's cattle. I can tell you, without reservation, we would not be where we are without ATX's involvement."

"Thank you, ma'am", responded Randy. "Mom and Dad hold you in high regard, as do I. While we would have just as soon avoided this malady, we are happy to cooperate and willing to participate in learning as much as we can about this disease and how to best manage the issues it brings with it."

Clare smiling said, "Now, let's address the elephant in the room, carcass disposal. Randy, you are the technical and practical expert on this problem. Please participate in this discussion. It is my understanding we cannot deal with DVE infected carcasses in a traditional manner because prions are so difficult to inactivate. This was also a major problem in Great Britain when they dealt with BSE. Do you have any suggestions?"

Randy began the discussion saying, "When I was doing postgraduate studies I learned of the problems Great Britain was having with carcass disposal. I explored several options. Digesters have limited capacity and there are issues regarding residual chemical disposal. Trenches with wood or coal as fuel simply do not burn hot enough to destroy prions. I concluded that only a giant crematorium would provide even burning at high enough temperatures to ensure total carcass disposal. I spoke with my brother Bobby, he's a mechanical engineer. We brainstormed design, practicality, fuel source, and related requirements. Bobby developed a design and he made six, one for each of the feedlots. In my opinion, they do the job we need. We additionally harvest the resulting oils and minimally process them into biodiesel which we use to fuel our equipment and vehicles. Our units have a capacity of about 65 head, depending upon carcass size. This process works well for us, even now when we're using frequently. Penny reviewed the process; making some recommendations which specifically address the challenges of dealing with massive volume increases. I'll let her discuss those recommendations."

Penny continued, "Perhaps the first thing I should mention is Bobby Bennett had the foresight to patent the crematorium design. I basically made three recommendations. The first is to remove the hides and viscera prior to putting the carcasses into the incinerator. This significantly reduces or eliminates the noxious odor of burning hair and hide, which might pose problems in some locations. If we skin the carcasses, we can market the green hides to a third-party processor. My second recommendation is to run the eviscerated carcasses through a pre-breaker and hasher, then auger the material into the incinerator. Pre-breaking and hashing reduce particle size, thereby increasing capacity, and reducing cycle time. I included eviscerating carcasses and conveying the viscera to the crematorium in my recommendations. This procedure allows the pre-breaker and hasher to function efficiently. It may increase the necessity for clean-up between batches. My third recommendation is to explore the possibility of designing and building mobile modular units to use where multiple smaller operations are located. Honestly, I don't know if this is feasible. However, from my cursory review of the investigative reports, particularly the more recent reports, indicate we need to plan for the destruction of carcasses from small and very small operators as well as large operators."

"Penny your recommendations are thoughtful and practical. Does anyone have any idea of how many stationary units and mobile units we are talking about", asked Clare.

Bobby replied, "Ma'am, I don't think anyone has given this any thought, unless it would be Penny or Randy."

Both Penny and Randy indicated they had not.

Clare stood making eye contact with Randall she asked, "Do you and Philip have a moment to join us?"

Both men joined the discussion on carcass disposal. Clare brought them up to speed on the discussion. She then said. Randall, I'm told your son Bobby designed, patented, and constructed the crematoriums for ATX's feedlots. Would he be interested in constructing some for the government? We don't know how many we will need, or where they might ultimately be located. We would also like you to design and build mobile units. Does Bobby have the time for such a project?"

Randall hesitated a few seconds before responding, "Clare, I don't know specifically what Bobby has on his plate. I know he has a crew salvaging an old refinery down by Midland. As I remember Bobby made those incinerators out of salvaged materials. Someone needs to discuss this with Bobby and he is out-of-pocket for a few days. His daughter has been ill; they've taken her to Mayo Clinic in Rochester for some advanced diagnostic testing and evaluation. He expects to be back Tuesday or Wednesday of next week. However, I'll say we'll do what we can to help you get this equipment made. I should tell you, if you are planning on making them stationary units like we did, you'll need them close to a good source of natural gas. I don't know what type of permitting is necessary or who would have regulatory oversight. Philip do you remember what Bobby made those units from?"

"You're right, they were made from something Bobby salvaged", said Philip. "Clare, if I may suggest; you might consider locating the units on property already owned by the US government, preferably the military. That will cut through all the red tape in permitting, air quality, etc. Because the funding originates from an emergency appropriations bill, DVE is a national emergency. In these situations, the government has wide latitude implementing its response. You can side-step that further by locating them on government owned lands. I'm sure your legal staff can help you with that once you pull the right political strings. If one considers piles of cattle carcasses lying around decomposing at numerous locations awaiting disposal, and being hamstrung to do anything because of regulatory concerns; the situation quickly becomes a sanitary problem and a public health emergency."

"Regarding the patented design of the crematoriums, I will speak for Randall and Bobby; saying ATX will charge a token royalty for each unit constructed by a third party, if Bobby is unable to take on the task. It may be necessary to have multiple contractors constructing these units to meet legitimate time constraints. It will also clean up the transaction between ATX and the USDA. Neither ATX, nor you, want the appearance of conflict of interest or appearance of favoritism."

"I don't know what I would do without you two. Once again, you've both demonstrated the wide view of your problem-solving skills accompanied with comprehensive solutions. Philip, I appreciate your suggestions and advice. Bobby, why don't we have Penny contact Bobby Bennett, once he gets back home? She knows the issues and maybe you can have someone determine how many we'll need and the ideal locations for the crematoriums, so Penny will have that information when she meets with Bobby. I'll work on the political side, getting them on military reservations."

"With that, I need to visit with Rose and Larry, as well as my girlfriends. We have about an hour before we leave for lunch in the faculty dining room at the University of Wyoming. You will meet my good friend Dr. Lucy Ingram, the university's president, and the deans of the college of Arts and Sciences and Agriculture. Wyoming's congressional delegation could be there, but I think they're in DC."

Clare left the table sitting down between Beth and Kay. Looking across the table she said, "Larry and Rose, please don't leave. I came over to talk specifically with Larry. I must thank you from both me and President Smyth. Without your collaboration, we as a nation would not be where we are today. Larry your efforts alone led us to uncover a highly technical and brilliantly designed act of bioterrorism. I will share with you, and everyone at this table, that Homeland Security is investigating this as an act of bioterrorism. It appears DVE is part of a larger plan involving an effort to manipulate the cattle commodities market and commodity ETF trading on the London Stock Exchange. These investigations are underway as I speak. I would not be surprised if you are not contacted by an FBI agent soon."

"Again Larry, I wanted to convey thanks from me, President Smyth, and a grateful nation. We're going to have a short news conference after the meeting this afternoon where I will recognize Ray and the other University of

Wyoming scientists. We will let the press know these scientists discovered absorption of the tainted fertilizer by alfalfa plants and then consumption of the alfalfa by cattle. When the reporters ask more specific questions, we'll decline citing we're not going to interfere with an on-going investigation. The president and I spoke about involving you and the Bennett family now. We chose not to do so because we did not want you to endure an onslaught of investigative reporters."

"That's fine Clare, we don't need any recognition", said Randall. "But we're certainly pleased that you chose to recognize these fine scientists."

Bobby, still sitting with Randy and Penny, asked, "Penny, I was wondering if we could meet tomorrow with Dr. Yu instead of next Monday and Tuesday?"

"Sure, I don't know we're doing anything specific tomorrow; do you have anything planned", she asked Randy.

"No, I thought we might just kick back and relax. We've been busy ever since we arrived in Wyoming. We do have a full Saturday with Junior roping in the performance, then going to see your parents in Denver."

"Where are you staying tonight", asked Penny.

"I thought I would get a room there somewhere in Cheyenne."

"Do you have reservations in Cheyenne already", asked Randy.

"No, my secretary tried a couple of places, but they were full. I told her not to worry, I would find a room somewhere."

Randy said, "Let me make a call and see if we can get you in the Cheyenne Club Inn where we're staying. During the rodeo, the town fills up and motel rooms are hard to come by. Over the years I have always stayed at the Cheyenne

Club Inn. I think the desk clerk knows who we are; she'll help us, if she can."

Randy stepped away from the table and searching for the number to the motel. Penny asked, "Are we planning on going to Fort Collins tomorrow to meet with Dr. Yu?"

"Yes, I thought it would be good for you to meet him in person; and I think you will provide valuable input to our discussion from a field and lab perspective as we do the postmortem on the in-depth investigations. I'll rent a car and then return it in Fort Collins or Denver."

"Rental cars may be harder to come by than motel rooms. We rented the Escalade we're driving in Denver. We can use that vehicle tomorrow, if you like. Randy and the guys will have Randy's pickup to run around in when they feed."

"I hate to impose; but if you don't mind, that will work out fine for me. I'll have Dr. Yu sign a GSA car out to me and then he can take me to the airport on Sunday."

Randy returned smiling. "The Cheyenne Club Inn was able to find you a room, if you don't mind sleeping in a heart shaped bed with a mirror on the ceiling? Randy could tell by his hesitant look Bobby was not comfortable with the arrangements. Before he could answer, Randy said, "Not really, Bobby. You've got a regular room with a king size bed...I just couldn't help seeing your reaction."

Bobbie walked over to the other table to remind Clare it was about time to leave for the university. He also told the group what Randy had done in jest, telling them about the honeymoon suite. Everyone broke out in laughter as they walked to the door.

Chapter 29

Anne Burke, Director of Plant Protection and Quarantine (PPQ), was holding a video conference call with her Area Managers about the tainted nano-fertilizer contaminating Alfalfa. Bobby Laporte had tasked her with tracing down the adulterated fertilizer and the affected farm products and fields. Her team began by gathering information from the investigation reports that were available online. The United States Federation of Farmers Cooperatives (USFFC), a central distribution warehouse Oklahoma City received the nano-fertilizer.

Conrad Sutherland, an Investigative and Enforcement Services officer, traveled to the firm and met with the cooperative's general manager. Conrad first told the firm's general manager, Gerry Erickson, recent research demonstrated adulteration of nano fertilizer with nanoparticles containing the DVE prion. Erickson was shocked, initially becoming defensive of the product. Sutherland stated his purpose was not to place blame; rather to gather information hoping to control the devastating DVE outbreak. Conrad requested the firm's cooperation and assistance by providing information. He inquired if USFFC had records showing purchase of the fertilizer by USFFC and to whom they sold the product, including the volumes received and sold. Erickson said they kept complete computerized records of their inventory, but he would have to get permission from USFFC's president before he could release such information. Erickson made the call with Sutherland sitting in his office. Dean Fortenberry, USFFC's president, answered. Erickson informed him of the allegations and the information requested by Conrad Sutherland. Fortenberry listened intently before responding. He said the allegations were very serious and he wanted to consult with USFFC's legal counsel before doing anything. Fortenberry said he would call Erickson back within thirty minutes.

Twenty minutes later, Erickson answered the call by pushing the speakerphone button on his phone and advising Fortenberry he was on speakerphone with Sutherland in the room. Fortenberry said that was fine. Erickson requested to see Sutherland's credentials. Sutherland reached into his right hip pocket pulling out a thin tri-fold wallet. It showed Sutherland was an Investigator with the USDA, displayed a color photograph of him, and a brass shield identifying him as a USDA Investigator. Erickson relayed the information to Fortenberry who then said, "Gerry, give him anything he requests. We want to cooperate fully with the USDA on this issue."

After ending the call, Erickson apologized for the delay saying, "Nothing like this has ever happened; I didn't know how to respond."

"That's fine", responded Conrad. "I don't want anyone to get in trouble. It may take a few minutes to get things cleared, that's just part of doing business. Do you have any questions about what information I am requesting?"

"No, I don't think so. I'll get you all the invoices we paid when we purchased the fertilizer as well as a summary and I'll do the same for sales of the fertilizer to our members. The sales invoices will include the addresses and phone numbers of our customers. You know, I remember something that was out of the ordinary about when the fertilizer was delivered."

"What's that", asked Conrad.

"The fertilizer came from Advanced Fertilizers" in Salina, KS. "When their salesman came here last fall about purchasing the fertilizer, he gave us a bunch of information and brochures to distribute. After we agreed to purchase the fertilizer, he said it was Advanced Fertilizers' policy to pay for the product on delivered by giving the truck driver the payment. He said Advanced Fertilizers required payment to be in the form of a certified check or cash. Saying it is Advanced Fertilizers' policy to not accept business or personal checks. For every truck load of fertilizer delivered, I had to go down to the bank and get a certified check. Every time a delivery was made they were waiting when we opened. I'd have to wait for the bank to open to get their check."

"I have never heard of anything like that before", said Conrad. "Were the checks made out to Advanced Fertilizers?"

"Yes, another unusual thing I noticed was the certified checks were all cashed at the same bank in Laredo, Texas. According to the labels on the five-gallon buckets, Advanced Fertilizers makes the nano in Salina, Kansas."

"Were the trucks sealed when they arrived here at your warehouse?"

"I don't know. We can check with the guys down at the dock, maybe they will remember. Let me give the information you requested to my assistant, Justin. He'll get to work pulling the information together. I think it will take him an hour. Do you want to stay while he puts it together or come back?"

"I have a few more questions for you, but after we check with the guys on the dock, I think I will leave and come back."

"What other questions can I answer for you?"

"Gerry, do you recall how many five-gallon containers of the fertilizer you purchased?"

"We ordered 25,000 containers", said Gerry looking at a computer screen on his desk. However, we only received 24,999 containers. They must have lost or broken one."

"Of the 24,999 containers did you sell all of them, or do you have some still in inventory?"

"Let me see, my inventory shows we sold all the containers, but then we had 287 returned from Razorback

Cooperative in Magnolia, Arkansas. We sold 225 of those to Greenfields Coop in Garden City, Kansas and the remaining 62 to Circle Coop in Imperial Nebraska. So, we do not have any in inventory."

"Let's see what your dock guys have to say about whether the trucks were sealed", said Conrad.

Gerry called all the dock workers to the receiving/shipping docks asking, "Do you guys remember that fertilizer that we received in the five-gallon buckets from Advanced Fertilizers?"

All the dock workers nodded their heads yes. Gerry then asked, "Do you remember if the trucks were sealed when they arrived here?"

A worker spoke. "I remember that none of them had seals that we had to break. Some of the drivers said they broke the seals before backing up to the docks, but they didn't show us the seals. Those trailers always arrived during the night hours. Every time they were ready to unload as soon as we came to work in the morning. I don't mean to sound racist or anything; but all the drivers were Mexican, and everyone had a relatively new truck. All the trucks had different magnetic signs on the truck doors with their DOT numbers. The drivers could speak and understand English, but not well. It seemed like they all were in a hurry to unload and leave, but they didn't help us unload. Most stood over by the trees in the shade, away from their trucks and trailers. Most drivers don't get very far away from their rigs. These guys were different, kind of nervous. Once they got their checks, they got the hell out of Dodge. I think I saw one driver twice. All the others only delivered one load. I also noticed, all the trailers were unmarked and a couple had refrigeration units on them. I wondered at the time; why would a guy who could haul perishable items be hauling five-gallon containers of fertilizer. It just didn't make sense. Refer units can charge almost double per mile what straight freight charges."

Conrad thanked Gerry and the dock workers for their information. He told them he would have lunch and would be back to pick up the information they were getting for him. He also said if they remembered anything else about the trucks or deliveries, he would listen to them when he returned.

On return to USFFC warehouse, Conrad picked up the information he requested. Gerry said he had no further comments, but he would contact him if something pertinent came up. Conrad waved to several of the dock workers as he left the warehouse. None attempted to stop him or get his attention. Looking at his watch, it was 12:45PM. He drove to Salina, Kansas to request Advanced Fertilizers shipping documents. Maybe they distributed the fertilizer to other vendors and USFFC. He punched 3800 West Interstate Road into his rental car's navigation system and headed north through Oklahoma City to Wichita and then on to Salina.

According to his navigation system, Advanced Fertilizers was near I-70 on the west side of I-135. Driving north through Salina he came to Interstate Road where he turned left. Soon he arrived at 3800 and pulled into the Smoky Hill Wildlife Sanctuary. There was no Advanced Fertilizers at 3800 West Interstate Road. He turned around driving to a nearby convenience store where he asked the salesperson for directions to Advanced Fertilizers. The salesperson did not know of the business. Conrad drove to the Salina Police Department inquiring about Advanced Fertilizers. No one knew of the company. After looking at their 911 directory, they found no such business. A heavy-set police sergeant came to the counter and said, "I was born and raised here. I have never heard of Advanced Fertilizers, but just to be thorough, why don't I call the fire department. If it's a business in Salina they will know about it."

From the counter where Conrad was standing he dialed the fire department's non-emergency number. "Hello Frank, say I have a federal investigator here who's looking for Advanced Fertilizers. I never heard of the place; I thought maybe you could help him out. I'm putting you on the speaker phone.

His name is Conrad Sutherland. Conrad this is Frank Kelly on the phone, he's Salina's fire chief."

"Good afternoon Conrad", said Frank. "I'm not familiar with Advanced Fertilizers in Salina. I'm checking to see if there's anything like that in our data base. I'm sorry, we do not show an Advanced Fertilizers in our data base either. Are you sure you have the name correct?"

"I'm positive the name is correct", said Conrad. "I have billing invoices from this business where they billed a firm in Oklahoma for several semi-trailers of fertilizer. I tried calling the phone number on the invoice and I got a message saying the number is no longer in service or has changed. Thank you both for your efforts. I'm convinced there is no Advanced Fertilizers in Salina. I've run into a dead end."

Conrad found a motel where he could spend the night. He needed to regroup and develop a new plan of how to proceed. He drafted a report of the day's activities and scanned the records he received from USFFC. He e-mailed everything to Anne Burke at PPQ headquarters.

Awaking early the next day, Conrad began his plan. He would drive to Wichita to visit the Wichita Farm Cooperative. His invoices showed them receiving one-hundred-fifty units.

Driving south toward Wichita, he input the Wichita Farmers Cooperative into his GPS and continued driving. The cooperative was on the west side of Wichita in a newer style metal building. Entering the store, he asked for the manager. Conrad went to an office overlooking the retail space from a second story office built over the sales counter area. Conrad walked up the stairs and knocked on the door.

From the other side of the door he heard a gruff sounding voice on the other side of the door bark, "Enter."

Conrad looked across a desk at a man around 50 with graying temples and a wide greeting smile with the phone placed next to his ear. He pointed toward a chair with a welcoming gesture. He continued listening mostly interjecting a few comments as if trying to appease the party on the other end. After a few minutes, he said, "Don, I understand what you're saying; we'll try to make it right, if we've done something wrong. Let me check into it; I'll get back to you this afternoon." He then rose from his chair again with a smile and an extended arm. "Chuck Himmler", he said.

"Conrad Sutherland, I am an investigator with the USDA. Here's my identification."

"Conrad, I didn't expect a badge", said Chuck with a smile. "How can I help you?"

"I am here regarding some fertilizer my list shows you ordered from USFFC. They described it as a new, environmentally friendly product containing nanoparticles of titanium dioxide. Are you familiar with the product?"

"Yes I am. Matter of fact, the call I was on when you walked in concerned that product. Don Mathews called me; he's a banker here in town. He owns a farm and a medium sized dairy. He's complaining the alfalfa hay which he raised on his other farm is causing his dairy cattle to wobble around. Their eyes are twitching back and forth and some are aggressive when they take them to the milking parlor."

"What kind of fertilizer did you sell him", asked Conrad.

"It was some of that new stuff that supposed to be easier on the environment. They call it nano-fertilizer. Don has a kid that's a junior at Wichita State that's doing his farming. The kid is majoring in chemistry and came in specifically requesting it. His name is Curt Wepner. He said he had heard about it and claimed it increased alfalfa yields by fifteen percent and required less water to make the crop. He's really a good kid and works hard for Don, but he's still a little wet behind the ears. He had calculated he needed 150 of the five-gallon containers. So, I ordered it for him. He wanted us to deliver containers in three 50 container loads about three weeks before each cutting. We delivered the last fifty about a month ago."

"To confirm, you ordered 150 containers in the spring. Is that correct?"

"That's right."

"And you delivered all 150 containers in 50 container lots about a month apart with the last delivery about one month ago?"

"That's right."

So, no other customers ordered or used any nanoparticle fertilizer except the kid?"

"That's right."

"So, you have no nano-fertilizer in your inventory?"

"No Conrad, we do not have any in our inventory. All your questions are starting to worry me. Is there a problem with the fertilizer?"

"There is a concern the fertilizer is adulterated. I'm assigned to investigate and follow up on those Coop's who purchased the nano-fertilizer. I'm interviewing those coops and farmers who purchased the fertilizer. What's the name of the kid who bought the fertilizer?"

"His name is Curt Wepner and he farms Don Mathews' farm?"

"Where is the farm located?"

"Don Mathews' farm is located south of here, near Haysville. Let me look up the exact address and Curt's phone number. As I recall Curt does not have a phone at the farm house and uses his cell phone exclusively." Chuck went to his computer and quickly he printed a single page. "Here's the farm's address with Curt's phone number and Don's phone number as well as the address of the dairy farm."

"Chuck, thank you for your cooperation. You have been a big help. I think I will head to the farm and see if I can find Curt. By the way, do you happen to have any printed literature on the nano-fertilizer?"

"I'm sorry, I did not keep it. I gave it to Curt. There was only one brochure and a couple of research studies that came with the delivery. I don't want to interfere with your methods; but it might be expedient to give Don a call. I'll bet you he will meet you there and I don't know if Curt will provide much information without Don being there. I get the feeling Don's got him on a pretty short leash."

"Thank you. I will give Don a call on my way to the farm."

"Conrad, there's probably something you need to know about Don. He's the excitable type and gets riled quickly; but it's all a show. He has a big ego and is well-to-do; but he's in no way dangerous or mean. Sometimes he lets his mouth runoff before thinking."

"Thanks again, Chuck. I appreciate your candor."

Getting back in his sky-blue Chevy Malibu rental, Conrad called Don Mathews. "Mr. Mathews, I am Conrad Sutherland. I am a federal investigator with the USDA. It is my understanding you purchased 150 containers of nano-fertilizer from Wichita Farmers Coop."

"Your name is Conrad Sutherland and you are with the USDA?"

"Yes sir, I need to go to your farm and visit with Curt Wepner. I understand he does the farming for you on your Haysville farm. Before I go to see Curt, I wanted to give you the opportunity to meet us there. Is it possible you could meet us there, in say 30 minutes?"

"It seems you know a whole hell of lot about my farm. Why do you need to talk with Curt? What's this about?"

"Mr. Mathews, I'm with the USDA. I am investigating the farms that used nano-fertilizer this spring and summer. I have questions I wanted to ask Curt. Again sir, you are welcome to be present. I may have questions for you. Is 30 minutes convenient for you sir?"

"Yeah, I can be there in a half an hour. Have you talked with Curt?"

"No sir, I called you first. You are the land owner. Curt will be my next call."

I'll call Curt and have him meet us at the farm. He has class from 8:00AM to 10:00AM. Sometimes he goes to the library for a while. I'll have him meet us at the farm; he should be out of class now."

"That's fine Mr. Mathews. I look forward to meeting you in person. Drive safely."

Conrad pulled into a gas station/convenience store and filled up with gasoline; getting a sandwich and a bottle of water for his drive back to Oklahoma later that afternoon. He had plenty of time, so he thought he would get ready to continue his travels south after leaving the Mathews' farm. After he put the address into his navigation system he drove south on Highway 81 and then turned west through Haysville. The farm sat on the west edge of town near a school and a church. A black Cadillac sedan pulled into the property just ahead of Conrad.

The Cadillac pulled up next to a small white farm house with green shutters and a green roof. As he looked to his left Conrad saw an equipment shed and a covered hay shed. They too were white with green trim matching the farm house. Conrad parked the Malibu next to the Cadillac. Getting out of his car, he said, "You must be Mr. Mathews.

I'm Conrad Sutherland", Conrad said showing him his credentials. "Were you able to get in touch with Curt?"

"Conrad, it's nice to meet you. Curt should be right behind us. Wichita State is located on the north side of town; so, he has a little further to drive. He was walking into the library when I spoke to him, it will take him a few minutes to walk back to his truck as well."

"This is a nice farm you have here. It seems to be kept up very well."

"Curt does a nice job around here. He farms, irrigates, and takes care of the place. He's also going to school full time in the fall and winter, and only part time in the summer. He's a chemistry major and wants to go on to medical school. Curt's bright and a hard worker as you can tell from the looks of the place. His dad is a farmer near Scott City. They farm quite a bit of ground, mostly wheat, with some corn."

Into the farmyard drove a green two tone older Chevy pickup. "Here's Curt now", said Mathews.

Curt jumped out of his truck walking over to the two men. "Hi Mr. Mathews, I got here as soon as I could."

"Curt, meet Mr. Conrad Sutherland. Mr. Sutherland is here to ask us some questions regarding the nano-fertilizer you applied to the alfalfa this year."

Curt extended his hand saying, "It's nice to meet you Mr. Sutherland."

"It's nice to meet you as well, Curt. I am an investigator with the USDA and I'm interviewing those customers who used the nano-fertilizer purchased from Wichita Farmers Coop. Here are my credentials. I understand you purchased 150 containers. Is that correct?"

"Yes sir. The coop delivered it in three 50 container shipments. I applied the fertilizer about three weeks prior to cutting the alfalfa for hay. I put it up in large square bales, then hauled the hay to Mr. Mathews dairy."

"Curt do you have any of the fertilizer left over", asked Conrad.

"Not now sir, I had about a quart left over from the first application. I used it on my garden. I planted a garden this spring to raise my own vegetables. It saves on my grocery bill and I like fresh vegetables better than those at the grocery store."

Trying to be nonchalant Conrad inquired, "Have you eaten anything from your garden yet?"

"You bet. I planted carrots, peas, radishes, beans, lettuce, tomatoes, cabbage, potatoes, and a little sweet corn. The tomatoes are just coming on and the corn is not quite ready, and I haven't dug any potatoes yet, but I have eaten some all the rest. The carrots, peas, and radishes are all about gone. I've been harvesting the beans as they mature, so they don't get tough."

"I see", said Conrad. "Have you been feeling well recently?"

"Yeah, I've had some headaches, but I think that's because I've been working out in the sun, probably not been drinking enough water. Why do you ask?"

"Oh, I was just wondering, I noticed you have a twitch in your left eyelid. Have you had that a long time?"

"No, it's kinda bothersome. It developed about two weeks ago. I used to get eye twitches back home when I got too tired. They always went away. Anyway, I thought it's a long way from my heart, and I've just been ignoring it and trying to get a little more sleep."

"Mr. Mathews, I happened to walk into Chuck Himmler's office while you were on the phone with him. I gathered you have some dairy cattle acting abnormally. Is that right?"

"Yes, some of the cattle are walking abnormally, some run into fences and gates; others seem agitated and are hard to get into the milking parlor. Milk production has decreased. My manager first thought it was Milk Fever and treated them with calcium, but it didn't help and some of them were heifers and had not calved yet. It's really been baffling him. He said the only thing different was he's been feeding the new alfalfa Curt put up. That's why I called Chuck. Do you have any idea what it might be?"

"I am not a veterinarian; so, I wouldn't want to speculate. When we finish, I am going to call the USDA-APHIS-Veterinary Services area office in Topeka to ask them to have a veterinarian come look at the cattle at your dairy. There will be no charge for their services. They may be able to help you figure out what's wrong."

"Conrad, I would appreciate their help. Paul, my manager at the dairy, doesn't get along with the vets around here and won't call them. He says they are too expensive and never available when you need them. He knows how to pull a calf and treat cattle. He went to Vet Tech School for a while, but I don't think he ever graduated. He's a good dairyman-works hard, is dependable, and doesn't drink."

"What percentage of your herd would you say is acting abnormally?"

"I have not been out there to look for myself, but Paul says it's about 20 percent", Don responded.

Conrad faced Curt again asking, "How did you hear about this new fertilizer?"

"I have a friend in Colorado. He told me about it on a social media site. I went on-line, but did not find out very much. It's new so that didn't surprise me. I asked Chuck

Himmler at the Coop if he would get some information. I ordered enough to fertilize this year's first three cuttings of alfalfa. My friend in Colorado is also using it. The main Coop in Oklahoma City sent copies of a couple of journal articles showing testing data. The articles were in trustworthy peer reviewed journals. They showed the fertilizer reduced cost, used less water, and reduced soil nitrates. Two respected researchers from large agricultural universities published the articles. Mr. Mathews, remember I dropped copies by your office for you to read?"

"Yes Curt, I remember. I read the articles but I didn't understand a lot of the scientific stuff they were talking about. Remember I am a banker, not a scientist like you."

"Do you happen to have a copy of the journal articles", asked Conrad.

Curt thought a moment and then said, "Yeah, I think I saved them in a file in the house. I'll go get them." Curt walked to his pickup, opened the door picking up his books and notebook from the seat, and walked into the farm house. In a few minutes, he walked back out carrying a manila file. "Here they are."

"Would it be possible for me to take these for a few days, then send them back to you", Conrad asked.

"Sure."

"I'll make copies of your file and send your file back. I really appreciate you giving them to me; it will save me driving back to Oklahoma City to get a copy."

Conrad then said, "That's all the questions I have for now. Mr. Mathews expect a call from one of the veterinarians in Topeka this afternoon. They will schedule a time that will be convenient for you and your dairy manager, Paul. I have your number at the bank, is that the best number to reach you at later this afternoon?"

"Let me give you my cell phone and home phone number. That way they will be able to reach me, where ever I may be. Conrad, thank you for getting in touch with the USDA veterinarians in Topeka; if you need any further information just give me a call."

"If you can't get in touch with Mr. Mathews, or if you have any further questions for me, just give me a call on my cell. I have it with me all the time. My number is..."

Conrad interrupted; "Curt I have your number. Thank you both for your cooperation."

Chapter 30

The two full-size SUV's arrived parking in a visitor parking area in front of the Student Union building. Larry led the group to the faculty dining room stating he and Ray previously ate lunch there. Dr. Ingram; Floyd Van Hoof, the Dean of the College of Agriculture; and Claudia Black, the Dean of the College of Arts and Sciences met Clare at the door. Clare introduced everyone to Dr. Ingram and the deans. Before entering the dining room, Dr. Ingram informed everyone the Wyoming congressional delegation was inside. Smiling Lynn informed Clare this was an event Wyoming's two senators and one congressman would not pass up. As everyone walked into the room, Randall noticed a large table tastefully setup on the far side of the room near the windows. The politicians were busy shaking hands and visiting with some of the faculty eating lunch. Everybody walked to the table and sat down. Soon the politicians joined the group sitting at the far end of the table from Lynn and Clare. Randy and Bobby Laporte sat next to the two senators with the congressman sitting between them at the end. Shortly the elected officials stood up and introduced themselves to everyone individually. As they worked themselves down the table one on the far side of the table and two on the nearer side making introductions and shaking hands they met at the end of the table where Lynn Ingram stood. Before they could greet her, she stood to address them eye to eye. Lynn began, "Good afternoon gentlemen. Welcome to the university once again. As you know, we have Secretary of Agriculture Clare Johansen joining us today. This event is to recognize five of our senior faculty. She is here to recognize their significant contributions to the DVE problem infecting our nation's cattle. Four of the folks sitting at our table will meet with them at 1:30 this afternoon to discuss additional research. We will drop in on them unannounced about three o'clock. It's meant to be a surprise. Following the recognition ceremony, there will be a brief press conference held by Secretary Johansen and her technical experts. As you may know a novel prion causes DVE. Unless you have technical expertise in novel prion diseases, I suggest you listen and make no comments to the press. I do not intend to tell any of you what to say, or not say; although it may sound like it. Rather, let's all keep in mind whose holding this important press conference. Gentleman, the stakes are much higher than they may appear to you. Please be seated and the wait staff will start serving our lunches. After lunch, you will learn more as we will adjourn to a private conference room."

During lunch, everyone visited casually in groups along the table. Randy took a phone call excusing himself about midway through the meal. Returning a few minutes later, he relayed to Penny and Bobby that Dennis called to let him know that Panhandle Cattle Feeders between Dumas and Dalhart had just broke with DVE and Glen Rogers was on his way there now. Randy said he relayed information to Dennis regarding the new terminal study and that it would begin today. Dennis was to call Bud and Jim Bob to let them know the change.

****

As lunch concluded Lynn Ingram led the group to a small rarely used conference room on the third floor of the Student Union building. Larry, Randy, Penny, and Bobby separated from the group and walked to Ray's office to meet him prior to going to the small conference room in the basement of the Biology building. "Randy", said Ray, "it's great to see you once again. I hope the cowboy state has been treating you well while you've been here."

"Ray, meet Dr. Penny Adams and her boss Dr. Bobby Laporte. Penny is my girlfriend and we're enjoying the cool evenings and the great weather. Bobby is with APHIS and is here from Washington, DC. How have you been?"

"I've been doing great. We just got back from over near Saratoga where we played golf and did some fishing. As you know, Rose and the kids are here. We've been having a great time."

"That's good to hear. Hey, I want to thank you for choosing such a great group to work on the fertilizer/DVE project. They did some remarkably good work in a short amount of time. Penny and I found it amazing that right out of the box they essentially did critical studies and identified the fertilizer as the culprit. Do you have any idea what their proposals may be?"

"Not really. I know they have met a couple of times and Dr. Edwards who runs the imaging lab is going to work with me on the upcoming soils testing and Dr. Fong is going to collaborate on the corn trials we're going to be doing at ATX. Other than that, we headed to Saratoga for a few of days. I have not heard anything. I suppose it's about time to walk over to the Biology building to see what they propose."

"Sounds good", said Larry.

As Ray and his "entourage" walked into the small basement conference room they noticed the white boards covered with explanations of different proposed studies. The University of Wyoming team were much better prepared than when Larry and Ray initially met with them.

After introductions, Dr. Schwartz asked everyone to sit down. He started with a summary of the previous experiments and noted promised follow up information. Dr. Schwartz stated, "On that note I will yield the floor to my colleague Dr. Brenda Edwards."

Dr. Edwards explained that the dilutions she had initially performed were not dilute enough to gain good visualization of individual NP under the SEM. She determined a dilution of 1:16,000 optimized visualization of the NPs in the fertilizer. She clarified the NPs contained both titanium dioxide and the proteinaceous residue, described by Dr. Thorpe. After visualizing and measuring several nanoparticles she determined with a remarkable consistency the nanoparticles were 30 nanometer spheres.

Ray commented, "Thank you Dr. Edwards. Thirty nanometer spheres are small indeed. By the way, I want to also thank you for the disks of the SEM photomicrographs you took during our last session."

"You are most welcome", said Dr. Edwards as she sat down.

Dr. Fong rose and walked to the front of the room and began. "You may recall we viewed the presence of NPs in the leaf and stem of the alfalfa plant samples Mr. Shelton sent from Texas. However, we did not view the presence of any NPs in the root specimens we examined. For my own satisfaction and in the interest of being thorough I repeated this trial with other randomly selected root samples. Again, I did not view any NP spheres in the root sample. I think it is safe to conclude the NPs are likely too large to absorb through the root hairs or there were no NPs in the soil. I postulate the NPs we viewed in the leaves and stem relocated to those areas of the plant through absorption when initially applied with the surfactant. Does anyone have any questions?"

Penny asked, "The plant samples you received were from early growth and first cutting Alfalfa plants. The plants received subsequent treatments of nano-fertilizer prior to the second and third cuttings. Would you care to speculate whether NPs would be present in leaf and stem samples from the forth cutting as there has not been further fertilization after the third cutting?"

"That is a very good question, Dr. Adams. I would reason the quantity of NPs less prevalent due to the previous harvests of leaves and stems. Without conducting further testing on samples from the fourth cutting, I would not speculate. The infectious dose of NPs for DVE is unknown. Under those conditions, I would want to verify the leaves and stems are devoid of NPs before speculating on whether the forth harvest could safely be used as feed."

"If there are no other questions, I will be seated and Dr. Thorpe will speak."

Dr. Thorpe stood and began his summary. "As I recall Ray and Larry asked if I would quantify the number of vacuoles containing titanium dioxide vs. those vacuoles containing the proteinaceous residue. The quantification performed both on the dilute fertilizer and the alfalfa plant composite yielded 33 percent titanium dioxide nanoparticles and 67 percent nanoparticles containing the proteinaceous residue. However, I must credit my colleagues Dr. Lin Fong and Dr. Brenda Edwards for doing this work. I thank them for their assistance and these data I summarized. Are there any questions?"

Randy commented: "Dr. Thorpe your experimental design was brilliant. You made it very easy for us and the USDA to determine the fertilizer was indeed adulterated. Absorption of nanoparticles into the alfalfa adulterated the hay. In turn, the cattle consumed the alfalfa hay. About sixty days later, the cattle developed DVE. That is excellent work sir!"

Dr. Thorne returning to his seat humbly said, "Thanks".

Dr. Schwartz stood, faced the group and said, "The next portion of our presentation will be to proffer continuing studies that will provide ATX with additional information. Of course, Dr. Shelton will be traveling to Texas to conduct additional studies on soil from the fertilizer exposed fields. He will also take samples of corn fertilized with the adulterated fertilizer. Dr. Fong will be conducting studies on the exposed corn samples. These studies will follow the same protocols as she used with the alfalfa samples taking samples from the leaves, stalk, root, as well as corn or the fruit of the plant. Dr. Edwards will be supporting both Dr. Shelton and Dr. Fong in operating SEM. All three professors will be involved in viewing the various samples and interpreting the results. Dr. Thorpe, I will let you explain your proposal."

At this time, there was a knock on the door of the conference room and Claudia Black, Dean of the College of

Arts and Sciences, peeked her head in the room asking, "May we listen in on your meeting?"

Dr. Schwartz immediately stood up and said, "Yes ma'am, come in and make yourselves comfortable."

As the group entered the room Dr. Schwartz noticed there was not space for everyone to have a chair. "We can relocate into a larger conference room upstairs to allow everyone a seat."

"That's not necessary", said Dr. Ingram. "We've been sitting quite a bit; standing will actually feel good. Don't let us interrupt your meeting. We just want to listen for a few minutes."

Once everyone had entered the room, Dr. Schwartz said, "Dr. Thorpe, continue with your proposal."

"Thank you, Dr. Schwartz. Although you may initially think this proposal is too research based, I think determining the composition and structure of this novel protein is a primary. We must first determine its size, weight, and composition and shape to thoughtfully study how it acts. My proposal is to conduct a series of tests to determine its amino acid sequence by using a protein sequencer, Edman degradation methodology, and mass spectrometry. Because now we think the DVE prion is unique, it may also provide us information into how it originated. If one considers the DVE prion may be a product of cleaving or manipulating existing proteins, this information will be most valuable. This concludes my proposal. Are there any questions?"

Penny waited to see if anyone else had questions, then raised her hand. "Dr. Thorpe, I think your proposal is clearly a good starting place not only from a classic molecular biology perspective; but also from an investigative perspective. Determining if this novel prion protein is the product of manipulating proteins would be most helpful in determining the level of knowledge and sophistication used by the folks manufacturing it for use as a biological weapon.

However, that leads me to ask, have you developed a method of isolating and purifying the proteinaceous residue from the fertilizer?"

"Dr. Adams, I have not considered the methodology that would be needed to isolate and purify the nanoparticles in the fertilizer. Indeed, the initial step in these studies must be to isolate and purify the nanoparticles containing the proteinaceous material. My initial thoughts would be to try both magnetism and centrifugal force. Thank you for your question. Considering Dr. Adams' helpful question, I need to amend my proposal to first include methodology to isolate and purify the proteinaceous material contained within the nanoparticles. Once I complete this step, I can then determine composition and structure."

Dr. Schwartz stood thanking Dr. Thorpe and said, "You have heard our proposals. One involving Dr. Shelton, Dr. Edwards, and Dr. Fong; the other proposal is Dr. Thorpe's to first isolate and purify the nanoparticles containing the proteinaceous material and then determine its composition and structure. Are there any questions or suggestions?"

"Dr. Schwartz", said Randy, "we have heard proposals from everyone on the team except you. Is there anything you want to propose?"

"Dr. Bennett, I did not proffer a proposal as I am transitioning into retirement. I am just finishing my second year of that transition. At the University of Wyoming when one chooses to transition into retirement they reduce their workload to 75% for year one, 50% for year two, and 25% for year three. With my existing commitments, I would not be able to give any proposal the necessary time. I'm sure you understand."

Randy shook his head yes as Dr. Ingram interrupted. "Ladies and gentlemen, we came today to recognize the efforts of five senior scientists on the faculty at the University of Wyoming. Let me make some introductions. On my right is Clare Johansen, the United States Secretary of Agriculture.

Standing next to her are Beth and Randall Bennett and Kay and Philip Granger. They are all involved with ATX holdings as is Larry Shelton, Ray's younger brother, and Dr. Randy Bennett. Attending your meeting is Dr. Bobby Laporte the Administrator of the Animal and Plant Health Inspection Service, a division of the USDA. Also with APHIS and sitting between Dr. Bennett and Dr. Laporte is Dr. Penny Adams. Standing behind them is Wyoming's congressional delegation, Senators Phillips and Swanson, and Representative Thompson. Without further ado, I will turn this over to Secretary Clare Johansen."

"Thank you, Dr. Ingram. I'm pleased to be in Laramie today to recognize Dr. Ray Shelton, Dr. Marty Schwartz, Dr. Eugene Thorpe, Dr. Brenda Edwards, and Dr. Lin Fong. The first set of experiments you performed for AXT Holdings were not only important to them, but also to United States Agriculture. The DVE outbreak currently involves cattle in eighteen states, many different entities within each state and millions of cattle. It was through your efforts that we learned cattle developed DVE after consuming tainted alfalfa fertilized with adulterated fertilizer. Armed with this knowledge, we will be able to contain and manage DVE. It is for these efforts I am presenting you with the USDA Secretary's Honor Award and a USDA research grant for 250,000 dollars for continued DVE research. I congratulate you all and want to extend congratulations from President Smyth. Thank you all."

"Now before we leave", said Dr. Ingram, "Secretary Johansen is going to hold a press conference out on the front lawn. Everyone please join us for Secretary Johansen's press conference."

Everyone walked out of the Biology Building to where a podium sat on the grass adjacent to the walkway. There were about forty members of the press including television cameras from the major networks, and CNN, and Fox News. As Secretary Johansen walked out and viewed the crowd she said to Bobby, "Well so much for expecting a small crowd."

"Ladies and gentlemen of the press, it is a proud day for the University of Wyoming to be visited by the Secretary of Agriculture, Clare Johansen. Without further ado, it is my honor to present Clare Johansen the United States Secretary of Agriculture."

After Clare made her announcement about where DVE had come from she said, "Now I will take a few questions. My technical expert Dr. Bobby Laporte will field those questions that are of technical nature. Please state your name and affiliation prior to your questions."

"Harvey Good, ABC-Denver. Madam Secretary, am I to understand the DVE agent was mixed in fertilizer used to enrich alfalfa was the source of the infection?"

"That is indeed the case. The alfalfa plants' leaves and stems absorbed the adulterated fertilizer. As the plant grew and matured prior to cutting the infectious agents were inside the plant leaves and stems. When cattle consumed the tainted alfalfa, they digested the prions and subsequently developed DVE."

Melissa Lopez, CBS-Cheyenne. Secretary Johansen, you used words like adulterated and tainted in your last response. Does the USDA think this was an intentional act? If so, what actions have been taken to identify the culprits?"

"Melissa, you are an astute listener. At this point, we have deduced DVE appears to be an intentional act. As soon as we got the results from the University of Wyoming, we initiated a criminal investigation into this matter. Because this is an ongoing or active investigation, the details will not be released to prevent compromising the ongoing investigation."

"Ben Dell, Fox News. Madam Secretary, where was the adulterated fertilizer made and how was it distributed?"

"Ben as I said earlier, there is an ongoing investigation in progress. We will not divulge information that may compromise our investigation."

"One final question said Secretary Johansen."

"Mary Wright-Laramie Daily News. Madam Secretary, how did the University of Wyoming become involved?"

"Mary, that is a fascinating question. One of the first premises to encounter cattle with neurological symptoms was a large, integrated, and very progressive cattle feeding operation in Texas. The owners happen to be long time personal friends of mine. The feeding operation uses feedstuffs produced by their farming operation, in this case alfalfa hay. USDA had an investigative team detailed to the feedlot gathering information to help in determine what was causing these cattle to develop neurological problems. It was through excellent communications of a USDA investigator with feeding operations management and the farming manager that concern arose regarding the new fertilizer and the alfalfa fed to their cattle. It was this concern that brought them to a trusted scientist they knew very well at the University of Wyoming. In collaboration, these scientists brilliantly designed and conducted the experimentation we are honoring today. After hearing the results of these experiments, the owner of the feeding operation called me."

"Thank you for your time and questions", said Clare as she walked away from the podium.

The reporters attempted to extend the news conference as they followed Dr. Ingram and Secretary Johansen as they walked toward Administration Building. The Wyoming congressional delegation, ATX management; Bobby, Penny, and Rose quietly walked in the opposite direction to their vehicles.

One reporter followed the congressional delegation asking, "Senator Swanson, what are your thoughts on this issue?"

Senator Swanson stopped to address the reporter. "It makes me proud a team of scientists from the University of Wyoming has made such a timely and significant discovery. I am very pleased Secretary Johansen took time out of her busy schedule to personally present them with this high honor. From my perspective, the next challenge she faces is getting the Emergency Supplemental Funding Request bill passed by congress. Let me assure you, my esteemed colleagues and I will fully support her efforts."

****

Lynn reserved a private room at a local restaurant so everyone could have a meal before departing Laramie. During the press conference Larry and Rose decided they and their children would return to Texas on the charter. Randy called Rick Phillips to advise them of the additional passengers telling Rick he would pick them up in twenty minutes for supper prior to departing to Amarillo.

"Randy, it's really nice of you guys to think of us", said Rick as he and Buzz jumped in the rear seat of the Escalade.

Randy introduced Rick and Buzz saying that Rick was an old friend of the family and that his brother Mike and Rick still see each other with regularity. "Penny, it's Rick's plane that Mom and Dad, and Philip and Kay rode up in", said Randy. "Rick normally keeps himself busy running Caliche Oil and Refining."

"Yeah, but today I played hooky and went flying", said Rick. "It's been fun and I've learned my golf game has suffered enough that I won't be playing for money anytime soon. Buzz beat me like a drum. I only won two holes; and I think that was because Buzz was feeling sorry for me."

Arriving at the restaurant, Randy pulled up behind Ray's Tahoe on a side street. As they all got out of the Escalade, Rose walked up to Rick with Larry trailing behind her. "Aren't you Rick Phillips?"

"Why yes I am."

"I'm Rose Shelton, it used to be Bennett. You ran around with my brother Mike. When you were both seniors at Tech, I was a freshman. I had the biggest crush on you. What brings you to Laramie?"

"Buzz and I flew your folks up here."

As they walked into the restaurant's private dining area Randall said, "Randy why don't you and Penny join us at our table. Your mother and Kay want to visit Penny."

Randall had chosen a table for eight and set two napkins on the back of two chairs for Lynn and Clare. As Randy and Penny walked up to the table, Beth said, "Penny, please sit down; and call me Beth. I feel like I know you. Between Sarita and Rose, I have heard so many nice things. Sarita thinks of you as the big sister she never had."

"Sarita and Rose have both been so kind to me. I think of Sarita as the little sister I never had. I have two older brothers, but I am the only girl in our family. Rose is so fun to shop with; we had such a good time when she went shopping with me. Her tastes are much like mine. She knew exactly where to take me. You know, I found most of my new clothes at a quaint resale boutique."

Kay said, "I know where you mean. Rose has Beth and me shopping there as well. Most of the clothes are designer labeled and in new condition. We like that place as well; and the prices are reasonable."

"May I interrupt you for a moment", said Randall. "While we have a minute, I want to update Randy and Penny on what Philip and I have been working on recently."

Randy and Penny both turned giving Randall their attention. "Since we talked with you at lunch after the board meeting, Philip and I have been busy working on your request. Penny you should know that Texas Tech University in Lubbock is planning to develop a National Prion Center. It'll be a joint venture between the College of

Agriculture and the Health Sciences Center. The concept will maximize the known synergies between the College of Agriculture, the School of Medicine, and the Graduate School of Biomedical Sciences. The Board of Regents and the Chancellor approved the idea at its last board meeting. Our plan is to have the program up and running within a year, and within two years we will have a research and teaching facility up and running. Our experience with the Amarillo hospital project taught us the need for consensus building and selecting the director early in the process. The board thinks the director should be someone from the agricultural side, with broad education and research experience in studying prions. This, we feel, is necessary to attract the grants and research funding that will soon become available. We visited with Clare this morning to enlighten her of the plan. She is supportive of the concept and its location. Both Philip and I foresee the Director of Texas Tech's National Prion Center to be Dr. Penny Adams."

Penny's jaw dropped open with overwhelming surprise. "Oh my God."

Philip began, "Both of you need to understand there's still lots of work to be done. In some respects, we are waiting on the DVE emergency funding bill to pass, we also need to meet with the Chancellor and Deans of the three Colleges, shore up some things, and initiate a consensus building campaign. There are still too many unknowns and variables to be able to provide a timeline. However, I am quite confident both of you have enough to do to keep yourselves busy for a while. Penny, please send me a copy of your resume. I'll hold it in confidence; it will help Randall and me to speak of your strong points. Do either of you have any questions?"

Penny said, "I'm so overwhelmed, I don't know what to think. Thank you both so much."

"I too am overwhelmed. Is there anything I can do?"

"Yes Randy, there is one thing", said Randall. "Don't let Penny get away. Penny, we all think you are a wonderful young lady."

Rising from his chair, Randall said, "Excuse me for a minute. I just figured who our co-pilot is. I need to go apologize for not recognizing him sooner. He's an old friend of Mike's and his Dad was an old friend of mine in the oil business."

"Rick Phillips, you old scallywag, you were going to fly me back to Texas and not say a word. Let me think, it's been twenty or more years since I have seen you. It was that day Mike and I helped you and your Dad mud in that well up north of Amarillo. Since I spoke to you as we were getting off the plane in Laramie, I've been thinking; who is that guy? I know him from somewhere. As I was talking with Randy and Penny, it finally hit me. That's Rick Phillips. How are you?"

"Mr. Bennett, I am fine. I didn't expect you would recognize me; it's been a long time since we worked on that well. You may not know it, but it was your generosity on that day that made Caliche Oil. That was going to be Dad's last hole, if it was dry or if it had blown out. He was totally out of funds. It was you and Mike that that helped us make that well; if you had not loaned us your mud, the well would have blown out. The well continues be a good well for us, after all these years. We call it Caliche One."

"Rick, you may not have known it at the time, but it was touch and go for a while, even with the mud. I worried about both you boys; but it all ended well. Although you've grown into a fine man, I think one of the reasons I did not recognize you sooner was that you were out of context for me. Had you walked into a board room I think I would have recognized you sooner, but flying second seat on our charter took me by surprise."

"Mr. Bennett, I have not been out of my office at the refinery for over three months, our CFO took another job and I have been riding herd on the refinery. I'm about to hire another CFO. So, I will soon be able to travel more. The regular co-pilot had a dental emergency last night. There was no way I was going to cancel, so I stepped in to replace him. I needed to get out of the office for my own sanity. It worked out well. It's been a fun day for me too. They delivered this plane to me about four months ago. For the most part, it has sat in the hanger. It did the plane good to give her some work. How do you like her?"

"I don't know a lot about private planes, but it's by far the nicest one I have ever flown in. It's got lots of space. Randy told you that we were planning on taking Rose and Larry and their kids back with us? Just add the additional charge on to the bill."

"Mr. Bennett, I'm glad you like the plane. It does not matter whether there's one passenger or a plane full the charge is the same. I'm just pleased Mike called me-it means a great deal to me to be able to fly you up here today."

Chapter 31

Randy was up early Saturday morning to meet Sonny and Junior at the pickup to go feed the horses. After the horses finished their oats, everyone saddled up to give the horses exercise. The horses unaccustomed to standing in small stalls. Randy wanted to ride Blue so he wouldn't get too full of himself from lack of exercise. They rode down the track that surrounded the expansive arena. By the time everyone finished the horses had broken a sweat and were breathing hard, more from the increased altitude than from hard work. Sonny noticed Junior was getting a little excited about roping in the performance that afternoon and suggested they gallop along the back stretch and then go put their horses up. After giving them a bath and allowing them to dry in the warm morning sun, they fed the horses hay. Randy seemed within himself, not saying much, seemingly in deep contemplation.

Arriving back at the motel room he found Penny awake and dressed in matching pale pink shorts and blouse. After he entered the room she smiled saying, "Hi cowboy, how's Blue this morning?"

"He's fine. After feeding them grain we went for a ride to give them some exercise. Blue just takes everything in stride. I think enjoys the excitement of everything around him. Junior's getting his game face on a little early; but Sonny is ever so subtly keeping his mind occupied about everything but roping. One thing you may find interesting happened while we were riding. Sonny got a phone call from Sammi Downey."

"Really?"

"I don't know much of what was said as Sonny pulled up to talk with her. He seemed pleased with the call, but didn't provide any details. I suppose they talked for maybe ten minutes. I know you don't know Sonny that well, but that's an eternity for him to be on the telephone. I think Sonny may have a girlfriend."

"Sounds like it", said Penny. "Hey, I'm hungry. How about you?"

"Yeah, I'm ready to eat. Sonny and Junior are already in the coffee shop; they're supposed to have gotten a booth for all of us."

After Junior roped, Randy and Penny left for Denver. By leaving early they were ahead of the traffic and would get to Penny's parents' house in Cherry Hills by about 5:00PM.

"I thought Junior had a good run this afternoon, said Penny. What did you think?"

"With his 16.0 today that put's Junior at 31.8 on two head. That should be fast enough to get him into the finals. Thumper worked OK, but took an extra step as Junior strung the steer's front leg. That cost Junior about a half-second. Also, he didn't pull his string tight before raising his hands. I was afraid the steer would get up, but it just laid there. Junior was lucky the steer didn't strain. For his first time at Cheyenne, I think he should feel good about himself. If we can just keep him cool for the finals. That's when everyone feels the pressure."

"What did you do yesterday while I was in Fort Collins with Dr. Laporte and Dr. Yu?"

"I really didn't do a whole lot. Of course, I went to feed and rode Blue. Then I came back here and chilled. I took an afternoon nap; then went and fed again. I ran into some old friends; we sat around their trailer visiting. They have living quarters in the front of their trailer and once they're at the rodeo grounds they just stay there. It's a nice trailer, but I like getting away from it a little. I'm sure it's more difficult to get a good night's rest with all the activities going on nearby. How about you; did you have a good meeting with Bobby and Dr. Yu?"

"We covered a lot of ground yesterday. I'm sorry about getting back late; it was either stay late or come back Monday to finish up. We just worked until we finished. It was really an interesting experience. We did a postmortem look at the entire investigation period of the outbreak. Sam had all sorts of data that I had never imagined they kept. We evaluated each team individually and collectively to identify major commonalities of the investigation. All the pathology and other laboratory data as well as water and feed sample results were available. They asked me lots of questions regarding the software and how it could be more effective. They have productivity monitoring software integrated into the programs to see what each team has completed within a given timeframe. We also discussed DVE in detail, taking a very critical look at why APHIS did not detect anything with all the testing performed in comparison to the information that Ray's team uncovered. One conclusion we came up with was when we see an outbreak indicating an important event, the software is not flexible enough for the investigators to intuitively modify the investigation. You know it was when we saw symptoms in your roping steers that were on exclusive alfalfa hay ration, we should have been able to modify our investigation and thought process. The current software does not allow the flexibility to alter our thought process. It did with you and I and Larry and you guys acted on it quickly. I continued to follow protocol, but the protocol's inflexibility would not allow us to redirect our thought processes given new information. We agreed the software needed modification."

"An unexpected conference call interrupted our progress. We were on with Secretary Johansen, Anne Burke, the Director of Plant Protection and Quarantine division of APHIS, Dr. Roy Jackson, the Secretary of Health and Human Services, and Dr. Susan Gray, the Director of the CDC. Anne Burke called Bobby to tell him one of the investigators running down the nano-fertilizer and hay producers, interviewed a young man near Wichita, Kansas that used the fertilizer on alfalfa hay. Having about a quart left over, he used it on his garden. A nearby dairy is feeding the hay he produced. Reportedly those cattle are symptomatic. The young man is a student at Wichita State. The investigator reported the young man has experienced headaches and has a persistent eyelid twitch. The discussion concerned how we go about notifying this young man and getting him into a diagnostic center for evaluation and follow up. They are going to notify him today and setup initial exams and testing with local physicians. CDC is sending a team as well."

"I also had an interesting visit with Bobby on the way down to Fort Collins. He asked if I found it unusual that the agency administrator was so involved in this outbreak. I told him I hadn't given it any thought. He told me the Director of Veterinary Services would normally be doing this work, but he recently found out he has pancreatic cancer. He's in the process of retiring and enduring chemotherapy. Bobby said since he had held that position prior to becoming administrator; he stepped back into his old role during the outbreak. He said he'd been thinking about what qualities the VS Director should have to best serve the agency. He said all the Deputy Directors were strong leaders, bright, experienced, and willing to serve; but they all fell into the mold of being reluctant innovate. Bobby said he thinks the agency needs someone who is innovative and willing to help lead the agency into a new and more modern era. He asked me if I had ever considered moving to Washington; very subtly hinting I would be a good fit for director. I tried to act like I was nonchalantly listening, but I almost drove off the road."

"Wow. What did you say?"

"Randy, it was very subtle, so I didn't have to say anything. I was shocked. I wanted to tell him you and I are in love, and me taking a job in Washington, DC was the farthest thing from my mind. First, your Dad and Philip talking to us at the restaurant totally blew me away. With Bobby riding back to Cheyenne with us and me being gone yesterday, we really have not had an opportunity to talk about that discussion. What do you think?"

"When I asked Dad and Philip for help, I had no idea that they would conceive the idea of a National Prion Center located at Tech. Once I thought about it, it made sense. You need to understand their thought processes. If they are going to spend their time doing something, they begin with identification of the significant problem; their solution is what produces the most good. Experiencing the DVE first hand and finding out there was so little actually known about prions, they identified that as the problem. How best to attack this problem is through a central collaborative information gathering and sharing center, but there is not one. Therefore, they need to develop that center. They are both very loyal to Tech, although that is obvious since they are regents."

"Dad foresees lots of funding coming available for research through the research portion of emergency funding bill for DVE; he and Philip think what better place to spend some of it than investing in a National Prion Center at Texas Tech. I think that was the main topic of discussion when Clare spoke privately with Dad and Philip at the country club in Laramie."

"Dad really likes you, as does Philip. They both are good judges of character and talent. I think you have impressed them both with your work ethic, intellect, humility, class, and education. I can tell you when I asked Dad if there was anything I could do and he responded don't let her get away, he was serious. Mom thinks you're special as well. While you were in Fort Collins yesterday, I called the office and spoke with Sarita. It was maybe 11:00AM Texas time. Mom had already spoken to Sarita and told her what a wonderful person you are. Apparently, you were the topic of discussion for Mom, Kay, and Rose on the flight back to Amarillo."

"I think I may know a little about how you feel. You think being the Director of the National Prion Center is more of a job than you can handle. I felt the same way when I was home for Christmas during my senior year at vet school. Dad and Philip pulled me aside telling me ATX planned to build an integrated cattle feeding operation and he wanted me to run it. I was initially overwhelmed, then Dad said they expected to start building the first lot in January and thought it would take about six months to get it built. After that, they would start on the second lot. Their plans called for six lots initially, with expansion when it was necessary. I stayed an extra year getting my masters. When I returned home with two lots finished and they were working on the third. I did Jim Bob's job and mine. It was busy, but not overwhelming. Dad and Philip helped me learn the financial end of the business. As we started filling the third lot, that was Dimmitt, Bobby and Tony began building the first of the northern feedlots. As I got busier and busier, I needed help doing the veterinary work and hired Jim Bob. Basically, what I'm saying is I think they're planning on doing the same thing with you. Bring you in early in the process, Dad called it consensus building, to let you grow with the job. Putting curriculums together, advising facility on grant opportunities, collaborating on the direction of research, etc. The Deans, Provosts, the university president, and the chancellor will help you learn those aspects that you need to know. I also think you need to consider what Bobby Laporte asked you. Not about moving to DC; but inquiring about your interest in being the Director of Veterinary Services. Bobby recognizes talent when he sees it. He has recognized your qualities as well as Dad and Philip. I think you must consider if these people want to use your talents in these jobs, they must think you can handle them and succeed. Don't sell yourself short. You're good at what you do, you're very smart, and everyone, including me, sees your potential."

Penny smiled and said, "You make it all so easy for me to understand. That's why I love you. By the way you're getting close to the exit for Mom and Dad's house. It's not this exit, but the next. Get in the right-hand lane of the off-ramp and take a right at the light. Stay on that road about two miles and then turn left on University."

After a few minutes Penny and Randy drove into a brick paved driveway of a large rambling brick and rock constructed home. Besides the three-car attached garage, there was a brick structure about the size of another three-car garage with no overhead doors. Rather, there were large windows in the front and on one side with a double walk-in door. Randy parked in front under the portico.

They walked to a set of hand carved hardwood doors where Penny knocked as she walked in saying, "Hello, is anyone home?"

"I'm back in the kitchen, dear. Come on in", said Pam Adams.

Holding Randy's hand, she led him to the back of the house where the kitchen was located. Entering the kitchen Penny said, "I'm sorry if we're late, we left the rodeo early and drove straight here."

Pam and Penny hugged and then Pam hugged Randy. "Penny you guys are not late. I got a call from your dad a little while ago. He was leaving the hospital. He should be here soon. I have him making a beer and wine stop on the way home. You guys make yourself at home; I'm just finishing up some stuff here. How about some iced tea?"

"That sounds great, Mom. Randy, you want a glass too?"

"Yes, please." You have a very nice home Pam. Did you design it?"

"Yes, almost forty years ago. It took two years after that for us to save the funds to begin construction. We've lived here ever since. It's too big for Ken and I now, but we can't bear the thought of moving to a smaller place and leaving all our memories behind. Great neighbors have become good friends. Ken enjoys his time in the backyard gardening and mowing. Penny since you were here last, we turned the barn where you kept your horse into Dad's equipment shed. He's got a riding lawn mower/tractor in there with all the attachments. In the winter, he puts on the snow blower attachment and clears the drive way. I've used it twice, it's fun. Here's Dad now, I hear the garage door opening."

Penny walked toward the door to the garage meeting Ken soon after he opened the door. "Hi, Dad, how was your day?"

"Hi, Penny, I am sorry I am late. The case took a little longer than I anticipated. Randy, it's good to see you again", Ken said as he hugged Penny and then shook Randy's hand. Have you been here long?"

"Not long at all. Maybe five minutes. Just long enough to have a glass of tea and hear about you blowing snow with your tractor."

Ken smiled saying, "You know I have more damn fun on that tractor. In the summer, I cut the grass and in the winter, I blow snow."

"Dad, do you want some iced tea?"

"No Penny, I have been craving a beer since I stopped to pick it up. A beer sounds better. How about you Randy?"

"I'd drink a beer with you. I've almost finished my tea. A beer sounds good to me too."

"I'll get them, said Penny. Are they in the fridge in the garage?"

"Yes, I also picked up some wine for you and Mom, if you want some. You have a choice of red or white wine; I didn't know what we were having for dinner."

"I thought we would grill hamburgers and corn on the cob. I've made German potato salad; we'll top it off with apple pie alamode. It's such a nice night, I thought we would eat on the patio."

"How can I help", asked Randy.

"Really there's nothing for you to do. Ken can grill the hamburgers and corn. Maybe keep him company."

Ken washed his hands in the kitchen sink asking, "Are we ready to put things on the grill?"

"Whenever you are ready dear, you can start", replied Pam. "I lit the briquettes a few minutes before Penny and Randy arrived. They should be ready by now."

Ken placed the hamburger patties on a paper plate and put the corn on a second plate. The sliding door to the patio was open. He set both plates next to the grill; then reached in turning on the patio lights and the indirect backyard landscaping lights. Ken opened the cover of the grill to find the briquettes to be perfect. Placing the hamburgers close to the heat he placed the corn adjacent allowing it to cook more slowly, yet still have the char marks. Ken returned to the kitchen to get a small bowl containing melted butter with a touch of cayenne added to baste the corn.

As the burgers cooked, Penny set the place settings on the table and Pam brought out the potato salad. Penny placed another beer next to Ken and Randy's place setting with frosted mugs from the freezer. She and Pam would drink the remaining portion of the bottle of wine she had placed in an iced champagne canister adjacent to the table between her and Pam.

Ken cooked the hamburgers and corn to perfection. The cool tangy potato salad was the perfect accompaniment to the meal. Everyone visited casually as they enjoyed the meal. "Who's ready for warm apple pie alamode", asked Pam. Everyone responded in the affirmative. As Penny cleared the table, Pam prepared the pie. During dinner, it warmed in the oven and the cold vanilla ice cream melted immediately. After dessert, everyone's attention drifted to the backyard where the indirect lights hidden in the shrubbery seemed to heighten the relaxed mood.

"What is the plan for tomorrow", asked Randy. "I seem to recall brunch with you both and Penny's brothers and their families."

"That's the plan as far as I know", said Ken. "You both can sleep in if you wish; we'll need to be at the club at 11:00AM. Pam isn't that the time you requested when you called?"

"Yes dear, but it's approximate. We don't have to be there exactly at 11:00."

Randy continued looking around the back yard taking in everything, yet nothing. He soon yawned. "This excellent meal, a couple of beers and such a relaxing setting has made me sleepy. If you don't mind I am going to excuse myself and go to bed."

"Not at all Randy", said Ken. "I'm going to be right behind you."

Penny said, "Randy let me show you our room. While you were out with Dad cooking the hamburgers, I brought our luggage in." Penny rose from the table and took Randy's hand and led him to their bedroom. Once there, she showed him the attached bath, gave him a kiss saying, "Good night sweetheart, I'll be in later."

Penny returned to the patio table, sat down, and poured the remaining wine into her glass. Pam said, "Penny I am so glad you and Randy were able to come down. Dad and I really like Randy. He's so laid back, yet it seems like he's eons ahead of you when you ask him a question. He has such good manners and treats you so nicely. We know he is involved in feeding cattle, but that's about it. Have you met his parents?"

"Randy is the man of my dreams. He's so kind to me, actually to everyone. He's considerate, loving, and to a fault humble. Yes, he is involved in feeding cattle, which is one of his family's businesses. He is the Director of Feedlot Operations. He operates six feedlots each of which hold 65,000 head of cattle. As you can imagine, it's a big operation. They own a large portion of the cattle they feed. His little brother, Skip, runs the ranching division. They have ranches in several states and that's where a lot of the feeder cattle come from. I have met his parents, they are very nice people. Over their lifetime Randall, Randy's Dad, had put together several synergistic businesses. Each one of his siblings runs one of the businesses. Beth, Randy's Mom, is so sweet and considerate. I think that's where Randy gets his sensitivity from, but his Dad is also considerate and always willing to help."

"Are there just the two boys, Randy and Skip?"

Penny smiling said, "You know I asked Randall that same question the first day I met him. Randall and Beth have eight children. All their children run a different business. A holding company owns the businesses. Randall is the Chairman and CEO of that company. Mike, a petroleum engineer, runs the oil and gas company; Mary runs the bank; Tony, also an engineer, runs the construction company; Bobby, a mechanical engineer, runs the salvage and industrial design company; Rose is a radiologist, but her husband Larry oversees the farming operation and trades commodities; Kate is a housewife, but her husband Harold runs the equipment and transportation businesses; then there's Randy and Skip who you know about."

"Goodness they are so diversified and yet talking to Randy you would have no idea", said Pam. "Are all these businesses fairly good size?"

"Yes, I think so. Randy told me the oil and gas company is fairly good size. With the revenues from that company they started the bank. Once the bank became successful, next came the construction company, and so on. The equipment and transportation company includes the Amarillo John Deere, Caterpillar, Peterbuilt and GM dealerships. I don't know how large the construction company or the salvage and industrial design companies are, but I know they built the Amarillo hospital."

"My God", said Ken. "This is quite a family. Do they all get along?"

"The best that I can tell, yes. I know Randall knows generally what's going on with each company, but he leaves it up to the children to run their companies. Randy said at this point all the businesses are mature and expected to pay their own way with the profits go into the holding company. Randy told me that all his brothers and sisters, or their spouses, draw the same annual salary from their business. The holding company keeps a war chest of funds that helps even things out if someone has a bad year. Randall draws his salary from the holding company. Also, Randall's best friend since childhood is Philip Granger. He's an attorney and is almost always at his side. Philip married Kay who is Beth's twin sister. Randall asked Philip to join his business early on and Philip declined. He wanted to focus on his law practice. It's now the largest and most successful firm in Amarillo. It's managed by his son. Philip is on a retainer with Randall, who is now his only client."

"So how serious are you and Randy", asked Pam.

"Mom, we're both pretty serious. We have both told the other that we love them. We also realize that we have only known each other for a short time and both of us feel like we need to get to know each other better before getting married; but I think that's where it's headed."

"How is that going to work out when you return to Iowa", asked Ken.

"We're trying to avoid a long-distance relationship. I commented to Randy I would have an interest in doing prion research and teaching, if I could find a tenure track position somewhere close. A while ago Randy met with Randall and Philip asking for their help in finding something for me. Texas Tech University is about 90 miles from Randy's house in Happy. I had not given it much thought until Randall and Philip called Randy and me aside when we were Laramie a couple of days ago. They gave us a status report on their progress. Both Philip and Randall are regents at Texas Tech. They proposed developing a National Prion Center at Tech. The regents approved the proposal as did the Chancellor.

They envision it being a joint venture between the College of Agriculture and the Health Science Center. Anyway, they want the program up and running in about a year and have a new teaching and research facility constructed within two years. They envision me being the Director of the National Prion Center."

"Wow", said Pam as she reached over and hugged her daughter.

Ken said, "My God Penny. That is wonderful."

"Philip says it's still some ways off, they are waiting for the emergency supplemental budget request to pass. That will fund the DVE indemnification program and the research funds that are included in the bill. Philip said to send him my resume, so he and Randall would have specific talking points. They both talked with Secretary Johansen earlier that day before they spoke with Randy and me. Randall says they are in the consensus building phase now; and he wants me to be involved in that phase. Needless to say, I am excited about maybe getting closer to Randy; but I'm a little scared. It is a big and important job."

"These men would not set you up to fail Penny", said Ken. "It will certainly be lots of work, and a continual learning curve, but I know you're up to the challenge. Being close to Randy is important. I do like the idea of you both getting to know each other better before jumping directly into marriage. You need to make sure you are compatible. However, from what I've seen, your mother and I think you both are. I like Randy as a person and being humble to a fault is not necessarily a character flaw."

"Thanks for listening to me this evening. I wanted to explain some things about Randy's family, our relationship, and what might be happening. Now, I think it's time that I also go to bed; we've had a very busy week with a lot of things going on in our lives. To say I am tired is an understatement."

"Honey, we also need to get to bed", said Ken. "Thank you for filling us in what is happening in your life. You seem happy; that is gratifying to us. Good night dear."

****

Randy was up, showered, and drinking a cup of coffee on the patio when Ken came out to join him. Randy enjoyed the cool mornings he knew in Cheyenne and now Denver during the mid-summer's heat in Amarillo. Ken was also an early riser and enjoyed the solitude of the early morning.

"Good morning, Ken", said Randy as Ken sat down next to him.

"I see you have found my favorite spot in the early morning. I enjoy listening to the birds as I sip my coffee. For me, it's the best way to start the day. I thought I would get up early this morning and make rounds before everyone was up and going. I was surprised that you were up and dressed when I walked into the kitchen."

"I've always been an early riser. I like the early morning and to wake up slowly before I start my day. I have been this way all my life. I too enjoy the solitude. I thought you would have a resident making rounds for you", said Randy.

"I do; but I also like to see my patients. It's not that I don't trust them; rather, it's more that I enjoy seeing and interacting with my patients particularly the day after surgery. It's a time that the patient's parents are less anxious over the surgery and often have questions. I don't think it's fair to have the residents answer their questions. It will take me an hour or less to make rounds and travel time will be about the same. You're welcome to ride along if you wish. I could have someone give you a tour."

"Thanks, but if you don't mind, I think I'll go buy a paper and see what's been going on in the world", said Randy.

"We have the paper delivered. There is an opening in the right-hand pillar outside the gate. It will be in there."

"That sounds good to me. I'll walk out and get it after you leave. You want another cup of coffee?"

"No thanks, I'm going to finish this one, then go to the hospital. That way I will be back by the time the gals get up and going."

As Ken departed for the hospital, Randy walked out to the street and got the paper. He looked around the tastefully landscaped front yard. Reaching down he felt the fine bluegrass blades, they were much softer than the Bermuda grass at his house. He thought, *sometimes it's the smallest things you notice first*.

"You look comfortable", said Pam as she walked out onto the patio in her robe and slippers clutching a cup of coffee. "Did you sleep well?"

"Oh, yes ma'am", replied Randy as he put his paper down and took his feet off the chair opposite him. "My head no sooner hit the pillow than I was asleep; and I slept soundly. I didn't even hear Penny come to bed."

"I'm an early riser and enjoy the early morning. I've been up for a little while. I had a cup of coffee with Ken before he left to go make rounds. When he left I went out to pick up the paper and have been catching up on what's been happening in the world. Did you sleep well?"

"I slept like a baby. I usually awaken when Ken gets up, to fix him breakfast. I never heard him make a sound. I don't know when I have slept so soundly. It's a nice morning, isn't it?"

"I really like the mornings here, they're cool. I've been listening to the birds singing in the trees and watched two robins fight over a worm in the grass. There was a yellow tabby cat that walked through the yard like he was making his morning rounds. It's been very relaxing. I got to thinking; I hope there is no dress code where we are going for brunch, the only thing I brought was Wrangler jeans. I hope that will not create a problem."

"That will not present a problem. We planned on dining in the patio area. They have the buffet set up, and it's more casual there. If we were going to the dining room, there is a dress code."

"I'm back", said Ken walking into the kitchen pouring another cup of coffee. He joined Pam and Randy on the back porch. My patients are all doing well. The little boy I operated on yesterday asked me when he could get up and play. I asked him if he would play quietly and not run around. He responded ever so solemnly, 'Dr. Ken sometimes I have a problem with that.' His cheeks are pink and it appears the surgery did not slow him down, even temporarily. Where's Penny?"

"I think she's still sleeping", said Randy. "She's had a couple of very busy and long days. She needs the rest; I've been down here enjoying the coffee, weather, and your paper."

Randy sat up straighter in his chair and looked at both Pam and Ken. "I don't know if you have had an opportunity to visit much with Penny, but I wanted to tell you our relationship is becoming serious. We're working on getting her a job down in Lubbock at Texas Tech so we will be closer to one another. While we haven't known each other long, our relationship has grown into love. We both feel like we need to get to know each other better before we commit to marriage, but that's where I want it to go. Therefore, I wanted you both to know where I stand and my intentions. I would like your blessings. We're not contemplating marriage soon. However, Penny needs more of a commitment from me, if she will leave her job to move closer. It is my plan to propose to her, with your blessings. I see that happening sooner rather than later."

Pam smiled immediately and looked at Ken. Ken also was smiling and began, "Randy we had an opportunity to visit with Penny last night. She told us she loved you and wanted to move closer so you two could get to know each other better. Pam and I both think you two are approaching this relationship in a very mature and thoughtful manner. It was obvious to both of us when we met you that Penny had found someone she loved. And you've responded in kind. I think it's wonderful you thought enough of us to ask for our blessing. We know you didn't need to do that. Randy, both Pam and I would be very pleased to have you as our son-in-law. I think it's a good thing you will make this commitment before Penny uproots herself and heads her career in a different direction. That tells us a lot about your character. Visiting with us this morning indicates your high character. Last night Penny told us what your Dad and Philip were planning. I think it scares Penny a little. But, I have no doubt she will do a good job. Pam and I are most pleased."

"Thank you both. I will do my best to take care of her and make her happy."

Chapter 32

"Good morning everyone, please be seated", said President Smyth. Security issues were the initial topic of discussion at the cabinet meeting.

Fred Robinson summarized Homeland's terrorism investigation. Much of what he had the FBI doing was retracing the steps the USDA had accomplished and was available to him through the DVE investigation link sent to Secretary Robinson. Treasury (the Commodity Futures Trading Commission, and FinCEN) continued to drill down on the financial side of things; working toward determining true ownership of the foreign investments. The DEA reported intelligence from eight months ago about a substantial volume of fertilizer reportedly smuggled into the US through Mexico. The fertilizer accompanied a large shipment of heroin across the Mexican border at Nuevo Laredo.

President Smyth commented, "From my perspective it seems like the DVE issue started out very complex and just worsens the deeper we investigate. Since we're talking about DVE, let's hear from Agriculture."

"The DVE outbreak continues to expand. Research on non-symptomatic cattle fed the adulterated hay has shown what I'll describe as pre-DVE lesions. Based upon this evidence, we intend to depopulate all exposed and infected premises. This presents a huge problem with carcass destruction. Additional studies are currently underway to see how long cattle showing symptoms will live with no interventions. Once these cattle cannot function normally they will be humanely euthanized. These trials will determine how much time we have before we need depopulate to avoid creating a public health emergency. Cremation seems the most practical method of destruction. The location of these crematoriums needs thoughtful consideration. Construction of these crematoriums awaits passage of emergency supplemental funding."

"Another division of APHIS is the Plant Protection and Quarantine Division (PPQ). They acquired a list from the national distributer identifying distribution of the tainted nano-fertilizer to the individual cooperatives. We're working on getting the list of purchasers from the local cooperatives. From the local stores, we'll determine specific farmers who purchased the nano-fertilizer. Then we will interview those farmers. We know some of the farmers have grown the alfalfa as feed to their own cattle. Others have unknowingly grown the tainted alfalfa to be sold to others."

"According to the product's label and other literature distributed with the fertilizer, the responsible firm is Advanced Fertilizers in Salina, Kansas. Our investigator attempted to visit the manufacturing plant. When he arrived at the address, he found it to be a wildlife sanctuary. Both the police and fire departments of Salina were unaware of Advanced Fertilizers."

"One of our investigators interviewed a young farm worker who had applied the fertilizer to alfalfa. Having about a quart left over, he fertilized his personal vegetable garden. The investigator was very astute noticing the farm worker, a pre-med student at Wichita State University, had a persistent tick in one eyelid. Dairy cattle on a separate farm, also owned by the proprietor, were reportedly symptomatic. Veterinary Services examined the cattle with one testing positive for DVE. We discussed information on the young man with Secretary Jackson and Dr. Susan Gray, Director of the CDC. We attempted to have Secretary Robinson join us on the call; but he was unavailable and his secretary was unaware of a designee in his absence. I am unaware of what has happened to the boy."

"Our investigator acquired copies of two scientific articles from the young farm worker. The scientific articles were alleged copies from two very reputable agronomy journals and written by respected research agronomists. However, we discovered, the agronomists did not author the articles and the journals did not publish them. The firm that reportedly made the fertilizer does not exist and the literature provided to the distribution warehouse is spurious."

"I also heard something in Secretary Robinson's report that may be a coincidence. There may be an association between intelligence regarding smuggling of fertilizer across the border at Nuevo Laredo and cashier's checks used to pay for the nano-fertilizer. Reportedly, Advanced Fertilizers required payment upon delivery of the fertilizer in the form of cash or cashier's check to the driver delivering the load. The national cooperative warehouse paid by cashier's check. All of the cashier's checks were cashed at the same bank in Laredo, Texas."

"Excuse me for interrupting Madam Secretary", said Secretary Robinson. His face appeared flushed and his voice slightly elevated. He was sitting upright on the edge of his chair giving the impression he was very angry. "Why are you interfering with my criminal investigation? You have no business continuing your investigation. Once identified as a terrorist act, it becomes the responsibility of Homeland Security to go forward with the investigation. If I need your help, I will ask for it!"

Clare sat dumbfounded for a moment looking at Secretary Robinson. President Smyth appeared about to intercede when Clare spoke. "Secretary Robinson, while I don't think this is the forum for your accusation, I am compelled to respond. Mr. Secretary, I am not nor have I ever interfered with your criminal investigation of terrorism. I too have mandated responsibilities that go along with the DVE outbreak. They fall in the line of protecting animal and public health. It is my responsibility to identify all affected premises, make proper disposition of infected livestock, and attempt to minimize the effects of this outbreak. I have and will continue to do just that. Now that we know the source of prions, I must identify those growers that fertilized their fields with the tainted nano-fertilizer. We must track whether the farmers used the alfalfa as feed or sold it to other feeders. It is my responsibility to determine if, in the public's interest, I quarantine the infected farms and agricultural products produced. Sir, that is what I am doing. If I have added information or evidence that your investigation has not yet developed, it was information that came forth while my Department was conducting official business under its legal authority. That information, sir, has been shared with you, in total."

President Smyth began, "Clare thank you for your thorough description of what the Department of Agriculture has developed since our last meeting. It appears that as we go forward the complexity of the DVE issue only increases. I think it's time we get together, as a group, to further study this issue and investigation. I include Secretary Robinson, Secretary Johansen, Secretary Jackson of Health and Human Services, Secretary Cohen of Treasury, Geraldine Green, the Attorney General, and anyone else that either you or Secretary Robinson wish to invite to the meeting. Let me know if I need to invite anyone else after this meeting. We will meet in my office for starters at 2:00PM sharp this afternoon. We'll go from there."

"Now let's move on", said President Smyth. By this time the entire cabinet had sensed President Smyth's ire and rationalized there would be a better time to discuss ongoing issues. "Are there any other national security issues? Are there any international issues, or domestic issues? ...OK we're adjourned. Thank you all for attending."

President Smyth sat in his seat a minute and timed his exit to meet Clare about at the door. He recognized Clare was angry, but it was well hidden. Clare said, "Mr. President, there is one person I would like you ask to attend, if we are going to discuss DVE in-depth at the meeting. That person is General Clark."

"Clare, this is going to be an in-depth discussion. We're going to get down and dirty on DVE and what needs accomplished and who is responsible for what. Secretary Robinson had no business attacking you like that. For that I apologize."

"Mr. President you have nothing to apologize for."

"I should have interrupted before you began your response."

"Actually, I sensed that you were going to. That's why I began. I may have been too blunt; but, he needs to know he's not going to push me around."

"I thought you made that abundantly clear in a polite manner, albeit fiery and succinct. Perhaps you didn't notice, but right after the meeting adjourned Secretary Robinson rushed out the back door. I think he'd had enough humiliation for one morning. I'll see you at two and I will notify General Clark."

"Thank you, Mr. President."

Chapter 33

Randy and Penny stayed an extra day in Denver. Randy spent most of the day on the back porch making phone calls checking on things at the feedlots. Cattle continued to develop CNS signs. Unexpectedly, there were very few cattle requiring euthanasia due to advanced symptoms. Jim Bob had visited the northern feedlots and on careful examination found no symptomatic cattle. He had been spending most of his time at Dimmitt with Sonny and Junior gone; however, operations there were routine. Bud Thomas and Dennis Young reported routine operations at Tulia and Hereford. Randy called Skip checking in on the ranching operation. Skip Bennett stopped shipping cattle to the feedlots. Grass cattle pasture rotation increased more than usual. Skip leased additional pasture in northern New Mexico for about fifteen hundred head of yearlings until he could ship them to the feedlots. Bobby Bennett had not returned to Amarillo yet. The Mayo Clinic were performing additional diagnostic testing. Randy also checked in with his Dad. Randall mentioned he had spoken with Bobby filling him in on perhaps making crematoriums. Bobby was interested; saying he had a big inventory of scrap. He also said Philip and he had been working on the National Prion Center concept in Lubbock. He said everything was progressing nicely, given they had not presented the DVE emergency funding to congress. He said he expected congressional approval. Once that happened, Tech's Chancellor would be ready with a comprehensive proposal. Included in the request was a tenured and endowed chair for the director. Randall said Ray and Kate were leaving in two days to head down to collect samples of corn and soil. Rose has taken a week off, so she and Kate can go back-to-school shopping for the kids.

Penny and Pam returned from shopping. Penny tried to call Bobby Laporte; only to find he was in a meeting all afternoon and would be unavailable. She left word she would call tomorrow. She called Pat Rhodes-Voss. Their conversation centered primarily on the laboratory. Penny and

Pat then discussed DVE. Penny asked Pat, "Who do you think could be responsible for such a heinous act?"

Pat replied, "I have thought quite a little about that. Whoever it may be, they possess cutting edge knowledge of molecular biology, biochemistry, and have a very sophisticated laboratory."

"I agree", said Penny. "There's a guy at the University of Wyoming that's going to be working on isolating and purifying the nanoparticles containing the prions from the fertilizer. He then is planning on determining the size, weight, and amino acid sequence of the proteinaceous residue. Once he completes this work we will have the necessary information to postulate about the structure of the DVE prion."

"So, what all have you been doing?"

"As you know we went to an art show. We met my folks there. I watched Randy rope his first steer and he did very well, winning the first go around. He ropes his second steer Saturday. If he does well, he will qualify to rope in the finals on Sunday. We went to Laramie and met Secretary Johansen and Bobby there. I spent the next day with Bobby and Dr. Yu in Fort Collins. So far, it's been a mixture of work and vacation, but it's mostly work."

"How are things going with you and Randy?"

"Things are great, we're in Denver now. We came down Saturday afternoon. We're staying with my folks. Yesterday we all went to brunch with my two brothers and their families. Everyone really likes Randy. I'm glad he gets along with everyone so well. The Denver Broncos football team is starting their pre-season practices today. After Dad gets home from the hospital, they're going to go watch practice. It's not too far from here."

"I'm making enchiladas for everyone tonight. They are Randy's favorite and my parents both like Mexican food. I suppose I should let you get back to work, but I wanted to see how you were doing."

"Penny thanks for calling. I hope you and Randy have fun this week. I miss you."

****

Randy and Penny left the following morning returning to Cheyenne. While driving north Randy asked, "Well, do your parents approve of me-of us?"

"Oh, my yes, Mom and Dad think you hung the moon. It was interesting when we were shopping, Mom told me about the same as your Dad told you-"don't you dare let Randy get away. I almost laughed at the irony."

Randy laughed and said, "I really like your parents, they're good people. Your Dad works too hard; I think that goes with the generation. At the Bronco's practice one player came to say hello to your Dad after practice. Your Dad had done heart surgery on his daughter. He was so appreciative he stopped to tell your Dad if he ever wanted tickets, to call him. He also introduced him to the Defensive Coordinator. Apparently, his son had experienced cardiac problems. He told him if his son ever needed surgery, Dr. Ken was the only one he should consider. I think it embarrassed your Dad a little. It was nice of your Dad to take me to watch the practice. I couldn't believe the physical shape those guys are in and how big they are. I swear the center was as big as a Volkswagen when he bent over the ball."

Penny laughed and said, "Remind me, I need to call Bobby Laporte today. I tried to reach him yesterday; he was in a meeting all afternoon and could not be interrupted."

"OK." Randy teased, "Are you going to tell him you'll take the job in DC?"

Penny laughed, "Not hardly, cowboy. I'm not that easy to get rid of."

"I spoke with my Dad yesterday. He told me a couple of things that will interest you. He said my brother Bobby and his family are still at Mayo Clinic so they can run additional diagnostic tests. Dad said he spoke with Bobby about building the incinerators and he was interested. He told Dad he had lots of scrap around and would talk with you once he returned to Amarillo. I think he will be back about the same time we get back."

"Dad said he and Philip had been spending quite a lot of time working on the National Prion Center concept and it was progressing nicely. The chancellor was working on a comprehensive proposal which would be ready for submittal when the funding bill passed and became law."

"God, Randy they are moving a lot faster than I expected. Am I going to have time to finish my work before I have to resign?"

"Probably most of it; but that's just a guess. I think Dad and Philip will have their ducks in a row, but it may take some time for USDA to review and hopefully approve the proposal. I also think they have Clare Johansen's ear so it won't get pigeon-holed in bureaucratic red tape."

"Once we get to Cheyenne, I'd better update my resume and get it sent to Philip. I really don't have too much to do to have it ready. I thought I had at least a few weeks to work on it. Apparently not. And you told me you think my Dad works too hard. Between your Dad and Philip, they are unrelenting."

As they were nearing Cheyenne, Randy called Sonny. "Hey Dude, where are you guys now?"

"We're about to leave the motel for the rodeo grounds. Where are you?"

"Penny and I are about five miles from the motel. Would you mind waiting a few minutes? I'd like to catch a ride with you. Penny has some work to do this afternoon; and I want to ride Blue a little to get him used to the crowds."

"That's fine, Randy, we're in no rush. I've been doing the same thing with Gus. Although he's been everywhere, the first crowd noise and the cannons going off during the National Anthem did break his focus, he jumped a little. We'll see you in a few minutes."

As Randy drove up in the Escalade, Junior pulled out of a parking space near Randy and Penny's room allowing them to park close. Once Randy pulled in to the parking space, Sonny walked over to help unload their luggage. He asked, "Did y'all have a good time in Denver?"

"Yes, it was a good time. It was nice to spend some time with Mom and Dad and just chill", said Penny.

Randy kissed Penny good bye saying, "We're out of here. We'll let you work in peace."

"You guys have a good time. I'll see you when you get back."

"Hi Bobby, it's Penny. How are you today?"

"I am doing great. How was your trip to Denver? Did you and Randy have a good time?"

"We had a wonderful time and good visit with my parents. In fact, we stayed an extra day. I tried to call you yesterday, but you were in a meeting, so I told your secretary I would call again today. We just got back to Cheyenne. Randy went to the rodeo. I can't believe the preparation and detail that goes into preparing to compete. Randy leaves nothing to chance."

"I didn't ask while I was with you; how has he done so far?"

"He's only roped one steer so far. He won the first go-round and set a new arena record. I watched him practice roping a couple of times and had no idea he was so good. The guys that came up with him also placed in the first go-round. Junior roped his second steer in a good time and Randy says he will make it into the final fifteen that rope for a third time on Sunday. Sonny ropes his second steer tomorrow, during the rodeo; Randy ropes his second steer Saturday, also during the rodeo."

"I had no idea he had done so well when I met him in Laramie. I noticed he was wearing a new shiny buckle."

"Randy's very humble. He would not tell you unless you specifically asked. The buckle you're talking about he won earlier this month at the Prescott, Arizona rodeo. I didn't know that until I asked before we went to the art show. Randy is superstitious. He thinks discussing winning will bring him bad luck."

'I have a meeting in about twenty minutes; do you have anything we need to discuss?"

"Actually, I do. Randy spoke with Randall yesterday. Bobby Bennett is still at Mayo Clinic with his daughter. They're doing additional diagnostic testing. However, Randall mentioned the crematoriums to him. Bobby's interested in the project. Randy and I will be flying back next Monday. Bobby is due back about the same time. I plan to meet with him as soon as I can after we're all back in Amarillo. Has anyone considered how many incinerators will be needed and where they will be located?"

"I had folks working on it while we were in Laramie and Fort Collins. The number they determined is around four hundred. That shocked me, until they went through the numbers with me. Now I think that is a conservative number. If Bobby can design mobile units, the mobile units will replace the stationary units, but not in a one to one ratio. I may have more information after my upcoming meeting."

"My God, four hundred units! I don't think anyone was expecting that number. Bobby's operation is not large enough to build and install that many units; nor would he have that volume of salvage. Do you have locations identified yet?"

"I'll have more information after the meeting. Call me tomorrow."

"OK I will give you a call tomorrow morning. Thanks Bobby."

Penny had a copy of her resume in her laptop files. She had taken Pat's advice a few years ago. Pat suggested Penny should update her resume every six months and keep track of her publications and accomplishments as they happened. Looking at her resume she found she only needed to add four publications. Then, she began to critically review the resume. Penny felt the resume was too detailed; she needed to edit portions. Government service, prefers long, comprehensive, and detailed resumes. In academics, a resume needs to be concise capturing her knowledge, experience, and publications. The interview process brings out further detail. Penny modified her resume for about three hours. After editing and polishing, she e-mailed a copy to Philip.

Knowing it would be awhile before Randy got back, Penny walked to the motel's gift shop. She found upscale clothing and jewelry. A delicate turquoise and gold necklace caught Penny's eye. She noticed there were matching earrings and a bracelet. After looking around, she returned to the jewelry counter and purchased the matching set.

Penny finished getting ready for dinner when Randy walked in. "Hi there cowboy, is there a chance you would take a girl to dinner?"

"Well maybe, but I've got to shower first", responded Randy. "Hey, is that a new necklace?"

"Yes, I found it at the gift shop. Do you like it?"

"It's really nice, very feminine and looks great on you. I like turquoise set in gold. Of course, I think you could hang a soup can around your neck and you would look good."

"You're saying all the right things. If you keep it up and clean up, you have a good chance of getting lucky tonight", said Penny as she kissed Randy.

Randy held her close and whispered, "I love you."

Penny held Randy in her arms and said, "I love you too. Why don't you shower and get ready for an early dinner?"

Chapter 34

President Smyth met everyone at his office door. As he suspected, the assembled group was larger than the oval office's capacity for a working meeting. The group moved to the cabinet room. President Smyth began, "Our first goal for today is to share information. Everyone in this room holds a need-to-know position. They need to know all the information. There can be no compartmentalization. Are we understood on this point? Our second goal is to determine where the investigation needs to be going; and develop realistic timeframes for completion based upon the information we have now. Our third goal is to work together to find synergisms and capitalize on them. What I don't want is withholding of information. We're not putting ourselves in the same situation that allowed 9-11 to occur. I intend to meet these goals before we adjourn.

I requested the Attorney General to attend for two very important reasons. The first, to gain first-hand information from the investigation and its progress. She will be the one leading the resulting prosecution. Therefore, her sage comments will help lead us to our best legal position. The second reason she is here is to guide everyone regarding our responsibilities and limitations, from a legal perspective. Are there questions before we proceed further?

I want to start with a historical perspective of what has led us to where we are today. Please provide detailed responses and be open to questions as you proceed. Secretary Johansen why don't you start us off?

Thank you, Mr. President. Roughly six weeks ago we received reports of cattle, both beef and dairy, displaying symptoms of central nervous system disease. USDA used established protocols to initiate testing all cattle displaying these symptoms for BSE. During a few days, we identified 122 cattle on seven premises in five states displaying CNS symptoms. After euthanasia, their brains were tested for BSE. Inclusive test results were reported. We then sent tissues and slides to an international reference laboratory in England. They also reported inconclusive results deducing we were not dealing with the BSE or any known spongiform encephalopathy. Electron microscopic studies revealed we were dealing with a novel infectious prion protein. The English lab named it Diffuse Vacuolating Encephalopathy or DVE."

"When we obtained this information, President Smyth and I held a joint press conference announcing to the public what we were dealing with. We also took some actions. I temporarily stopped the slaughter of all cattle in the US and stopped the transportation of cattle. Exports of cattle, beef products and byproducts became ineligible for export. Change of ownership of cattle was disallowed; this included selling of cattle by private treaty, through public auctions, including the commodities and futures markets."

"While we knew we were dealing with a novel infectious prion protein, we did not know the source of this prion protein. A subsidiary of a large holding company in Amarillo Texas feeds a substantial number of cattle. It's called ATX Feeders. They own and operate six feedlots. Three feedlots located south of Amarillo, and three northeast of Amarillo. While they diagnosed DVE in the southern feedlots, the northern feedlots were unaffected. The Director of Feedlot Operations is a veterinarian. He had some roping steers at his house he fed alfalfa hay exclusively. Some of his steers began to elicit central nervous system signs. ATX also has large farming operations near their feedlots. The southern feedlots began a new crop rotation program including a new fertilizer, called nano-fertilizer. It contained nanoparticles of titanium dioxide. The farming manager used the new nano-fertilizer to fertilize the southern field crops which are alfalfa and feed corn. After harvesting the first cutting of alfalfa they used it as feed on the three southern feedlots as well as the director's roping steers. The farming manager collected several samples of alfalfa from the southern farms. He sent them and a five-gallon container of nano-fertilizer to his brother at the University of Wyoming for further testing. University of Wyoming scientists determined the nano-fertilizer contained infectious prion proteins hidden in about two-thirds of the nanoparticles. The other third of the nanoparticles contained titanium dioxide. After applying the nano-fertilizer, the alfalfa plants absorbed the nanoparticles into the alfalfa plants leaves and stems. Subsequently cattle consumed the adulterated alfalfa. The cattle's digestive juices digested the nanocapsules surrounding the infectious prion protein. After digestion, they moved to the brain. In about two months central nervous system symptoms developed. This work was done solely by ATX, using University of Wyoming scientists."

"I was notified by ATX and contacted President Smyth. Later that morning I met with him and Secretary Robinson. There is no doubt this was an intentional act of bioterrorism. The terrorism investigation was handed off to Secretary Robinson."

"Mr. President, I can either stop here to let Secretary Robinson pick up his investigation or continue with what USDA has been doing and the additional information we have uncovered."

"Please continue Secretary Johansen."

"Sure. I traveled to Laramie to recognize the efforts of the scientists and I held a press conference to update the public regarding the source of the novel infectious prion protein. While I was traveling the Plant Protection and Quarantine division of APHIS began to investigate the distribution of the nano-fertilizer. Through our initial in-depth investigations, we knew a network of farmer's cooperatives in Oklahoma City distributed the nano-fertilizer. USDA sent an investigator to Oklahoma City. He acquired a list of all cooperatives purchasing the nano-fertilizer and the quantities purchased. Our investigator went to Salina, Kansas to visit Advanced Fertilizers' manufacturing plant. The address listed on the nano-fertilizer container labels and in their printed technical information brochures was spurious."

"Our investigator traveled to Wichita, Kansas to interview a coop manager who purchased some of the nano-fertilizer. A single customer purchased the fertilizer from the coop. The farmer applied all the fertilizer by the time our investigator met with a farm hand. After harvesting, dairy cattle consumed the alfalfa. Some of the dairy cattle were symptomatic and subsequently confirmed to be DVE positive. Tragically the farm worker, a young pre-med student attending Wichita State University, applied approximately a quart of fertilizer left after the first application of nano-fertilizer to his personal vegetable garden. Our investigator noticed the young man had a persistent eyelid twitch. When asked, said he had recently been troubled with headaches."

"I initiated a conference call with Secretary Jackson and Dr. Susan Gray, Director of the CDC. I am unaware of what has happened with the boy."

"The boy did provide our investigator with copies of two scientific articles written about the nano-fertilizer. It appeared two very reputable scientific journals reported research conducted by two well respected agronomists. However, further investigation revealed the two agronomists did not author the articles and the named journals did not publish them. The nano-fertilizers scientific documentation was bogus. We've confirmed the firm allegedly manufacturing the fertilizer does not exist and the scientific literature provided to the distribution warehouse is phony."

"The primary focus of our ongoing investigation is dealing with three issues. First, tracking down and quarantining the alfalfa produced using the nano-fertilizer to contain further exposure to the novel infectious protein. Secondly, we are in the process of ascertaining all the premises requiring total depopulation and dealing with proper carcass destruction of those depopulated premises. This is a huge undertaking. Finally, the emergency funding request bill, which will be on President Smyth's desk soon for presentation to congress."

"Clare thanks for the very descriptive accounting of USDA's investigation. We must all remember it was through the fine work of the USDA that we were able to determine a novel prion is responsible DVE and its source is adulterated fertilizer. The USDA has substantial work to do on many fronts. Clare has brought to light we may be facing possible human exposure and disease development. Reading between the lines, we don't know yet if other crops are also involved. All these concerns fall under the purview of the Secretary of Agriculture. Mrs. Attorney General, am I correct in making this statement?"

"Yes, Mr. President you are correct. All the work Secretary Johansen described, as well as the future work described, falls under the responsibilities of the Secretary of Agriculture. She has the legal authority to act in the best interest of the public's health as well as animal health, and plant protection in taking whatever actions deemed necessary to do so. Her powers to do so are wide, as exampled by the actions she has already taken concerning DVE."

"Secretary Robinson, if you don't mind, I would like to hear from Secretary Jackson; then we'll hear about your terrorism investigation. Secretary Jackson please enlighten us on what's happening with the young man in Wichita, Kansas."

"Thank you, Mr. President. The young man's name is Curt Wepner. For the past two years he has lived on Don Mathews' farm near Haysville, Kansas which is a few miles south of Wichita. I contacted the director of the Sedgwick County Public Health Department regarding Curt. We involved his academic advisor in contacting him. I also contacted a large local neurology practice providing one of the neurologists there with brief history of our concerns. I asked her to examine Curt as soon as possible. We also told her physicians from the CDC would be traveling to Wichita. Dr. Ward saw Curt the following day. Curt underwent a complete panel of diagnostic tests to include CT and MRI scans of the brain as well as a series of metabolic tests and an extensive neurological examination. The MRI demonstrated multiple small vacuoles. The eyelid twitch continues; nerve conduction studies demonstrate diminished peripheral nerve signal in both legs and in his left arm. The consensus of the neurologists and the CDC team is these symptoms and test results are consistent with DVE in cattle. Realize this is the index case in humans; we don't know what to expect. Local neurologists will examine Curt monthly, more often if necessary, quarterly the CDC team will examine him. Curt has chosen to continue with his education at Wichita State; he's promised he will inform his family."

"Thank you, Dr. Jackson. Well described. Curt will be in my prayers", said President Smyth. "Now Secretary Robinson please provide us a status report on what Homeland has been doing."

"Thank you, Mr. President. The FBI began conducting interviews with those people we know have used adulterated fertilizer. We're in the process of tracking it back to its initial distributer so we can determine the location of manufacture. This morning I became aware that the USDA has already contacted the national distributor, gotten a list of local coops receiving the adulterated fertilizer, and have begun contacting the local coops. The USDA reported the manufacturer of record is a business that does not exist. We will confirm this information is accurate."

Dick Kline and Bill Franklin are diligently digging through a very complex network of dummy corporations, investment trusts, and other entities, some of which are interrelated. They are located around the globe. They initially identified twenty international investments in fat cattle commodities and futures. Efforts to decipher ownership in each of the twenty entities have led the forensic accountants and senior financial intelligence officers to a maze of other investment entities. The Commodity Futures Trading Commission and FinCEN are continuing drilling down to determine the true ownership of the twenty international investments. Bill Franklin says in his thirty-eight years of experience, he has never encountered such complexity in determining ownership of commodity contracts and put options. In his opinion, this complex investment strategy attempts to deceive and protect the principals. These two teams also uncovered irregularities, involving these same twenty investment entities, involving live U.S. cattle ETF trading on the London Stock Exchange. Clearly, this complex network of ownership points to an international effort to manipulate the cattle commodities market."

"Ryan Anderson, DEA Administrator, reported intelligence developed about eight months ago. Reportedly, a smuggling operation brought a substantial volume of fertilizer into the US through Mexico. There is an association between the fertilizer and a large shipment of heroin also smuggled across the Mexican border at Nuevo Laredo. This investigation is ongoing; however, the Texas Rangers, ATF, and other Texas law enforcement authorities made a raid in Laredo, Texas where they recovered one five-gallon container of the nano-fertilizer. It was seized as evidence in an unrelated case involving smuggling firearms into Nuevo Laredo."

"Mr. President, this is the extent of the information I have now."

"Thank you, Fred, let's take about a ten-minute break. Next, we'll change focus to our second goal-determining where the investigation needs to be directed and developing realistic timeframes for key parts of the investigation to be completed."

****

"Before we continue, does anyone have any questions or thoughts", asked President Smyth..."If not, let's continue."

"Secretary Johansen, will you share where you think your portion of this investigation needs to proceed? I know you referenced your upcoming plans in the first portion of our meeting. I think it is worthwhile to go over it again, this time in more detail. As I recall you said your plans were a 'huge undertaking', please quantify your comments as best as you can."

"Yes, Mr. President. The first order of business for the USDA is to have the emergency funding request ready for you to present to congress in two days. The bill is requesting a total of thirty-two billion dollars. We anticipate wide support from both sides of the isle; but, I will likely need to testify before the bill is approved."

"Of the total amount, twenty-five billion is earmarked for DVE indemnification. Our research shows us that total depopulation of the DVE infected herds is necessary. We have determined through economic analysis, the fairest method to indemnify is based on an algorithm considering weight, sex, breed, and other factors for beef cattle; and a lump sum per head for lactating dairy cattle based on another algorithm which considers age, milk production and other factors. Non-lactating dairy cattle, bulls, and younger stock will be indemnified using the beef algorithm."

"DVE Research is earmarked for four billion. We know very little about this novel prion specifically, and about prions in general. These monies will fund research at academic institutions throughout the US. We'll also fund academic endowments for principal prion researchers. We're also developing a new program where Agricultural Research Service employees performing prion related research can participate onsite at academic research institutions. The term of these USDA funded post-doctoral sabbaticals is one to five years. A portion of the research funds can be used for capital improvements at institutions of higher learning."

"The remaining three billion will be used for proper carcass destruction. It is important to know that prions, although very small, are very resistant to normal methods of carcass destruction. We calculate there are going to be more than 12 million cattle carcasses requiring destruction. There are six incinerators in existence at six feedlots in Texas. These natural gas-powered units each have a capacity of 65 carcasses per load. Their designer and builder patented the design. However, he is willing to cooperate with the USDA. We estimate we will need around four hundred of these incinerators strategically located to do the job. We are checking to see if mobile units are feasible. The USDA has suggested a way to increase capacity and decrease cycle time. Obviously, it is going to take time to construct these units, deliver them to their locations, and complete their installations before they are ready for use. We know most units will require a set of cattle pens adjacent to the incinerators. As you can imagine locating them strategically could likely result in public outcry and delays due to permitting, local ordinances, etc. Therefore, the USDA has determined the best locations for these huge incinerators would be on land already owned by the federal government, preferably on military reservations. We can sidestep state and local regulations by locating them on federal lands. In the case of an emergency, and this is both an animal health and public health emergency, we can avoid intense scrutiny from other federal agencies. General Clark, this is where we will need your help."

"In a nutshell, that's what is contained in the emergency funding request bill. I will answer questions you may have."

"Madam Secretary", commented General Clark. "I have to say you may be underestimating the size of your undertaking when you considered it huge. I find your carcass disposal plans to be creative and well considered. The military will provide such lands as necessary for this important undertaking. There may be additional synergisms to discuss later."

"Thank you, General Clark, I look forward to us working together. I welcome your thoughts on additional synergisms. If there are no other questions, I will proceed with USDA's second focus identifying the farmers who have purchased and applied the nano-fertilizer.

"The containers of nano-fertilizer were sold and delivered to 283 local cooperatives. We have the names, addresses, and quantities delivered to each local coop. Our first order of business is to contact each of these local cooperatives to determine the individual farmers who purchased the nano-fertilizer. We plan to send USDA officials to interview each farmer/user of the nano-fertilizer. From the farmers, we will find out where the alfalfa went. If used as feed, we will quarantine the cattle. If sold, we will have to track down and quarantine the buyers premise."

"Madam Secretary", asked Secretary Jackson, "are you potentially concerned about other crops, or do you think nano-fertilizer was exclusively on alfalfa?"

"Based upon what we currently know, we consider any crop fertilized with nano-fertilizer to be adulterated and will take enforcement action. We will seize the crop will and most likely destroy it. We aim to keep it out of both the human and animal food chains. In addition, until we have further information concerning the soil, USDA will quarantine the fields that have received the nano-fertilizer."

"Madam Secretary, do you have the authority to put land under quarantine and seize harvested crops whether they have been sold or not", asked Dr. Jackson.

"Let me answer that Secretary Johansen", said Geraldine Green, the Attorney General. "Secretary Johansen has the legal authority to act in the best interest of the public's health as well as animal health, and plant protection. Her legal authority is much wider than those provided you Dr. Jackson, as well as most other members of the cabinet. Treasury and State have wide legal authority, but not quite as much as Agriculture."

"Perhaps I should clarify something. I don't know I have mentioned", said Clare. "When we first began seeing cattle displaying CNS signs the USDA, the USDA quarantined the entire premises and all the cattle involved. Basically, what we are doing now is extending that quarantine to the farm ground and any crops produced on that farm ground. In doing so, we are following the principles of epidemiology by attempting to control DVE before is spreads further."

"As you can imagine, now that we have a list of those cooperatives that purchased the nano-fertilizer, we are moving to an onerous phase. Identifying and interviewing individual farmers is time-consuming; but we must specifically identify the land fertilized. If harvested crops are involved, we need to locate those crops. As I said earlier, our actions will be to quarantine land contaminated with DVE prions, and we'll seize or limit the use of harvested crops. Such actions require significant personnel and integrated real-time communications."

"How and why would the USDA limit the use of harvested crops", asked President Smyth.

"The situation would have to specifically warrant the use of adulterated crops. For instance, if there are cattle in a feedlot or a dairy found to be positive for DVE, the owner of the cattle could continue to feed the cattle the adulterated crop, in this case most likely alfalfa hay. Obviously, this requires strict controls and accountability. It makes no practical sense to require the owner feed non-adulterated alfalfa to cattle destined for depopulation and destruction. Movement of adulterated feedstuffs to a positive herd will require special permitting and done only with the oversight of USDA officials."

"If there are no further questions, this concludes USDA's plans."

"Thank you, Secretary Johansen. As you said initially, these actions are huge undertakings", said President Smyth. "Secretary Robinson, please share you upcoming plans with us."

"Mr. President, as you know terrorism investigations develop based upon hard evidence. Our investigation is not as concrete or as advanced as USDA's. Terrorism is a crime usually involving individuals experienced in being covert; they are good at performing stealth operations."

"I plan to have The Commodity Futures Trading Commission and FinCEN continue drilling down to identify the true ownership of the twenty international investments in live cattle commodity contracts and futures contracts. We will also check to see if these entities have additional investments in our financial or commodity markets."

"The DEA will continue to investigate the historical evidence of fertilizer and heroin smuggling across the Mexican Border into the US. There is a tentacle of evidence indicating there may be an association with illegal firearms trade."

"ATF will investigate that lead further. Secretary Johansen also provided information this morning regarding the fertilizer payments cashed at the same bank in Laredo, Texas. We will be investigating that lead. Before contacting the bank, we will interview USFFC to obtain exact dollar amounts, and other specific information that will be helpful. We may further involve Treasury and request a complete examination of the Laredo bank."

"We need to verify Advanced Fertilizers does not exist as a business. We need to question individual state agencies that regulate fertilizer and investigate any records involving Advanced Fertilizers."

"As we develop credible information, we will further investigate that information. Our investigation is basically trying to follow the money using a multi-Department/Agency approach to uncover further evidence. There is no doubt this will be labor intensive and time consuming."

"That is all that I have."

"Thank you, Fred. It appears you also have some huge undertakings ahead of you. Let's take another break for those of us with weak bladders and need additional caffeine."

****

"Our final goal for today is to find existing synergisms and capitalize on them. The intent of this portion of today's meeting is to be a brainstorming session where everyone participates. Everyone has now heard the facts and plans concerning the DVE outbreak. Now we should be asking themselves, 'How can I help?' It's now time for you to share your thoughts, experience, and resources that might be helpful. Let me start it off."

"Fred, your investigation appears to be two pronged, in addition to following up on information. Because you mentioned a large shipment of heroin, I wondered if you have made additional international contacts, specifically in Mexico and in southwest Asia. Further, have you contacted the CIA or the military?"

"Mr. President I will defer to Ryan Anderson, DEA Administrator, concerning DEA's portion of the investigation. Ryan is here with me this afternoon."

"Mr. President", said Ryan Anderson, "according to our source in Mexico, the fertilizer and the heroin came from the same source-a southwestern Asian businessman. Reportedly, there were twelve to fifteen container loads that came into Mexico through the Port of Tampico to Monterrey for processing and then to Nuevo Laredo. An informant reported the Los Zeta cartel paid 100 million dollars for the heroin and received the price of the fertilizer upon delivery to a US location. From what I learned today, that location was Oklahoma City. Although, I suspect the heroin distribution in the U.S. originated in San Antonio, Texas. The Zeta's have a distribution operation there. My investigative strategy was to attempt to back track this shipment to its origin."

"Mr. President, I have not contacted the Director of National Intelligence or the military. It now seems obvious there may be significant intelligence available that I have not attempted to garner. I will do so."

General Clark added, "Secretary Robinson, if you will give me a call when I get back to my office, I will give you some names and numbers to contact in Intelligence Support Activity. I'll also need to call those individuals to personally introduce you. Their security is pretty tight."

"Secretary Johansen or Secretary Robinson", asked Dr. Jackson, "have you begun any investigation into who may be responsible for adulterating the fertilizer? It seems to me, whomever did this purposeful act must have advanced knowledge and molecular biology skills. Prion science is a relatively small field. As I reflect on the knowledge level required to develop or modify an infectious prion protein, propagate it, and then hide it in nanocapsules, there are only a few folks in the world having such expertise."

"Secretary Jackson", said Clare, "I concur with your assessment. USDA has not focused any efforts toward that end. While we are willing to participate, our priorities have focused on other objectives."

"Frankly, Dr. Jackson, I am still attempting to grasp what a prion is and what it does", stated Secretary Robinson. "My education and experience is not in a scientific field. Although Homeland has both physicians and veterinarians, their expertise does not include molecular biology or prion science. Early on when Homeland first became involved, Secretary Johansen suggested I find an expert in this field to advise me. To date, I have been unsuccessful in locating anyone with this expertise. At this point, I'm flying by the seat of my pants; trying to assimilate as much information and understanding as possible. I am finding that to be a daunting task."

"Secretary Robinson", said General Clark, "Let me do some checking with our folks at USAMRIID at Fort Detrick. We probably have someone there I can temporarily have assigned as an advisor. Those folks also work closely with CDC. If we don't have someone with this expertise, maybe CDC does."

Dr. Jackson commented, "I will do some checking as well. If General Clark can't find anyone, I will assign someone from

CDC. One way or another, we will get you some scientific and technical expertise."

"Thank you both so much. I feel like I have been spinning my wheels and not making any progress."

"Fred", said President Smyth, "we are all here to help you. The issues and problems that rise to our level are difficult and complex; we need everyone's efforts and expertise to solve them. At our level, it can't be about turf or ego. We must work together to make the progress the public expects. As one encounter problems, it's expected they ask for help. I can't tell you how many times I have sought help from members of my cabinet. It also works the same way between departments. Don't be hesitant to ask for advice, help, or additional technical staff. No one can know it all. None of us do."

"Are there further questions or comments regarding DVE or where we're headed? If not, let's adjourn. I think this has been a very productive and valuable meeting. We'll meet again in a week. Thank all of you for attending and your participation."

Chapter 35

Not long after Randy went with Sonny and Junior to go feed the horses Penny was on the phone calling Bobby Laporte. "Hi Bobby, how are you this morning?"

"Penny I am fine. I just returned from another meeting. The Secretary is keeping me running, and that's just to keep up with her. We had a meeting yesterday with the President and some other Cabinet Secretaries and staffers. Discussion was the DVE investigation. That was the meeting I was heading to after I spoke with you. This morning we met with General Clark, Chairman of the Joint Chiefs. The emergency funding request bill must be on President Smyth's desk tomorrow."

'Well, bring me up to date on the status of the investigation."

"Most of what's been going on with the investigation you already know. The purpose of the meeting was to ensure all departments were sharing information and working cohesively with one another. A couple of things occurred."

"We spoke about carcass destruction and the need for about 400 crematoriums. They will be placed on military land to eliminate the paperwork and circumvent a lengthy approval process."

"Yes, that was Philip's recommendation", said Penny.

"Right", said Bobby. "General Clark was at the meeting. He was very receptive to the idea. He told the Secretary that he also wanted to discuss some other synergies. The Secretary and I met with him this morning. As I recall you expressed concern that Bobby Bennett's operation was not large enough to meet the demand. General Clark solved that issue this morning. He explained the military has people trained in all phases of construction including engineering officers to oversee the work. The concept we developed was for Bobby Bennett to manufacture as many units as he thought possible. The others the military will construct on site, with Bobby's company monitoring and overseeing progress. This also gives us access to all the military's equipment. If Bobby Bennett agrees to this concept, we should be able to greatly hasten the carcass destruction process. Penny, I want you to oversee and manage this project start to finish. If you need help, let me know. Once you visit with Bobby Bennett, and if he agrees, we'll have you both fly to Washington and finalize the whole thing. Are you up for the challenge?"

"Sure, I think it will be a learning experience", commented Penny excitedly.

"Great, I think you will enjoy General Clark. He's a nice and thoughtful man, it's amazing when he mentions something, there are generals jumping all around. That's why I wanted to wait until today for us to speak."

"Penny, there is something else I want you to consider. There's not been a focus on who may have adulterated the fertilizer. We know it takes a high level of expertise in prion proteins and molecular biology. Now there is a shred of evidence pointing to the Middle East or Pakistan, I would like you to approach the issue from the perspective of someone who possesses the knowledge and skills that may have a reason to contrive putting infectious prions in nanoparticles in fertilizer. As I thought about it overnight, I think at least two people are involved. One a gifted scientist with expertise in prion proteins and molecular biology, and at least one other who is equally brilliant in business and investing."

"I'll give that some thought and maybe make a few calls. Maybe I can develop some sort of short list. I know when I was going to college there were a substantial number of Middle Eastern and Pakistani graduate students everywhere I went to school. Wouldn't it be horrible if the U.S. educated and trained the people responsible for this atrocity?"

"Yes, it would Penny. Why don't we visit again in a few days? I want you to enjoy your time in Cheyenne. I hope Randy does well roping in the rodeo."

"Thanks, Bobby."

****

The public-address system crackled to life as the rodeo announcer broadcast the steer roping was forthcoming. "First up in the steer roping is Sonny Thompson. Sonny hails from Dimmit, Texas where he manages a large cattle feeding operation. Sonny was fourth in the first go round pocketing a little over $2500 for his 15.3 second run. His first steer attempted to get up as Sonny got to him; big Sonny laid him flat on the ground and tied him like a calf. He is riding a steel gray horse he calls Gus. Sonny is one of the most consistent steer ropers going down the road. Last year Sonny was fifth in the year-end standings, with less than $50 separating him from the fourth-place roper."

Sonny backed Gus into the left-hand box swung his rope twice and flipped the loop under his arm. Gus was standing square. Once the steer looked at the chute gate, Sonny nodded his head. The chute gate opened ever so slowly. Out walked and then trotted a red and white steer with wide flat horns. Sonny judged the thirty-foot score perfectly; Gus ran to the steer's left hip rating off about twelve feet behind him. Sonny was standing up in his stirrups and dipped his loop slightly to assure he would rope the right horn. The loop traveled around the right horn, passed around the left horn with a slight rise as Sonny pulled his slack placing the rope about halfway between the steer's right hip and hock. As Gus turned hard to the left the steer veered slightly right. After the rope came tight, Sonny lifted his right leg over the saddle and rode two more jumps standing in the left stirrup. Once the steer flattened out, Sonny stepped off as Gus ran past him placing the steer at Sonny's feet. Sonny reached for the bottom front leg, placing his piggin string over the steer's fetlock, he gathered the hind feet up in one swoop placing them over the steer's front leg. Then it was one, two, and a half hitch around all three legs. Sonny threw his hands in the air. Walking back to Gus, Sonny patted him on the rump, reached up to the rein to turn Gus around slackening the rope. Once the rope came slack, the steer strained his feet trying to get up, but Sonny's tie held tightly for the required six seconds. Sonny loosened his rope from the saddle horn, coiling it after the untie men took it from around the steer's horns. Sonny mounted Gus, reached for the piggin string and trotted out the arena gate with a wide smile on his mustachioed face.

"I told you Sonny Thompson was consistent. His time on his second steer is another 15.3 seconds. That makes Sonny 30.6 seconds on two steers. We'll see Sonny in the finals on Sunday. Congratulations Sonny."

Randy was horseback on Blue standing in the exit alleyway for the ropers, just outside the arena. Randy raised his hand pumping it in the air while letting out a few whoops. As Sonny rode into the alleyway, Randy reached over and shook Sonny's hand. "Nice run, man!"

"Thanks", Sonny said exiting the alleyway. He dismounted to loosen the cinch and make Gus more comfortable.

"I've got you sitting third in the go round and third in the average", said Randy. You'll be roping one more on Sunday. What do you say we tie the horses to the fence and go find Penny and Junior? A round of tall lemonades is in order. I'm buying."

"That's a great idea, but we're not going to have to look too far." Here came Junior in a slow jog with Penny in a fast walk behind him. "We're heading for some lemonade; y'all want to join us?"

Randy had placed his hand over Penny's shoulder. Junior was excitedly talking with Sonny. "Great run Sonny. Gus worked perfect. I thought you were going to stay in the stirrup too long, but as soon as he was flat, you baled, Gus brought 'em right up to you. Your tie was fantastic. Right now, you're third in the average and in the go round. Great run."

Sonny grabbed Junior pulling him close by putting his arm around his shoulder almost in a headlock. "Junior, you're more excited than I am. Slow down son, we both have another steer to rope before it's time to get excited."

Randy walked to the concession stand with Penny while Sonny and Junior sat at the end of a nearby picnic table. "Four lemonades please", said Randy. Soon they returned with the lemonades. Handing lemonade to Sonny, Penny commented, "This is so good. I don't know how long it has been since I have had fresh squeezed lemonade."

Soon the rodeo was over for the day. Sonny walked to Randy saying, "I was talking with one of the Cheyenne committee guys. He invited us over to their private bar after the rodeo. Why don't I pony Blue back to the trailer and unsaddle him and Gus, then meet you two at the bar? Junior's already there."

"I've got a better idea", said Randy. "Since you were the one that got the invitation, we'll have Penny ride Gus to the trailer and I'll ride Blue. Once we get them unsaddled and feed them all some grain, we'll meet you at the bar. Let Junior know we are going to grain Thumper."

Sonny responded, "That sounds OK too."

Randy and Penny walked over to where Gus and Blue stood tied to the fence. Randy tightened the cinch a little on Gus helping Penny aboard. He tightened Blue's cinch and jumped to the left stirrup swinging his right leg over the saddle. The two horses leisurely walked back to the barn. Once they reached the trailer Randy unsaddled both horses and put their saddles in the locked tack compartment in the trailer. Penny brushed Gus and then Blue while Randy got the grain.

They would feed the horses hay when they returned from the bar. Penny led Gus into his stall and took off his bridle. She scratched him under the ear on the side of his head. Gus preferred Penny's attention to the filled grain bucket. When Randy returned, he watched Penny and said, "I think Gus has found a friend."

Penny said, "He's such a nice gentle horse. I like Gus."

"What do you say we walk over to the bar?"

"Something cold to drink sounds good. Where is it at?"

"It's under the main grandstand. There is a small unmarked door between two vendor booths. If you don't know where it is, you would have difficulty finding it. It's air conditioned, reasonably quiet, and usually they have something light to eat while you have a drink. It's kept exclusive; an invitation from a committee member is the only way you get in."

"Well how are we going to get in then?"

"I'm planning on your good looks getting us past the bouncer", Randy said with a big smile.

Penny punched Randy in the upper arm saying, "No you're not. How are we really going to get in? I don't want to crash someplace where we're not invited or welcome."

"OK really, I have a standing invitation to come in whenever I want. The committee called me a few years ago in the fall looking for enough roping and steer wrestling steers coming over from Mexico to use during the rodeo. I found them some, leased some wheat pasture for them to graze, and then fed them at Tulia until late spring."

"Do you do that every year?"

"I did it two years in a row, then someone got jealous and raised a stink that there was no competitive bidding. So, the guy that raised hell, got the bid. I didn't even bid. I was trying to help the committee. They put up the money for the cost of the cattle, rent on the pasture, and I cut them a deal while they were in the Tulia lot because we only fed them haylage. I arranged for ATX Transportation to haul them to Cheyenne. I knew the guy that was complaining couldn't do it as cheaply as I had, but I didn't want any hard feelings over something I was doing just to help the committee. He'll end up losing money or try to take advantage of the committee. They'll be giving me a call again. I told them they could call, if they needed to. That's how we will really get in."

Soon they were at the non-descript door. Randy knocked and the security guard opened the door. Randy identified himself telling the guard which committee member invited him. It was spacious without being too big, dimly lit with a definite ambiance of an old western bar with memorabilia from days' past. Several large tables, made from old wagon wheels with Plexiglas tops, sat around the room. Western music was playing in the background. Randy and Penny joined a group that had pushed two tables together. It was a mix of committee members, their wives, and contestants including Sonny and Junior. Randy introduced Penny to everyone he knew and met those he didn't. The room was mostly full with a mix of cowboys, dignitaries, event sponsors, the committee, and night show performers. Sonny took drink orders and walked with Randy as he went to get Penny and him a drink. As they returned to the table, Randy with two drinks in each hand and Sonny with three drinks in his right hand and sipping from the drink in his left hand, noticed a man sitting next to Penny.

Randy walked up with a smile thinking this was someone Penny knew, placing her drink on the table and one for Junior who was intensely listening to the conversation. "What the hell; are you too good to dance with me", the man asked Penny. The smile washed off Randy's face as if he had just stepped on a rattlesnake.

Penny replied in a slightly elevated voice, "I told you; I am here with someone and I don't want to dance with you. That's all you need to know. You're sitting in my boyfriend's chair and he's standing behind you. Please leave."

Sonny saw the color leave Randy's face and said, "I got this", as he set the drinks down on the table. Two committee members stood. Sonny reached over grasping the man near the neck on the top of his shoulder with his ham-sized hand lifting the man right out of the chair. "Pal", Sonny said, "it's time you found somewhere else to be. This chair is taken."

The man struggled to free himself from Sonny's grip, to no avail. "Keep your hands off me. This is none of your business."

"The lady is my friend, which makes it my business. Pal, you have a better chance of shedding your skin than me letting go of you."

About that time three of the man's friends arrived to help. As one man took a swing at Randy, Junior lunged to his feet hitting the man on the bottom of his chin before Junior had extended his legs. The blow violently struck the man knocking his head backward. The man lost his feet, landing on the far edge of the table behind him knocking the table over. Randy positioned himself to protect Penny. The men bent on avenging their friend's failed pass at Penny. As another man dressed in shorts with thongs on his feet stepped in, Randy placed a powerful blow to his solar plexus knocking the wind out of the man. As "shorts and thongs" bent over, Randy hit him with a dominating uppercut landing squarely on his nose. Blood immediately gushed from his widened nose. To add exclamation, Randy stomped down accurately on the bridge of the man's unprotected foot. Everyone at the table heard bones breaking. By this time Sonny had the man who had bothered Penny face down on the floor with his knee in the small of the man's back. Sonny had incapacitated the man and crouched like a mountain lion waiting to pounce. "Knife" yelled Junior who could not get around Randy.

Sonny sprung like the jaws of a bear trap; grabbing the third man's arm with both of his meaty hands just above the man's wrist flexing the man's elbow backward and slightly outward until the man's hand was well behind his shoulder. However, the man's wrist and forearm did not stop until there was a sickening tearing sound immediately preceded by a loud pop. The knife dropped to the floor. Sonny dislocated the man's elbow in an instant. The security guard from the entrance door and two uniformed policemen arrived. Sonny positioned himself immediately to the left of Penny still sitting in her chair. Randy was directly behind her, with Junior to her right. Penny had seen nothing; it was over in an instant.

The two policemen immediately began to arrest Randy, Sonny, and Junior. The chairman of the committee stood and said to the police. "The three cowboys are OK; they were protecting Penny, the lady sitting there. It's the others you need to arrest. The man with the bad elbow had a knife and was planning on using it. All of four of them need medical attention."

Penny's eyes widened. She immediately turned around to Randy and asked, "Are you OK?"

"Yeah, I'm OK; how about you Sonny?"

"I'm fine", said Sonny with a grin.

"Junior how are you", asked Penny.

"I'm OK; my hand's a little sore. I was worried about that guy with the toad sticker."

"No need to worry any about him. It's going to be awhile before he's able to use his arm", said Randy.

The police called an ambulance that stationed on the grounds. In a few minutes, the EMTs came in with a gurney. The guy Junior punched had not yet regained consciousness.

The EMTs called for another ambulance, as all four required transport to the hospital.

Everyone sat around the table-just looking at each other. Sonny thinking the mood was much too somber said to Junior, "I think I'm going to start calling you 'Punch'...Punch Thomas; it has kind of a nice ring to it."

"We don't need to tell Dad about this."

"We don't need to tell anyone about this; but I'll bet you a steak dinner Bud knows about it, before we get back home. Look around the bar; there are plenty of folks in here who know your daddy. Any one of them would be proud to share your KO with Bud. And, when Bud finds out what really happened, he'll be proud of your actions. Isn't that right, Randy?"

"I think Sonny's right. I know I am proud of you. I didn't see that guy coming. He would have sucker punched me into next week."

"Enough", said Penny. "I am shaking like a leaf. It all happened so fast that I truthfully didn't see anything. My God, all of you could have been hurt badly."

"Penny, I'm Vick Walters, general chairman of the committee. I saw the entire thing. I apologize for such a thing to occur in here. We bring our wives in here to have a drink and a snack before attending the night show. We enjoy having our invited guests join us. We see Randy once a year, when he comes up to rope. He's helped us out of some tight spots over the years, and we look forward to seeing him, Sonny, and Junior. They're true cowboys, competitors, and gentlemen. Please accept my apology not only on my behalf but that of our committee. We're sorry such a thing happened."

"Thank you, Mr. Walters. I'm just happy everyone in our group is OK", said Penny as she put her arm around Randy's and held it tightly.

"Penny", Vick said, "in all sincerity I'm glad Randy, Sonny, and Junior were not injured as well; but those guys made a tragic mistake attempting to take a cowboy's girl away. It was over nearly as soon as it started. I started to come around the table. Before I could push my chair back, the entire ordeal was over. It was like college vacation meets delta force."

Sonny stood, smiled, and said, "Now that I've worked up a little appetite, I think I'm going to get some of those meatballs and little sandwiches."

"Me too", said Junior.

Penny, still tightly holding onto Randy's arm said in a scolding voice, "I don't understand how you can be so nonchalant. You just sent four men to the hospital and now you're ready for hors d'oeuvres? How many men do you have to injure before you're ready for supper?"

Sonny stopped, turned around to face Penny and bent down on one knee. "Miss Penny, it was not me or Junior who were rude or ugly. Those guys were here to cause trouble, and they picked the most beautiful girl here to use as bait. It was them who exhibited poor manners and judgment, but by God I was not going to let anyone hurt you or Randy. That's behind us now. I was planning on eating some of those meatballs and little sandwiches before this whole thing started. It's not that I am insensitive; I'm hungry. I never eat before I rope."

Penny loosened her grip on Randy's arm, kissed Sonny on the forehead, saying, "Thank you for making sure we were not hurt. Now go get some of those meatballs and little sandwiches."

As Sonny got to his feet Junior quipped, "Hey Sonny, do you think if I piss Penny off, and seek forgiveness, she'll kiss me too?"

Chapter 36

"Major Merle Harris from USAMRIID at Fort Detrick reporting as ordered, Secretary Robinson."

"General Clark certainly acts fast. I spoke to him late yesterday afternoon and he said you would be here to act as my technical liaison. I had no idea it would be first thing this morning! Welcome to your TDY assignment at Homeland Major Harris."

"Sir, if the Chairman of the Joint Chiefs calls your commander directly and says he needs to send someone, things happen fast. I am glad to meet you Mr. Secretary. How can I be of assistance to you?"

"Major Harris, I don't know how much briefing you have been given, but we're currently investigating an act of bioterrorism. It has to do with DVE involving cattle in several locations across numerous states."

"Mr. Secretary, my briefing consisted of telling me that I needed to report to you first thing in the morning. I would be your technical liaison in a matter of national security."

"Major, please sit down. Would you like a cup of coffee?"

"Yes, sir; black please."

Secretary Robinson handed him a steaming mug. "Major, please call me Fred when we are working together and you can call me whatever your protocol calls for when we are not alone."

"Fred, call me Merle. I know a little about DVE from what I have heard and read, but information in the press is rather limited. Hopefully you can fill me in on that information, or have someone I can contact to allow me to get up to speed."

"I have two contacts for you at USDA. One is Dr. Bobby Laporte, he is the Administrator of APHIS; the other is Dr. Penny Adams, whom I have not met. According to Dr. Laporte she's up to date on USDA's investigation and knows more about prions than anyone at USDA. Here are their contact numbers."

I know Dr. Adams; she is a top-drawer scientist. I was a little surprised when she went to work USDA a few years ago. I'll call Penny."

"Merle, tell me about yourself."

"Like Dr. Adams I am a veterinarian and have a PhD in Molecular Biology. I had a scholarship provided by the Army to attend veterinary school at Kansas State University. When I graduated I owed the army four years; and started in the Veterinary Corps. After two years the Army provided me with another opportunity, to get a PhD in Molecular Biology at Stanford. That's where I met Penny. She was a grad student getting her Masters in Molecular Biology. I'm married and we have three boys. We live in Fredrick, Maryland near the Fort. My wife is a pediatrician and partner working with five other docs in a pediatric practice."

"Merle, I arranged an office for you down the hall. I would like you to accompany me to the meetings I attend concerning DVE and the terrorism investigation, and of course to all our senior staff meetings. I want you to feel free to ask questions and provide scientific clarification when you think it will add to the discussion. Hardly anyone here has a scientific background; so, you may find we are wandering from where we need to be going. It will be up to you to get us back on track. I would also like you to listen in the conference calls regarding the investigation. What kind of security clearance do you have?"

"I have a TS/SCI/CI/FSP clearance. Recall USAMRIID's operational mission is to research and develop medical solutions to protect military service members from biological threats. We work in a Biological Level three and four environments. We work with the nastiest of the nasty biological organisms."

"That clearance level will certainly gain you access to all of the information we are dealing with and more. What if I show you to your office and give you some time to arrange things where you can work comfortably. Did you bring a laptop?"

"No sir, I thought about it, but did not know the security level of your communication system. There's stuff on my computer that doesn't need to get out. I thought you probably had something around I could use."

"Let me make a call. I'll have one brought up by one of our IT folks and they can walk you through the details of getting it operational. We have a conference call with the DEA at 1:30PM and a staff meeting at 2:15 PM. I will introduce you to the group at that time. Will you require secretarial assistance?"

"No sir. You will find I rarely print anything for distribution. However, if you want the information I will gladly share it with you, using secure e-mail."

"Let's show you your office?"

****

Secretary Johansen called Bobby and advised, "I have read through the final draft of the emergency funding request bill. I also had our attorneys look it over from a language perspective to assure it gives me the latitude and authority to do the things we discussed. Have you finished your review?"

"I have", said Bobby. "We're very comfortable with the indemnification program; I gave the carcass destruction part of the bill particular attention. I also had a Department attorney review that portion closely. I can confidently say it gives us wide latitude to do what we need to do regarding carcass destruction. I asked Penny Adams to review the carcass destruction portion. In her opinion it provides sufficient latitude to modify our basic plan when necessary to accomplish the mission."

"I'd like you to ride with me to give it to the President. You and your staff put it together; I think you ought to be there when we hand it to President Smyth. How about I meet you at the side door in about ten minutes?"

"I'll see you in ten."

****

Penny had been racking her brain trying to remember more details about a Pakistani graduate student she had briefly encountered while working on her masters at Stanford. He received his PhD and was leaving after her first semester. She couldn't remember his name, but recalled he made racist accusations against some of the graduate students and the male professors. As she remembered, he waited until he had graduated; then reported several individuals made racial slurs regarding his heritage. Before the investigation was complete, he left for a fellowship at Harvard Medical School in Neurobiology. However, she could recall no further details. Penny was becoming frustrated when her cell phone rang.

"Hi Penny, I don't know if you remember me. We were at Stanford together for two years. My name is Merle Harris. I was working on my PhD and you were working on your masters."

"Of course, I remember you, Merle. How are you?"

"I'm doing fine. You may recall, I was in the Army when I was at Stanford. I'm still in the military, now I am more or less permanently assigned at USAMRIID in Maryland. However, I am on temporary loan to Secretary Fred Robinson at Homeland Security. I started this morning. I'm serving as his technical advisor regarding the terrorism investigation into DVE. They gave me your name as someone I could contact to brief me about the investigation. Can you help me?"

"I'll do my best ", said Penny. "I don't know anything about the terrorism investigation; but, I can tell you about USDA's involvement. Penny then summarized APHIS's investigation, providing details about the investigation and what had gone on subsequently leading them to discover the source was adulterated nano-fertilizer. She brought Merle up to speed on the alleged association between the nano-fertilizer and heroin smuggling. Penny provided what she knew about the emergency appropriations funding bill and carcass destruction.

Penny asked, "Merle, do you have any questions?"

"I don't think so. You covered a lot of details succinctly, but I have a general idea of what USDA is doing. This afternoon, they will brief me on what homeland is doing with the criminal investigation. I am impressed USDA has made so much progress so quickly. You have a big job ahead of you. It's not going to be easy to kill and completely destroy twelve million cattle."

"I have a question for you. Remember during our Stanford days there was a Pakistani graduate student who received his PhD and then caused a big stir about racial discrimination. As I remember, he was going to Harvard to do a fellowship in Neurobiology. That occurred at the end of my first semester. I can't remember much about it or who he was. Can you refresh my memory?"

"Yeah, I was one of the graduate students who allegedly showed racial bias toward him. His name is Mohammed Aziz. He was an active member of the Islamic Students Organization at Stanford. He said a few of us referred to him as a 'rag head' in front of students in the labs we taught. After the dust settled on the investigation, we were all exonerated. As I remember, he did not stay at Harvard very long. He made similar allegations there and moved to

England to work with Graeme Pennington and Ian McLaughlin. I don't know where he is now, but it's not at the Animal Health and Veterinary Laboratories in Worcester. Mohammed ran around with another Pakistani guy from the business school. His name is Mushtaq Shakir. He was a trouble maker; always keeping things stirred up between the Islamic students and the Christian students. I think he was a radical Islamist before it was cool to be one. Why do you ask?"

"Bobby Laporte and I were visiting a few days ago. We both agreed, given the degree of complexity used to adulterate the fertilizer, whoever is responsible must have advanced knowledge and experience with prions to essentially create a novel prion. As we both know, our field of expertise involves a small number of people who have that degree of knowledge and expertise. Bobby asked me to give it some thought to see if anyone stood out. Merle, he's the only one I can think of. As I remember, biochemical and structural manipulation of proteins was his specialty."

"Penny, now that I think about it, he would be my top candidate too. He was arrogant, seemed to have his own religious bias. He demanded the Stanford faculty make accommodations for his religion. He wanted time off in the middle of his undergraduate lectures to pray, the same when he was teaching a lab. He was one of the leaders of a student Islamic group demanding the cafeterias serve Halal meals. That happened before you arrived at Stanford."

"Merle let me do more checking. If he appears to be a viable person of interest, I'll let you know."

"That sounds good to me. Thanks' for the briefing. It was wonderful talking with you again. If you're ever in this area, please let me know. We can have coffee or go to dinner or something."

"Actually, I may be in DC in a couple of weeks. We need to put together the crematorium plans with the military. I don't know how much time I will have; but I will at least call."

****

Penny thought, *I must find Mohammed Aziz's current location. He's likely at a university somewhere conducting research and teaching. That would be most likely and would provide him with access to a laboratory. I wonder what he may have published recently.* A quick primary author search using several search engines revealed no publications within the past 14 years. The last article published was his PhD research while at Stanford. Penny found that to be strange. She opened a new window and used a popular search engine and typed in Aziz's name. She found him a faculty member and Head of the Department of Biochemistry and Molecular Biology in the Army Medical College at National University of Pakistan in Islamabad. Penny dug deeper into the department's website looking at published articles. While she could find no articles that named Aziz as an author or coauthor, she found what he was teaching his graduate students by the research papers they had published. There were papers on developing proteinaceous nanoparticles, sequencing of amino acids, and creating structural stability of small protein molecules using disulfide bonds. V*iewed independently these papers would not raise attention from the scientific community nor from investigative software. However, when viewed collectively it became apparent they researched all the components to synthesize a misfolded prion. This brilliant, yet sneaky bastard, kept his research compartmentalized. One graduate student independently worked on one portion while another graduate student worked on another component. He purposely omitted his name from participating in the research. Once his students developed the technology, he used the information to collectively synthesize misfolded prions and put them in proteinaceous nanoparticles, which he added to the fertilizer.*

Penny thought about how to incorporate the titanium dioxide nanoparticles into the fertilizer. Searching the web, she found numerous sources for reagent grade titanium dioxide. It was available in quantities of one kilogram up to metric tons. And it was inexpensive; less than ten dollars per kilo for reagent grade. She reasoned one kilo would be enough to make all the titanium dioxide nanoparticles needed for the 25,000 five-gallon containers. Penny found making 30 nanometer proteinaceous nanoparticles was like the protocols for making nanoparticles encapsulating chemotherapeutic drugs. It was a relative easy process using bovine albumin, which also is relatively inexpensive and readily available. Aziz's plan was ingenious, inexpensive, and potentially devastating when used as a weapon of terrorism.

Penny tried to locate Mushtaq Shakir using the same methodology. However, she could develop no useful information.

Penny was excited about her discovery regarding Dr. Mohammed Aziz; calling Bobby Laporte.

"Hi Penny, today has been very busy. Yesterday we took the emergency appropriations bill over for President Smyth to present to congress. That's a big load off our backs. I'm taking a short breather, before getting back to work. What's happening?"

"I think I may have figured out who may be responsible for the DVE prion."

"Hold on, I'll be right back."

A couple of minutes later she heard a door close. Bobby put Penny on the speaker phone at his desk. "Penny are you still there?"

"Yes Bobby, I'm here. We're in Cheyenne."

"Penny, I put you on speaker phone. I have Secretary Johansen with me. I wanted her to listen. You just said you think you've figured out who may be responsible for the DVE prion. Is that right?"

"Hello Madam Secretary. Yes, that's right Bobby. After we talked a few days ago, I started thinking about who had the knowledge, expertise, and maybe the motivation to do such a heinous thing. I remembered a Pakistani guy who was just finishing his PhD as I was starting my masters at Stanford. After he graduated, he made accusations about racial and religious discrimination concerning some graduate students and the molecular biology faculty. He caused a big investigation at Stanford; then he left for a fellowship at Harvard. However, I could not remember his name."

"A friend of mine from my time at Stanford, Major Merle Harris, who now works at USAMRIID at Fort Detrick, is on temporary assignment to Secretary Robinson. I briefed him on the technical side of what we have been doing and where we're headed. Anyway, I asked Merle if he remembered this guy's name and he did.

It's Dr. Mohammad Aziz. I dug into where he is now and what he has been doing. He is the Head of the Department of Biochemistry and Molecular Biology at the Army Medical College at National University of Pakistan in Islamabad. Oddly, for someone in his position, I found he's not published anything since he left Stanford, over a decade ago. I dug a little deeper, finding his graduate students have published good work. The subject, when viewed separately, is nothing that would raise any flags; however, when looked at collectively, it's a definite flag raiser. His graduate students have published papers on the manufacture a novel infectious prion protein to hide in a nanoparticle. I also looked in to making titanium dioxide nanoparticles. We could cook up a batch and put them in proteinaceous nanoparticles in your kitchen over the weekend. The supplies are readily available and inexpensive. Merle also said Aziz ran around with another trouble-maker Pakistani while at Stanford. He was getting an MBA at Stanford's School of Business. His name is Mushtaq Shakir. I could find no information about him. While I can't be certain that Aziz is the one who adulterated the fertilizer, it's very suspicious and I wanted you to know. I also told Merle I would let him know if I found anything out."

"Penny, this is Clare. The information you have just shared may be the key to discovering who's ultimately responsible for making the adulterated fertilizer. Call your friend Major Harris and tell him what you found. I will write you an e-mail. It will capture the information you just shared with us. I will cc Secretary Robinson, General Clark, and President Smyth. I'm certain they will treat it as top priority. Penny, thanks so much for calling."

Chapter 37

"Hello Bobby, how are things with Rachel", asked Randall.

"Dad, that's why I'm calling. The doctors here have put her through a battery of diagnostic tests. They say she needs open heart surgery to repair a hole in her heart between the bottom two chambers and she may require a heart valve replacement. Honestly, we don't know what to do. Caroline and I want another opinion from an expert. I thought you may know of one, and I needed to tell you where we are with Rachel."

"Let me make a few calls. I'll call you back as soon as I know something."

"Sounds great. Thanks Dad."

****

"Rose, it's Dad; how are you today?"

"I'm fine. Ray and Kate are due in today; but they haven't arrived yet. It's going to be great to see them and have the kids together again. I also know it will relax Larry to find out the extent of damage the new fertilizer has done. You know he blames himself, regardless of what everyone is telling him. I think not knowing bothers him more than knowing. Larry can react to the facts presented to him; but it's the waiting he finds difficult. With the cattle markets still shut down, he is unable to keep himself busy. So, he worries."

"I wondered if you would do me a favor?"

"Sure Dad, anything. What do you need?"

"As you know Penny's father is a pediatric thoracic surgeon in Denver. I want you to check him out very quietly.

Determine if he's top notch. Rachel apparently needs open heart surgery. They found that out at Mayo Clinic. Bobby and Caroline want another opinion. I want us to determine if Penny's dad is someone they could take Rachel to for the other opinion. Can you do that for me honey? Bobby's waiting for my return call."

"I'm on it. I'll make a few calls and get back to you soon. Let me know if there's anything I can do for them."

****

"Dad, I made calls to folks that know Dr. Ken Adams in Denver. He specializes in pediatric cardiothoracic surgery and is on staff at the University of Colorado Medical School. Dad, he's a real heavyweight in his field. He continues to help set the bar for pediatric surgeons and cardiothoracic surgeons. He is board certified in both specialties and is on the board of governors for the American Association of Cardiothoracic Surgeons. One person I spoke with says he continues to work hard every day, although from a financial perspective he could have retired long ago. I think I know where Penny gets her work ethic, or at least part of it. As you may know, Penny's mother is a successful architect who was responsible for designing the new Denver Children's Hospital. I would not hesitate to take one of my children to him if they needed heart surgery. I hope this helps. How's Bobby holding up?"

"Bobby sounds stressed. I think he feels like he needs to be back here. I'm going to give him a call now and have him call Randy. I think it would be best if he spoke to Randy and Penny and get the appointment set up that way. When he speaks with Penny, I think she can relieve some of his stress. Thanks so much for your help."

"Bye, Dad; please keep me in the loop on Rachel. Let me know if Larry or I can do anything. I love you."

"I love you too honey. I'll be in touch."

****

"Randy, it's Bobby; did I catch you at a bad time?"

"Not at all; Penny and I went to the rodeo today. I'm riding back to the barn to unsaddle Blue. How's Rachel, I heard you needed to stay for additional testing?"

"Rachel is doing well for a little girl, who has been poked, prodded, and constantly being told lay still and do not move. The doctors here found a hole between the lower chambers of her heart. They told us she may also need to have a valve replaced. We're going to get a second opinion, that's why I'm calling. Although I have not met Penny, I understand her Dad is a pediatric cardiothoracic surgeon. Randy, I wondered if Penny could speak to him, and best-case scenario, we could have him examine Rachel on our way back to Amarillo. Do you think Penny would do that for us?"

"There is no doubt in my mind. Penny is with me; would you like to talk with her?"

"That would be great! Thanks."

Randy handed his cell phone to Penny riding Gus. "Penny this is my brother Bobby. He wants to talk with you about his daughter Rachel and getting her in to see your Dad."

"Hi Bobby, this is Penny. I understand Rachel has some problems. How can I help?"

"Penny the doctors here at Mayo Clinic have examined Rachel and done a lot of diagnostic testing over the past four or five days. We met with her main doctor here and another doctor who is a surgeon. They say Rachel has a hole between her bottom heart chambers and she may need a new heart valve. We want a second opinion before having Rachel undergo such a dangerous surgery. I know your Dad is a top pediatric cardiothoracic surgeon. We wanted to see if you could help us have him examine Rachel?"

"Sure, that's not a problem Bobby. Would you like to have Dad see Rachel on your way back to Amarillo, or come up later? I'm sure he would be glad to examine Rachel when it's most convenient for you guys."

"Penny, I can't tell you how much this means to me and Catherine. Do you think he would have time on our way back to Amarillo? That would be in two or three days, but that's also over the weekend."

"Bobby, weekends don't mean much to Dad; but I don't know his schedule. Do you have some paper and a pen available? I want to give you his contact numbers. I'm going to call him when we hang up; but, if he's in surgery or making rounds, he is not available. I will call to keep you informed."

Penny provided Bobby with her Mom and Dad's home phone number, his cell phone, office phone, and the hospital phone numbers. She told Bobby he would have to ask the hospital to page Dr. Ken Adams. She added, "I doubt you will need anything except his office number, but it's better to be safe than sorry. I need to tell you one other thing before I give him a call. It's about Rachel's medical records. Before you leave Rochester, you need to sign a form for Mayo to release Rachel's records to Dr. Ken Adams, Denver Children's Hospital, Cardiopulmonary Department, 26246 East 29th Avenue, Denver, CO 80064. Ask them to expedite the records and tell them when you have your appointment. That way, all her records and test results will be available for Dad to review when he examines Rachel. Do you want to talk with Randy again? I'm going to call Dad right now on my cell phone."

While Penny was talking with Bobby, Randy unsaddled Blue, brushed him off and fed grain to all the horses. Sonny and Junior walked up as Penny was sitting on Gus talking on the cell phone. After handing the phone to Randy, Penny dismounted. Sonny walked over to unsaddle him. "You're going to spoil Gus", said Sonny with a big smile on his face.

"How's that Sonny, have I done something wrong? I'm sorry."

"Well you weigh about half as much as I do. You don't ask him to do anything except walk next to his best friend, Blue. I heard you even brushed him down after you rode him yesterday. I'm getting worried he'll buck my butt off and come running to you one of these days."

"Oh Sunny, I thought you were serious. I've got to give my Dad a call."

****

"Hi Dad, how are you today?"

"Fine, dear. I got out of surgery about an hour ago, just finished rounds. I'll head home in a few minutes. It's an early day for me. How about you?"

"We're fine. We went to the rodeo this afternoon. It was fun and no one has yet bested Sonny's time on his second steer. That leaves Sonny third in the second go round and third in the average. Randy ropes again on Saturday. I need to ask a favor from you."

"Anything for my little girl."

"Seriously Dad, I need a favor. Randy's brother Bobby has a little girl, Rachel. They're at Mayo Clinic right now. Mayo's diagnosed her with a ventricular septal defect and she may need a new valve. They want a second opinion and called me to see if you would examine Rachel on their return from Rochester to Amarillo. I told them that you would. That's my favor. Please examine Rachel. They plan to leave tomorrow and make it a two-day trip to Denver. That would put them in Denver some time on Saturday. I told them about signing a records release, gave them your contact numbers, and your address at the hospital to send the expedited records. They stayed several days in Rochester; it sounds like they have done a complete workup. I also told them you would give them a call. If you would examine Rachel over the weekend, it would mean a lot to me; if you and Mom don't have any plans."

"Penny, Mom and I don't have any important plans. I would be happy to examine Rachel. How old is she?"

"She's about four. She's not going to school yet, but does go to pre-school. I've not met Bobby or his wife Catherine. Rose told me about them and Rachel when we were shopping. They sound very concerned about Rachel. I'm sorry, but I just couldn't say no to Bobby, and I really didn't think you would mind."

"Penny, I don't mind. I'm concerned about seeing Rachel sooner rather than later. If she has a large defect there may not have been a mummer evident when she was younger; but she may be developing ventricular hypertrophy thus causing the valvular insufficiency. If the hypertrophy is not advanced, we can repair the defect and we will not need to replace the valve. Her repaired heart will grow into the hypertrophy. I will see her as soon as they get in town. Do you have a contact number for Bobby?"

"Yeah Dad, if you can give me five minutes after we hang up before you call. I told them I would call them back. I'm just going to say that you will be calling them in a few minutes. Thank you so much."

"Anything for my little girl. I better go, if I'm going to call Bobby in five minutes. I love you dear."

****

"Hello, this is Bobby Bennett."

"Hi Bobby, this is Ken Adams. Penny asked me to call. I understand Rachel has some heart problems."

"Thank you so much for calling us back right away Dr. Adams. I can't tell you how much this means to me and my family. Rachel has been getting too tired to play with her friends and gets out of breath very easily. She has always been an active girl; lately we have noticed she would rather sit playing quietly by herself. Our family physician referred Rachel to the Mayo. Rachel's doctor up here says there is a hole between the bottom chambers of her heart and recommended surgery. The surgeon also said that he may need to replace a heart valve, but he wouldn't know until he was able to see her heart. We're planning on leaving Rochester tomorrow morning to head back west. Would there be a possibility you could examine her as we traveled through Denver?"

"Bobby, I would be happy to examine Rachel on your way back home. Penny said you were planning on being in Denver in a couple of days. Is that correct?"

"Yes, Dr. Adams we thought we could make it easily in two days, if everyone travels OK. You know how it is traveling with little kids. We're worried about Rachel; but could try to make it in one day, if necessary."

"There's no need to rush. I'll be around all weekend. It is better not to get Rachel too tired or stressed. If it takes longer for you to get here, I'll work her exam into my schedule. I want you to come directly to the hospital when you arrive. I'll meet you there. I understand Penny gave you the information about getting Rachel's medical records from the Mayo Clinic here for me to review. It's important you sign the release prior to leaving Rochester. Tell them to express ship them by FedEx for Saturday delivery. I understand Penny gave you my contact numbers. Don't hesitate to call me anytime if you have a question or if it appears Rachel is acting differently."

"Dr. Adams, thank you very much. My wife Catherine and I have not met Penny yet; but we have heard nothing but good things about her. When I spoke with her, I could not believe the information she gave me. It had to be from memory. She gave me all your contact numbers and knew the address of the hospital from memory. I know my brother Randy really thinks she's special."

"When Penny was in college and veterinary school in Fort Collins, she worked in my office during the summers. I'm sure she had to provide the hospital information so many times that it's still ingrained in her memory. I've had the pleasure to spend a few days with Randy. I know Penny thinks a lot of him and so do I."

"I have some colleagues at Mayo Clinic. Actually, I did part of my residency in Rochester. I will have my office text you the directions from Interstate 76 to Denver Children's Hospital. If you have time, please give me a call on my cell phone as you travel by Fort Morgan, Colorado. You will be about an hour or so from the hospital; it will give me time to travel to the hospital. Again, make your trip as easy as you can on Rachel; there is no need to rush on my account. I will see her as soon as I can after you arrive."

"Dr. Adams, thank you very much for your help and willingness to see Rachel. In just the few minutes we have spoken, I feel much better about making the trip. I look forward to meeting you. Thank you for your kindness."

"I look forward to meeting you, Catherine, and Rachel when you arrive. Drive carefully. I will see you when you get here."

Chapter 38

It was finals Sunday at Cheyenne Frontier Days. Penny sat in the contestants' bleachers near the roping chute alone and anxious. Randy roped yesterday as the last person to rope his second steer. He had drawn another good steer; Randy roped him quick, Blue worked perfectly. Randy, the guy who knew he needed to tie his steer in less than 22.6 seconds, did not pass up his first good shot. He threw his hands in the air marking a 14.4 second official time. The time placed him first in the second go round. Randy's aggregate time on two steers was 27.7 seconds. It moved Sonny to fourth in the go round and forth in the average with his 30.6. Junior moved to ninth in the average with a two-head aggregate of 31.8. All three were now horseback warming up their horses preparing to rope in finals.

It is Cheyenne tradition at the finals that the top fifteen ropers rope in reverse order. The roper with the fastest time on two steers ropes last. Randy would be the last roper.

Penny's cell phone rang. She answered, "Hi Dad, I'm glad you called. I'm sitting in the bleachers alone getting anxious. The guys all made the finals; and are off warming up their horses. What's new with you?"

"Penny, Mom and I were tentatively planning on coming up to watch Randy rope yesterday or today and spend a little more time with you. But it didn't work out as we planned. I examined Rachel yesterday afternoon. She is such a sweet little girl. Bobby is much like Randy, laid back, courteous, considerate as is his wife, Catherine. Rachel has a large septal defect that requires repair. As you suspected Mayo did a complete work-up. I'm going to repair Rachel's defect tomorrow morning. She is showing significant signs of fatigue with exertion. Bobby, Catherine, Rachel, and their other two kids are staying with Mom and me. I wanted you and Randy to know; thinking you may want to delay your return to Amarillo to be with Bobby and Catherine during and after surgery. They are very concerned and anxious. I think it would be good them to have family around. We've got the two boys, Robby and Mack, lined up with a great day care center that's close to our house. We know the people that own it and it's first rate. That will reduce some of the pressure on Catherine and Bobby. I purposely called when I thought you'd be alone. Randy doesn't need to know about this until after he competes; there nothing either of you can do until tomorrow. As you know, we have plenty of room for everyone to stay here. You and Randy plan on staying with us. I hear the rodeo announcer in the background. I'll let you go for now. Please call and tell us how Randy did."

"Dad, thank you for calling. Count on Randy and me being at the hospital tomorrow morning. We'll go to the house from the hospital. I'm going to cancel our flight right now. Could you stand to have Randy and me around another couple of days?"

"We would love to have you around for as long as you feel comfortable staying. I'll tell Mom the plan. She's out in the back yard playing with the kids. Rachel is sitting on a patio step watching with Catherine. Bobby is taking a nap. We'll talk with you and Randy later after the rodeo is over. I love you dear."

As Penny disconnected her cell, her anxiety diminished. She reflected; *here I was getting all nervous and excited about the guys roping. They all know how to take those emotions and use them to their benefit. If anyone should be nervous or excited, it should be Dad. He's operating on a little girl's heart tomorrow morning. Dad's thinking of what's best for Bobby, Catherine, and Rachel. I must train myself to be more like him. I must handle stress better, if I'm going to be the Director of the National Prion Center.*

Each event in the rodeo had two sections on the day of the finals. The competitors in fifteenth through ninth places compete in the first section; eighth through first compete in the second section. Junior was the last roper in the first section.

"The next steer roper is Junior Thomas from Dimmitt, Texas. Junior is a second-generation steer roper. His father, Bud Thomas competed at Cheyenne for many years. He won the steer roping, calf roping, and All-Around titles here in 1968. Junior placed seventh in the first go round and came back with a sixteen flat on his second steer. Junior travels with two other cowboys who are also in the finals this afternoon; Sonny Thompson and Randy Bennett who will rope in the second section."

Junior backed Thumper in the box. Sonny stood in the back of the box holding the jerk line. Randy was horseback on Blue watching from the alleyway. Junior appeared relaxed and focused. Junior nodded his head. Thumper made a mighty lunge and was soon behind the steer. Junior took an extra swing placing it smoothly over the steer's horns. He pulled his slack throwing his trip all in one motion. Thumper turned sharply left dropping his left shoulder preparing for the jerk when the rope came tight. The steer was airborne landing flatly on his left side. Junior reined Thumper slightly left stepping off smoothly. As Thumper dragged the steer up to Junior as he reached down picking up the jerk line while he jumped over the steer's midsection. As Junior yelled whoa Thumper stopped. He tied the steer smoothly throwing his hands to the side signaling for time. Hopping over the steer he quickly walked back to Thumper. Patting him on the butt as he jumped into the stirrup turning Thumper to slacken the rope, Junior waited for the six seconds to expire before hearing his official time.

"Junior Thomas, your time is 15.1 seconds. Your aggregate on three head is 46.9 second. Currently that is placing you first with only eight more ropers to go. By the way Junior, you are also winning the final go round." Junior coiled up his rope and was walking Thumper toward the exit gait as he heard his time. He pumped his fist in the air in celebration. As Junior rode through the exit gate, Randy met him in the alleyway shaking his hand and then patting Thumper on the rump. He rode down the alleyway with Junior receiving handshakes and congratulations from everyone.

Penny walked out of the stands meeting Junior and Randy just outside the alleyway. Junior dismounted; Penny ran up and hugged him. Then, almost as an afterthought, gave him a kiss on the cheek saying; "and you didn't even have to piss me off or beg for forgiveness."

Randy and Sonny laughed. Junior blushed; he didn't think Penny had overheard his comment from a few days ago. Noticing the blush another round of laughter ensued.

Penny walked back to the stands to her seat as Junior loosened the cinch on Thumper.

Randy and Sonny walked toward the backstretch of the track talking to each other about Junior's run.

"Thumper worked great", said Sonny. "Junior had the jerk line in his hand but didn't need it so he dropped it. Things are starting to slow down for him. He's had a memorable first year at Cheyenne."

"Yeah, he made a good, smooth, and efficient run", said Randy. We can only wish for the same."

"Did you see which steer you drew", asked Sonny.

"I looked at him over the fence. He's a stagy looking black steer. His hair looks a little rough. I think he'll be OK."

"It's the steer I roped in the first go round. I thought he was a good steer. He wants to stay down once he's flat and he can't run very fast. I think you drew the pup of the herd."

"Don't jinx me, Sonny", Randy said with a smile on his face. "What about your steer?"

"They won second in the first go on him. They missed him with an early shot in the second go round. I'll just have to see how he runs. He looks OK."

Soon the roping box announcer said, "One more saddle bronc rider to go. Steer ropers be ready."

Sonny rode into the alleyway saying, "I'm fourth up." Once in the alleyway Sonny tightened up the cinches. Attached the end of his rope to the saddle horn, and began his routine checking of all his gear. It was time for Sonny to focus on the job ahead. The eighth placed roper missed roping the horns, as did the seventh placed roper. The sixth placed roper roped the horns tripping his steer quickly, but the steer never laid flat, jumping to his feet before the roper had gotten his front leg strung. Sonny was up to rope his third steer.

The arena announcer said, "Next up is Sonny Thompson of Dimmitt, Texas. His traveling partner, Junior Thomas, is currently winning the go-round and the average. Big Sonny is one of the most consistent steer ropers competing. In last year's world standings Sonny finished fifth. This year he won the steer roping at Guymon, Oklahoma. Sonny roped both of his steers at Cheyenne in 15.3 seconds. How's that for consistency. He comes to the finals in fourth place."

Gus was standing squarely in the left-hand box; the steer's nose was pointing toward the middle of the roping chute gate when Sonny nodded his head. The steer jumped out of the chute and trotted to the 30-foot score line. Gus had gathered himself ready to lunge when the steer jumped; but Sonny held him back, timing his release. Gus was quickly on the steer's hip, leveling off when Sonny threw his rope. Roping both horns, Sonny pulled his slack and threw his trip in one smooth motion. They had drifted left and the left arena fence would become an issue. Sonny turned Gus sharply left and the powerful horse dropped his left shoulder readying himself for the rope coming tight. Sonny positioned Gus so he would come to the fence at an angle allowing Gus to run down the fence line back toward the roping chute. In an instant after the rope came tight the steer landed on his right side; Sonny stepped off as Gus drug the steer to him. Sonny strung the bottom front foot with the piggin string. In a smooth motion, he gathered the rear feet smoothly throwing on the wraps with the half-hitch tightening as his hands were moving forward to call for time. Sonny walked up the rope, patted Gus on the rump, turned Gus's head around slacking the rope. Sonny loosened the cinch, released the rope from the saddle horn as the six seconds expired. Sonny coiled his rope and reached for his piggin string as he mounted Gus and rode out of the arena.

"Folks, we discussed Sonny's consistency. Sonny you recorded your third 15.3 second time. I don't think I have ever seen that before at Frontier Days. Your aggregate of forty-five point nine; putting you a full second ahead of your traveling partner Junior Thomas, but you're placing second behind him in the final go round. Good roping Sonny. I'm sure your trip back to Dimmitt will seem shorter with the money you both have won."

The fourth-place roper recorded a time of 15.8 seconds and didn't move Junior or Sonny in the final go round. However, his aggregate time on the three steer is 46.6 seconds. Moving Junior down one place to third in the average. The third placed roper's steer got up leaving him with a no time and putting him out of the average money. The second placed roper was last year's world champion. He had won the world title five times. He roped and tied his steer in 14.9 seconds but was a full three seconds behind Randy on two head. However, he was winning the final go round moving both Junior and Sonny down one notch. It was Randy's turn to rope. He had gone through his routine of cleaning his sunglasses and checking his equipment.

"Ladies and gentlemen, the final roper this afternoon is Randy Bennett from Happy, Texas. Dr. Bennett is a veterinarian and operates several large feedlots in the Amarillo area. Randy is currently leading all other steer ropers in the chase for the world championship. So far, Randy has set a new arena record for steer roping and is the winner of both the first and second go rounds. That's also something that has never happened in the history of the Cheyenne rodeo. Randy also won the steer roping at Prescott, Arizona earlier this month. Randy's job keeps him very busy; he does not compete at all the rodeos, but he sure makes his presence known when he enters."

Blue stood flat, quartered in the back of the left roping box. Randy waited until he steer's head was straight and nodded his head. Unconsciously, Penny was holding her breath as Blue dashed out of the box rating off behind the steer. *Sonny's right* Randy thought as he readied his loop- *the steer can't run very fast*. Randy roped the steer's horns as the steer ducked to the right. Reactively, Randy pulled his slack and set his trip. The steer was airborne for an instant before landing on his right side. Randy smoothly stepped off Blue who drug the steer up to Randy stood and stopped leaning into the rope to keep it tight. Randy tied the steer in a smooth motion. As Randy walked quickly back to Blue, he thought, *well I've done my best, I just hope it was good enough.* Like Sonny before him, Randy reached for Blue's rein and turned him around to slacken the rope. Penny was standing still breathless waiting to hear his time. Randy coiled his rope, stepped back on Blue, and walked up to the untie men to get his piggin string soon after the six seconds expired.

"Well folks, it's a day of records for Dr. Randy Bennett. He has broken his own arena record of 13.3 seconds with a 13.1 on his third steer. That gives him 40.8 seconds on three head. That's also an arena record. With the 13.1 on his third steer he has won the third and final go around. Another record; no steer roper has won all three go rounds at Cheyenne in its long history. Dr. Randy Bennett is your new steer roping champion. Congratulations Randy!"

As Randy rode out the gate he looked up in the bleachers at Penny. Penny found herself breathless from holding her breath. When Randy looked at her all she could say as she jumped up and down was, "Oh my God, Randy." Her pent-up emotions gushed; Penny cried as she walked out of the bleachers and ran toward the end of the alleyway. By the time she reached Randy, he dismounted and reached to loosen the cinches. The other contestants crowded around Randy congratulating him. Penny stood at the periphery of the crowd around him. Sonny walked to Penny's left encompassed her hand in his and walked through the circle of cowboys. As he cleared the path for Penny, big Sonny put his arm around Penny and made room for her directly in front of Randy. Penny excitedly jumped into Randy's arms giving him a big kiss and hug.

Penny felt Sonny as he reached over her shoulder to shake Randy's hand saying, "Well, I guess you just showed us all how to rope steers at Ole Cheyenne. Congratulations Champ!"

Junior was in the crowd that encircled Randy, but ended up on the opposite side of Blue. He waited a moment until the crowd dispersed. Then, he ducked under Blue's neck and shook Randy's hand congratulating him. About that time a rodeo volunteer came up to Randy saying, "Congratulations, immediately after the rodeo please come to the front of the main grandstands for the buckle presentation."

"We'll be there."

"We can pony Blue back to the trailer, unsaddle him, and give him some grain", said Sonny. We'll take our horses out right away so we can get back for the buckle presentation."

Randy said, "That would be great, if you don't mind. I need to go get my rope bag; it's right over there. I'll be right back." Momentarily Randy returned with the rope bag placing his rope and both piggin strings into the bag he zipped it and put the handles over the saddle horn. "Thanks guys. We all did well; let's go enjoy ourselves after the ceremony."

Randy reached over hugging Penny again. Penny said, "I am so proud of you. There had to be a lot of excitement and pressure roping last. I can't believe you roped the last steer so quickly. It didn't look like it but it was all so smooth. Blue worked perfectly."

"When I got back on Blue I just told myself I've done my best, I just hope it was good enough."

"I thought you would play it a little safer."

"When I nodded my head that was my plan. Then I had a good early shot and I took it. When Blue turned left and the steer landed flat I just stepped off and kept telling myself, 'slow down and be quick' and muscle memory just took over. When I heard my time, I was surprised."

"Well, you did good, cowboy. I'm so happy for you."

Randy lowered his head and kissed her. "I'm so glad you are here today. I knew I couldn't screw up with you watching. That was in the back of my mind all day."

"Where are we walking? We're now under the announcer's stand at the roping chute."

"Oh, we're going to walk through a gate back here and go across the track to the sponsor's tent."

"Oh, Dad will be so excited to hear about your run. He called just before the rodeo started. He examined Rachel yesterday late afternoon. She has a large ventricular septal defect and is teetering on heart failure. Dad will repair the defect tomorrow morning. I've cancelled our tickets for tomorrow and extended our rental car to be with Bobby and Catherine. I left Sonny's ticket as it is; as I didn't know what he would want to do. When you have time, call Bobby. Dad purposely called when he thought you would be busy, so this information would not affect your roping. He and Mom planned on coming to see you rope today, but Rachel changed Dad's priorities. Everyone's staying at Mom and Dad's house. I will call Mom and Dad in a little while and tell them how you did."

"Is it going to cause problems with Dr. Laporte if you stay a couple of days?"

"Heavens no, the first thing I have to do is meet with Bobby. If he's up here I will have nothing to do. I'd rather be up here with you to help you support them and help Mom. If I returned to Texas, I would have to find stuff to keep me busy. I have plenty of vacation days, so that's not a problem either."

"Thank you for taking care of everything so we can stay. I know Bobby and Catherine will appreciate us being there. I'm also sure your Mom can use the help. Is she going to take care of the boys while everyone is at the hospital?"

"Mom offered; but Catherine insisted they go to a day care. It's owned by some of Mom and Dad's friends. That will make it a little easier on Mom; however, she's used to taking care of my brothers' kids."

"Before Sonny and Junior get here, I want to tell you that I'm not going to drink after the rodeo. I'm the designated driver. I think you three may need one. We've had too good of time in Cheyenne and you all did so well up here, I don't want to risk having it end badly. We'll celebrate a little when we get back to the motel, if you're up to it."

"That's cool; thanks ahead of time for taking care of us", Randy said with a smile. "Although, Penny you just gave me a lot incentive not to imbibe too much", Randy said chuckling as he gently pulled Penny to his side. "I don't want to have a hangover when I'm with Bobby and Catherine at the hospital tomorrow. What time is Rachel's surgery?"

"I don't know. I'll ask Dad when I speak with him in a little while."

Immediately after the rodeo ended the presentation of buckles to the event champions began. Randy made his way to the center of the grandstands at ground level with the other event winners. Everyone walked closer to the grandstands. The arena announcer stood at a podium in front of the event champions. The committee members stood beside and behind the cowboys. The first event champion to receive his championship belt buckle was the steer roping champion.

Cheyenne Rodeo's General Chairmen Vick Walters began Randy's introduction. "Dr. Randy Bennett is from Happy, Texas. Randy set so many records at this year's rodeo I don't have time to name them all. He is rodeo's undeclared steer roping ambassador. He symbolizes the dedication, humility, and integrity of today's professional cowboys. Until this year, I would have told you he was rodeo's most eligible bachelor; now, I think he's off the market. This year Randy won over $28,500 roping three steers. This is the most money ever won by a cowboy competing in a single event in the history of the rodeo. Randy, come on up here. It gives me great pleasure to present this championship buckle and saddle to you. Congratulations. We hope to see you again next year."

Randy replied, "Vick, thank you and all of the folks who work so hard to make Cheyenne the best rodeo of the year for us contestants. I also would like to pay particular thanks to whoever drew the steers. I drew three really good steers. I also want to thank the crowd who witnessed the best rodeo production you will see anywhere. I'll wear this buckle proudly."

As awards ceremony continued, Penny called her Mom and Dad. Ken Adams answered the phone. Penny told him to also have Pam pick up an extension.

As Pam picked up the phone she said, "Hi dear, we've been waiting to hear from you. How did Randy do roping?"

"Mom, Randy roped great! He roped his second steer yesterday winning the second go round. Today he roped his steer faster than the other finalists. Randy is the champion steer roper. Just a few minutes ago, he received a beautiful silver and gold championship buckle and a saddle. He also set a bunch of records."

"That's wonderful Penny. Tell him congratulations from us. What are your plans for tomorrow", asked Ken.

"We plan to be at the hospital with Bobby and Catherine. What time is surgery?"

"We'll take Rachel into surgery about 7:30AM and start surgery about 8:00AM. I know Bobby and Catherine will appreciate you being there. Naturally, they're concerned for Rachel; your support will be most helpful. I have not told them anything yet, but I will let them know."

"We'll try to be there about 7:15AM so we can say hello to Rachel before she goes into surgery. I know Randy would want to do that."

"Dear, thank you for calling and telling Randy what is happening with Rachel. I know you need to go and do a little celebrating, just be careful."

"Dad, I already told Randy that I am the designated driver tonight. Randy said if he was going to be at the hospital with Bobby and Catherine, he didn't want to do that with a hangover; I think the extent of our celebrating will be a couple of drinks and a good dinner. I do have to go. The awards ceremony just ended. I love you both. We'll see you tomorrow."

Randy walked back to Penny, Sonny, and Junior with a big smile of satisfaction on his face holding his new buckle in one hand and his new saddle nonchalantly draped over his hip.

"Hey Champ, said Sonny. "Let's see what one of those Cheyenne buckles looks like up close."

Randy set the saddle down, handing the buckle to Sonny. Sonny scrutinized it carefully as Junior moved in to get a closer look. The saddle was custom made by a well-known saddle maker. The fully tooled saddle displayed a unique floral design, a silver horn cap, and engraved silver plates on the rear skirts.

"That's one nice buckle. I hope someday to have one like it", said Sonny.

"Me too", said Junior.

"Sonny, Bobby's little girl Rachel is having heart surgery tomorrow in Denver. Penny and I are going to stay in Denver a couple of days before we go back home. We will be glad to take you to the airport before we go to the hospital; but we'll need to leave the motel by about 5:00AM."

"Randy, I think I'm going to ride back with Junior. We're going to the same place, it makes no sense for me to get there a few hours before he does. I'm going to cancel my ticket. We'll leave the motel about the same time as you. We'll be back to the feedlot in the afternoon. If it's OK with you, we'll take Blue back to Dimmitt. You can pick him up or we'll bring him to Happy once you're home. That way Junior and I can keep an eye on him while you're gone and Sarita doesn't have to worry about taking care of him."

"That sounds like a good plan. I'll call Jim Bob and let him what's going on. I appreciate you and Junior looking after Blue. Now, I think I'm going to lug this saddle over to the trailer and lock it up. Penny, you can carry the buckle."

"Junior and I can carry the saddle over to the trailer. We will meet you in the committee bar. That way, you can hopefully have everybody whipped before Junior and I get there", teased Sonny.

"No, why don't you guys check out the committee bar and we'll meet you there. There's something I need to do."

"OK, if you insist, we'll go get things riled up and ready for you. Ole Punch is pretty good at needling the tough guys", Sonny said hoping to get a rise out of Randy.

"If you don't quit about another fight in the committee bar, I won't be able to get Penny to join us. If that happens, I'm going to get Vick Walters to throw both of you guys out on your ears." Picking up the saddle by the saddle horn, Randy threw it over his right shoulder starting his walk to the trailer. Penny walked beside Randy.

At the trailer, Penny opened the back gate so Randy could place the new saddle into the tack box. The extra saddle filled up the tack box. Randy locked it up again. After closing the back gate, he walked over and sat on the narrow fender of the trailer. Penny followed and sat next to him. "Are you a little tired packing that saddle all the way here by yourself?"

"Maybe a little", replied Randy. "Mainly, I was reflecting that today was a pretty good day."

"A pretty good day? I'd say you had a perfect day."

"No. It's not a perfect day, at least not yet", said Randy.

"Here, put on your new buckle."

Randy put on the buckle saying, "How does it look?"

"Great. I'll put your Prescott buckle in my purse." Penny hesitated a second, then asked, "What would make your day perfect?"

Randy scooted off the fender, turned toward Penny and got down on one knee, like he would remove his spur, reached up took Penny's hand in his and said, "To make it a perfect day, you would have to agree to marry me." Randy looked up at Penny's eyes.

"Oh My God; Yes, Yes, I will marry you Randy Bennett."

Randy stood and kissed Penny lovingly. Penny returned his kiss, placing her arms around his neck holding him tight. "Randy, you had this planned, didn't you?"

"Yes, I did. I thought Sonny was going to ruin it when he volunteered to carry the saddle to the trailer", Randy said still holding Penny close to him.

Penny laughed.

"Now, it is a perfect day."

Penny teased, "Where's my ring, cowboy?"

Randy laughed, "We'll get you one while we're in Denver. I thought you may like to have a little input into it, since you're the one who's going to be wearing it. You've been around me long enough to know I don't have much taste."

Penny again put her hands around Randy's neck, kissed him passionately and said, "I love you, Randy Bennett! I've got to call my parents and tell them."

"Penny, why don't you wait until you have a ring to show them?"

"OK, but we're going back to the committee bar; I'm at least going to tell Sonny and Junior. I'm the happiest girl in Cheyenne, and I've got to tell someone."

"Let's go have a drink and celebrate?"

Chapter 39

This was the first meeting of the multi-department/agency DVE investigation group since meeting in the cabinet room with President Smyth a week ago. Attorney General Geraldine Green was in attendance and presided over the meeting.

"Good afternoon ladies and gentlemen. I'm glad to see everyone invited additional members from their departments or agencies. Today, our goals are the same as they were when we last met with President Smyth. Our first goal is to share information; the next to determine if the investigation is on track and set or amend timeframes, and finally to find synergisms and capitalize on them."

"Secretary Robinson, let's start with you this week. Please share with us the status of the DVE terrorism investigation."

"Mrs. Green, I want to defer first to Dick Kline and Bill Franklin. Collectively, they have been working to determine who owns the 20 foreign accounts that have invested in market cattle commodities, put options through the Chicago Mercantile Exchange, and live cattle ETFs through the London Stock Exchange."

Dick Kline began, "After reviewing our progress, both Bill and I felt like we needed additional personnel to hasten our progress. We asked Ryan Anderson from the DEA for additional forensic accountants. He sent twelve additional senior forensic accounts to our part of the investigation the next day. We informed them of the apparent 100-million-dollar heroin purchase by the Zeta cartel asking them to find where those funds originated and where they went. Using DEA's special access to financial transactions, they determined the 100 million originated from ten international bank accounts, each contributing ten million dollars. The banks releasing these funds are in the Cayman Islands, Hong Kong, Zurich, Mexico City, Monterey, and Buenos Ares. Each of the banks transferred five million US dollars into two separate investment accounts. The location of the accounts is global. They exactly match the twenty locations from where subsequent five million-dollar investments in U.S. market cattle contracts, put options, and live cattle ETF investments on the London Stock Exchange originated. They also determined none of the twenty global investment accounts invested the entire five million dollars in these various investment vehicles. This led the team to attempt to determine if additional investments occurred in either U.S. Stock Markets or the London Exchange. The team uncovered additional investments in corn contracts and futures as well as triple inverse ETFs in Dow Jones Industrial Average. Each of the twenty investments in total was five million U.S. dollars. Collectively, the entire 100 million dollars was invested."

"After DEA forensic accountants put the pieces together, each investment was frozen. Whoever is responsible for these investments will have to come forward providing legitimate explanations for each investment or the entire funds will be seized."

"I will let Bill Franklin describe FinCEN's activities and progress."

"We also decided that we needed additional manpower; thanks to the FBI we received an additional dozen senior financial intelligence officers. The two groups integrated well investigating the financial entities involved. As it turned out, for each of the twenty initial investment entities, there were three entities at the next level. It was like peeling an onion. After the second level, the sixty second level entities became intermixed. We completed our investigation this morning. The money ultimately is directed to fall into three accounts. One in the Cayman Islands, the Grand Cayman National Bank. The other two accounts are at separate private banks in Switzerland-The Sion Bank, Ltd. in Lugano; and Vorab & Landquart, banquiers in Bern. All three accounts owned by a Pakistani businessman from Islamabad. His name is Mushtaq Shakir."

Secretary Johansen and Bobby Laporte looked at each other in surprise. Major Merle Harris appeared astonished. Secretary Johansen spoke first. "That name was given to us a few days ago by Dr. Penny Adams. Major Harris, I think you and Penny visited about this man in relation to a Pakistani prion scientist, Mohammed Aziz."

"Yes, Madam Secretary. They were both students at Stanford when Dr. Adams and I were students there. He was known as an activist member of the Islamic Students Organization. Shakir was a troublemaker."

"When I received the two names from Secretary Johansen", said Secretary Robinson, "I sent them on to General Griffith, Director Quinn, and Director D'Amico of the FBI."

Director D'Amico commented, "Shakir made our terrorist watch list before 9-11 happened. At Stanford, he was indeed a troublemaker. He was known for his very extreme jihadist views of Islam. When he graduated with his MBA from the Stanford School of Business, he returned to Islamabad, Pakistan and has not attempted to return to the United States."

"Mushtaq Shakir is also on the CIA's list of terrorists as someone who would or has financially supported terrorist acts", said National Intelligence Director Quinn. "I reviewed his dossier after I received his name from Director Robinson. He returned to Pakistan shortly before his father, Mohammed Shakir, died. Mushtaq is a businessman in Pakistan with several successful business interests. He is allegedly a key figure in the drug trade from Afghanistan to Pakistan. From what I read, it appears Mushtaq inherited his father's business interests and has made them much more profitable, including his father's involvement in the poppy/opium/morphine trade. Mushtaq's operatives are the primary smugglers of morphine out of the northern half of Pakistan. His business interests have led him to become very wealthy and powerful. Mushtaq Shakir is known to be reclusive, although he routinely attends Asr, the afternoon prayer, at a mosque near his Islamabad home. Often, he meets Mohammed Aziz at the mosque. Later they go to a nearby coffeehouse for reflection and to visit."

"Shakir has made his way into our intelligence reports; however, Aziz is new to special operations intelligence", said General Griffith. We suspect Shakir of trading arms for morphine with Afghan al Qaida. Intelligence sources say Afghani nationals and Al Qaida process the poppy stems into opium, then refine the opium into morphine bricks. After the morphine bricks travel through the Torkham area of the Afghanistan/Pakistan border Al Qaida trades for arms or cash. The morphine moves to Peshawar, then on to Islamabad where it's smuggled out of Pakistan under the guise of legitimate business products from one of Shakir's businesses. One of Shakir's legitimate businesses is a transportation company that operates throughout Pakistan and into Kabul, Afghanistan and Amritsar, India. His transports routinely travel to Karachi, the port city of Pakistan."

Attorney General Green commented, "My, my, haven't we learned a lot in one week's time. I should point out that while this is excellent intelligence, little of it is the hard evidence needed to prosecute a terrorism case."

Secretary Robinson continued, "Ryan Anderson can you share any new information with us?"

"Not a lot", said Anderson of the DEA. "We spoke with ATF regarding their firearms smuggling bust. Their intelligence prior to the bust said the Zeta cartel smuggled arms into Mexico for use by the cartel. We have no evidence suggesting shipment of the arms to Pakistan or Al Qaida. One informant did produce some general information regarding the shipment of fertilizer and heroin into the port of Tampico. Reportedly, the origin of the shipment was from the Nigerian port city of Lagos. That's all I have to offer."

"Thank you, Ryan, for your new information", said Secretary Robinson. "We have not yet checked into the bank in Laredo, Texas. When this other information began to develop, my focus was primarily on this new information. Secondly, I did not want to compromise the information flow we were getting by examining the bank."

"That is certainly understandable, Mr. Secretary", said Mrs. Green.

"Secretary Jackson, do you have updated information on Curt Wepner, the young farmer who fertilized his vegetable garden with nano-fertilizer?"

"Sadly, I do. Curt is not doing well. He is in the hospital in Wichita, KS. Within a week he has lost significant motor function and is unable to walk or talk. He is blind in one eye and he's lost control of his bodily functions. We have never experienced a prion disease this aggressive. He was unable to visit his parents to advise them of what was going on; although they are with him in Wichita now. Follow up MRIs have progressively shown increased vacuoles in his brain. Our CDC team has traveled back to Wichita and are working hand-in-hand with his local neurologists. If he continues declining at this rate, it is only a matter of days."

"Thank you, Dr. Jackson. Young Curt and his family will certainly be in our prayers", commented Mrs. Green.

"Secretary Johansen what do you have to share?"

"In the past week, Agriculture has not made nearly as much progress as Homeland", said Clare. First, the emergency supplemental funding bill was on President Smyth's desk last Wednesday. He presented it to congress the following day. I testify in front of the joint appropriations committee tomorrow morning. We anticipate expedited passage, perhaps by the end of the week."

"Dr. Anne Burk, director of the Plant Protection and Quarantine division, and her group has been very busy investigating each co-op that received the nano-fertilizer, and then following up with those farmers who actually purchased the fertilizer. Recall 283 local cooperatives received nano-fertilizer. PPQ as of this morning had contacted 238 cooperatives. We have found only one or two farmers per co-op purchased this fertilizer. From the 238 cooperatives, we have interviewed farmers who purchased the fertilizer. We issued quarantines to all farmers; 46 additional cattle feedlots, dairies, and other livestock producer premises received quarantines. Most producers were operators newly identified to USDA and their animals. These animals are all non-symptomatic and the animal depopulation list is current. I have no exact count on the number of cattle involved. We hope to complete the local cooperative investigations and hopefully the farmer interviews by the end of the week, and all the interviews of cattle producers who purchased the adulterated feedstuffs by the end of next week."

"At the request of General Clark, any unused nano-fertilizer is initially being placed into secure inventory at APHIS area offices. There is an area office in each state. Once the investigation has is complete, USAMRIID at Fort Dietrich will destroy it. They possess specialized equipment for disposal of such materials."

"The manufacturing of carcass destruction incinerators is at somewhat of a standstill. The engineer owning the patient and engineering company who manufactured the existing crematoriums has been away dealing with a serious medical condition involving his young daughter. If all goes well, we will probably meet with him and Dr. Penny Adams, the lead person involving cattle destruction, at the end of next week. If it works out to be easier to hold that meeting in Texas, General Clark and I will travel there."

General Clark and I had a very productive meeting last week. Construction of 400 plus industrial-size crematoriums for cattle is not a small project. General Clark and the military are going to partner with USDA on constructing the crematoriums on government owned lands. This affiliation will significantly decrease construction time, expense, and bring the crematoriums on line much sooner. General Clark thanks for recognizing this synergism."

"That is all that I have."

Geraldine Green spoke, "Thank you all for your participation. Group progress this past week is remarkable. I am going to report to President Smyth the significant progress you all have made. We will tentatively plan to meet next week. This meeting is adjourned."

Chapter 40

The sun had not risen yet as Randy and Penny left the motel room. "Sonny and Junior must have left already. I don't see my pickup. They're used to waking up early. I'll bet when they woke up they just hooked up, loaded the horses, and headed south."

"I checked out last night while you were in the shower. All we have to do is load up and head to Denver", said Randy.

"Do you want some coffee for the road?"

"Yeah, I thought we'd get big cups to go at the restaurant before we left."

"Why don't I walk over to get some while you finish loading the Escalade? I'll meet you out in front of the restaurant entrance."

"Sounds good to me.

After loading up and getting on I-25 south, Penny made a call. "Good morning Bobby, it's Penny. How are you this morning?"

"Penny, I'm fine. You're up early. How did Randy do at the rodeo?"

"Randy won the steer roping championship. He's wearing a brand new shiny belt buckle and won a new saddle along with the prize money. He says hello. The reason I called this morning is to let you know something has come up and I'm not going back to Amarillo today. Randy's niece Rachel, she's Bobby's daughter, is having open heart surgery in Denver this morning. If it's OK with you, we will spend a few days with Bobby and Catherine as Rachel recovers. My first order of business is to talk with Bobby. So, if I returned to Texas, there's really nothing for me to do until Bobby gets back. Once things settle down, Randy and I will fly back. I have plenty of annual leave hours, so that's not a problem. I'll call you daily to check in, and you know you can call me anytime if something goes haywire."

"Penny, it's fine for you to take an additional few days, considering the circumstances. You can also use accrued sick leave or comp time, and save your annual leave. It's up to you. I appreciate you checking in, when it is convenient. There are lots of things happening, but nothing we need you for. Getting the cattle destruction project up and running remains your primary focus. Maybe later, you will have time to visit with Bobby about our plans. How is everything going with you?"

"Things could not be better. Yesterday Randy told me he had the perfect day. He won the steer roping at Cheyenne and I agreed to marry him. It was a perfect day for me as well."

"Penny, congratulations to you and Randy. You're both good people and I wish you both much happiness. I now understand your reluctance when I mentioned the Director of Veterinary Services job. When is the wedding? I know Clare will want to know all the details."

"We haven't discussed wedding plans. I can tell you I don't want to think about marriage until this DVE thing is behind us. Both of us think we must get to know each other better before getting married. I'm just so excited and happy; I had to share this news with you."

"Thank you for including me among the first to know. If you don't mind I will tell Clare the news? We're going to a multi-department DVE meeting. I should have additional information for you when you call tomorrow. Again, congratulations."

"Thank you for your well wishes. I think it will be OK to tell Clare, but please tell her our parents don't know yet. We want the opportunity to tell them ourselves. I'd better let you get back to work; I'll give you a call tomorrow."

****

Penny and Randy arrived at Denver Children's hospital a few minutes before 7:00AM. Remembering how to get to the cardiac wing, Penny held Randy's hand as they walked toward the elevators. Arriving on the floor, they walked to the nurses' station where Penny inquired, "We're looking for Rachel Bennett's room. She is a new arrival and is scheduled for surgery this morning."

"She arrived about an hour ago, and is in room 407. Dr. Adams is in with Rachel and her family now; you might want to wait a few minutes."

"Thank you", said Penny. "I think it will be OK if we walk down. I'm Dr. Adams' daughter; this is Rachel's uncle."

Randy knocked on the door and then opened it. "Come on in", said Bobby.
Rachel was lying on the bed being still as Dr. Ken, as she called him, had placed the stethoscope in Rachel's ears. She was listening to her heart with an amazed expression on her face.

Ken Adams turned around and said, "Hi guys, you arrived a little earlier than I expected. Rachel, I want you to meet someone. That girl with your uncle Randy is my daughter, Penny. Penny, this is Rachel Bennett. We're going to fix her heart in a little while." Ken stood giving Penny a kiss on the forehead and introduced her to Bobby and Catherine.

Bobby standing in the corner walked first to Randy and gave him a hug and said, "Thanks for sticking around; we appreciate y'all coming. Penny it's very nice to meet you. Catherine and I have been anxious to meet you. Randy, congratulations on winning the steer roping at Cheyenne. Ken told us the news last night."

Catherine was sitting on a bench seat near the head of the bed with a large window behind her. It was obvious her anxiety level was high. She looked exhausted. Penny sat next to her shaking her hand, then holding it between her hands. "I have heard so many nice things about you from Rose, Beth, and Sarita. I feel like I know you already. You are as beautiful as Sarita said. Is there anything I can get for you or Bobby, perhaps some coffee?"

"Penny, thank you for all you've done for us. You're so kind and considerate, just like everyone has told me. Thank you for offering; but coffee right now would only make me more nervous. We had some at Ken and Pam's; so, I think Bobby has reached his limit, he's not much of a coffee drinker. Maybe a little later."

"Rachel", Dr. Ken said, "I am going to go change into the green shirt and pants I wear in surgery. I will see you in the operating room, before they put you to sleep. Before I go, do you have any questions for me?"

"Dr. Ken, after I wake up, and my heart is all better, will you be with me?"

"Rachel, I will be close by. A nurse whose name is Sally will be with you waiting for you to wake up. After you wake up I will come see you. While you are still asleep, after we have fixed your heart, I need to go tell your Mom and Dad how you are doing. We would not want them to worry about you, would we?"

"Oh no, Dr. Ken. I don't want Mommy and Daddy to worry about me. I'm probably going to be sleepy anyway; but I want you to wake me up when you come to see me, OK", asked Rachel said with a big smile.

"OK Rachel, I will wake you up. A nurse will be coming soon to give you a pill and a little water to swallow it with. Bye for now; I will see you in the operating room."

As Ken Adams walked out of the room Catherine squeezed Penny's hand, "Your Dad is such a wonderful man. He has all the time in the world for his little patients and tells them things that put them at ease. After he examined Rachel on Saturday afternoon and reviewed the entire records sent by Mayo Clinic, he sat down with us near a miniature playground and explained what was going on with Rachel's heart and why surgery was necessary. He said we did not have to do it right away, but he did not want to wait until she was experiencing more signs of heart failure before he interceded. Bobby and I feel so comfortable with your Dad. As you can tell Rachel thinks the world of him. While we were discussing everything, the kids were playing quietly. I would have never believed my two boys would settle down and play quietly after traveling in our Suburban for seven hours. Dr. Ken told them there were some very sick kids in the rooms near the play area and that it was important not to be loud or disturb them. He is such a kind man; I know you are proud of him and have every right to be."

"Catherine, I am very proud of Dad. You should know he gets such pleasure from his work. He told me recently that he has the best job in the world. Mom thinks he works too hard, but Dad would not have it any other way. He still makes his own rounds twice a day; because he feels he owes it to his patients and their families. He's been like this for as long as I can remember. It's easy to forgive him for missing a recital here and there when you know what he is doing instead. It never bothered my brothers or me when Dad was unable to attend an event."

At 7:30AM a nurse came to give Rachel her pill. The pill, a mild sedative, would relax Rachel to prepare for placement of the IV catheter in about ten minutes. Rachel relaxed as the medicine did its work. Soon the IV fluids were slowly dripping into the vein in her arm. It was now time to roll Rachel's bed down the hall to the elevator. The two couples followed the bed into the elevator and out into a small area near a pair of double doors stating "No Admittance-Surgical Personnel Only". Momentarily, the doors opened and Dr. Ken walked out. He said hello to Rachel who appeared very relaxed as she softly said "Hi Dr. Ken."

"Are you ready to get your heart fixed?"

"Yes, sir," Rachel whispered.

Ken Adams looked up at Bobby and Catherine. "I'm going to say the surgery will take about four hours, but that's only an estimate. Do not read anything into the timeframe if it takes less or more time. Surgical procedures take as long as they take. Do you have any questions?"

Bobby and Catherine both answered "no". Dr. Adams smiled saying, "we'll see you in a few hours. If you want to have breakfast, now would be a good time to go to the cafeteria. Should something unexpected happen, I'll have you paged." He rolled the bed toward the surgery wing; the double doors opening automatically. A nurse met him at the doorway to assist turning the bed into the surgical suite.

Randy noticed Bobby visibly tighten up as he turned walking away from the doorway. Penny had put her arm around Catherine's shoulder as a few tears found their way down Catherine's cheeks. "What do you say about sitting up here for a few minutes. Then, get a bite to eat in the cafeteria", said Penny. "Once Rachel is out of surgery, you will want to be with her. You won't feel comfortable leaving her to get something to eat."

"That sounds like a good plan", said Catherine needing a few minutes to compose herself.

After a few minutes sitting mostly silent in the surgical waiting room, Catherine looked at Penny and asked, "How bad is my mascara?"

"It could use a touch up", said Penny. "Let's find a restroom; the large cup of coffee I had on our way down this morning has worked its way through." Catherine and Penny walked down the hallway a short distance and found the women's restroom.

Bobby visited with Randy. "I really like Penny. She is very kind, like her Mom and Dad. Dad had told me she was very special, I now think that was an understatement."

"Bobby, we've fallen in love. Yesterday after the rodeo I asked her to marry me; she accepted. No one in either family knows yet. After Rachel's surgery when she's stable, we're going to go buy her a ring. I wanted Penny to help pick it out. She's the one who's going to be wearing it. I don't know anything about rings or diamonds."

"Congratulations brother, I think you picked a great gal. Have you talked about when you're going to get married?"

"Not really. We have not known each other very long; we both think we need to get to know each other better before we get married. Due to the DVE outbreak, Penny's working out of Amarillo; but she lives in Ames, Iowa. We're trying to get her closer to Happy. That may take a little time. I feel if I am asking her to uproot herself and change career paths, I needed to demonstrate that I'm seriously committed. We're both very busy right now. I doubt we will even discuss it until things slow down for us."

"Randy, you look as happy as I have seen you. I think the approach you and Penny are taking is very sensible and practical. I wish you nothing but happiness. Dad told me he told you, in front of Penny, not to let her get away. I think it was good advice, and a display of very good sense on yours."

"Listen, Catherine and I really appreciate you guys being with us. You can't imagine the stress and anxiety we have gone through in the past week or so. It was a Godsend when we met Ken Adams. Not only did he examine Rachel on a Saturday afternoon, but he insisted we stay at his house with all the kids. He and Pam have treated us like royalty. My stress and anxiety level is significantly on the down slope, even with Rachel currently undergoing open heart surgery."

"Bobby, there's no place we'd rather be than with you and Catherine. It's all about family. Hey, here come the girls. It looks like they have become fast friends. I suppose you're not very hungry, but you really should try to get something in your stomachs. Penny was spot on when she said you guys need to eat something before Rachel gets out of surgery."

"Hey cowboy", said Penny, "Why don't we get these folks some breakfast before they starve to death?"

"We were just talking about that. I think I've talked Bobby into it. How are you doing convincing Catherine?"

"Catherine is convinced. OK, you guys head toward the elevator; I'm going to let the nurse behind that counter know we've gone to the cafeteria. I'll meet you at the elevator."

"Sounds good; we'll see you there," said Bobby.

At breakfast both Bobby and Catherine ate more than they expected. Although concerned about Rachel, there were spurts of laughter as Bobby and Randy reminisced about their childhood. Penny and Catherine visited, generally getting to know one another. In a little more than 20 minutes the four were back in the surgery waiting room. Again, a nervous silence ensued. Bobby broke the silence saying to Penny, "When Dad and I spoke a few days ago, he said we needed to talk about the carcass burners I made for the feedlots. It's my understanding from Dad that you wanted me to build some to destroy the cattle affected with DVE."

Penny replied, "Bobby we don't need to talk business now."

"Penny, I need to take my mind away what's happening in that operating room where my daughter's chest is laid open and her heart is exposed. If you don't mind, let's talk about it now. I need the distraction."

"OK, that's fine, if it helps you. I just didn't want you to think it was necessary to do so for my benefit", Penny said as she moved over to sit next to Bobby on the waiting room couch.

"It's a large project and we need your help and guidance. Because of the studies we conducted on cattle not showing central nervous symptoms, the USDA has concluded all cattle on infected premises require complete destruction. There is no one in the U.S. besides ATX that has large crematoriums. As you may know, a novel prion causes DVE. Prions are very resistant proteins. The most practical way to inactivate them is by incineration. You displayed excellent foresight when you patented your invention."

"This sounds like a big project. How many burners are we talking about?"

"We calculated a little over 400 units about the size of the ones at the feedlots."

"Penny, that's too big a project for me. If we stopped everything else, it would take me over a year to build that many. That would be if I could gear up and produce one per day. I'm sure you're on a much shorter timeline."

"That's what I thought too, when I heard the number. However, what if you had help? A lot of help. All you'd be doing is overseeing construction. How many units could you build at your shop in 90 days without shutting down all the other activities that you are involved in presently?"

I don't understand where you are going. Where's this help coming from? I have supplies on hand and more coming when we complete the salvage of a refinery. We might do six to eight, ten if we're lucky. But there's more to it than just constructing the units. It takes ground preparation, hooking in to a natural gas source, site construction, etc. If we had to do these things, we'd be talking more like three or four units."

"Let me digress and start at the beginning. The USDA estimates twelve million cattle require complete destruction.

This is not a big project, it's gigantic. We recognized there was no way a single contractor can build this many units within a 90-day timeframe. Because of permitting and other issues, Philip Granger suggested locating them on military owned lands. That allows us to sidestep the local, state, government requirements because DVE is a national emergency. The military, through General Clark, agreed to their placement and offered their help in construction, installation, and operation. With that in mind, our thoughts changed to constructing them near their installation sites. There will be multiple crews working at different sites simultaneously. With the military, there's another benefit. They have their own equipment and a specialized chain of command to supervise each site."

As Penny described the USDA/Military concept, the light came on in Bobby's eyes and he began to smile. "Penny this is an ingenious plan. Where does ATX Salvage and Industrial Design fit in to your plans?"

"There are many ways ATX can fit into the plans. First, we want your company to build as many burners as you feel comfortable building. Second, we want your company to serve as a consultant to the military as they build the units. I liken this to being a general contractor who's checking on subcontractors. The military will have a construction officer at each site that will oversee the personnel on that site, and will construct everything to your specifications. Third, we would like you to design and consider building portable modular units to service smaller producers. Fourth, we want you to remove the oils produced. Fifth, we would pay you a nominal royalty for each unit produced. Finally, I want to talk with you regarding modification of the design of the burners somewhat. I think it would make sense to skin, eviscerate, pre-grind and hash the carcasses before loading the material into the burner. This should reduce particle size before cremation allowing them cook faster. I think it will also decrease cycle time and increase the number of animals cremated per cycle. This is negotiable. Once Rachel gets home and you feel comfortable traveling, we'll go to DC and negotiate the final deal. If you don't feel comfortable traveling, I think we can get the USDA and the Military to travel to Amarillo. What do you think?"

"Let's first talk about the design changes you suggested. In my initial design, I had a skinning and evisceration stations, a pre-breaker, and a chopper in the design. Randy had me take them out. His reasoning was that his cowboys would be doing this nasty work. He did not want them returning to the feedlot and being a source of contamination. You are correct these changes will increase efficiency in both cycle time and throughput. Having a workforce that wouldn't be returning to the feedlot eliminates that concern. I think I still have those early designs, so making the modifications will be easy."

"You also mentioned picking up the oils produced. That's something my company doesn't have the equipment or desire to do. I'm sure we could get Mike to do it. It's a better fit with ATX Oil and Gas. He has the equipment and what he doesn't have he can get. But there are lots of folks around who can perform that service. The government watchdogs may view it as monopolizing a contract. I want to get Philip's view on this. The same applies to getting rid of the hides. That doesn't fit into any of ATX's business plans."

"Coming up with a modular design is not a problem. I'm thinking about a three-trailer unit. One for skinning and evisceration, another for the pre-breaker and chopper with augers into the burner. Constructing the modular units would probably be all that my small company could handle; and I would want to build the first few anyway, to ensure they worked as intended."

"It is probably best for the folks from USDA and the Military come to Amarillo. I've been gone for several days with Rachel at Mayo Clinic and traveling. I don't know how long we will be in Denver. When we return home, work will consume my time, particularly if this project is to start soon. I'll want Dad and Philip involved in the negotiations. Often their schedules won't allow them to be gone for several days.

I know they have been spending a lot of time on a new project down at Tech that's high priority to them."

"Penny, I am glad I asked you to visit with me about this carcass destruction project. I did not understand the magnitude. You have given me a lot to think about. The concept of government, the Military, and private industry working together is brilliant. Where do you fit in to the project?"

"I was asked to oversee and manage the project for the USDA", said Penny.

"Wow, that's a big job, Penny. I guess you'll be sitting in on the negotiations then?"

"Yes, but I will not be one of the decision makers. My job is to understand the agreement and to make sure it's implemented as agreed. Then when the carcass burners become operational, we'll start destroying twelve million cattle."

"The magnitude of the project astounds me. My mind is now trying to wrap itself around the project. I am really interested in helping in the best way I can. To tell you the truth, I need to give this some serious thought to determine what that may be. I think it's going to take me a few days to digest what you have told me. I do have a question."

"What's that", asked Penny.

"The whole concept behind my salvage and industrial design company is to repurpose salvaged materials in the projects we're involved in. To me, this concept is very important. The cattle burner portion of the project will fit my reuse concept; although I probably won't be building any of the stationary units. Do you think USDA and the military would consider using salvaged materials?"

"Personally, I don't see why they'd object. It would mean lower costs per unit. The burners will run at maximum capacity for a period of about 90 days. After that, I don't foresee much use. I'll check and get back to you, so you'll know for sure."

"To clarify, I wouldn't be using substandard materials. As you know, we made the burners at the feedlots from salvaged pressure tanks. Pressure tanks require a higher standard; so, we use premium steel of greater thickness than required to engineer a new tank for this purpose. They cost about ten percent of a new tank. We don't scrimp on quality or safety; it's just that we repurpose existing used materials. I know the military has huge scrap yards with materials that would be suitable. In this time of emergency, it seems to me repurposing scrap is an optimal concept. It would save the taxpayers a significant amount of their tax dollars."

"I don't know anything about military surplus or scrap materials. I do know Secretary Johansen is responsible for getting the most bang for the taxpayers' buck spent for this project. I have not met General Clark; therefore, I don't know his thoughts, or government or military regulations dealing with surplus supplies and equipment. But I will do my best to find out these answers. It seems both practical and logical to me. I am amazed at your creativity."

"We are such a wasteful nation. I'm trying to do my part to maximize our resources. It is very important to me to utilize what we already have before creating more stuff from new materials. That was the premise I brought to Dad and Philip when I wanted to start the salvage and industrial design business. You would not believe what we have built from things we've salvaged."

"Actually, I have seen some of your work; and I think it is amazing. The feedlot headquarters in Canyon is impressive. It is beautiful mixture of the old and new. I had to ask Randall whether the building was a newly remodeled old building or a new building. When he explained where all the different materials came from, I was astonished. I know Tony constructed the building; but, I bet the materials came from what your company salvaged. Randy's house and barn are other examples, aren't they?"

"Yes, they are."

"Look", said Penny. "Here comes Dad. I think he's bringing you good news."

Penny moved over next to Randy. Ken took her seat between Bobby and Catherine. "The surgery went well. The defect closed nicely. I used a Gore-Tex patch that will allow Rachel's own heart cells to grow over the patch. When we started her heart, it beat with a normal rhythm and has maintained that rhythm post surgically. She has a little right ventricular hypertrophy, which means the right lower chamber of her heart is a little thicker than normal. She has a slight heart murmur now; that's due to the surgery. It will go away as her heart heals. I did not replace the valve. As her heart grows the hypertrophy will dissipate. Rachel's resting comfortably in the recovery room. She still has an endotracheal tube in place; however, she is breathing on her own. Once she awakens a little bit more, she will begin swallowing. Then we will remove the tube. I am keeping her sedated with morphine for pain. If she continues to progress at this pace, and I expect she will, we will move her into ICU in about two hours. At that time, you can see her and be with her. She will be sleeping due to the morphine. We'll taper her morphine dose down over night. I anticipate we will keep her on a low dose for a few days to make her more comfortable. I will be in and out checking on her throughout the rest of today."

'If you have not eaten, this would be a good time to do so. If you have, I would recommend you have lunch in a while and take a walk to get your blood circulating and loosen up a little. I know you all have been in a stressful situation waiting for the surgery to end. That's been a little hard on your bodies; walking will help you. Do you have questions?"

"Dr. Adams I can't thank you enough for all you have done for Rachel", said Catherine. "We are going to take your advice and take a walk. You have both Bobby and my cell phone numbers, if anything changes." Catherine turned in her seat and hugged Ken in appreciation. "After our walk, we'll get something to eat."

"Take your time, Rachel is resting and the anesthetic is slowly dissipating from her system. A nurse assigned to care for her is monitoring her constantly. As I said, I will be in and out, but never far away. You guys have a nice walk."

"Thank you Dr. Adams", said Bobby. "We know Rachel is being given the best care possible. She is in good hands."

Penny got up and walked over and gave Ken a big hug and whispered into his ear, "Thanks Dad."

****

After their walk around the Children's Hospital campus, the two couples stood at the entryway to the hospital. "If it's OK with you, we'll let you two have lunch by yourselves", said Randy. "We have a little shopping to do. We'll be back in a little while. In the ICU, they will limit the number of people in Rachel's room so she can rest comfortably. We will stop back and check on her and you guys, but we won't stay long. Is there anything we can bring you when we return?"

"I can't think of anything, how about you Cath?"

"No, I'm fine."

"Penny thanks for filling me in on your project. You took my mind off what was happening and I really appreciate that. I feel more relaxed now and in the best state of mind I have been in since we left Texas. That's because of you, and of course your Dad. Thank you again."

"Bobby, I'm glad it helped. We shouldn't be gone long."

Chapter 41

Penny received an e-mail from Bobby Laporte as she was walking around the Children's campus. She opened the e-mail on her smart phone. The message read, "Call me when you can-Not an emergency-News to share." Penny handed the phone to Randy to let him read the message.

After leaving Catherine and Bobby at the hospital, Penny called Bobby Laporte from the parking garage.

"Hi Bobby, it's Penny. Rachel's out of surgery and stable in the recovery room. All is going well for her. Randy and I are sitting in the parking garage about to go shopping for my engagement ring. What's the news?"

"I'm glad you called as soon as you could. Clare and I went to a meeting regarding the progress on the DVE investigations. There are some interesting developments that I wanted to share with you. I have meetings all afternoon and will be out of touch."

"The terrorism investigation has made a lot of headway. On the financial side of things, the Treasury department has identified the true ownership of the 20 foreign investment entities that invested in cattle contracts and futures. The owner is your old buddy Mushtaq Shakir. The money in the investment accounts originated from the Los Zeta cartel in payment for $100 million dollars of heroin."

"Come to find out, Mushtaq Shakir is on the FBI, CIA, and military intelligence watch lists for suspicion of funding terrorist activities. I won't go into a lot of detail, but they were able to track the heroin from Afghanistan to Pakistan and then to the port of Karachi, Pakistan. Somehow the shipment then ended up in the Nigerian port city of Lagos and from there to port of Tampico, Mexico. DEA intelligence sources have linked the smuggled heroin with the fertilizer. There is also evidence showing the payment checks from the cooperative distributorship in Oklahoma City for the nano-fertilizer were cashed at the same bank in Laredo."

"That's the good news. The bad news according to Geraldine Green, the Attorney General, is very little of this information contains the hard evidence needed to prosecute a terrorism case. Clare and I think the hard evidence may be impossible to obtain. International smugglers don't keep records. Eye witnesses willing to testify against Al Qaida or the Zeta cartel will not come forward in fear of their life and those of their entire families. I don't know of any other way to obtain the hard evidence we'll need."

"Just as I thought the investigation was going so well it hits a dead end", said Penny. "How are we going to proceed?"

"That's for Homeland to determine. We will just keep plugging along in identifying the farmers who used the nano-fertilizer on the fields and crops. We've just about finished identifying the farmers and still have quite a few parties that purchased alfalfa for feed. It's too soon to know if fields of corn, sugar beets, soybeans, etc. fertilized with nano-fertilizer will have the prions cross over from the nano-fertilizer to those crops. Those fields are quarantined. We have identified another 46 infected premises for depopulation. I don't know yet how many cattle that represents."

"Thanks for the information. I do have some good news for you, although I do not have time to go into a lot of detail. I had a meeting with Bobby Bennett this morning while Dad was operating on Rachel. He was very positive about working with us. I think we'd better plan on holding the meeting in Amarillo, rather than in DC. Bobby wants to have Randall and Philip involved. He told me something that we need to keep in mind going forward. That is, when Bobby formed his salvage and industrial design business his mission was to was to reuse salvaged materials in his projects. He wants access to military surplus and government salvage materials. This is a key prerequisite or we may not get his expertise. He appears willing to participate fully in overseeing the construction of all the crematoriums and does not plan on his company building any of the stationary units. He wants to build at least some of the mobile modular units and will design them. Bobby has some earlier designs that include skinning, evisceration, a pre-breaker, and a hasher. He is not interested in the collection of oils or hides. He thinks his brother Mike might be, but thinks there are a lot of folks that would have an interest. He doesn't ATX's involvement to have the perception of an insider deal. It is very important to Bobby to utilize what we already have before creating more stuff from new materials. This is key to getting Bobby on board. It will certainly have a positive impact on the budget; which he pointed out is being paid for with the taxpayers' buck."

"That's all I have. I know you will pass it on to all the parties involved. I think it would be safe to set up a meeting in Amarillo the week after next toward the middle or end of the week. I can take care of getting a place to meet and lodging arrangements if you tell me how many will be coming."

"Thank you for calling. I'll pass your information on and maybe we will have more time to talk tomorrow. I think Wednesday through Friday of the week after next would give us time to negotiate and finalize a deal. You might run that timeframe by Bobby Bennett, if you think it's appropriate."

"You guys have fun and make Randy buy you a nice ring; he's got a pocket full of money from his winnings at the rodeo."

Chapter 42

Penny provided the directions as Randy drove to the jewelry store.

Upon entering the jewelry store, Randy said, "We're here to buy an engagement ring; but if it's OK, let us look around a little and we'll find you when we're ready to have you show us something."

Randy said to Penny, "I want you to choose a ring you like and want to wear for a long, long time. Don't make your selection based on price. I look at buying your ring as a long-term investment; it's my initial investment our future."

"Just as I've become accustomed to the cowboy side of you, I hear something so sweet and sensitive. That's part of why I love you."

"OK, you have some decisions to make. What do you like best yellow gold, white gold, or platinum?"

"I've always been fond of a traditional yellow gold ring", said Penny.

"Yellow gold it is then. Let's look at different settings. Do you want a single stone setting or do you want a large stone with smaller ones set around the large stone?"

"I've always thought a single stone or a solitaire and a single gold band looks the most feminine."

"So, we're looking for a yellow gold solitaire setting. What about the shape of the stone? There is round, oval, square, emerald, pear, marquise, cushion, and heart-shaped."

"I actually like either an oval or round shaped diamond. Hey, I thought you told me you did not know anything about engagement rings", Penny said teasingly.

"No, I told you I had poor taste; it's not that I don't know anything about them. Although I must admit, it never hurts to do an internet search", replied Randy with a big smile.

"Color is next; there are lots of different colors. Some of the..."

"It's got to be white. I'm sort of a traditional girl, gold ring, oval solitaire in a low setting so it won't catch on everything, and a white diamond. What's next Mr. Diamond expert?"

"Nothing, I think it's time to ask the saleslady to help us."

They walked to where the saleslady was sitting on a stool. "I think we're ready for you to show us some rings", said Randy. "We're looking for a yellow gold ring with a low set solitaire setting to hold a white oval diamond."

"You make my job easy. I wish everyone knew what they were looking for. I am Mary, by the way. Let's go over to that counter and look at some low set solitaire settings in yellow gold." Mary set out four different setting styles all in size seven, Penny's size. "Don't worry about the prong size we can adjust that to the size of the stone." Penny selected a ring/setting with a narrow yet flat band she thought looked feminine and would wear well. "Did you have a carat size in mind", asked Mary.

Penny looked at Randy and did not answer.

Randy said, "Let's start somewhere between three and five carats and go from there."

Again, Penny looked at Randy but her eyes were a little wider as if to say, "Are you sure about this?"

Mary said, "Please give me a moment, I have to go in the back and get our larger diamonds. With the robberies these days, I don't display these size stones. I wouldn't want them stolen."

As Mary walked into the back of the store Penny said, "These are going to be too expensive."

Randy responded, "Just keep in mind what I said earlier. It's your job to select what you want. Are you saying you want to limit my investment in our future?"

"Of course, not", answered Penny realizing Randy had thought this through to the extent that he was prepared for Penny becoming price conscious.

Randy selected almost the largest stone on the tray to look at first. It was almost five carats. He placed it between his fingers and delicately placed it above Penny's left ring finger. He studied the stone's size compared to her finger and said, "Penny what do you think? I think it's a little too large and would easily get in your way."

"I think it's too large too. I also think it would look out of place in the setting I have chosen. I want it to look feminine and classy. On me, I think it would look excessive."

Mary selected one three and a half carats and held it on top of Penny's ring finger. The diamond shone brilliantly and was more size appropriate for Penny's taste. "I like this one, but I also want to look at one that's smaller, just to compare."

Mary selected two and a quarter carat stone and placed it on top of Penny's finger. It also shone brilliantly, but is was noticeably smaller and did not look more feminine. "I like them both", said Penny. I thought the smaller one might look more feminine, but not really. Which one do you like the best Randy?"

"I like the larger one of the two. It looks more striking and brilliant. Both look feminine, but I'm partial to the larger one. What do you think; you're the one that's going to be wearing it?"

"I think I like the larger one the best, but I would be very happy wearing the smaller one. I agree with you the larger one is more striking and brilliant. I think it will look good in the low setting", Penny said.

"Mary, I think we have settled on the ring and diamond. What are we talking in price", asked Randy.

"The 24-carat gold engagement ring and matching wedding band is $2,600 and the 3.5 carat diamond is $27,500 for a total of $30,100 plus tax."

Penny was speechless. Randy however was not; "Mary, I'm not trying to offend you, but I'm willing to give you $25,000 plus tax right now for the rings and diamond."

"Randy, my husband and I own this store. I want to consult with my husband before I make a decision like this. How do you propose to pay for the rings and the diamond?"

"I will call my bank and have the money wired directly into your account. That way there's absolutely no worry or risk to you. Your account will be funded within 30 minutes of the call."

"Let me go talk with my husband", Mary said.

As Mary walked into the backroom Penny whispered, "What made you think to do that? Do you think they will take your offer?"

"I think they may comeback with a counter; if it's close, I'll take it. If we're too far apart, I may put some pressure on them. Penny, remember I trade a lot of cattle. It's all about negotiation and I learned there is a wide margin in jewelry. It was worth a try, particularly when you took me into a privately-owned store."

"Randy, you never cease to amaze me."

Mary returned with her husband. "This is my husband Sam. Sam this is Randy and Penny. I'm sorry I do not know your last names."

"I am Penny Adams and this is my fiancé Randy Bennett."

"Randy and Penny our last name is Nichols. After hearing you will have the money directly wired into our account, you have a deal", said Sam. We normally do not negotiate prices, but we normally do not have people come in and buy $25,000 worth of merchandise and pay for it with cash. How do you propose to do the transaction?"

"I'll make the call on my cell phone with the speaker on; when they answer I will ask for Mary. She's the president of the bank. Once Mary is on the line I will tell her what we're doing and you can take the phone into your office to provide her with your bank information. That way we will not be privy to your private information."

"That is satisfactory to us", said Sam.

The transaction went off with no problems. Sam had gone back into his shop area to set the brilliant oval diamond in the setting and polish everything. He brought it out and gave it to Randy who put it on Penny's finger. "That was a surprisingly smooth transaction. We have not done anything like that before; but, I'd like to do it that way every time. By the way, Mary at your bank said to tell you both congratulations."

Both Penny and Randy laughed. Penny looked at the ring on her finger and then at Randy and gave him a kiss.

"Hey, you kids don't leave yet. We need to get you the paperwork and a box for your rings and put the wedding ring in the box."

After getting the box and the wedding ring, Randy handed it to Penny as they walked out of the jewelry store hand in hand.

"I'll tell you what, you to keep the wedding ring until you think it's time we start planning the wedding. When that time comes, you give it back to me. We'll start making the arrangements and set the date. That way there's no pressure on either one of us. Does that sound OK?"

"Perfect", replied Penny.

****

Penny and Randy returned to the hospital. They got off the elevator on the surgery floor to find the waiting area empty. The volunteer at the desk informed them Rachel was doing well and was in the ICU. At the ICU nurses station, they learned Bobby and Catharine were with Rachel.

Randy and Penny quietly walked into Rachel's room. Bobby and Catherine were sitting next to the bed quietly visiting, almost in a whisper. They both stood as Penny and Randy entered.

"They moved her to this room about a half hour ago, said Catherine in a soft voice. She is doing well according to her nurse. Your Dad has not been in since they moved Rachel. We expect him soon. Did you have a good time shopping?"

Penny held up her left hand with the back of her hand facing Catherine.

"Wow", said Catherine in a full voice. Realizing what she had just done, she lowered her voice saying, "When you guys go shopping, you do some serious shopping." Holding Penny's hand in hers she said; "It is absolutely gorgeous. Penny we're glad to have you joining our family. Bobby and I felt we already knew you before we met you this morning. I never got the opportunity to thank you for getting Rachel in to see your Dad. We really appreciated all you've done.

Now, I find out we're going to be sisters-in-law. I'm elated. Have you set a date?"

"No, we're going to take our time."

Bobby walked up to Penny and looked at her new ring. "It's really beautiful. While Catherine and I were having lunch, I told her. I now know why Dad told Randy not to let you get away. Randy, for once in his life, listened to Dad. I'm so happy for you both. Bobby hugged Penny and whispered congratulations into her ear.

Randy and Penny were about to leave when Dr. Ken Adams walked in the door. "How is my patient doing", he said as he walked up to the head of the bed to examine Rachel. He looked at the monitors and the chart. "She's doing great. She's sleeping due to the pain medication. All the anesthesia has worn off and I see she is comfortable. I'm going to slowly back her off the pain medicine, but I also want her to get a good night's rest. She's been through a lot the last week or so, and today is no cakewalk for her. It will be a slow taper down to a base level of narcotic. I expect her to be awake tomorrow morning and ready for breakfast. We're keeping her nourished through the IV fluids. She will feel hungry tomorrow and we will begin feeding her semi-solid foods. Once she is eating well and her bowels are moving normally, we'll take out the tubes. Then she will be ready to go home. I'm thinking in about a week she can leave the hospital. Plan to stay at our house that night. If all goes well, I think she will be well enough for you to travel back home."

Ken walked from the head of the bed over to Penny putting his arm around her shoulder. "How's my little girl this afternoon?"

"Your little girl is fine this afternoon. I do have something to show you", Penny said lifting her hand to show off her new ring.

"Oh God, Penny it's beautiful. Does your mother know yet? Congratulations are to both of you."

"Mom doesn't know yet. We were about to go to the house to surprise her."

"She will be elated, as am I."

"When we get home, we're going to celebrate", said Ken. "That reminds me, Bobby and Catherine, I know you want to spend more time with Rachel, but I would recommend you come home in a little while and plan on staying home tonight. Your boys will want your reassurance that Rachel is doing well; and she is. She's going to sleep through the night and you can do nothing here but watch her sleep. Come home, be around the boys and get a good night's sleep. If anything unexpected happens, I will be the first to know and you can return to the hospital with me. After tonight, Rachel will be awake and she'll bounce back to normal faster than you think."

"That's my sermon for this afternoon. I hope to see you all home for dinner and a celebration. I am going to make rounds; check on Rachel one more time, and then I will be heading home."

****

"Hi Mom, we're back." There was no response. She and Randy walked into the house walking back to the kitchen. Penny walked toward the garage. Pam's car was not in the garage. "I think we're alone. Mom's car is gone."

"Let's get our luggage out of the car. Do you know where we will be sleeping?"

"I don't know, let's go look around and see what appears to be empty."

"I think we're moving in to the right room; if not, we can move easily."

Randy headed to the back porch after finding the newspaper. He walked back into the garage for a beer as the garage door elevated. In drove Pam with both Bennett boys. When they saw Randy they both got excited.

"Uncle Randy, what are you doing here", asked Robby.

"We were nearby at a rodeo. When we heard Rachel was having surgery, we came to be with your Mom and Dad." Both boys ran to Randy hugging him.

"I'm glad you're here Uncle Randy", said Mack. "How's Rachel? We've been thinking about her all day. Is she done with her operation?"

"I'm glad to see you both. Rachel is through with her surgery and is sleeping. The surgery was very successful. I think your Mom and Dad may be home a little later. Tell me what you did today."

"We went to this cool day care center. Miss Pam took us this morning. They have lots of neat playground sets and two really tall slides. We played on the slides a lot. When it got hot this afternoon we went inside to watch a video and some cartoons while the babies took their nap. We also helped watch the little kids; so, they wouldn't go up the big slides. Those slides are just for big guys like us", Mack added.

"Let's go inside. There is someone in there that I want you to meet." As they walked in from the garage Penny was helping Pam put away the groceries. As Penny reached up to put away a cereal box, Pam noticed her hand saying, "Oh Penny, is that what I think it is?"

"What's what", Penny asked.

"Don't play coy with me young lady. On your left hand, the ring finger."

"Yes, it is", Penny smiled. "Randy asked me to marry him yesterday after he won the steer roping. He said it would make his day perfect, if I would marry him. Of course, I said yes. We got this ring this afternoon. Randy said he wanted me to pick it out as I would be the one wearing it."

"Penny it is beautiful; but, you didn't have to pick the biggest one in the store."

"It wasn't like that", interrupted Randy. "I chose the stone, but Penny had to approve. This is what we came up with. I like it, it looks good on her."

"When the saleslady went into the back to get some stones to look at, I told Randy they were going to be too expensive. You know what he said to me? He said, 'Are you saying you want to limit my investment in our future?' I learned right then, he meant what he said about it being my job to pick out what I wanted. And he negotiated a good deal on it too. I learned something there too; he's a tough, but fair, negotiator."

"I want to hear the whole story, but let's wait for your Dad to get home. Has he seen your ring yet?"

"Yes, I showed it to him at the hospital. He said it was beautiful. I think he should be home soon. He was just starting rounds when we saw him. I think Catherine and Bobby will be coming home for dinner. By the way, we put our bags in the room we stayed in when we were here before. Is that the right room?"

"Yes, dear it is. I did not put anyone else in that room because I had not yet put fresh sheets on the bed and I didn't want anyone sleeping in there without clean linens on the bed. Don't tell anyone-not even your Dad."

Penny laughed and said, "Randy...we got the right room."

Pam laughed and said, "I thought you were going to tell him, just to spite me."

Randy was in the back yard with Robby and Mack playing catch with a football. The boys were the receivers and Randy was the quarterback. It helped the boys run off some of energy. They liked playing with their Uncle Randy. Mack had thrown the ball back to Randy who noticed the football appeared to be new. On closer examination, it had the NFL logo burned into the ball. On the side of the ball there was an inscription. It said, "To Dr. Ken, Thanks for everything. John Elway #7." Randy called both boys in close and asked, "Where did you guys get this ball? It's a real NFL game ball."

"Yeah, we know; Dr. Ken gave it to us yesterday to play catch with", said Robby.

About that time Ken walked off the porch joining Randy. "Ken, this is a real game ball", said Randy.

"Yes, it is", said Ken. "John gave it to me several years ago. It's just sat around on the mantel above the fireplace in the family room for years. From time to time I take it down for our grandchildren to play with. Footballs are for play, not to sit on a mantel. The boys can't hurt it, and if they do, well it's just a football."

Randy threw the football to the boys again as Ken sat on the stairs of the patio reminiscing to when he would come home from work and throw a football with his boys. While time has marched on, some things remain the same-boys and football.

Bobby and Catherine left Rachel's room as Ken left the hospital. They trusted Dr. Ken. Soon Bobby walked into the back yard. Both boys came running to him; hugging his legs asking about Rachel. After Bobby confirmed Rachel was doing fine and sleeping comfortably in her hospital bed, Bobby took over throwing the football to his boys. Randy returned to the stairs and sat next to Ken as they watched the play. Normalcy overtook worry and tension.

As the sun began its decent over the Rocky Mountains the western sky displayed broad strokes of dark blue and orange, the colors of the Denver Broncos. During dinner Penny detailed Randy's marriage proposal, buying the ring, and Randy giving her the wedding band. After dinner Ken brought out a bottle of aged bourbon. A patient's father gave it to him years ago. The adults had a celebratory drink. Ken called the ICU on his cell phone putting it on speaker so everyone could hear. Everyone, including Robby and Mack, heard the nurse as she said, "Rachel is resting comfortably, and she is sleeping. Her blood pressure is normal, heart rate normal and steady, EKG is normal as is her oxygen saturation." Rachel's heart is fixed, just as Dr. Ken said early that morning.

Chapter 43

"Tex, come on in", said General Clark.

"Sir, I have compiled the existing information available on Dr. Mohammad Aziz and Mr. Mushtaq Shakir. The deeper we drilled the more we found. Our challenge was putting it together in a meaningful manner. We completed the project yesterday afternoon, just before I called requesting a meeting with you. There is no formal report. I don't think we want a record of what I am about to tell you. Let me give you the rundown and I'll finish with my recommendation."

"That sounds great Tex. Let's hear what you've got."

"Mushtaq Shakir's home is located near the Faisal Mosque in an exclusive neighborhood of Islamabad. The home is large and modern. There is a large screened porch across the entire front of the home. A ten-foot white cinder block wall borders the home on all sides. It's a two-story structure with a full basement housing Shakir's office. Connectivity throughout the house is wireless and is connected to a large contemporary mainframe computer housed in its own small climate controlled room in the basement. His communications system is sophisticated (computers and telephones) using encryption to ensure privacy. There's a hidden panel behind his desk leading to a safe room and an escape tunnel to a nearby garage housing his armored Mercedes S600. While he works from home; his home is a fortress with an armed security force and a state of the art security system that integrates hidden video cameras, laser alarms, and directional mines to fend off would be attackers."

"About a half-mile away, is the more modest home of Mohammed Aziz. As a university professor, his home is in an area of Islamabad that's above his stature and rank; however, he inherited the four-bedroom two story home from his father, a former General in the Pakistani army. He lives with his wife and two children, both teenagers. Mohammed's son, a bright young student, will be attending the University in two years."

"Three to four times a week Mohammed and Mushtaq meet at the Faisal Mosque for Asr, then go to a nearby coffeehouse. The men have a lot in common. They were both educated outside Pakistan. Mohammed secured a National scholarship which paid all his expenses when he attended Yale as an undergraduate, Johns Hopkins for his master's degree and Stanford for his PhD in Molecular Biology. He is known as a gifted scholar at the three institutions. His intellect carried forward to his laboratory work that resulted in his master's and PhD degrees. Prion science was his specific area of interest and study. Mushtaq's father paid for his education. He planned on Mushtaq taking over his business interests from the time he was a young boy. After leaving Pakistan, Mushtaq first studied International Business at the University of Cambridge in England. He then attended the Stanford Business School earning his MBA. He was a bright hard-working student. Mushtaq and Mohammed first met as young students at the Institute of Islamic Sciences, an exclusive boarding school located in Islamabad. After graduation, they did not meet again until they both sought advanced degrees at Stanford."

"At Stanford Mohammed and Mushtaq rekindled their friendship becoming steadfast in their hate for western society, its beliefs, and its citizens. At the Islamic Students Organization, they became more vengeful and activist dissidents. They were good at enticing other students to demonstrate and take actions they personally did not take. They used each other to fuel their hatred, which for the most part went unnoticed. Middle Eastern and Southwestern Asian students at the liberal university were frequently categorized with racial slurs such as camel jockeys, towel heads and rag heads. Such categorization happened to Mushtaq and Mohammed during those pre-nine-eleven times. At each incident, they appeared outwardly to ignore their verbal assailants; inwardly they became progressively more infuriated and vowed vengeance and retaliation against the infidels. While inwardly enraged they became paranoid of students, staff, and faculty. Both feared extreme retribution, such as expulsion from the university, if they brought their claims forward. Immediately after Mushtaq graduated, his father who was very ill called him home shortly before he died. Mohammed, however, stayed an extra few weeks in Palo Alto where he made false accusations against most of his fellow male graduate students and the Molecular Biology faculty. He charged the students with racial and religious bias and most faculty members. Additionally, he charged the faculty with knowledge of what was happening and encouraging the actions. The campus responded to these accusations by initiating an in-depth investigation of the entire department. The Dean of the School of Law and a university provost oversaw the investigation. It was thorough and exhaustive. In the end, the investigation exonerated everyone; but not before the leftist press attempted to tarnish the entire university as being racially insensitive. Excluded from the accusations were female graduate students and faculty. In Mohammed's strict conservative Islamic belief, women were lesser beings whose presence was to serve the wishes of men. In Mohammed's view, they were not worth mentioning."

"Before the tumult reached its crest, Mohammed moved to Boston. He received a fellowship in the Liao laboratory at the Harvard Medical School to further study the structure and function of membrane proteins. Within a few weeks Mohammed made identical accusations to the university's civil rights department. A second firestorm erupted to include a complete investigation of the medical school and its culture. As in Palo Alto, once he incited the vengeance he and Mushtaq had planned, he resigned his position moving to Worcester, England. He began work as a fellow at the Animal Health and Veterinary Laboratories. He stayed there several months, but he was unhappy. There were few Muslims in England's countryside. He felt isolated."

"Prior to Mohammed Aziz leaving Worcester, he obtained and accepted an assistant professorship in the Department of Biochemistry and Molecular Biology at the Army Medical College at National University of Pakistan in Islamabad. Soon after Mohammed arrived in Islamabad, he and Mushtaq began meeting after Asr."

"As always with good friends, their conversations and thoughts picked up where they left off in Palo Alto. They discussed vengeance against the infidels and soon began planning it. They came to an early consensus that the vengeance, whatever it may be, must occur in the United States and be wide spread. Mohammed was responsible for designing the stealth biological attack while Mushtaq's responsibilities included finance and logistics."

"Within six months Mohammed presented his idea to Mushtaq. He wanted to manipulate prions into slightly smaller misfolded proteins with enhanced infectivity. However, the technology to do so did not exist. As they continued their visits over coffee, they refined their plan. They both thought it was better to have someone other than Aziz conduct these studies. After more thought, he separated the idea into three very compartmentalized experiments to be conducted by graduate students pursuing their PhD degrees under Mohammed's tutelage. Funding for these studies came from World Health Organization grants. Mushtaq provided subsistence grants for the three students under the guise of three separate business interests he owned. The first graduate student learned how to enhance the replication of the prions in vitro, or within artificial culture media. The second student learned how to cleave small units of peptides off the protein molecule and alter where they folded by manipulating the position of the disulfide on the protein molecule. The third student learned developed methodology for making proteinaceous nanoparticles. To further deceive, no two experiments occurred simultaneously. It required nine years to fruition and enhanced compartmentalization. It also provided Mushtaq time to acquire the necessary funding estimated to be over 50 million dollars."

"Mushtaq began expanding his narco-trafficking by increasing the capacity of his morphine processing laboratories and building a new heroin processing facility in Mogadishu, Somalia. The addition of this laboratory opened new markets and new business partners, like the Los Zeta cartel in Mexico. His reputation as a reliable, high quality manufacturer grew as his business grew and expanded. This allowed him to demand a premium for the high-quality heroin. Narcotics smuggling became his primary business concern with profits soaring as a result. He concealed much of his profits awaiting the day Mohammed produced enough modified infectious prion protein to implement the plan. They were both patient and intelligent in stockpiling their resources. However, Mushtaq was greedy; he developed a supplementary plan to leverage his capital using the international stock markets. Thus, allowing him to exploit the financial mayhem created in the U.S."

"They projected it would take the U.S. years to uncover their plot. By that time, they would be extraordinarily wealthy and divested of any illicit business that could tie them to their contrived heinous act. Their plan was to capitalize on the infidels' greed and plentiful food resources to devastate the U.S. cattle herd and cripple the economy."

"After a decade of working diligently and living under the radar, Mohammed Aziz and Mushtaq Shakir implemented their plan. Mohammed developed a very sophisticated laboratory at the university and began replicating novel highly infectious prions. Which he then covered with proteinaceous nanoparticles. He also manufactured the titanium dioxide nanoparticles. He combined them in a two-part prion to one-part titanium dioxide ratio. The nanoparticles were added to generic five-gallon containers of surfactant."

"Mushtaq was charged with U.S. distribution. He hired a down-on-his-luck American salesman to sell the product. It was the salesman's idea to sell them to U.S. farm cooperatives by supplying their national distribution warehouse at a significant discount to comparable fertilizers. Mushtaq promised the salesman two million dollars for his efforts. He received a 230-grain hollow point slug that entered the bridge of his nose and blew off most of the rear portion of his skull splattering bone, blood, and brain all over a New Orleans motel room wall thanks to a Los Zeta cartel assassin."

"Mohammed wrote two technical articles, provided the agronomists names and locations, as well as the scientific journals where they would appear to have been published. Mushtaq used this information to counterfeit the supporting technical information. He also designed and printed labels for Advanced Fertilizers. The pressure-sensitive labels were applied at a warehouse where Mohammed added the nanoparticles to the surfactant."

"The nano-fertilizer was transported with a large shipment of morphine from Islamabad to Karachi using Mushtaq's trucks pulling sixteen container trailers. The trailers arrived at the Port of Karachi and were immediately loaded on a container ship destined for Mogadishu, Somalia. Reaching Mogadishu, they off-loaded the morphine and transported it to Mushtaq's laboratory. Here they processed the morphine into pure high-grade heroin. After reloading the heroin into the containers, they transported the containers back to the docks of the Port of Mogadishu. There they were loaded on a second container ship that navigated around the horn of Africa to the Port of Lagos. Another vessel carried the containers to the Port of Tampico. We know from there it went to Monterrey where the heroin was cut and repackaged prior to being smuggled through Laredo, Texas to San Antonio for distribution throughout the US."

"As we know the nano-fertilizer went to Oklahoma City where it was offloaded and distributed. It has been confirmed the bank in Laredo, where the fertilizer payment checks were cashed, is strongly associated with the Los Zeta cartel and is likely used to launder some of the cartel's money."

"You and I both heard the report of the Treasury Department's activities in determining the ownership of the multiple investments made to capitalize on the U.S. markets' response to DVE and adulterated feedstuffs. That too was traced back to Mushtaq Shakir."

"This intelligence was assembled through interviews with persons knowledgeable of their operations in the U.S., Pakistan, Afghanistan, Nigeria, and Mexico. We gathered most of the intelligence using collusion and other illegal interrogation techniques. In no way would it be admissible in a court of law. Mitch, I'm sure you recall the Attorney General's comments from our last meeting regarding information that had previously developed."

"It is my recommendation you seek approval for Dr. Aziz and Mushtaq Shakir to be terminated in a black op conducted by a Delta team. We will never be able to bring these two to trial in a court of law, yet we know they are the terrorists we're looking for."

"Considering what you presented, I agree. I will speak to President Smyth. Good work. I'll get back with you", said General Clark.

Chapter 44

Penny and Randy flew to Amarillo two days after Rachel's surgery. Bobby, Catherine, and the kids returned a week later. The representatives from Washington were traveling to Amarillo for the meeting. They planned to discuss carcass destruction and negotiate an agreement Wednesday through Friday of the following week. On Monday Penny was making final arrangements. She planned to meet with Bobby in the afternoon for the first time since he returned from Denver. The number of high-ranking officials scheduled to attend the meeting surprised Penny. From the USDA there was Secretary Johansen, Bobby Laporte, Dr. Sam Yu, and Penny. The military representatives included General Clark, and ten command and staff officers. ATX representatives were Randall Bennett, Philip Granger, Randy Bennett, and Bobby Bennett.

Randy assured Penny the Bank's board room was large enough to hold the twenty-one people. Penny made motel reservations at the Amarillo Suites. She also reserved three additional rented Suburbans. Helped by Rose and Sarita, they planned catered lunches. Wednesday's lunch would be at Rosa's in Canyon on the way to the ATX Hereford lot. There, they would gain an appreciation for the size and complexity of the incinerators. Thursday evening Penny planned dinner for everyone at the Amarillo Steak Ranch, a local landmark, famous for their "if you eat all 84 ounces, it's free" steak dinner.

Penny drove to Bobby's office and shop in an industrial area on the southeastern outskirts of Amarillo. A large sign stood in front of the parking lot identifying the office building and attached large precast and metal building. Bobby met Penny at the front door of his shop. "Hi Penny, it looks like you didn't have any trouble finding the place. How are you doing?"

"Bobby, it's nice to see you again. How's Rachel?"

"Rachel is doing much better. It was cute last night when Caroline gave her a bath, she did not want to put down the teddy bear you and Randy had given her at the hospital. She told me, Teddy needs a bath too. That was such a thoughtful gift; she hugged it all the way home while riding in her car seat. Hugging the teddy bear kept her arms together keeping pressure off her breast bone."

"Great, we're glad she enjoys her new Teddy. This is quite a place. I did not expect something as large, or so well kept."

"Thanks, the guys did a great job of cleaning up and organizing things while we were gone. The crew salvaging the old refinery in Midland should finish by the end of the week. We will be ready to give our full attention to the carcass burner project. There are some things I need to discuss with you. Let's go into my office."

Penny sat down in a comfortable leather chair adjacent to a coffee table where plans lay for viewing. "I'm so glad we had that discussion while Rachel was having surgery. It took me a few days to digest all you told me. I had breakfast with Dad and Philip the day after we returned. We visited quite a while about the project. Philip told me not to worry about using surplus and salvage materials. He said with this being an emergency, the decision makers have broad latitude to do what is most expedient. I foresee having a discussion regarding modifying salvage vs. using new materials. Even if we were to buy new tanks, they would still require modification. Dad told me Clare is a very practical person and would not want to throw money around just because it was appropriated. I feel more comfortable with my repurposing position."

"Philip has a concern regarding this project. Maybe you can get word to Clare. Philip's concern is the press may criticize the ATX for taking advantage of an emergent situation. He warned me to not to throw any big numbers. He recommends I structure pricing so my company fairly compensated for our time and expenses, plus a twelve percent profit. I intend to follow Philip's advice. However, I think Clare should know our concerns. She has a lot of influence in how things appear to the public and the press. Dad and Philip's main concern is ATX's reputation. They don't want to do this deal, if it compromises what they are trying to do at Tech."

"You should know when we begin to discuss the carcass burner project I am going to offer them various levels of involvement. I will offer to provide them with the plans for a royalty of $500/unit and they can acquire the materials and construct all the units themselves as one option. At the other end of the spectrum I will help find the materials and get them transported to the various locations and have my foremen travel to the various sites to personally oversee construction while we build the modular units here in my shop. We're open to negotiate anything in between."

"Bobby I'll get the message to Clare. Personally, I think Philip's concerns are legitimate. I also think your approach is equitable. From my experience, keep in mind some folks in government can make a simple deal complex. It's also been my experience if we plan three days for negotiations and signing an agreement, it will take three days. Regardless if both sides agree within the first hour of the meeting. I hope I'm wrong in this case. I also think Philip will be a big help in keeping simple things simple."

"I don't know if you've heard, Wednesday late morning we're all going to travel to Canyon for lunch at Rosa's, then on to the Hereford so everyone can see one of your carcass burner's. We'll start it up for them before leaving. Randy made this suggestion; I think it is a great idea. That way they will have a mental image of what's being discussed."

"That's a wonderful idea. I think having a solid visual image of not only the burner, but the entire site will be most helpful when discussing this project. I'm working on some PowerPoint slides. They will lead them through the entire construction process of building, ground preparation, and installing a carcass burner."

"If you have time, I would really like a tour of your shop. I've never seen anything like your operation. It fascinates me. I'm going to meet Randy near here in an hour or so. We are going over to Randall and Beth's for supper. They know we're engaged, but haven't seen my ring yet. Philip and Kay will also be there."

"I'd be pleased to give you a tour. We're between projects now so the shop is fairly empty", said Bobby. "Maybe before we go out to the shop, we should look at the modified plans for the stationary burners with skinning, evisceration, pre-breaker, and chopper in place. I looked at my old design; then enhanced it.

"I would like that, very much", said Penny.

Penny and Bobby reviewed the new drawings. He had modified the old design by adding augers and eliminating the clam shell type doors. He'd included a separate drawing of a method of conveying the viscera directly to the burner in a closed auger system.

"Bobby, you have captured everything I explained and more. These plans are great."

"I'm glad you like them. Let's go look at the shop."

As they toured the large shop area Bobby said, "It's really a big shop; but when we get busy, we use all the space. We constructed this building and the office/design studio using salvage materials. The steel support beams are from three interstate highway bridges. I know they look oversized. However, they support the overhead lifts and cranes we use. The lower precast walls we salvaged from an industrial building damaged by a tornado. The upper metal part of the walls and roof came from salvaging a train derailment southwest of Amarillo, almost due west from Randy's house. From that derailment, we also got four carloads of one by eight rough cut cedar. That was really a good job for us. The railroad paid us to haul off the contents of eight freight cars.

We used or sold the contents of the freight cars. That's about all to see here now."

"Bobby this is fascinating. What's that machine over there?"

"That's another brainchild of mine. It removes the mortar from bricks. When we remove a brick structure, we cut brick walls into sections that we load on a flatbed trailer using a forklift. We bring them back here and work through them as we have time. It works well. One person can clean the bricks on a large brick home in a day. They come out looking new. This part of Texas has its share of tornados; we get calls from insurance companies to demolish homes and buildings considered a total loss by insurance companies."

"Fascinating, just fascinating."

Penny's cell phone rang; it was Randy. "I need to leave soon to meet Randy. Would it be OK if I came back another time to look through your book of finished projects? When Mom and Dad come down, I want to bring them by. Mom, being an architect, would really appreciate what you are doing. I also have an idea, if there's a lull in the negotiations, particularly if there is concern about quality or strength; I think we should give the beltway boys and girls a tour of your business and shop. What do you think?"

"If you think it would help. It's probably as clean now as it has been in the last two or three years. My crew did a good job while we were gone with Rachel. Ken and Pam can come anytime they're in town. I would like it if you stopped by for coffee and looked over our past projects."

****

Penny met Randy in a grocery store parking lot leaving her Suburban before driving to Randall and Beth's house.

No sooner had Penny got into Randy's pickup than her phone rang. It was Bobby Laporte. "Hi Bobby, what's new?"

Penny, I just wanted to quickly tell you the senate passed the emergency funding request earlier this afternoon. President Smyth signed it about an hour ago. That's all I have, but wanted you to know as soon as it happened. We've got the funds; we'll start indemnifying DVE cattle producers in the morning. The prion research and carcass destruction parts of the bill, have just shifted into high gear."

"Thank you for passing that along. It sounds like we will be getting real busy now. I'm glad you called; I have something for you. I met with Bobby Bennett this afternoon. ATX's concern is they want to avoid the perception of capitalizing on an emergent situation. Because of this concern, Bobby intends to price things so his company receives fair compensation for time and expenses, plus a twelve percent profit margin. He plans to offer a range of goods and services they can provide. Basically, leaving it up to Secretary Johansen and General Clark what level of involvement they want."

"That's as fair a deal as anyone could hope for. Penny, I must go, but we will talk more tomorrow. Have a good night."

They pulled into the driveway as Randall was finishing watering his rose garden. As they walked to the house he said, "Hi son, how's that pretty fiancée of yours today? Go on in the house. Everyone else is in there, I just wanted to give water to my roses; it was hot this afternoon."

Penny stopped and gave Randall a quick hug before she followed Randy into the house. Beth met her near the doorway. There's our daughter-in-law to be; let's see that ring. Beth was smiling and overjoyed. Kay and I have been waiting all day to see you and your new ring."

Penny, slightly embarrassed, lifted her left hand and placed it into Beth's hand as Kay, Phillip, and Randall all leaned in to see the glistening engagement ring. "Oh, it's beautiful", said

Beth and Kay simultaneously. They then looked at each other and laughed.

"They say the same thing at the same time often. You'd think they were twins", Phillip said as he took a better look at the ring. "Penny that is a stunning ring for a stunning girl."

Randall looked at the ring and then at Penny and Randy. "Son, I'm happy you did not let Penny get away. The ring looks wonderful on her finger. Is there another to match?"

"Yes, Penny answered, and I have it for now." Then Penny shared the story.

Beth, touched by the story, came close and gave Randy a hug. "That is so sweet. We have one more guest to arrive, Sarita, and then we can start cooking. I hope you like fish Penny. Normally, I would not serve guests fish without knowing, but you are family now; and besides the fish is fresh salmon and halibut caught yesterday in Alaska and shipped to us by our neighbors. It was still frozen when FedEx delivered it. It's nearly thawed and looks so good, I decided we were going to enjoy it for dinner."

"I love fish, salmon and halibut are my favorites."

The women drifted toward the kitchen as the men sat down in the spacious family room adjacent to the kitchen. Beth poured Penny a glass of wine. Kay delivered a beer to Randy. In about five minutes Sarita walked into the kitchen, letting herself into the house.

"I'm sure you have seen Penny's ring", asked Beth.

"Yes, when Penny and Randy got in from Cheyenne, they stopped by the Canyon office. Penny asked me if I could help her get something out of Randy's pickup. I walked out into the parking lot. When she brought her left hand out of her pocket for me to see, I screamed. Penny had taken me outside to show me without the whole office knowing. That idea didn't work; when I screamed in joy, everyone in the office came to the windows."

Penny saw a carrot cake set out for dessert, she commented, "Carrot cake is my favorite dessert; I suppose Sarita told you."

"No dear, I called your mother. She was kind enough to share her recipe. We had a lovely chat this morning. She is so kind and open, much like you. I love that quality in you Penny."

After the women cleared off the table and loaded the dishwasher, Sarita excused herself saying, "I'm going over to Thomas' for a little while, then I'll head home."

The women joined the men in the family room as they visited about the upcoming meeting. Penny joined in at an appropriate moment saying, "I got a call on the way over from Bobby Laporte. He called to say the President signed the DVE emergency funding bill after it was passed by the senate this afternoon."

"Our timing was perfect", said Philip. "Penny, we told Bill Evans, the Chancellor at Texas Tech, to send the proposal packet for the National Prion Center this afternoon by priority FedEx. It will be there tomorrow morning. Randall and I will give Clare a follow up call."

"How did you know the bill would be passed today?"

"Senator Freidman gave us a courtesy call yesterday letting us know the senate would vote on it today. We already knew it had strong support and President Smyth fully supported the bill. He understood the urgency to initiate the indemnification program", said Randall.

"I find it fascinating how you both work. Not only is there a synergism in your thought processes, but I think you both know what the other is thinking."

"Kay and I have known that for years. What projects Randall and Philip become involved with continues to fascinate us. Over the years their projects have evolved. When Randall was younger and we were first married, his focus was making money so he could be a good provider, as was Philip's. Next came the desire to be able to finance the kid's education, and then came developing businesses so each of our children, or their spouses, could support their families."

"Over the last decade or so", added Kay, "Philip and Randall have become closer again. Much like they were in college. At that time, one was the other's shadow. Now, they have both developed other interests. I think the Amarillo Hospital project started them down the road of working on projects that resulted in improving Amarillo and Texas. Now, they're involved with getting the National Prion Center off the ground. Their minds still work hard every day. I can't tell you the number of times either Philip will get a call in the evening from Randall or vice versa. They find this work stimulating and satisfying."

"Over the years Philip and I have been very fortunate. First, we both had wives who fully supported our endeavors. Our friendship has grown over the years. We have sought counsel from each other as we've made important decisions in our lives. We have also been just plain lucky at times. We both think those times were when the Lord held us in his hand and helped us. Now, we think, it's time to give back; while we are able. We both live comfortably and hope to contribute to the good of our community and futures generations. Anymore, those are the only kind of projects that interest us."

Randy and Penny listened intently. Some things said Randy had never heard. To him, it was like now that you are starting down the road of life with your life partner, we want to share some thoughts with both of you. Penny felt included in sage advice from two couples who cared for them and wanted to share their secrets of success.

"Mom and Kay, thank you for such a delicious dinner. To everyone, thank you for a great evening. It's time we head home. We both have busy days tomorrow, before the big meeting on Wednesday. We appreciate you having us over. I'm glad you were able to finally see Penny's ring."

"Son, there is something we have not done tonight that we need to do; that is to congratulate you on winning the steer roping at Cheyenne. I had heard you won while Sonny and Junior were traveling back home. It was only today I learned about all the records you set while doing so. Congratulations Randy!"

"Dad, like you said earlier; sometimes you are just plain lucky and that's when the Lord holds you in his hand and helps. He also gave me the courage to ask this fine lady to share her life with me...and she said yes."

Chapter 45

"Mr. President, thank you for seeing me after today's cabinet meeting", said General Clark. "I want to talk with you about updated intelligence on the DVE investigation."

President Smyth walked to his chair in the conference area of the oval office to sit down. "Would you care for some fresh coffee? Mitch, it's always a pleasure to talk with you. Should we include the Attorney General and Secretary Robinson in this discussion?"

"No sir. I want this discussion to be between me and my Commander in Chief. After I finish, if you think you want to involve others, that's your call. This information comes as the result of intelligence I asked JSOC to develop. It was verbally reported by General Tex Griffith, Commander of JSOC."

"OK Mitch, let's hear the latest intelligence."

"Mr. President we have compiled comprehensive and compelling information on Dr. Mohammad Aziz and Mr. Mushtaq Shakir. This intelligence came from numerous sources we determined possessed high value intelligence. We interviewed some of the high value personnel using collusion and other illegal interrogation techniques."

General Clark summarized the information assembled by JSOC on Aziz and Shakir.

"We've both heard the Treasury Department's report detailing the ownership of the multiple investments made to capitalize on the US markets' response to DVE and adulterated feedstuffs. These investments traced back to Mushtaq Shakir. Mr. President, you are now current on the status of the investigation.

"This intelligence is not admissible in court. Further, it would not have been gathered without collusion. None of the sources would risk their lives, or the lives of their families, by testifying in court. Mr. President, I see our only option is to take out Aziz and Shakir in a Special Forces black op conducted by Delta. This is also the consensus of JSOC."

After a moment of solemn consideration and with more than a little surprise President Smyth responded; "Mitch, I fully appreciate your desire to keep this conversation private. Considering the damage these two have caused our country, the loss of life and property directly resulting from their endeavor, the mission is a go. However, I want to see if there is a way to eliminate the Los Zeta's as well. Both the Mexican government and the U.S. have allowed this cartel and others to poison our citizens long enough. If we're going to call it a war on drugs and terrorism, then let's treat it like a war, and not some ongoing back alley skirmish where one side plays by the rules and the other does not."

"With this objective also in mind, I want you to have JSOC plan the mission. I too have some work to do to get Mexico to allow such action to occur on the land of our neighbors to the south. If I am successful in convincing President Rodriquez to allow it, I want this mission ready to implement. You can use any additional government resources required for the mission. I will quietly get that ball rolling, if necessary."

"As I said before, the Pakistani mission is a go; but we will delay its implementation and attempt to dismantle the entire operation all at one time covertly. What are your candid thoughts on this plan?"

"Mr. President, it is this old soldier's dream to dismantle drug trafficking into this country. However, I think most of the heavy lifting will fall on your shoulders to gain the cooperation of the President of Mexico without the cartels getting wind of it. I also realize we cannot just invade Mexico. Your plan will likely require a series of well-coordinated simultaneous surgical strikes. To have this operational within thirty days will stretch our capabilities; but sir, it can be executed successfully."

"Mitch thanks for stopping by. It is always a pleasure visiting with you."

Chapter 46

At 6:30PM Tuesday an US Government Gulfstream 650 touched down at Amarillo's municipal airport and taxied to the private terminal where four Suburbans awaited the plane's passengers. Dr. Sam Yu, Dr. Penny Adams, and Dr. Randy Bennett were at the terminal to greet the fourteen passengers who deplaned. Secretary Johansen and General Clark led the delegation into the terminal. After introductions, Penny welcomed everyone to Amarillo saying there were four Suburbans waiting outside to take them to the Amarillo Suites where their rooms awaited. Three US Army enlisted personnel from Amarillo's Army Reserve Center drove to the tarmac and unloaded the luggage from the plane and placed it in an Army Reserve van which would follow the caravan to the motel. Penny explained she would lead them to the motel where they could pick up their room keys and luggage.

As they walked toward the awaiting Suburbans, Clare walked casually up on Penny's left side and put her hand in Penny's lifting it up. "I heard. Congratulations to you both. Penny the ring is absolutely stunning."

"Thank you Madam Secretary", said Penny.

Bobby Laporte and Sam Yu were walking behind them, as was General Clark and his staff officer General Elliott. Soon all four doors of Penny's Suburban were open and everyone was getting seated. After everyone loaded into vehicles, they traveled as a caravan to the Amarillo Suites. At the motel, everyone found a parking space and walked into the lobby. They visited quietly awaiting their luggage. Penny had maps of the area with nearby restaurants identified and on the reverse side a note about the restaurants and their phone numbers. Penny told everyone dinner tonight would be on their own. As soon their luggage arrived, everyone dispersed to their rooms.

The next morning Penny led the caravan to the AXT Bank building where they parked in reserved parking in the underground parking area. They took the elevators to the third floor. The boardroom table contained seating placards for everyone attending the meeting.

The meeting began promptly at 8:00AM with Randall standing and saying, "I am Randall Bennett and I am the Chairman of AXT holdings. I want to thank you all for traveling to Amarillo for this meeting. We certainly appreciate it. As I look around this room, I don't think I have ever seen so many general and staff officers in one place. Thank you all for your service and dedication to our country. Let's go around the table and have everyone introduce themselves."

"Before I turn the meeting over to my son Bobby, who you all really came to talk with, let me say that when DVE first appeared in this country we were one of the first premises involved. We were worried and wanted to determine the cause to minimize our losses. The best way to attain that goal, we thought, was to cooperate with the USDA. You should know Clare Johansen and I have been friends since our college days. When Clare called me asking for our cooperation, I told her we would help in any way we could. And we did. As we meet here today I tell you, we will cooperate in any way we can. Not one of us goes through life without walking across patches of rough ground. Collectively, I think we are all walking across one of those patches right now. We want to shorten that path as much as possible. With that, I will turn the meeting over to my son Bobby Bennett, President of AXT Salvage and Industrial Design."

Bobby stood and said, "Good morning ladies and gentlemen. The USDA faces the challenge of destroying approximately 12 million cattle infected with DVE. AXT faces destruction of almost 200,000 head in three of our six feedlots. Several years ago, as we were building our feedlots my brother Randy insisted we install crematoriums, or what I call carcass burners, at each of our feedlots. As a veterinarian, the spread of disease concerned him. Randy researched various methods of carcass destruction knowing of the challenges that faced England when they dealt with the BSE problem. After studying various methods, Randy concluded incineration, or cremation, was the most effective method. It was also the most cost effective. Randy asked me to design and build the six crematoriums for our feedlots. Using scrap materials from a refinery we tore down, we built the six units. We have a relatively close supply of natural gas to power the units. We constructed the units' large enough to have a capacity of around sixty carcasses. As it turns out, we can hold about sixty-five large heavyweight carcasses and as many as eighty lightweight carcasses; although, before DVE we had not encountered the need to destroy that many carcasses. We designed the burners in a manner to harvest the oils produced during the cremation process. Using a centrifugal pump, we further process the oil to remove residual water and filter out impurities. Then store it in a tank and use it to fuel our diesel equipment. Our primary problem, until we encountered DVE, was having enough oil to use as fuel. Currently, that is not the case."

Clare interrupted; "Bobby to your knowledge have others in the industry followed your lead and constructed crematoriums?"

"Secretary Johansen, to my knowledge, no one else has chosen to go this route. Feedlots typically use one of three primary methods of carcass disposal. One, they call an outside rendering company to come pick up their carcasses. The rendering company skins the animal and may render the carcass for products such as oil, tallow, and meat and bone meal used for fertilizer. The second method is to haul the carcasses to the operation's dump and allow the carcass to simply decompose over time. A third method used by some operators is to add the carcasses to their waste compost piles to decay there. Randy did not consider any of these methods acceptable due to potential for disease spread."

"Bobby, it is my understanding you patented the design."

"Yes, Madam Secretary, I did. I was hopeful the idea would catch on and my company could construct and install them. Regrettably, that did not happen. There has been absolutely no interest in cattle crematoriums."

General Clark said, "Bobby, this is a novel idea and shows a lot of foresight. I wonder what you think about the government coming to you in the middle of a crisis saying we need 400 plus of these units."

"General Clark, my first thought was my company is way too small to construct 400 units in a practical timeframe. In fact, that is what I told Dr. Adams when we first discussed this matter. It only became a realistic possibility to me when Dr. Adams explained we would have the help and resources of the military to construct and install the units. I have a relatively small company with a very well-trained crew. We stick very close to my original business plan. By following this relatively specialized plan we have been profitable from the first year we were in business. Honestly General Clark, as Dad said earlier, we are willing to cooperate and help the government, but I am not willing to abandon the business plan that has proven successful."

"Good answer Bobby", said General Clark. "It is my understanding that your business plan calls for salvaging and repurposing materials. Is that a fair statement?"

"That is indeed a fair statement. I think this nation disposes of a lot of materials that can be repurposed without compromising quality or aesthetics. For example, we are frequently called to demolish old structures such as private and commercial brick structures. We will go in, remove the bricks, and take them to my shop where we clean them of mortar and palletize them for reuse. We have done projects where the entire components of the structure come from salvaged materials and you would never know the structure was repurposed salvage. My largest customer is my brother Tony who runs ATX Construction."

"That sounds like a hell of a plan Bobby. Both Secretary Johansen and I have discussed your use of scrap materials. I'm told you have an interest in using military scrap and surplus materials in the construction of the crematoriums. As public servants reusing these types of materials presents us with both opportunities and challenges. An opportunity is we will not have to spend so much on materials; we already own them and they have been designated scrap or surplus. A challenge I see is convincing the public we have not constructed them from substandard materials. Would you please speak to the subject of substandard materials?"

"When selecting scrap materials, one needs to know what they are looking at and what are the project's design requirements. In my business, I either know or can quickly find out the specification of the materials I scrap. I can do the same when selecting military scrap. In the case of constructing carcass burners, one needs to be mindful of the pressures that will be present when the internal vessel temperature rises to 1800 degrees. If the scrap metal is not capable of holding up to those temperatures, then the scrap does not qualify for reuse. Selecting raw materials for any industrial project requires scrutiny of each component. It has often been my experience, for example, my design requirements call for half-inch plate steel that I may not have or can find easily. However, I have a ready supply of three-quarter inch material. We will use the three-quarter inch material in place of the half inch knowing that we have exceeded the structural requirements at a price that is say 75 percent less than what we would pay for half-inch material. Does that clarify material selection and use for you General Clark?"

"Very much so. You are building things, like we used to say in Kentucky, 'country boy stout' and using your education as a mechanical engineer as well as your experience and practicality to ensure it meets or exceeds specifications."

Philip interrupted, "Ladies and gentlemen we have extended our discussion through our first scheduled break. I will try not to let that happen again. Our plan is to take a leisurely break now. Then, rather than returning to this room, we will meet in the lower level parking garage. We're going to have lunch in Canyon, Texas on our way to AXT's Herford feedlot where you will see one of the crematoriums Bobby has built. Rosa's has the reputation of making the best burritos in north Texas. All their food is equally as good. We will see the crematorium as it fires up and begins the process. Please know, when we leave this room, it will remain secure while we are gone. Let's adjourn for now."

Everyone sat outside on the patio under umbrellas enjoying their lunch. After hearing Philip's recommendation, everyone ordered burritos finding them as good as he described. Soon they were back on their way to the Hereford feedlot. The four Suburbans drove to the top of the hill and turned left past the silos. They observed a large blackish-grey cylinder sitting horizontally, somewhat submerged into the ground. The dull grey structure gave off a distinct pungent odor of burnt hair and flesh.

First, the group got out on the concrete apron on the west side of the carcass burner. Nearly all the military personnel took photos using their cell phones. The engineers took several photographs from various vantage points including the open west end door. Randy was a little surprised as there were about twenty-five carcasses in the crematorium. He noticed a dump truck with carcasses ready for dumping at the top of the cylinder. Although the stench of the dead animals was prevalent, several brave souls stood next to Randy taking photographs of the inside the partially loaded vessel. As soon as those wanting photos finished, Randy swung the large heavy door shut and locked the door. Some wanted more photos of the locking mechanism. Others asked their colleagues to stand next to the concrete walls to capture the relative size of the cylinder and adjacent concrete walls. Next, the group walked to the east end the cylinder at ground level where more photos captured the gas line and plumbing.

Bobby answered technical questions from the group as they looked around the top level. Several military folks asked very technical questions to which Bobby's responses were consistently logical and thorough. Clare, Sam Yu, Bobby Laporte stood with Randall, Philip, Penny, and General Clark away from the large crematorium observing the rest of the group. General Clark commented, "This outing has been productive. I think it has helped get some who were on the fence about building crematoriums from scrap materials on board. In some ways, they remind me of a group of academy cadets on an outing to observe heavy artillery and then see it in use. For some of these folks, it's been way too long since they've been on a field trip. I think something as different as this is from their normal routines is sparking their interest and recharging their batteries. This will be a good project for us from top to bottom."

After everyone finished taking photos and asking questions, they drifted up to the top level. Bobby Bennett began, "The land each of our feedlots is on is near ATX oil and gas production. Our own natural gas through a high-pressure line fuel our crematoriums. They also fuel our feed mills."

With perfect timing Jorge and Lupe appeared and unloaded carcasses from the dump truck into the crematorium. A large electric wench mounted on an "A" frame picked up each carcass by a hind leg, then lowered it into the crematorium. Once the cable was slack, it unhooked from the hind limb and elevated back inside the dump truck. After unloading the carcasses, the dump truck pulled forward a safe distance. Jorge sprinted back to help Lupe close the hydraulically driven large thick metal clam-shell doors. Once closed, sealed, and locked, Lupe walked over to a wheel type valve rising from the ground adjacent to a pressurized tank. After opening the valve, Jorge opened a second valve housed in a separate enclosure. A loud hissing sound became apparent, almost immediately followed by ignition of the gas. They not only heard ignition but felt it while standing well away from the huge crematorium. Jorge flipped a lever mounted on the wall activating the automatic flue. For about two minutes the smoke rising from the pipe chimney was blue-black in color and had the strong pungent odor of burning hair and hide. The thunderous roaring sound was continual. Bobby estimated the actual cremation to be three hours. Then, another two hours for the unit to cool down to where people could work around it. As Jorge exited the control shack, he turned on bright red rotating lights like what one would see mounted on an emergency vehicle. Red lights around the concrete bunker of the crematorium also blinked. Without doubt, it was a dangerous area.

Bobby stood in front of the group speaking loudly so the military engineers could hear him over the roaring of the gas in the cylinder. "We've made some design changes to the crematoriums you all will be constructing. Rather than dumping in entire carcasses with the hides on them, the new design will have a shed for hide removal prior to evisceration. A large auger transfers the viscera into the crematorium. After cutting the skinned carcass into large pieces they pass through a machine called a pre-breaker followed by a chopper that will result in a small particle size yet. Then, the ground material enters the crematorium through a second auger. Using the pre-breaker and chopper increases the capacity of the crematorium while decreasing cycle time. Thus, improving efficiency. Skinning the carcasses also significantly decreases the resulting odors emitted from the unit."

"If there are no operational questions better answered on-site, let's get back in our vehicles and return to the conference room", said Bobby.

****

When the group returned to the conference room Bobby stood saying, "I have a little more I want to cover, and then I will open it up for questions before we break for the day."

"Now that everyone has had the opportunity to see one of these carcass burners up close and watch as it begins its cycle, I want to talk about what ATX Salvage and Industrial Design can do to help you with this project of destroying twelve million head of cattle. As I have said before, there is no way my company can build and install 400 burners. We are willing to cooperate and help as best we can. Our level of involvement, I'm going to leave up to you to decide. Minimal involvement is: I will provide you with the plans for a royalty of $500/unit. You can acquire the materials from whatever source you wish and construct all the units yourselves. At the other end of the scale, I will help find the materials, get them transported to the various locations, have my men travel to the various sites to personally oversee construction; while I build the modular units in my shop. Between the minimal level of involvement and the maximum, which is what I realistically think I can provide. We are willing to do anything you would like us to do. My company will complete tearing down a refinery we have been working on by the end of the week. For now, I will not start any other projects until you advise at what level you want us involved. Also, if you have other contractors who you want to interview or hire, that's fine. If you choose to design your own carcass burners, and not use my patented design, that's fine as well."

"I am concerned that while DVE is an emergent situation, the government may be criticized for showing favoritism toward ATX. And ATX criticized for taking advantage of an emergent situation. ATX enjoys an excellent reputation and I do not want to compromise that reputation. I am hopeful that the government is equally sensitive to this concern and will use its powers to negate my concern."

"Next, I want to tell you how I intend to charge for my company's services.
I will structure our charges so we are fairly compensated for our time and expenses, plus a twelve percent profit."

"That's all I have for you today. I have some PowerPoint slides showing the entire construction process of building and installing a carcass burner. If you would like, I'll go through these with you later. I think I've given you enough to digest and think about for today."

"Bobby thank you for the information you provided today and for your candor", replied General Clark. "We at the

Pentagon are not used to the plain talk that you communicated to us today. It is refreshing and frankly I value your assessment of your company's limitations. This is the first time the United States Military Services has partnered with the USDA. This project interests me personally for what it can provide to our soldiers, sailors, and airmen. I share your concern regarding compromising our reputation. Inside the beltway we are known as big spenders with hidden budgets and agendas. We in no way want that reputation to spill over into this project. I want it to be transparent and as cost effective as we can make it. I think that is the same thing you want as well. I have absolutely no problem repurposing military scrap or surplus toward getting these crematoriums up and running before we face significant public health problems. You have indeed given us a lot to think about and discuss. Tomorrow morning we'll be ready to discuss the project. I can tell you from my perspective we want your company involved."

"Bobby, I have known your family a long time", said Clare. "I expected nothing less than what you presented today. ATX indeed enjoys an excellent reputation. USDA will work hard to see to ensure its not tarnished. Many sitting around this table do not know it was ATX funded research that discovered the source of DVE, then shared it with USDA. I know your Dad, Randall, and Philip Granger very well. They like to work in the background and defer accolades to others. I am supportive of repurposing materials; but, we must be time sensitive. If something takes too long to find or modify, we need to be flexible enough to get the materials in place to complete and make a unit operational. We received supplemental funding yesterday. While we have a large budget for the project, we prefer anything that will lessen the overall cost. It's taxpayers' dollars we are spending. I can tell you from USDA's perspective, we want your company leading us through construction of the crematoriums. Hopefully, we'll divert a public health crisis."

Philip stood saying, "We have made good progress today. Bobby promised he would answer questions after his presentation. Does anyone have any questions for Bobby

Bennett?... OK, if there are no questions, let's adjourn until tomorrow morning."

Penny stood and said, "Dinner tonight is on your own. However, tomorrow we have made plans for everyone to enjoy a good steak at the Amarillo Steak Ranch. It's a local landmark, famous for their 'if you eat all 84 ounces, it's a free steak dinner.' Lunch tomorrow and Friday will be catered."

As the room cleared, Clare hung back to talk specifically with Randall and Philip. "I received a packet from Bill Evans yesterday morning. I found it thorough, thoughtful, and very well prepared. I made a copy to study on the plane ride out and in the motel last night. The more I studied and thought, the more sense it made. While I'm not surprised by your foresight; I am amazed at the size and depth of this project. I should tell you after I made my copy to study, I wrote a note to attach to the proposal. It said, 'this needs expedited approval through normal channels for the full amount. Be watchful for additional synergistic proposals from this institution. When they are received, please expedite through the process and copy me for review and possible recommendation.' Today during the meeting, I received an e-mail telling me Dr. Evans' proposal was approved and funded. I thought you both may be curious."

"Clare, thank you so much for the information", said Philip. "We'll let Bill Evans pass the information on to us without him having knowledge of our discussion."

Randall replied, "Clare this will mean a lot to a lot of people. Is there any way a couple of old reprobates like us could talk you into a quiet dinner with us and our wives?"

"Yes and No; I would love to have dinner with you both as well as Kay and Beth. However, tonight General Clark and I are going to discuss strategy, particularly as it pertains to talking a group of Generals into repurposing surplus and salvaged materials. Repurposing salvage is a new concept to this group of engineers."

"Clare, if it would help we could take another road trip tomorrow and visit some of the other things Bobby has done with scrap materials", said Philip.

"I like the idea, but let me run it by General Clark. He knows this bunch much better than I do. I'll let you know first thing in the morning."

Randy and Penny were on their way back to Happy. Penny's cell phone rang and caller ID said Randall Bennett. Penny answered.

"Penny, it's Randal and Philip. I've got you on speaker in my car. Have you and Rose planned a shopping trip anytime soon?"

"Not really, Randall. As you know we've been very busy since we returned from Cheyenne. Does Rose want to go shopping?"

"Oh Penny, Rose always wants to go shopping. We just thought you two might want to go shopping before you interview for the Director of the National Prion Center job at Texas Tech University."

"What are you telling me Randall?"

It was Philip who responded. "What Randall is saying is Clare just told us the proposal Bill Evans submitted to the USDA for building the National Prion Center was approved today. The whole package is fully funded. Clare put a note on Bill Evans' packet saying the folks who approve or deny the proposals should be watching for additional synergistic proposals from this institution and they need to be expedited, with a copy sent to Clare for her possible recommendation. We think you and Rose should plan a shopping trip sooner than later."

"Oh my God! You, Randall, and Randy were right, sometimes it's just plain luck. The Lord is certainly holding me in his hands. First, I meet the man of my dreams and he asked me to marry him, and now this! Thank you for calling to tell me. Of course, you know I won't be able to sleep a wink tonight."

"Please tell Randy the news. He might have something in mind, if you're unable to sleep", quipped Philip. Randall in the background was laughing.

"Good bye Penny", said Randall and Phillip still chuckling.

Chapter 47

"Good morning Larry, it's Ray. I have you on speaker phone. The rest of the Wyoming team is with me. We have worked through the samples I collected while in Texas."

"It is good to hear from you all. How is everyone in Wyoming? We have been exceptionally hot and dry down this way. I hope you all have some good news for me today."

"Larry, it's a mixed bag. I'll first give you the bottom line and then we can go through the details. The bad news is there is uptake of nano-fertilizer into the corn plants we tested. We found nano-capsules in the leaves, stocks, and kernels of the corn plants we examined. However, we did not find them in the roots or in the soil. Therefore, your corn crop is a loss, but there is no evidence suggesting you not plant new alfalfa this fall and corn next spring."

"In all, that is good news. At least the ground isn't contaminated. I can buy more corn. Have you spoken with Penny yet?"

"No, we tried, but the message on her phone said she was tied up in a meeting and would be checking her messages and returning calls as time allowed. So, we thought we would give you a call."

"Thanks, I appreciate that. However, let me see if I can reach her through Mary at the bank. They're holding the meeting there. Clare Johansen is there as well as a whole delegation of military folks. Maybe we can set up a conference call about 4:30PM our time. The meeting should be adjourning about that time. Can we reach everyone at your number about 3:30PM?"

"I am seeing everyone's head nodding yes on this side. I know you have my number. We will be waiting for your call."

"Ray, don't hang up yet. One thing I would like to know now is how best to manage my farming now that we have evidence that both the alfalfa and corn are contaminated."

"Larry, given that you still have lots of cattle that are destined to be destroyed I would green-chop the corn for silage; then feed it to the cattle along with the contaminated alfalfa. I see no harm in utilizing the contaminated feed on cattle scheduled for destruction. However, once the cattle are all destroyed, the guys at the feedlots will have to clean out the silage pits. I would treat them with high pressure water; then liberally with lye. That may not kill the prions, but hopefully it will dilute any residual and go through the waste removal systems. Larry, I would also get USDA's opinion or recommendations. This is new territory for all of us; I think it would be best to get a consensus. I think I would also have USDA involve the EPA in the decision-making process. Another thing, I'd recommend you to let your fields dry out substantially, then burn them to remove all the stems and hopefully destroy any residual prions in the stems. If you would like, I would be glad to participate in those communications with you and everyone involved at ATX."

"I would like that very much. Look for us to give you a call about 3:30PM your time at your office number."

"We'll be awaiting your call."

****

Mary walked into the boardroom, leaned forward beside Penny as she reached out handing her a note. She bent down smiling and whispered, "That is a beautiful ring, congratulations." The note read; UW Profs and Ray finished experiments-conference call with Larry at 4:30PM today.

Penny read the note and handed it to Randy who handed it to Clare and then on to Bobby Laporte and Sam Yu. Everyone nodded and looked at each other.

They made significant progress at the morning's meeting. General Clark addressed Bobby Bennett saying, "We discussed the options concerning your company's involvement with this project. First, let me say we appreciate you presenting us with options. Second, we appreciate you addressing the limitations of your company as it relates to the size of the project. Our conclusion is we want you and your company fully involved. We're dealing with an emergent situation. For us to attempt to find others who may have like expertise, would be cavalier given the circumstances of the situation. You possess the knowledge and experience; we want you to use it to help us prevent a public health crisis. Using your men, who also have knowledge of what we are building, we think we can decrease our learning curve and we'll become more efficient in getting these units built, installed and operational. Therefore, we want you and your company to provide us as much help as you possibly can."

"Last night my colleagues and I had a discussion on how we would expect you to react should you determine insufficient progress was being made at one or more locations. Of course, we would expect you to communicate this information to the engineering officer on site. Because this is a joint exercise from a military perspective, it presented some problems, but we've worked those out. We agreed we needed to provide you with one go-to person who would address any problem that arose, regardless of its cause. We determined that person should be General Timothy Bartlett, the Chief Engineer of the Army. We want you to go through our 'Bone Yards', Salvage depots, and Surplus depots to obtain as much material as possible for this project. Additionally, if you can provide us information on specifically what you might need, we'll have it sorted, cleaned, and ready to transport. We will disassemble and get the materials ready to ship. It's important to us to transport the salvaged materials to the construction sites. A secondary benefit to this exercise for us is to get our people to work in a coordinated and integrated manner with other government entities and the private sector. Bobby, we look forward to working with you."

Clare began, "Bobby, you actually made this very easy for us. The transparency of your compensation structure is certainly fair and equitable. The USDA will be compensating ATX Salvage and Industrial Design. I recommend you send monthly itemized statements. If you are not receiving payments in a timely manner, please contact me. There will likely be some new materials or equipment that will needed. We need to get your input on the most expeditious manner for this to occur. In addition, I will manage the press to ensure to the best of my abilities that ATX's reputation is not tarnished by the help your company is providing."

Bobby responded, "With consideration of General Clark's comments and those you made Madam Secretary, we have a deal and the full involvement of my company. May I assume you want me to design and build as many mobile units as I can?"

"That is correct", said Clare.

"Philip Granger, our counsel, will write up the agreement and have it ready to sign."

"Bobby", General Clark commented, "General Max Elliott, who is my Chief of Staff, is also an attorney. Perhaps he and Philip can work together on drafting the agreement. I don't want Max to feel I had him travel down here without earning his keep."

Philip Granger responded, "I would be glad to have General Elliott and I share this responsibility. We should be able to have it ready for everyone's signatures by noon tomorrow. General Elliott, what are your thoughts?"

"Noon tomorrow seems reasonable."

Noticing the caterers outside, Bobby said, "The caterers have arrived. As soon as we're finished with lunch, I will take you through a series of PowerPoint slides demonstrating construction of the burners, site preparation and burner installation."

Everyone thought this would be a valuable use of time while the attorneys drafted the agreement. Clare interrupted, "There are several of us that need to participate in a conference call at 4:30PM. If Bobby's presentation needs additional time, we will have additional time tomorrow morning."

****

After lunch, everyone huddled around the conference table, except Philip and General Elliott, to listen to Bobby's PowerPoint presentation.

Bobby took the group through a detailed set of PowerPoint slides explaining in a systematic fashion how to convert salvaged tanks into cattle crematoriums. Bobby was a good teacher. He explained the technical aspects in an easily comprehensible style. As questions came up, he responded descriptively. He used the slides to explain each step while he used a white board to identify the materials to construct the units. The crematorium construction phase of his presentation stimulated numerous questions as did the materials list. Discussions arose regarding equipment use and possible alternative equipment used for construction. Bobby learned the military possessed more equipment than he anticipated. By using some of the alternative equipment, it would reduce construction and installation time. After covering the construction phase of his presentation, everyone took a short break.

Penny, Randy, and many others used this time to check their phones for messages. Penny received an e-mail from Bill Evans asking her to call to set up an interview date for the position of Director of the National Prion Center. Randy read an e-mail from Larry. Prions contaminated the corn but not the farm ground. They both looked up and handed each other their phones and then broke out laughing.

"Hey you two", said Clare, "Do you have any idea what the Ray and his group found?"

"That was what I was just showing Penny", said Randy. "The corn is contaminated. However, the farmland is not."

"That's actually good news. Thank God, the farmland isn't contaminated. I don't know what we would do, if that happened."

"I'll text Anne Burk and have her on the conference call", said Bobby.

"If you have her contact information I will send it to Mary. She's going to get us connected with Ray", said Randy.

Penny felt like she needed to call Bill Evans; however, the call needed to be private. Her involvement with the group and Bobby's presentation was conflicting with what she wanted to do. She thought, *I'll sneak away for a few minutes. Mary has a conference room I can use. If not, the call must wait until after the conference call was complete. Oh well, when it rains it pours. I'll just slip out for a few minutes and return when I can.*

As everyone was returning, Penny walked into Mary's office. Mary walked from her desk with a smile. "Penny, as you know I'm Mary. While no one introduced us, we know each other. Congratulations on your engagement. I'm elated you will be joining our family."

"Thank you. I am excited about joining your family as well. When the jeweler told us that you said congratulations, Randy and I both laughed. You were the first one to know in either of our families. Thank you for keeping it confidential so we could tell everyone personally."

"Mary, I need to make a confidential phone call. Is there a conference room I could use for a few minutes?"

"Sure, let me get the key. We have a small conference room right across the hall. Opening the door and turning on the light, Mary said, "To get an outside line on the phone dial nine. If its long distance, just dial a one after the nine. When you've finished, turn the light off. I'll lock it later."

"Thank you so much." Penny sat down at the table to call Bill Evans. His secretary answered; on hearing the call was from Penny she immediately forwarded the call. Penny was nervous, but her voice was not affected.

"Good afternoon Dr. Adams. How are you?"

"Chancellor Evans, I am so sorry I have been so difficult to reach. I have been in meetings with my cell phone turned off. I do have a few minutes now though."

"Dr. Adams let me first congratulate you on being nominated for this position. Your qualifications as outlined in the nomination letter make you a most qualified candidate. Do you have knowledge of what Texas Tech University is planning regarding the study of prions?"

"Chancellor, I have a general knowledge. Texas Tech is planning to develop a National Prion Center. I know your plan is to have it be a joint venture between the College of Agriculture and the Health Sciences Center. It is my understanding the joint venture will attempt to exploit synergies between the two colleges. I know the Board of Regents and you approved the concept. I'm also aware your grant proposal has been approved by the USDA."

"Dr. Adams, you are well informed. Please call me Bill. We've put together an exploratory committee who would very much like to visit with you about becoming the Director of the National Prion Center.

Have you given any thought to a time that would be convenient for you?"

"Bill, please call me Penny. Frankly, I have not given it much thought; I'm sure we can arrange something when it's most convenient for the committee. If you don't mind, who nominated me?"

"Penny, I thought you might have known. It was Secretary Clare Johansen. She speaks very highly of you, as do several others inside USDA and in the academic world."

"The exploratory committee is trying to find the best fit for the Director position. We want to bring the Director on early in the process of developing the program. We would like to have our process completed and the Director named within the next three weeks. With that knowledge, when would you be available to visit our campus and meet with the exploratory committee?"

"I did not realize you were so far along. Let's see, how would the middle of next week work for you and the committee?"

"Penny the middle of next week is ideal. Please plan on spending about three days with us. I will make reservations for you at the Armadillo Suites. It is close to campus and they have the nicest rooms in town. Your reservation will be for Tuesday through Friday nights. If it's alright with you, I'll pick you up in the lobby about 8:30AM Wednesday morning?"

"That would be perfect Bill. I look forward to meeting you and the exploratory committee. I'll see you then."

"I look forward to it as well Penny. Again, thanks for returning my call. Have a good day."

Penny was so excited she could hardly contain herself; but, she must for the moment. Penny's mind began to race. *What must I do to prepare for this meeting? I need clothes. I must call Rose and Sarita to see if they will go shopping with me. I must let Randy and Randall know. I must thank Clare. I must get my hair done. I must let Mom and Dad know. I have to settle down and compose myself and then rejoin the group.*

Penny took a deep breath and walked into the conference room. She looked around and saw Clare smiling at her. Bobby soon completed the site preparation portion of his presentation. It was close enough to 4:30 that Bobby said they would adjourn. Leaving the installation portion of the presentation until tomorrow morning. As the military group was leaving Penny spoke up, "I want to remind everyone that tonight we have reservations at the Amarillo Steak Ranch for around 6:00PM. We'll see you all there."

Penny casually walked up to Clare putting her arm around Clare's and whispered, "Thank you. I had no idea who nominated me."

"Penny, it was my pleasure. After I wrote the letter, I kept it to myself until we got down here. I called Randall to let him know what I had done. He just giggled that little pleased giggle of his and said; this is a perfect surprise for Penny. I know you know it, but Penny you are joining a wonderful family who delights in helping one another. I am so very happy for you dear. It's being able to give others these little life surprises that makes it all worthwhile."

****

Those involved in the conference call and General Clark remained in the conference room. Larry Shelton joined them in the board room. "Mary set the call up and I thought I would join y'all here to make sure we got the best connection possible", said Larry.

Mary interrupted on the intercom saying, "Larry, your call is on line one."

Larry pressed the button saying, "Ray, the Amarillo contingent is on the line. Can you hear us OK?"

"We can hear you fine Larry."

"How about Dr. Anne Burk? Have you joined us", asked Larry.

"I am on and can hear you both clearly."

"To begin", said Ray, "let me first summarize the results of our experiments. We found nanoparticles in the leaves, stem, and corn kernels. We looked at them individually and as a composite. However, we were unable to find and identify any nanoparticles from the soil samples collected on the various farmlands. Now I'm going to turn it over to Dr. Thorpe who conducted the experiments."

"Good afternoon to everyone. Let me say Dr. Fong, Dr. Edwards, and of course Dr. Shelton assisted in conducting these experiments. I will first discuss the corn testing and then I will address the soil. We essentially conducted the corn testing using the same procedures we did for alfalfa. We previously established the nanoparticles are proteinaceous and one third contain titanium dioxide. Observing nanoparticles with the scanning electron microscope is proof of nano-fertilizer contamination in the corn. Each of the sixteen samples demonstrated the presence of nanoparticles from the composites. I must add at higher concentrations than we saw in the alfalfa. We reasoned this was because the corn had three applications of nano-fertilizer where the alfalfa only had one application per cutting."

"Knowing there were nanoparticles present, we decided to repeat Dr. Fong's experimental design to determine what parts of the plant are contaminated. Our next step was to macerate portions of the leaf, stem, root, and kernel individually for each of the sixteen samples. Then, we followed the same procedures we did for the sixteen composite samples and viewed all sixty-four samples under the SEM. We observed nanoparticles in each of the leaf, stem, and kernel samples; but we were unable to identify nanoparticles in the sixteen root samples. We think the nanoparticles are either physically too large to absorb through the root hairs or there were none in the soil. For the leaves, stems and kernels the nanoparticles were readily absorbed."

Moving to the soil samples Dr. Shelton collected from the fields of the southern farms, in total there were 128 samples collected. Areas of the fields sampled consisted of half alfalfa and half corn fields. He sampled each portion of the field using a spade. He divided each spade full of dirt collected into a surface portion and a deep portion. Our thought was the nanoparticles could move deeper with sequential exposures to irrigation."

"After slide preparation, we collectively viewed each sample under the SEM. We observed no nanoparticles in the 128 Texas soil samples. However, in the positive control samples we observed numerous nanoparticles. From these data, I think we have successfully demonstrated the Texas farm soil samples are devoid of nanoparticles. The positive controls gave us high confidence. If the nanoparticles were present, we would have observed them. Are there questions regarding our methodology or the results?"

"Dr. Shelton this is Anne Burk, I was wondering why you chose a separate source for the positive control samples?"

"Dr. Burk", responded Dr. Thorpe, "we wanted to ensure there was no possibility of the positive control soil sample being contaminated prior to adding the nano-fertilizer to the sample. I was in my garden the evening before we were to set up this part of the experiment. After harvesting some onions, I remembered we needed a positive control soil sample. I thought, this is as good as any and the ground is soft. Therefore, I collected that soil."

"Well done", said Clare. "We really appreciate you all doing this work in such a timely manner. Let me ask the group in Laramie, do you see anything unique in the soil samples collected in Texas? Maybe the question would be more concise if I were to ask it in a different way. Would you expect the same results if you tested soil samples from let's say Colorado and California?"

"I'll respond to that", said Dr. Shelton. "Madam Secretary, I would expect these results would be repeatable in samples from those two states as well as any other states and fields that were treated with nano-fertilizer. Initially, logic told me that we should find a few soil samples contaminated. However, I began searching the literature and found references relating to Chronic Wasting Disease in captive deer and elk, and others from small flocks of sheep that developed scrapie while held in a small confined area. In these cases, they collected and tested soil samples to determine ground contamination. It is known urine is a source of contamination for ground forage. In both cases, the investigators could not find any evidence of ground contamination. Does that sufficiently answer your question?"

Yes, Ray it does. I was wondering if we needed additional trials before developing policy regarding the farm ground. It sounds like with the results of the Laramie team and the reference articles you mentioned we should have enough scientific evidence to support our decision. Please send copies of those articles or references where they can be found to Dr. Burk?"

"I would be happy to Madam Secretary. Dr. Burk, please give me your address and contact information at the end of this call."

"Are there any other questions, comments, or subjects that we need to discuss", asked Clare. "If not, thank you all for time this afternoon. We appreciate the good work the University of Wyoming scholars continue to do for us. Everyone have a good evening."

Chapter 48

Antonio Rodriquez, the President of Mexico, is a handsome man of 41. His heritage traces back to the first Spaniards to settle in Mexico. He is from a family of privilege. Primarily through inheritance, he is one of Mexico's wealthiest and largest land barons. His vast holdings extend from farmland in the southern fertile Yucatan region to prolific grape vineyards and wineries in the northern reaches of Baja California in the Valle de Guadalupe near Ensenada. Between, he has vast cattle ranching operations raise over 400,000 cattle annually. Antonio attended college in the United States, first attending Yale where he received a bachelor's degree in Business Administration. He then earned a master's degree from Cal Poly in San Lois Obispo in Economics. Once he returned home from college, he centered the family's new investment capital toward oil and gas exploration and developing Mexico's communication network for computers and cell phones. These investments tripled his family's substantial net worth in a decade.

Internationally, Rodriquez has the reputation of being bright, an independent thinker, and a true Mexican patriot. When campaigning for the Presidency his views were middle of the road. He championed economic and educational initiatives that would lead to better and longer lives for its citizens. His top national priority was to improve the quality of life and life spans for Mexican citizens by reducing the death rates of children under age five and adults' due to diabetes, heart disease and stroke. Rodriquez viewed the need for social change directly related to the health of his constituents and prioritized spending on improving medical care over that of law enforcement efforts to control the cartels. His predecessors had unsuccessfully attempted these efforts to what Rodriquez felt was the detriment of his constituency. He viewed Mexico's drug cartels as contributing to a much smaller part of Mexico's public health problems. He was not naive to the horrors and violence caused by the cartels, nor was he politically or financially motivated to overlook their violence. Rodriquez simply felt there were larger priorities to which he should direct his government's resources.

President Smyth and President Rodriquez liked and respected one another, agreeing on most economic issues. Trade between Mexico and the US had increased. The Mexican government better controlled migration of illegal Mexican immigrants. However, illegal drug trade was one issue where their points of view were almost opposites and created friction between the two countries. It was now time for President Smyth to pull the scab off this wound.

"Mr. President, I have President Rodriquez on the line for you."

"Thank you for taking my call Antonio. I hope you and your family are doing well?"

"Yes, they are, President Smyth. Thank you for asking. I am also hoping you and your family are also well."

"Yes, they are President Rodriquez. The purpose of my call today is to apprise you of some new intelligence regarding the DVE outbreak we have been experiencing in our cattle."

"Yes, I have been following that with interest and concern for Mexico as well as my family interests in the ranching business. From what I have read, the disease is caused by a novel prion and was hidden in nanoparticles within a fertilizer."

You are correct. That is what our press releases have covered. What I am about to tell you is known only to a select few. We uncovered a financial plot associated with the DVE disease outbreak. Through a complex method of investment, the people responsible for causing the disease outbreak have made significant investments in our cattle commodities contracts and futures, corn commodities contracts and futures, cattle related ETFs on the London Stock Exchange, and in leveraged index funds on the New York Stock Exchange. If this investment went to fruition, we estimate the investment entity would have come away with over two billion dollars in profit.

If you don't mind, let me start at the beginning. We found a university laboratory in Islamabad, Pakistan manufactured the tainted fertilizer. The fertilizer and a large shipment of morphine both originated in Pakistan. The tainted fertilizer and morphine arrived in Mogadishu where they refined the morphine into pure heroin. Then, it sailed to the Port of Lagos in Nigeria and on to the Port of Tampico. After off-loading the containers in Tampico, the Los Zeta cartel transported it to Monterrey where they cut the heroin. Once complete, the heroin and fertilizer passed covertly into the U.S. at Laredo, Texas. After off-loading the heroin, they delivered the fertilizer to Oklahoma City for further distribution through a farmers' cooperative network. Our intelligence resources tell us the Los Zeta drug cartel smuggled it into this country. We have identified the individuals responsible throughout the distribution chain. I hope to eliminate this entire distribution chain from start to finish. I am seeking both your cooperation and authorization to do so within your country. I am certain we can cripple or eliminate the Los Zeta cartel during this covert operation."

"President Smyth, while the Los Zeta cartel is a thorn in Mexico's side and is responsible for more violence and deaths in Mexico than you can imagine, I cannot, in good conscience, allow your military to travel into my country to carry out such an operation. It would not differ from me calling you to say that arms originating in the U.S. covertly moved into Mexico and were used to kill Mexican citizens. If I asked you to allow our military to conduct a raid in say San Diego, you would not allow the Mexican army to conduct military operations in the U.S. In my view, you are asking the same of me. It is a request I must deny, for Mexican solidarity. I am sure you understand."

"Antonio, is there anything I can do to convince you to reconsider?"

"In this regard President Smyth, there is nothing that would change my mind. I do hope that we will be able to continue to work together on other issues between our countries. Thank you for calling Mr. President."

"Thank you for your time Antonio."

****

As the conference call with the University of Wyoming scientists was concluding, General Clark felt his cell phone vibrate. The caller ID identified the caller as POTUS. He walked toward the conference room door hitting three buttons on his cell phone. As the conference room door closed, General Clark answered the call. "Good afternoon, my line is secure."

"Good afternoon. The final leg is NO GO", said President Smyth. "The first three legs are green. Implement the first three legs as GO."

"I understand, first three legs are GO. Thank you, sir."

General Clark then hit a speed dial number on his phone followed by another speed dial number. "I am on a secure line."

"My line is secure", was General Griffith's response.

"First three legs of Puppy Dog are green. Fourth leg is red."

"Puppy Dog's first three legs are green. The forth is Red. We'll be hot in 30."

****

Anne Burk was still at work after the conference call. She was reviewing summary data from the farmers who had used nano-fertilizer on their crops. She had received word her investigators visited all 283 cooperatives and interviewed all 352 farmers who purchased the nano-fertilizer. Thirty-two additional cattle feedlots, dairies, and other beef producer premises received quarantines with their cattle added to the animal depopulation list. She reset the limits in her investigative software to identify those premises that fertilized crops other than alfalfa with nano-fertilizer. The new list populated. Of the 352 farmers that used nano-fertilizer on their crops there were 114 who had used it on crops other than alfalfa, or beside alfalfa. She then set the software limits to identify only those farmers who had used it on corn. Eighty-three farmers used nano-fertilizer on corn or alfalfa and corn. Anne printed the page. Once again, she reset the limits for crops other than alfalfa and corn. The 31 farmers in this subset included soybeans (19), wheat (10), hops (1), and tobacco (1).

Next Anne cross-checked her list of quarantined premises against those farmers on the two lists subsets she had printed. She felt confident her team accounted for all the nano-fertilizer and quarantined the cropland treated with nano-fertilizer. In the morning, they would issue additional or amended quarantines to 114 premises identified as using nano-fertilizer on crops other than or beside alfalfa.

She would send these two lists to her regional directors tonight. She hoped the amended or additional quarantines would be hand delivered to the farmers tomorrow. For the first time since the Wyoming scientists found infectious prions in the nano-fertilizer, Anne felt confident she had everything identified and under control.

Before leaving work, she had just one more task to complete. She wanted to determine total acreages of each crop treated with nano-fertilizer. As she set the computer program to summarize those acreages her phone rang.

"Hi Anne, it's Bobby; how are things going?"

"How did you know I would be working late?"

"I know you; and I knew you had things to do. So, tell me, what's new."

"Bobby, I feel confident all the crops have been identified and we have everything under control for the plants exposed to nano-fertilizer. We're issuing 114 additional or amended quarantines tomorrow to premises identified as using nano-fertilizer on crops other than or in addition to alfalfa. One farmer used nano-fertilizer on a field of hops. Other than that, I have just gotten the total number of acres fertilized with nano-fertilizer. If you like I will send you these data for review?"

"Absolutely, I was going to tell you we needed this information. Clare is going to hold a press conference tomorrow. I'm going to recommend she lift the bans that are in place for beef slaughter, transportation of cattle, and change of ownership. Everyone has agreed on the terms of constructing the crematoriums today. They'll sign the agreement tomorrow around noon. I also wanted to tell you, although don't make it public, Sam Yu is going to be the new Director of Veterinary Services. We'll first make him acting; then when David's retirement becomes final, he'll become the new Director. I just wanted to let you know what was going on."

"Thanks Bobby, I think Sam will make a good director. He handled the DVE outbreak well, I thought."

"Yes, he did. There were lots of good people who handled that outbreak very well. Frankly, I think we're very lucky to be at the stage we are now, considering how well hidden the novel agent was. I am proud to say we have some very fine folks working with us. I'm also including your group in that. If the alfalfa hay was not all traced and the other crops identified as adulterated, this could have gone on for a considerable time with additional loss of livestock and lives.

Can you imagine if those hops had contaminated a large brewery?"

"Bobby, I'm going to let you go and head home-I'm exhausted."

"We pulled up in front of a legendary steakhouse just before I called. I need to go in and join the rest of the group. I'll talk with you tomorrow."

****

Dinner at the Amarillo Steak Ranch was a fun and relaxed. Penny found the time to fill Randy in on the interview at Tech. Bobby Laporte announced Dr. Yu would be the new acting Director of Veterinary Services. Penny was happy for him; and thought he would do an excellent job. She thought his analytical skills would serve APHIS well. Clare sat next to Penny at dinner making polite conversation divulging no knowledge of what was going on in Penny's world. The entire group accomplished framing a new partnership between the USDA and the military. Bobby Bennett stimulated the engineers' creativity motivating them to think outside the box. It was something General Clark had not expected, but welcomed. He thought most spent way too much time taking care of administrative details and had allowed themselves to become stale in their professional areas of expertise. He hoped this trip and the project would broaden their perspectives. In his view, it was necessary for general officers to have broad perspectives and to be innovative, as it would carry over into battlefield situations. For everyone it was a very productive and enlightening day.

Chapter 49

General Griffith called Delta Force Commander, Colonel Norman Kennedy and advising him the first three legs of Puppy Dog were a go. The order came down to a six-man Alpha team from "B" Squadron who had been planning the mission for over ten days. Unlike other military missions, they provided Delta operators with the mission objectives and the operators, who were all counterterrorism experts, plan their own missions. The first leg of the mission is to destroy the morphine labs around Islamabad, destroy Dr. Aziz's lab in the Army Medical College at National University of Pakistan, and eliminate Dr. Mohammad Aziz and Mushtaq Shakir. The second leg of the mission was to destroy the new heroin processing lab in Mogadishu, Somalia. The third leg of the mission was to destroy the drug smuggling operations in Lagos, Nigeria.

The Delta team's plan was to divide into three two-man teams. Each two-man team would travel individually to Islamabad, Mogadishu, or Lagos. They would then meet up with their counterpart and conduct their mission. Flight origins were different for each operator, making traceability more difficult. Delta's intelligence was sound for each of the three legs. Appropriate weapons selected by the operators and explosives were in place for each mission.

Once on the ground, the two-man teams would be covert and operate independently. They would be responsible for their own extractions. Mostly, they preferred to operate in darkness while others were sleeping. Night vision goggles and other specialized equipment allowed them to conduct their mission in a stealthy manner. Once in place, they began their work.

In Islamabad, the two operators chose to first locate the three morphine processing labs. The labs were within a few miles of each other and all near the northwestern outskirts of Islamabad. Two labs were in small isolated warehouse buildings in Saidpur, the other in a rundown building that appeared to have been an automobile repair shop in Nurpur Shahan. On closer inspection, the labs were nonoperational; although, the equipment was in place and electricity was available at the flick of a switch.

They located the Army Medical College in the Rawalpindi section of Islamabad, south of the center of Islamabad. It was a more difficult target. However, they found security around the area to be lax with escape routes nearby.

The Islamabad team's plan remained the same. They would plant the explosives in the three morphine labs and wire each to detonate with a call to cell phones left as triggers. The same type trigger would destroy Dr. Aziz's lab. Last, they would deal with Aziz and Shakir at the coffee house in a more personal manner.

The Delta team wired the three morphine labs during night two of their stay in Islamabad. During the morning of day three Dr. Aziz's lab was laden with plastic explosives and wired in a similar manner while the operators posed as maintenance workers installing a new overhead fire extinguishing system. This work was complete in time for the two operators to make their way to the coffeehouse frequented by Aziz and Shakir after Asr at the nearby Faisal Mosque. Within ten minutes, the two operators left the coffeehouse and drove their stolen van west toward Peshawar. Their mission in Islamabad was almost complete. In the western outskirts of Islamabad, they drove to an elevated parking lot providing a panoramic view of the city to make four calls. From this vantage point, they viewed the results of their handiwork. After triggering the explosives, the operators drove through Peshawar reaching Kabul by early morning. From Kabul, they flew to Kandahar where they hopped a military flight back to the U.S. Leg one of Puppy Dog was complete.

The two operators conducting the Mogadishu (leg two) operation arrived at the airport within two hours of each other. It was about 10:00PM when the last operator arrived. They met each other at a predetermined location hotwiring an old Toyota pickup to pick up their supplies in an abandoned warehouse. They loaded the pickup with an assortment of explosives, wire, fuses, and a radio operated trigger. The location of the heroin lab proved challenging. As they drove by the lab they found it to be in a population dense area. The building's exterior appeared out of place with its brightly painted exterior, sturdy doors, and barred windows. Intelligence reported a security system they would have to disable. This was not a challenge for the highly trained and experienced Delta operators. Within a minute of parking adjacent to the building, they picked the locks and disabled the security system. What they hadn't expected was the additional level of security they observed coiled on the floor near a centrifuge. One operator jumped back after nearly stepping on an angry king cobra. Both shot the snake with their suppressed .22 pistols. Because they knew noncombatants were sleeping in structures adjacent to the lab, they set directional charges on the structural components of the building and incendiary devices below or in the laboratory equipment. While it took a little longer to wire the building in this manner, it would reduce collateral casualties. They also placed minimal quantities of explosives. Within twenty minutes the building was ready to blow. The team chose a detonator that would trigger when they keyed their radio microphone. The operators closed the door as they left the laboratory jumping into the stolen pickup. As they rounded the corner at the end of the block, one keyed the mike. The lack of noise from the explosion worried the operators. They backed up the pickup to get a better view of the structure which simply imploded. All four walls fell to the center of the building and the roof fell squarely down on the walls. Fire from the incendiary devices soon consumed the lab. The two operators returned to abandoned warehouse dropping off their firearms and leftover explosives. After ditching the stolen pickup, which was clean of fingerprints and any incriminating evidence, they took cabs to the airport. Both operators departed on an Emirates Airlines flight to Dubai. From Abu Dhabi, they flew to Kuwait where they hitched a ride on a military aircraft back to the US. Leg two of Puppy Dog was complete.

The Lagos operation did not start as planned. Due to the delay and eventual canceling of one flight, both operators arrived in Lagos on the same flight. They embedded with a CIA operative who met them. He provided them with fresh intelligence temporarily derailing their operation. Apparently, the Neo Black Movement, Nigeria's mafia, had a large-scale oil smuggling and human trafficking event scheduled to occur in about a week. Newly scheduled is a joint Delta/Seal operation aimed at eliminating the oil smuggling and human trafficking businesses. The scale of this joint operation dwarfed the heroin smuggling mission. The CIA expressed concerns the third leg of Puppy Dog may scare off the Neo Black Movement's operation. The two operators stood down and embed themselves with the CIA awaiting the full Delta squadron's arrival in five days. They would hopefully conduct leg three of Puppy Dog in conjunction with the larger operation, if that met the approval of the squadron commander.

"A" squadron arrived five days later via Delta Force's jet. A component of Seal team six arrived a day later. The seals planned to commandeer two large oil tankers scheduled to arrive in a couple of days to fill with oil stolen from the southern Niger Delta pipelines. Several smaller vessels storing the oil waited at dock in the Port of Lagos. As Delta "A" squadron began their surveillance activities, so did the two Puppy Dog operators. It soon became apparent the heroin smuggling ring was much larger than initially reported. They knew of a warehouse near the port stored both heroin and morphine. However, within that structure was a large processing lab not identified in their intelligence report. The Nigerian leaders of the narcotics smuggling ring rented office space in a high-rise office building near the dock. Two container ships involved in the heroin smuggling operation docked in the harbor. Puppy Dog's operators revised their plan.

Their new plan basically called for them to enter the high-rise office at night setting explosives which would destroy the contents of the office and its occupants without damaging the structural integrity of the 24-story building. The drug smugglers' offices were on the 18th floor on the northwestern corner of the building. They found building security was minimal, but on the northwestern corner of the 18th floor there were armed security guards, video cameras, and other electronic surveillance devices. While they could circumvent the electronic and video surveillance devices, the armed security guards challenged their plan. They feared detection of the explosives if they terminated the guards during a burglary. They revised their plan again. First, they would disarm the electronic and video devices. Then, rather than entering the office suite from inside the building, they would repel down the building, enter through a window, and place the explosive and incendiary devices. They hid the explosives without detection. This was step three of the plan. Step two incorporated the help of the seals. The seals' placed magnetically attached explosive devices to external key structural areas of the container ships' bilge and beam with remote triggers for detonation. This was a specialty of the seals and they completed it smoothly. Step one was to destroy the warehouse holding the heroin, morphine, and the lab. Due to the traffic and security, this step required careful planning and perfect timing. The plan was to carry out this step during the larger joint Delta/Seal operation to curtail oil smuggling and human trafficking. The larger operation would serve as a diversion for leg three of Puppy Dog.

The larger operation began four days later. Both large tankers were about half filled with the stolen crude. The seals forcibly took control of the large tankers assassinating their captains and crews. In a similar manner, two operators neutralized the smaller tankers captains and crews. Delta's "A" squadron hit the onshore smugglers neutralizing them while destroying their offices and setting free the captured slaves. Within fifteen minutes the entire operation was over. Six of the smaller tankers recognized what was happening and steamed out of port into international waters where their ships became disabled leaving them powerless and adrift. This was due to a backup plan the seals set up. The seals stealthy boarded all the smaller tankers re-routing the fuel lines from their main fuel tank into a smaller auxiliary tank allowing only enough fuel to travel into international waters;

then they ran hopelessly out of fuel. Navy vessels were waiting and promptly sunk the vessels using small torpedoes launched from a mini-sub.

The joint Delta/Seals operation served as the diversion the two Puppy Dog operators were hoping for. The two operators entered the warehouse quietly and terminated all who came into their sites using suppressed automatic weapons. Once they cleared the warehouse of enemy personnel, they planted explosives containing radio wave detonators. Once complete, they drove a safe distance away from the warehouse and hit the mike on their hand-held radio. The warehouse exploded shooting a plume of fire about three hundred feet upward, then settled down into red/orange hot inferno that turned the building and its contents into ash. Even the corrugated steel sides and roof melted. The extreme heat cremated the terrorists' bodies leaving small charred ruminants of bone and teeth as the only evidence of their existence.

Next, the charges attached to the two container ships detonated in unison. The ships simply rose in the water, broke in half sinking to the bottom of the harbor, leaving numerous containers floating in the harbor.

The end of Puppy Dog's third stage came as the two operators watched the key organizers of the drug smuggling operation return to their offices to regroup. Another key of the mike on a different frequency and the entire northwest corner of the eighteenth floor blew away from the building in a ball of fire. The corner pillar was undamaged. It appeared as the corner of the high-rise contained an open-air patio. The Lagos drugs smuggling operation failed to exist. Leg three of Puppy Dog was complete. The two Puppy Dog operators rode home with Delta's "A" Squadron.

General Griffith received word from Colonel Kennedy that Puppy Dog had returned home. General Griffith advised General Clark. General Clark drove to the White House where he walked up to the president's secretary requesting to see President Smyth.

"He's on the phone right now, General."

"If you don't mind, I'll wait until he has a minute."

"That's fine by me sir. How about a cup of coffee?"

"That would be wonderful...black, no sugar. Thanks."

As General Clark finished his coffee, President Smyth came to his door and said, "Mitch come on in."

The president and General Clark walked into the oval office shutting the door behind them. "Mr. President, it gives me great pleasure to tell you that Puppy Dog has returned home safely. We got 'em all. The entire drug smuggling operation from Islamabad to Lagos has been dismantled."

"And the two Pakistani's responsible for DVE?"

"They won't be causing any more problems, sir."

"I know it's an unusual request, but I would like to meet those two operators. Although it is perverse, I want to know how the two operators dealt with those two sneaky Pakistani bastards."

"I'll make that happen, Mr. President. You know they are currently in operational status. Their appearance helps keep them alive. If it's OK, I suggest bringing them in casually...none of the Delta operators are much for notoriety or accolades; but they are the best you have."

"Let's just do it that way. You bring them in. We will sit down, have a cold beer, and visit privately."

Chapter 50

The third day of the meeting started later than the previous two allowing time for packing and loading their luggage into the Army Reserve van. The van traveled to the airport and loaded the luggage well before the plane's departure.

Penny and Randy stopped at Rosa's on their way to Amarillo picking up breakfast burritos for everyone. They arrived a little early and the smell of the burritos permeated the board room and adjacent hallway.

Bobby presented the installation portion of his PowerPoint presentation. More discussion ensued retarding the use of propane rather than natural gas and harvesting the oils. General Bartlett, the Chief Engineer of the Army, said the military would use all the harvested oils in their equipment. Eliminating the need to find contractors to haul the fuel. He requested a copy of the presentation for reference and use in training the construction and installation crews. Bobby agreed it would be helpful saying he would e-mail the presentation by the end of the day.

Clare made calls earlier arranging a press conference scheduled for 2:00PM. They planned to hold it at Bobby's shop. This being the first step in making good on her promise not to have the press tarnish ATX's reputation. She decided not to fly back to DC with the plane; rather, she would stay another night in Amarillo, have dinner with Randall and Beth and Philip and Kay. One of Clare's morning calls was to Bill Evans at Texas Tech. While she was close to Lubbock, she asked if she could meet with him on Saturday. She was certain Randall and Philip would take her to Lubbock. She wanted to meet with Chancellor Evans regarding the recently approved funding. Clare would return to DC on Sunday.

Following a question and answer period regarding Bobby's PowerPoint presentation and additional technical questions, a discussion ensued regarding locations and general timeframes for construction, installation and to bring the crematoriums operational. General Clark and Clare participated in the discussion.

"Gentlemen", said Clare. "You need to keep in mind that we are facing a public health emergency. We need them built as fast as possible keeping safety in mind. If we fail to get them completed in time, we could face a catastrophic public health event. We cannot let that happen. Penny you've been conducting the survivability trial. Where are we at on that front?"

"Madam Secretary, while I don't have the specific numbers in front of me, for non-symptomatic cattle we are currently at about 145 days and counting. Once the cattle start developing central nervous system symptoms, our data shows we have about 95 days until about half of the animals' progress to a stage they must be humanely euthanized. Part of our strategy is to triage the cattle prior to sending them to the crematoriums. First priority, is for those showing central nervous system signs that are ambulatory. Second priority, are dead and down cattle on the infected premises because they are not ambulatory. Handling these cattle will be much more difficult and time consuming; so, we need to minimize the number in this category. The third priority will be non-symptomatic exposed cattle, because from our data, it appears we have more time to get them processed. Therefore, the first crematoriums need to be operational in about 70 days. In this scenario, the crematoriums will start with first priority cattle, and then intermix second and third priority cattle to the extent of not compromising efficiency by processing only second priority cattle. We'll finish up with third priority cattle."

"There you have it ladies and gentlemen", said General Clark. "This project is on a tight timeline. Bobby Bennett and I have spoken; he's leaving Monday to start lining up the scrap we will use. We're going to build these units on government owned lands as close as we can to where the highest concentrations of affected cattle are located. Over this weekend Bobby will be putting together a list of the type of scrap or surplus materials we need to locate. The most important thing you can communicate to your people is these timelines are firm. If it takes getting additional personnel and working two or three shifts, then that's what we're going to do. I expect all the military personnel sitting at this table to be actively supervising your personnel. I will be making unscheduled visits to various construction sites to see how things are going. If problems arise, I expect you to give them your attention and presence. You do not want me to arrive at a problematic site before you have been there. We need to treat this situation as an emergency. If we lollygag around, we will end up with a public health crisis. None of us want that. I have confidence in all of you and in the troops in your commands. This is our opportunity to work with the USDA on something that is real, not simulated. I know you will all give this project the attention it deserves. Are there any questions?"

The room was silent. There was no doubt in anyone's mind what General Clark expected. He had made himself abundantly clear.

Philip stood saying, "Let's all take a break. Return in about twenty minutes. We have completed the agreement. We will have everyone look it over, make any additions or revisions necessary, and get the documents signed."

Penny went to pick up a bottle of water and met Randall and Clare near the coffee pot. Randall smiled at Penny asking, "I'll bet you, Sarita, and Rose are going shopping tomorrow?"

"When is your interview", Clare asked.

"It's next Wednesday through Friday. I've been so busy, I haven't had time to even get nervous. I suppose that will change in the next couple of days."

"Penny", said Clare, "I have found a little bit of nervousness is advantageous-it keeps you sharp and focused.

If I can give you a little advice from my experience: be yourself, allow yourself some time to really think about where you want the National Prion Center to go, and how best it can get there. Respond to questions with answers that are what you really think. I know you will do fine. I want you to call me and tell me about your experience when it's over."

"I will. Thank you for your advice."

Philip said, "If everyone would please take their seats. We're going to pass around copies of the agreement so everyone will have a chance to read it. Please return the copies after reading the document."

General Elliott and Philip handed out the copies of the agreement. The document was two pages including the signature sheet and an area for the notary.

Clare and General Clark carefully read through the agreement finishing about the same time. Clare said, "I can always tell a Philip Granger document. It's clear, concise, easy to understand, and contains all the words it needs, but no more."

"Max, did it really take you two lawyers almost a day to draft this agreement", asked General Clark.

"No sir, it took us about twenty minutes. I learned a lot about wordsmithing agreements and got a wonderful tour of Philip's law offices."

There were no additions or corrections. Clare, General Clark, and Bobby Bennett all signed three copies of the agreement which Mary then notarized.

Clare announced; "This afternoon we are holding a press conference. It will be a joint conference with Bobby Bennett, General Clark, and me. We will announce our new agreement and I will provide an update on the DVE outbreak. I also plan to announce were lifting the temporary bans on cattle transportation, change of ownership and cattle slaughter effective Monday. I don't know what kind of press participation we will have. The Washington and local press received notification this morning. Dr. Penny Adams will be present to respond to technical questions regarding DVE, carcass destruction, and the research conducted at the University of Wyoming. Dr. Bobby Laporte will also be available to respond to technical questions as in the past. We will keep our responses general and refer to the ongoing investigation as appropriate. Is there anything else we need to include?"

"If not, it's time for lunch. We cancelled our catered lunch. Mary has reservations for us to have lunch at a restaurant within walking distance where she has reserved a private dining room for us. We will order off the menu. I must tell you all the restaurant's specialty is a Texas favorite, Chicken Fried Steak."

****

The news conference began promptly at 2:00PM with the press corps well represented. All the major networks including Fox and CNN sent representatives as did the Associated Press, Reuters, and newspapers from Dallas, Fort Worth, Houston, San Antonio, and the local newspaper.

Clare began with an opening statement. "This is a historic day for USDA. Today we signed an agreement with ATX Salvage and Industrial Design as well as the U.S. Military to cooperatively construct and operate about 400 industrial size crematoriums to be located on government owned lands throughout the US near where cattle stricken by DVE are located. As you may know dealing with disposal of prion stricken animals requires complete destruction of the animal carcass. These crematoriums will serve to accomplish that end. AXT Salvage and Industrial Design, located here in Amarillo, has experience building and installing these units. They also hold the patent. The size of this project is massive and is much too large for a private firm to handle within the necessary time constraints. Therefore, the US Military; the Army, Navy, and Air Force will be constructing these massive units for the USDA under the guidance of Bobby Bennett's Salvage and Industrial Design company. This is the first time the US Military has participated in a project with the USDA. To the extent possible, the construction of these crematoriums will be from repurposed salvaged materials in military salvage depots, bone yards, and scrap depots. We anticipate this to result in significant savings to the US taxpayers. Another unique aspect of this project is the oils produced in the process will be harvested and will be used to fuel military equipment."

"I also want to announce the temporary restrictions on transportation of cattle, cattle slaughter, and change of ownership in cattle will be lifted as of Monday. You may recall, we initiated these restrictions to contain the outbreak and minimize its impact on our nation's cattle herd. That goal has been accomplished."

"Earlier this week congress overwhelmingly passed the USDA's request for emergency supplemental funding for DVE. President Smyth signed the bill soon after congress presented it to him. The supplemental funding bill provides funds for indemnification of cattle lost due to DVE, the destruction of livestock stricken with or exposed to the novel DVE prion, and funding for prion research. USDA began processing indemnification claims the day following the bill's passage. We are reviewing research funding proposals and funding them based on their scientific merit. The agreement we just signed provides a mechanism for the construction, installation and operation of crematoriums that will be used to destroy stricken and exposed cattle."

"Regarding the progress of our efforts, USDA has identified and quarantined every premise that used the prion contaminated nano-fertilizer. Our investigations determined the nano-fertilizer primarily affected alfalfa; but other crops such as corn, soybeans, wheat, hops, and tobacco were also involved. We have quarantined these crops and they will eventually undergo destruction. We've sent the unused nano-fertilizer to Fort Dietrich. They have the equipment and experience to destroy it. I must tell you the acreages of crops other than alfalfa were minimal and should not impact commodity availability or prices. We have also conducted studies on the soil exposed to nano-fertilizer. I am very pleased to say the soil fertilized with the nano-fertilizer did not lead to soil contamination. These findings are consistent with previous research involving chronic wasting disease and scrapie; both prion caused diseases, where they demonstrated the ground was unaffected. These farmlands can go back into production the next growing season."

"Before I open the conference up to your questions, I must remind you there is an ongoing investigation associated with DVE. We will not be responding to questions that could in any way compromise this investigation."

"Now we will take your questions."

ABC News: "Secretary Johansen, you say the crematoriums are going to be located on US government land. Is there a specific reason?

Clare's response: "The government already owns these lands, it saves us time. We also can secure them; so, we won't have to deal with many of the concerns, particularly when the units are operational. As you can imagine these units generate a lot of heat. We need to ensure they are secure for public safety."

CNN News: "Four hundred units seem like a lot of units needed to destroy stricken livestock. How many animals are we talking about?"

Clare's response: "When I heard that number, 400 units, I was surprised as well. However, we're tasked with not only destroying the stricken livestock, but also those livestock who ate the prion laden alfalfa. The total number of livestock scheduled for destruction exceeds 12 million. When one focuses on that number, 400 units become a much smaller number. If we say each unit will destroy approximately the same number of livestock, it works out to 30,000 head per unit."

CBS News: "Why was the decision made to destroy all the livestock on an infected premise rather than just those that were showing signs of infection?"

Clare said, "I'm going to have Dr. Penny Adams respond to your question. She is a veterinary pathologist and a prion expert. She was involved in making this decision."

Penny's response: "Your question is valid. We conducted trials involving six premises stricken with DVE. We humanely destroyed 100 cattle randomly selected non-symptomatic cattle on each of the six premises located in Texas and California harvesting their brains. Subsequently, we observed the brains of these cattle under magnification. They all showed early signs of DVE. These data demonstrated it would irresponsible not to eliminate them from the food chains for both man and animals."

Fox News: "What will happen with the crops that have been quarantined?"

Clare's response: "The crops will largely be destroyed. Through special permitting and oversight, some of the crops can used as feed for cattle on infected premises. We will not allow sale or use of crops treated with nano-fertilizer to be fed or processed for consumption by non-infected cattle, other species of animals, or human consumption."

NBC News: "I don't understand why the military is taking the roll of private construction companies and construction workers. Would you please explain your reasoning?"

Clare's response: "This is an emergent situation. We simply do not have the luxury of time to seek and award bids. The only company we know who has experience making crematoriums for cattle is ATX Salvage and Industrial Design. We are using their expertise to the maximum. I will let General Clark comment on the military's roll."

General Clark's response: "As Secretary Johansen said this is an emergency. In the military, we have personnel trained in each craft required to construct, install, and operate the crematoriums. Additionally, we have the equipment and personnel in place. It also allows the military to work hand in hand with the USDA as we have in the past with other departments within the federal government. It will be a first for us to use scrap and salvage materials in a large project. That experience we consider valuable and will directly transfer to battlefield situations. Our involvement will allow us to be of direct service to our nation during this time of emergency. It allows us to test the effectiveness of our troops, distribution systems, engineering capabilities, in a situation that is on a short fuse. Where logistics, organization, and execution all matter."

NBC News: "A follow-up question. I have heard all of you refer to this situation as a national emergency. You also say you have contained the outbreak. Why is DVE a national emergency if the outbreak is contained?"

Clare's response: "The outbreak is contained. Distribution of the nano-fertilizer is known down to each farmer and field. That information allowed us to contain the farming portion of the outbreak quarantining and subsequently destroying the involved crops. We have also identified all the cattle fed the contaminated crop. Those cattle, and their premises, are under quarantine. Some of the animals have shown symptoms of DVE, others have not yet done so. We know, through studies we performed, the nonsymptomatic cattle are harboring the DVE prion. We must eliminate these animals and crops from our food chain. Doing so eliminates the worry to the public or our foreign trading partners. When we eliminate these animals and crops, it is necessary to destroy the prions that cause the disease. Only a small overall percentage of the animals infected have already died, but if we take too long disposing of the animals, they will die and we will have huge numbers of diseased and decomposing animals which we must destroy. Such an event would present a public health hazard of epic proportions. Our strategy is to get these crematoriums built and operational before we have to deal with a public health hazard."

Dallas Evening News: "Has there been any progress made in identifying those responsible for this act?"

Clare's response: "The investigation is ongoing. Therefore, I will make no comments on what progress has been made."

San Antonio Times: "Madam Secretary you mentioned the crematoriums will be made from repurposed salvaged military materials. Are you concerned this may result in equipment that is not able to perform as intended?"

Clare's response: I am not the least bit concerned. However, Bobby Bennett may speak to your question better than I."

Bobby's response: "My company specializes in repurposing salvaged materials. This nation disposes of a lot of materials that can be repurposed without compromising quality. The previous crematoriums we have built were all made from salvaged materials. They have been in use for several years without experiencing any issues. It is key to know the specifications of the scrap materials. In the case of constructing the crematoriums, one needs to be mindful of the pressures that will be present and internal vessel temperatures as well as its structural limitations. We will not use scrap, or for that matter new material, that will not meet or exceed the required specifications."

We will take one more question.

Amarillo Tribune: "What is time frame are you dealing with on this project?"

Clare looked at Penny who responded, "We need to have the first crematoriums built and operational in 70 days. We're planning on constructing several simultaneously. The logistical issues are currently in the planning stage. I am hopeful as we gain experience we will increase our efficiencies. Perhaps we will find minor design changes will also improve efficiency."

"I want to thank all of you for coming this afternoon", said Clare. "You will find the press release on the USDA-APHIS website under the DVE heading. APHIS personnel continue to man the phones to answer your DVE questions."

"Well done", Philip said to Clare. "I hope you are planning on dinner with us this evening or we are going to have two very disappointed wives."

"I'm looking forward to dinner tonight; and a good visit with Beth and Kay. Would it be possible for you two to take me to Lubbock tomorrow? I have a meeting with Bill Evans regarding the grant we just approved. I think you will be interested in attending."

Chapter 51

"Hi there beautiful. I'm in a meeting with Jim Bob and the managers of the northern feedlots. We're working on getting a slaughter shipping schedule put together for the next week or two. The packing houses in this area are scrambling to get cattle to slaughter. We have a whole bunch that we need to send off to make room for cattle Skip has on grass. Are you finished at the hairdresser's?"

"Yes, I'm just coming into Canyon. I thought I would stop if you were in the office. Since you are not, I'm going to head home, and then to Lubbock. I'll give you a call this evening. Say a prayer for me. I love you."

"I wish I were at the office, but we have a lot of heavyweight cattle to ship to the packers. We're shipping twenty-eight loads today. Tomorrow will start a very busy time for us. Good luck with the interview, although I am confident you will blow their socks off. Let me know if you want me to come down to spend some time with you. I shouldn't be too late getting home tonight. We've got a solid tentative plan put together. I love you. Drive carefully."

Penny had taken Clare's advice and given a lot of thought to her vision of the National Prion Center. She had laid out her goals for one, five, and ten years. She'd given thought to the research she wanted to conduct. She wanted to study what triggers amyloid precursor protein to form in some diseases and not in others. Penny postulated understanding this process could be key to learning how to manage multiple neurological diseases.

Bill Evans walked into the lobby of the Armadillo Suites promptly at 8:30AM. He found Penny's beauty astonishing. They introduced themselves to each other and walked toward Dr. Evan's car. "Penny I want to take you on a little tour of the Texas Tech campus before meeting with the committee. Have you been on our campus before?"

"I drove around a little bit when I got into town yesterday afternoon. The campus is larger than I expected; it's so attractive. I like the Spanish Renaissance style of architecture. I also like campuses that are deep in tradition, and Texas Tech has its own traditions."

"In front of us now is the Animal Science building. It was one of the first buildings constructed second only to the Administration building. Next we will go to the Administration building where my office is located."

"That sounds great. Tell me who is on the exploratory committee."

"The committee is rather small. There is Norman Theodoresen, the president of Texas Tech; Billy Henderson, Dean of the College of Agriculture; Barbara Mendoza the Dean of the Graduate School; Caroline DeCastro, the Dean of the Medical School and me. You will meet them soon, we're just pulling into the parking lot."

Walking into the Chancellor's office, Bill introduced Penny to his secretary, Polly Black. Penny casually visited with Polly. Adjacent to the secretary's office through a solid oak door Bill led Penny into his conference room. They walked in and the members of the exploratory committee stood to meet Penny. Bill made the introductions and everyone sat down.

"Penny", said Bill Evans, "we have looked over your academic credentials. Your accomplishments are impressive. I was somewhat puzzled why you chose to go to work in a USDA laboratory with your academic background."

"Actually, I made that choice to gain some practical experience to help me pass my specialty boards in veterinary pathology. It also allowed me to do some practical laboratory related research and publish my results."

Billy Henderson requested, "You were involved in the DVE investigation. Please describe your involvement."

"Dr. Henderson, initially I served as a veterinary pathologist on an investigative team based out of Amarillo. The team conducted in-depth investigation at the involved feedlot. Symptomatic cattle were isolated, humanely euthanized, and I performed limited necropsies collecting samples for laboratory analysis. Soon after we started our investigation, two additional nearby feedlots broke with DVE. We expanded our investigations to include these feedlots. A few days later the Director of Feedlot Operations reported seeing CNS signs in his own roping steers. Alfalfa hay was the only feed these steers received. While delving further into the production of this individual feedstuff, we found a new fertilizer containing nanoparticles of titanium dioxide was used."

"In only a few days our laboratory in Ames, IA was inundated. We needed to determine if we could omit sampling some of tissues. I read photomicrographs of the tissues collected providing a second opinion on which tissue samples could be eliminated."

"When the investigative teams completed their investigations, they were disbanded. I was one of two investigators who continued working on DVE. At my suggestion, we began a study of 300 randomly selected non-symptomatic feedlot cattle. My colleague did the same with dairy cattle. We sampled the brains and submitted them to the laboratory for histopathology. I also read photomicrographs of the slides. The purpose of this testing was to determine if all cattle would require destruction. Essentially all we brain tissue we examined displayed early DVE pathology. Therefore, we recommended depopulation of the entire premise. I participated in making that policy decision."

"Next, I designed and began two additional trials. The first trial involved cattle showing symptoms of DVE to determine how long they would live with symptoms before they became non-ambulatory requiring euthanasia. The second trial involved cattle that were not symptomatic to determine how long they would live before becoming symptomatic. This work is ongoing. From this work, we estimated the time USDA has before nonsymptomatic cattle become non-ambulatory. I'm currently managing the cattle destruction aspect of the DVE outbreak."

Norman Theodoresen, Texas Tech's President was next to question Penny. "Penny, what are your guiding principles?"

The guiding principles I try to live by are: One, work hard; nothing of substance is accomplished without hard work. Two, listen to understand. Unless I listen actively, I may not understand the true meaning of what someone is trying to communicate. Three, be fair-minded. Great things require me to be honest with myself and my colleagues. Four, take responsibility for my shortcomings and mistakes. No one is perfect; everyone makes mistakes occasionally. Five, take time to enjoy myself and my victories. Life is short and full of challenges; but what makes it worthwhile is the fun I've have along the way. Six, collaborate. Work together. Seven, do the right thing. Most often I know what's right; although it may be the most difficult."

"Well stated", said Bill Evans.

"I have a question for Penny", said Caroline DeCastro. "If we select you as the Director of the National Prion Center, do you see yourself conducting research? If so, specifically what kind of research would you like to conduct?"

"I certainly hope I would be able to conduct research. I hope the expectation is not for this job to be totally administrative. I enjoy research and find it stimulating. As far as what I would like to study, I have an interest in how molecular structure causes different cellular responses. For example, what modulates amyloid precursor protein production? It appears if there are high levels of amyloid, it induces neurotoxic properties. If amyloid levels are low, it elicits neurotrophic properties. By better understanding these processes, we might be able to develop strategies to improve management of neurodegenerative diseases in man and animals. It may also tell us why diseases like transmissible spongiform encephalopathies and DVE affect the brain in different ways. It may also provide answers to why neurodegenerative diseases such as Multiple Sclerosis appear to have an autoimmune component to them."

"Penny, I have one final question for you", said Bill Evans. "Please share with us your vision for the National Prion Center."

"I think I lack scope to provide a detailed vision for the National Prion Center. I have not had the opportunity to read the recently approved USDA grant. Therefore, my response today will be in broad terms."

"My current vision is the National Prion Center should be a repository of information on prions. In my view, any national center should contain the most current cutting-edge science available. This is not to say the research must occur at the center. The National Prion Center needs to be inclusive of various scientific disciplines and species. There is room in the study of prions for those who have an interest. We know so little about prions major breakthroughs could come from any scientific discipline."

"The National Prion Center needs to be a center for consolidated learning including everyone from skilled brilliant researchers, to teachers, to students just beginning their careers. Collaboration is a crucial element and needs to occur at all levels. Academics, design of the physical building structure, academic management, innovation, and creativity must serve to encourage everyone. Long-term funding should come from non-discretionary sources, such as line items in the USDA's and the Department of Health and Human Services portions of the federal budget. Private funding through various sources will compensate the center for more specific areas of research and development. Through these private funds we can also set funds aside for scholarships and fellowships. The National Prion Center should also take advantage of existing synergisms and develop others at Texas Tech. It is my vision that open mindedness, goal setting, and teamwork will lead to consensus management."

"Thank you. Your responses this morning have been through and well communicated. We are now going to deviate from most normal interview processes. We want to provide you the opportunity to get to know Texas Tech better as well as the individuals in this room."

"This afternoon we have arranged for you to spend time with Barbara Mendoza our Dean of the Graduate School. Tomorrow, Billy Henderson will be spending the morning with you. Tomorrow afternoon, Caroline DeCastro and you will be at our Medical School. Tomorrow evening, is a little more laid back at Norman Theodoresen's home. Norman is well known as competitive grill master. He is going to share some of his famous barbeque with us. Friday morning, we will meet back here. There will be no need for you to drive to campus. Barbara will take you back to the motel this evening; Billy will pick you up at 8:30AM tomorrow; Caroline will take you back to the motel tomorrow afternoon and will pick you up at 6:30PM to go to Norm's barbeque as well as return you to the motel. I will pick you up Friday morning at 8:30AM and return you to the motel when we finish that afternoon."

"Now it's time for us to go to lunch."

****

As Penny walked into the lobby prior to going to Norman Theodoresen's barbeque, she looked over at someone sitting in the lobby-it was Randy.

"Well, hi there cowboy! This is a welcome surprise", Penny said walking over to give him a hug and kiss. "I've missed you."

"I got lonesome and thought maybe you could use some company. How are things going?"

"I think everything is going good, but it's hard to tell. I've never been through an interview like this one. I met with the committee for about three hours where they asked me some general questions. The committee consists of the Chancellor, Texas Tech's President, and the Deans of Agriculture, the Medical School, and the Graduate School. I have spent a half-day with each of the deans. Tonight, there's a barbeque at the President's house. Did you bring some clean clothes?"

"Yeah, I was going to take you out to dinner. They're in the truck. I'll go get them. By the way, I like the way you have your hair done."

"Thank you. Rose's stylist gets all the credit; I never thought of fixing it this way. I'll wait here and walk with you to the room."

As they walked to the room Penny asked, "What has been going on at the feedlots?"

"We've been shipping a lot of cattle from the northern lots to make room for cattle Skip has been holding on grass. It's good to get some cash flowing again. At the southern lots, we are starting to see more cattle breaking with DVE. Larry called me yesterday. He wants to start cutting corn on the southern farms to use for silage. I gave Glen Rogers a call and he said it would take him a day or so to get the paperwork processed, but we're good to go as of this afternoon. Larry's going to start on Monday. We'll put the silage in a single pit at each lot; so, it will be easier to clean up after we have depopulated the lots. Larry bought enough corn to make up for what we would have produced on the southern farms. He hit the market at a good time and got us a good deal. It won't be delivered until this year's crop comes in; so, we'll have enough silo space."

While Penny showered, Randy turned on the TV to watch the news while he changed into a pair of newer starched jeans, his dark brown alligator boots with a light blue oxford western dress shirt with a small AXT embroidered on the left cuff. He also wore his new buckle from Cheyenne.

Penny walked out of the bedroom wearing her new bone white casual dress. To Randy she looked stunning and Randy felt underdressed to accompany her to the barbeque. Penny felt comfortable both in the dress and with Randy's attire.

Caroline and her husband, Tom, picked up Penny and Randy at the motel driving them to President Theodoresen's home in their midsize SUV. After introductions Caroline commented, "Penny, you look absolutely gorgeous in that dress."

"Thanks, this is a dress that I bought recently when Rose and I went shopping. She helped me pick it out."

"Randy, Caroline was Rose's roommate through medical school."

"Does Randy know Rose", asked Caroline.

Randy responded, "Yeah, she's one of my older sisters."

"Randy, I remember you now; you used to come over to our apartment for dinner occasionally. I think it was when you were a freshman and sophomore. As I remember you were in pre-vet. Did you go on to vet school?"

"Yes, after I got my B.S., I went to veterinary school at A&M."

"We're here", announced Tom as he pulled into the circle driveway of a large Spanish Renaissance style house adjacent to campus. Norman Theodoresen greeted the two couples at the door and introduced himself to Randy before Penny could make the introduction.

"Everyone is out on the patio. Caroline and Tom, you know the way. Penny you look lovely tonight."

Randy felt better once they walked out on the patio and saw everyone in casual clothing. Caroline introduced Randy to everyone commenting that it was such a small world. "You know Randy was my med school roommate's little brother. He's now a veterinarian."

The intent of the barbeque was so Penny (and Randy) could socialize with the committee and their spouses in the relaxed environment of Norman and Betty's back porch. Theodoresen prepared an excellent barbeque dinner which he served buffet style. Everyone enjoyed the meal and the opportunity to get to know Penny and Randy in a more relaxed setting. Penny and Randy felt comfortable with the rest of the group as they visited and got to know one another.

Billy Henderson knew Randy. After shaking hands he said, "You know you've got quite a girl there. Penny just blew us away in the interview."

Randy said, "Thank you Dr. Henderson, I think she's pretty special too. I'm glad she has done well."

Caroline introduced Penny and Randy to the spouses they hadn't met.

Returning to the motel room, Penny said, "Thank you for coming down and surprising me. What did you think of the barbeque tonight?"

"I thought the food was excellent. The fellowship among the group was extraordinary. It's been my experience when you get university staff at that level together, there's usually a little tension. I did not see or feel that at all. Everyone seemed to genuinely have a good time and enjoy each other. From what I saw, I think it would be a good group to work with."

"Tomorrow is the last day of your interview; how do you see your chances of getting the job?"

"I feel comfortable so far, but it's hard for me to tell. The questions they've asked were all open ended with essentially no right or wrong answers. I think I interacted well with everyone I spent a half-day with. They were all open, honest, helpful, and willing to share information. I really liked Caroline; I think we could become good friends as well as colleagues. Everyone told me what they had written into the grant proposal. I also don't foresee problems working closely with any of them. They each bring a lot to the table. I guess I just don't want to get too hopeful, and then not be selected."

"That's a good answer. Now, I have one more question for you. Given that you have had to spend the last two nights sleeping alone, what would you say to us snuggling up together in that big king size bed?"

"Honestly Randy, that's the best offer I've had in the last two days." Randy stood lifting Penny into his arms where he kissed her passionately.

****

"Good morning. I thought we might drive around a little this morning to look at three prospective sights for the Prion Center."

"Good morning. That sounds great."

"The three locations are relatively close to each other. After much discussion, the regents and I thought the Prion Center should be located close to the medical school, health sciences center, and medical library."

"Location one sits right north of the medical school. As you can see it's currently parking, primarily for the medical school and the medical center. If we construct the Prion Center here, there will be little room for growth or expansion."

"At location two the Prion Center would face the medical school and health science center with the boulevard separating the two. At this location, there is room for expansion. It also provides better parking access."

"Location three is the plot sitting to the northwest of the medical school and health sciences center. It sits on the corner of two highly traveled thoroughfares. It too has room for expansion and sits across the street from a USDA-Agriculture Research facility. Again, there's better access to parking."

"Penny, tell me which of the three do you prefer?"

"Without the benefit of giving it more thought, I like location three. It's on a corner of two relatively busy roads, with a stop light already in place. I think it is important we keep expansion as an option. I totally agree with locating it near the medical library, medical school, and health sciences building. There is already existing equipment and laboratory space which we might use without additional expense. With further thought and collaboration, I'm sure we could identify additional synergisms to support the location."

"Let's head back to my office. I want to talk with you privately, then the rest of the committee will join us about 11:30AM."

"Before we go into the conference room can I get you a cup of coffee or some cold water?"

"Water would be great, thank you."

Chancellor Evans and Penny sat in the conference room. "I must confess, I had a conference call this morning with the committee. You have impressed us all with your education, knowledge, achievements, and experience. There is no one who hasn't described you as very smart, hardworking, and dedicated. We listened to the news conference held in Amarillo last week. We thought you handled yourself very well responding to the press. What I'm trying to say is you were the committee's unanimous selection to be the Director of the National Prion Center. Congratulations!"

"Wow, thank you very much. I promise to work to the best of my abilities representing Texas Tech and The National Prion Center. Please understand, I'm going to need some help. I hope I can count on you and the committee to help and guide me in the right direction."

"I will respond for both myself and the committee when I say that we are here to help you. Before everyone arrives, there are some details I need to go over with you. First, your position is endowed and tenured. That was part of the proposal that we submitted. Next, I should tell you we offer all employees coming to Texas Tech at your level, which is basically at the Dean level, a relocation package. This package includes the purchase of any real estate you may own in Iowa, moving expenses, and assistance with finding you a place to live here in Lubbock, as well as assistance in finding financing for your new home. We want to make the transition as seamless as possible for you. Your salary will start at $250,000 plus full medical, dental, and ocular insurance. You will participate in the university's retirement program. The sick leave and vacation days you have accrued with the USDA transfer to your sick and vacation accounts at the university. Your position qualifies for performance bonuses based upon meeting established goals. Your appointment is on a twelve months/per year basis. After five years, you qualify for sabbatical studies, if you so choose. We anticipate your position will require a degree of travel. The university will fully reimburse your travel expenses. Do you have questions? Is there anything we need to negotiate?"

"Ah, I don't think so. I'm hoping you have all of that written down for me to review. I'm elated. However, I don't think I can remember it all. Thank you so much."

"I do have it written down. I want you to review it carefully. It's all in your employment contract. I recommend you have your attorney look it over. If there's something we need to discuss, please let me know. We're pleased to have you aboard. Without reservation, I can tell you everyone is looking forward to working with you."

Chapter 52

"Madam Secretary, Penny Adams for you."

"Please put her through. Hi Penny, how did the interview go?"

"It went very well. I got the job. I wanted to thank you for all that you've done for me and Randy. You're so kind."

"How did you find the interview process?"

"It was nothing like any other interview process I have gone through. I met with the committee for about three hours, then spent a half day with the Deans of Agriculture, the Graduate School, and the Medical School. Norman Theodoresen, Tech's President hosted a barbeque Thursday evening. I met privately with Bill Evans this morning after looking at possible sites for the Prion Center. He hired me soon after we got to his office. He went over the details of my contract suggesting I have it reviewed by my attorney. I was thinking about either Philip or his son; I want to see what Randy thinks. About noon, the rest of the committee came to congratulate and welcome me. We all went to lunch. I'm headed back to Happy now. I have to call Bobby to tell him I will be resigning; however, I wanted to call you first."

"Bobby is sitting in my office; so, he has heard everything we've said."

"Congratulations Penny. I'm very happy for you and wish you nothing but the best. Do you know when you will officially be starting?"

"Bobby, I don't. I was so shocked and happy we just didn't talk about it. They know I'm involved with the carcass destruction project. You know I won't leave you high and dry."

"Penny, I appreciate that, although I had no such thoughts. You're too classy for that. Once I became aware of your relationship with Randy and wanting to move closer to him, I knew I had to find someone else to be the Director of Veterinary Services and promoted Sam Yu quickly. I'm going to have Sam work with you; hopefully it will make your transition, as well as his, as smooth as possible. Let me know when you've negotiated an official starting date. If you could give us 30 to 45 days for the transition that would be ideal."

"I'll do my best to make it 45 days. Know I will miss working with you, but this opportunity is one I can't pass up. I am confident it's part of God's plan for me."

"That's a wonderful way of looking at it dear", said Clare. "I wanted to ask which of the three locations did you think would be the best for the Prion Center?"

"I liked the one on the corner across the street from the medical center."

"That's the one I liked as well. It's also the one Randall and Philip like. I think it's also the one the committee has chosen."

"When were you in Lubbock", Penny asked.

"The day after the press conference Randall, Philip, and I drove down to meet with Bill Evans. We saw the proposed site locations at that time. I wanted to make it clear to Bill that I expected the entire grant money to go toward research and the Prion Center. There would be no administrative fees deducted for managing the funds, etc. I also told him I expected the Director to receive 100 percent of what they requested in the grant proposal as well as the first endowed chair and of course the position needed to be tenured. Their proposal left a little wiggle room. I wanted to make sure he knew where I stood."

"I was unaware that you stayed in Amarillo and went down to Tech."

"Penny, that was intentional. I did not want my presence to influence the committee in any way; however, I did feel that I needed to meet Bill Evans to clarify my expectations. I had dinner that evening with Philip, Kay, Beth, and Randall. Having them, as regents, with me provided the leverage I thought I might need when I spoke with Bill. Our meeting went smoothly. I anticipate no problems concerning the funding."

"We need to get back to work. Thank you for calling and again congratulations."

****

The following week there was a cabinet meeting on Monday. At the meeting Clare gave an update on the progress of DVE. Basically, more non-symptomatic cattle were developing signs. Those cattle showing symptoms were faltering. General Clark added that Bobby Bennett had visited fourteen military bone yards, salvage and scrap depots finding a substantial inventory of supplies for the crematoriums. General Clark also said site preparation was underway and by the end of this week he anticipated the raw materials to be on-site at about 140 locations. He noted his military personnel were having a difficult time keeping up with Bobby. When he hit the ground, he knew what he was looking for. Once identified, he already had a plan for where to send it. The delivery location was always least cost. They reported he worked on the plane preparing for the next location. He reviewed inventory and developed shipment plans. The officers were learning a lot about working efficiently and cost efficiency. The cooperative efforts impressed and pleased President Smyth. He asked Clare to stop by his office after the meeting.

533

"Clare, thank you for meeting with me", President Smyth said as he excused his Secret Service detail from the room. I wanted to meet with you this morning regarding two DVE issues. First, there is a veterinarian who works for you that seemed on top of everything going on with the investigation. You once told me she knew more about prions than anyone in the USDA. As I recall, she's also the one who identified the two Pakistanis. I think you told me her name was Dr. Adams."

"Yes, Mr. President, Dr. Penny Adams."

"I want to do something special for her. In my assessment, she probably contributed more to minimizing this catastrophic event than anyone. I am going to award her the Presidential Early Career Award for Scientists and Engineers. As you know, the Department of Agriculture is a participating Department in those awards. I explored awarding her the National Medal of Science. A group of twelve appointed scientists and engineers evaluate nominations for that award. I'm told Dr. Adams research is top quality, but her experience limits the body of her research. She has only been conducting independent research for three years. Therefore, the Presidential Early Career Award for Scientists and Engineers is intended for someone like Dr. Adams."

"Mr. President that is a wonderful honor. I spoke with her a few days ago. She will be leaving USDA in about six weeks. She's been selected as the Director of the National Prion Center at Texas Tech University."

"I am happy for Dr. Adams. I am also very pleased that there is going to be a National Prion Center. We know so little about those agents that as a nation; we need to have a greater focus in that area of science. The award generally carries research funding for three to five years. I'm going to see she receives five years of funding for her research. I'll let you know the details of when she will receive the award. I would like to have you there when she receives it."

"I would be honored to attend."

"What about the folks from ATX", asked President Smyth. "I think we need to do something special for them as well. They have done so much involving this DVE outbreak."

"Mr. President, the ATX folks are close friends of mine; they shun the limelight. I think if you invited to a private dinner at the White House, perhaps when Dr. Adams receives her award, they would appreciate that much more than any form of public recognition. I also think you would enjoy spending an evening with them."

"Please get me their contact information. I'll make sure it happens."

"Secondly, I wanted to visit with you about the terrorism investigation. Although you have been silent, I know you well enough to recognize you've been wondering about the status of the terrorism investigation. Concerning the financial end of things, you know we traced ownership back to the same Pakistani identified by Dr. Adams. We have frozen all those investments. We will eventually end up with all the money they invested, which appears to be about one hundred million dollars. I turned the investigation over to the military. They developed substantial intelligence regarding these two men also linking them to a heroin smuggling operation. We've dismantled their operations in Pakistan, Somalia, and Nigeria. While there was not enough solid evidence to present a legal case, I can assure you those two men will not be conducting any further terrorist acts."

"Mr. President, thank you for sharing this information. I was wondering what was going on. There were no further joint meetings. Can you tell me what happened to the Pakistanis?"

"Clare, I don't know what specifically happened to Dr. Aziz and Mushtaq Shakir. I was assured they were no longer a threat to the United States."

"Thank you, Mr. President. That is reassuring to know."

******

As Secretary Johansen exited the oval office she saw General Clark waiting to see the President Smyth. They said hello to each other. Sitting on an adjacent couch were two men appearing to be tourists. Both were wearing black short sleeved golf shirts and held ball caps in their hands. One was wearing chinos and a climbing type of boot. The other wore blue jeans and tennis shoes. Both men had long hair and dark long beards. Their clothes were clean, but they looked scruffy and out of place. Clare thought to herself; *they are not with General Clark.* Clare walked toward the west portico where her driver was waiting.

A few minutes later, President Smyth walked out of his office saying, "General Clark, please bring in your guests."

In the oval office President Smyth introduced himself. One man responded, "Nice to meet you Mr. President. I am Bill Brown."

The other man responded, "It is an honor Mr. President. I am Greg Green."

"Mr. President", so you are aware, "for operational security these are not these two men's names. They identified themselves to me the same as to you. If you think about, we really don't need to know their real names."

"How about a beer", asked President Smyth.

"That sounds good", said Green.

"Yes, please", said Brown.

In about thirty seconds, a porter delivered four bottles of beer and four frosted mugs to the oval office. He handed everyone a beer and a mug and left quietly.

"I know this is a highly unusual request. I have never made such a request before; but, I would like to hear about your recent mission in Islamabad", said President Smyth.

The men looked at General Clark. He responded, "Men, he is our Commander in Chief."

Brown began, "Sir, we flew into Islamabad and acquired a vehicle. After confirming our intel was good; we entered the three labs, wired them with high explosives and incendiary materials. We used cell phones as triggering devices. The following morning, we drove to the Army Medical College at the National University of Pakistan and found the Department of Biochemistry and Molecular Biology. We packed Dr. Aziz's lab with high explosive and incendiary materials wiring it together with another cell phone trigger."

"Next, we went to the coffeehouse where Aziz and Shakir frequently go after Asr. We arrived shortly before they did. Following our original plan, we left twenty minutes later.

"So how did you take them out in the coffeehouse? Why did you stick around after?", asked President Smyth.

"When we were planning, we considered typical methods, such as assassination including using poison. We thought those methods exposed us to a high risk. We settled on giving them a dose of their own medicine."

Brown summed it up another way. "In Galatians 6:7-9 it states: Do not be deceived, God is not mocked; for whatever a man sows, this he will also reap."

Green clarified, "We had the guys at Fort Detrick make us up an ampoule of purified nanoparticles. We dumped it in their coffee pot. We stayed around while they both drank a cup of coffee each. We left as they were pouring a second cup. Intel reports both men are very ill with a mysterious disease. They are no longer able to walk, talk, or control their bodily functions. Their time on this earth is limited."

Acknowledgements

Thank you for selecting and reading ATX: Outbreak. If you enjoyed the book, please take a moment to leave a review. I really do appreciate your time, particularly for this my first novel in the ATX series.

I would be remiss if I did not thank my friend and colleague Dale Hansen, DVM for his encouragement, candid recommendations, and editorial suggestions. Without his help and gentle nudging, ATX: Outbreak would not have been published.

I also want to thank my loving wife, Pat. She keeps me grounded and has kindly allowed me to let my mind wander and pen this novel. It is to Pat I dedicate this book.

Made in the USA
Columbia, SC
08 March 2024

32872132R00321